SOUTHERN
GOLD

SOUTHERN GOLD

James Alan Vitti

THOMAS NELSON PUBLISHERS
Nashville • Atlanta • London • Vancouver

Published in Nashville, Tennessee, by Thomas Nelson, Inc., Publishers, and distributed in Canada by Word Communications, Ltd., Richmond, British Columbia.

This is a work of fiction. Any similarity to real life in the scenes, characters, timing, and events is merely coincidence.

Library of Congress Cataloging-in-Publication Data

Vitti, James Alan.
    Southern gold / by James Alan Vitti.
       p. cm.
    "A Jan Dennis book."
    ISBN 0-7852-7781-1
    I. Title.
PS3572.I82S65 1995
813'.54—dc20   95-2256
                                                CIP

Printed in the United States of America

1 2 3 4 5 6 — 00 99 98 97 96 95

Thank you, Rophe.
Thank you.

PROLOGUE

Gavin Duke thought he was dead.

He couldn't move—paralyzed by fear and shock and, perhaps, a slew of fractured bones. He tried to lift his head, but it was useless. Tried to pry his eyelids open, but that was futile too. Tried to make a sound, a noise, anything.

Maybe, he shuddered, *maybe I really am dead.*

No, the pulsing scream in his ears was too painful. And besides, he knew where he was—flat on his back, lying on his bed of gravel and ancient buckled pavement, seconds after the explosion had angrily slammed him down. Gavin Duke was far from dead, but equally far from the shining success story he had become. He imagined how he must have looked, tattered and torn and peppered with scrapes and cuts and welts, lying in the dust in the middle of nowhere, an unimaginable leap from the silk-suited golden boy who used to wink back at himself from the mirror.

So this, this is what it comes to? he heard himself thinking, wondering, calling out. *Or will I get another chance? Just one more chance . . .*

It had been only a few months, months that had lately stretched into centuries, or millennia, for his meticulously planned life to fall so far from center. Only a few months since the campaign began. Only a few months since his meeting in the ninetieth-floor screening room at Carolina Gates Advertising . . .

BOOK
1

Waiting for G-Day

One

Gavin Duke sank back into the plush VIP seat, licking his chops for the show that was about to begin. He looked cool and calm, as always, but inside he was a churning, twirling keg of dynamite. He knew what he was about to see, and what it was going to mean. Thirty seconds was all it would take. Thirty seconds that would forever alter the course of his career . . . and his life.

The giant screen sat before him like a sumptuous feast and came to life as digital sound bathed the room and swept goose bumps across his clammy skin.

It began gently, softly, and increased imperceptibly to a passionate pitch. Drums off in the distance. A fife playing. Cannon fire. Shouts of men—young boys, actually—walking into battle against their cousins and uncles and brothers. Haunting silhouettes of America at war with herself, packaged like toothpaste by the finest practitioners of advertising money could buy.

A rich, warm, somewhat familiar voice joined the chorus—with words rolling up the screen to match the audio and to hammer home the impact of their meaning:

"In May of 1865, one train after another steamed away from Richmond with fury. The Civil War was about to come crashing down on the Confederate Army, and its leaders bid a hasty retreat south.

"One of those trains contained a treasure so vast, historians cannot begin to fathom its worth today. Gold bullion. Precious jewels. The finest silver. This was the treasury of the Confederate States of America, and legend holds that it was hidden somewhere in the Deep South.

"To celebrate this greatest of Southern mysteries, First Southern Bank is pleased to announce Southern Gold, a one million dollar treasure hunt open to anyone who has an account with us.

"First Southern. Discover your dreams . . . with Southern Gold."

The spot faded to black, and the lights returned.

Gavin took a deep breath. He was a million miles away, already spending the treasure he would be due for concocting this, the most brilliant of promotions.

Yes, yes. This campaign is about to seal my fate. The marketing director who created this masterpiece would be the darling of two industries. He was on the verge of writing a ticket to wherever he wanted to land, whether in the ad business or high finance.

"So, Mister Duke," a voice said with the grin of the Cheshire cat, "what's the verdict?"

Gavin came back to earth. He angled his head slightly to the left and met Carolina's piercing ice-blues. The drama of the moment required some airspace. He cleared his throat slowly, very slowly, for added impact. Carolina Gates laughed.

"Carrie, my dear," he finally said, "we are about to grab some 'Southern Gold' ourselves."

"I couldn't agree more," the ad agency president said.

"Awesome," Gavin shook his head. "That's one super-dramatic execution. Sure to win us another Clio," he smiled wryly.

"I suspect," she volleyed back, "that a few more little statues are actually the farthest thing from your mind right now."

He laughed. "Okay, you got me. It's another kind of gold that's got me preoccupied." He ran his fingers through his thick black hair.

She flicked her gaze back toward the screen and asked, "Do you want to see it again, or were there any final tweaks you wanted to make before it goes to 'The Man'?"

"I think we're there," Gavin nodded. "But I definitely want to see it again. And again. And—"

She interrupted him by chuckling and pressing the button next to her chair, and the two were once again cast back in time, with blue and gray woolen uniforms before them. Yes, The Man was gonna love this.

Gavin settled in. *This will be even sweeter the second time.*

"In May of 1865, one train after another steamed away from Richmond with fury. The Civil War was about to come crashing down . . . "

This time, when the lights came up, he was the first to speak. The energy of the moment partially dissipated, it was time to map out strategy.

"Do we bring him up here for the preview, or have you got something else in mind?"

"Up here" was a room Gavin affectionately called "The Space-ship." The private screening room for Carolina Gates Advertising, it was perched atop the penthouse at the Peachtree Tower—a gleaming new monument that laid claim to the title of being the fifth tallest building in the world.

Inside this sanctum of virtual reality, your wildest imaginings were but the push of a button away. Giant screens appeared and disappeared with hushed efficiency. The roof could open to reveal a massive domed skylight—watch your new commercials under the stars. And add to that every Disney-esque sensation you could possibly dream up—the room could shake and roll, for instance—and there you have it. The Spaceship, just two doors down from the executive washroom.

"Hmm—last time he was here, he got kinda nervous. Maybe the boardroom at the bank would be better," Carolina mused.

"Sounds good to me. I'll set it up. Is tomorrow afternoon okay?"

"I'll keep it clear," she said, handing him a videotape in a black plastic box. "Here's your dub—I know you'll want to watch this a few hundred more times tonight."

"Or a few thousand, maybe," Gavin deadpanned.

They grinned, and there was another pause. But this was no Gavin Duke pause-for-dramatic-effect—the enormity of it all was sinking in.

Carolina broke the silence. "I've never seen one this big, Gav," she said.

Another pause. "You're so right, it's unnerving," he replied. "Absolutely unnerving."

"I'll pass the good words onto the creative team," she said, standing up and straightening her electric blue dress—which had somehow managed to stay permanently-pressed through an eleven-hour day.

"Yeah, uh, right. Okay," Gavin agreed absentmindedly, unconsciously wincing at the thought of having to pass around so much credit for his idea. He sprang up, clutching the tape. They walked into the hall, the automatic mahogany door closing behind them. Gavin reached over to gallantly push the down button on the elevator. "See you out?" he asked.

"Thanks, but no," Carolina said, nodding toward her office at the other end of the hall. "I've got another half hour of papers to crash through."

Odd, he thought. *You could usually set your alarm clock by Carrie— don't stand outside her office door at five o'clock, or you're liable to get run over.* How could a woman have single-handedly built a $250 million ad agency—far from the hallowed halls of Madison Avenue, no less—by putting her personal life first?

He thought about a dinner party at Carrie's a few summers back. He'd wandered inside, looking for a bathroom, and stumbled onto Carrie and her husband sitting on a sofa in the darkened den. Funny, Gavin squinted, for a couple in their early forties to sneak away like a pair of love-struck teenagers. He dared to listen for a second before he realized they weren't getting romantic but were instead praying together. He felt his face flush and he tiptoed back out, unseen. He never could quite bring himself to mention it, but he never forgot it. Not a praying man himself, he found it interesting that a couple would actually pray together. And out loud, at that. Must be something to it, though, he concluded—since Carrie had managed to stay happily married more than twenty years. *Ah, well, different strokes. Glad it works for them.*

"Paperwork, huh?" he said, blinking. "Still working on adding this little shop of yours to the daily feeding frenzy up on Wall Street?"

"Now, Gavin, you know I can't fuel the rumor mill, can I?"

"Gimme a break," he laughed. "The whole town's buzzing about it."

"Mmm," she smiled back. "Is it, now?"

"Yeah, I just hope nobody gets confused. I mean, 'Carolina Gates'—who's gonna know that's an ad agency? Everybody's gonna think it's some residential development outside Charleston."

"I refuse to accept criticism from a man who has his fingers manicured. Your nails are prettier than mine, mister!"

"All right, all right. Let's not get vicious now. Back to the issue at hand. Are you sure you won't let me buy a few dozen shares before you go public, darling?"

"Wish I could," she said, "but you know the rules. The regulators would frown rather heavily on that one."

"Too bad," he said. "I'd say the success of this little campaign of ours could boost the value by a good half mil or so."

She leaned in, with a mock whisper. "Three quarters," she said.

He grinned, then bowed at the waist for emphasis. "Glad to be of service, mum."

They shared a laugh, and he looked straight at her. "Seriously, Carrie. I'm glad for you. Thrilled. It's nice to see a good person get ahead."

She swallowed hard, and for once looked a little ruffled. "Thanks, Gavin. That means a lot." She squeezed his elbow and looked down at the floor before determining to peer into his dark eyes again. A man so full of bravado, slickness, and charm masking the unsure heart of a vulnerable little boy. *One day*, she thought. *One day, you'll let the mask down long enough for someone to break through and actually get inside your head—and your heart.* She'd only seen a few quick glimpses of Gavin's hidden inner man, and only when he was tired enough to let his well-entrenched guard slip. Like now.

Ding! The light on the elevator announced its arrival, and Carolina smiled to herself.

"Finally," Gavin complained. "You'd better call your building maintenance guys. These blasted elevators of yours seem to be getting slower every day!"

"I'll jump on it first thing," Carolina chuckled. "G'night!"

"G'night," Gavin answered, stepping onto the elevator. The door closed as a glimpse of electric blue marched off down the hall.

He took a deep breath and leaned back against more mahogany. Quarter to eight already, doggone it. *The only trouble with skyscrapers,* he thought, *is it takes an awfully long time to go down ninety stories.* He wished elevators could move faster, then chuckled when he realized that'd be the last thing he'd want in an elevator: *Devilishly handsome marketing exec perishes while setting elevator shaft speed record,* he thought, and laughed just a little out loud, before a minor bump at the fifty-first floor made the whole thing a bit less funny. Not one to ponder matters as weighty as death, he quickly switched subjects.

The bell went off again, and Gavin emerged. He headed through the ten-story atrium lobby, out to the parking deck, and into his jet-black Mercedes. He stopped at the exit gate and just before accelerating onto Peachtree Street caught a glimpse of a flower vendor, wrapping things up for the night.

"Hey," he called out as the window glided down electronically. "Hey! Got any roses left?"

The little man perked up. "Have I got roses for you, mister! Red roses! Real American Beauties!"

"Gimme a dozen," Gavin answered. He twisted back to grab for his billfold from inside the tailored jacket, which was nattily suspended from a curved cherrywood hanger on the hook behind his head.

"Your lady's gonna love these," the man said with a tired smile.

"Yeah, sure," Gavin said, passing him a crisp bill and pressing the button for the window to seal him off again. "Keep it," he said as the man nodded. A fifty-cent tip was better than nothing.

"Good night, sir. And thank you," he said, stuffing the bill into his pants pocket and shaking his head as Gavin roared off in a puff of diesel exhaust. "Big shots," he muttered, rolling his tiny cart off into the dusk.

As Gavin sped home, his mind raced with thoughts. *What if the New York cats laugh at us Southern hicks and manage to keep this labeled a regional nothing? Nah. It's too big; the numbers are too big. We'll grab a billion in new deposits—Chase or Citi never did that with a single promotion. We'll double the size of the credit card portfolio. And what about the trade press—Adweek and Ad Age? Will they have the "no life west of the Hudson" mentality, and bury us somewhere on page nine? No, they can't; this stuff does have Clio written all over it. And besides, it's got to get bigger than itself . . . it's just got to . . .*

Suddenly, a flashing blue light just ahead pinched Gavin's attention. *Oops. Got a little excited there. Eighty-five! Good thing that cop wasn't on this side.* He eased up, leaned back into the plush interior, and smiled the rest of the way home.

"This," he said aloud, "is gonna be better than hitting a home run in Yankee Stadium."

Marni's Porsche was in his driveway when he pulled in. Gavin sighed deeply and looked at the flowers, which didn't seem such a good idea any more. He sat in the car for a moment, back down to earth after a fast-lane trip through the stratosphere. *Wonder how long she's planning on hanging around tonight,* he sighed to himself before crawling out, moving slower than he was half an hour ago. Once he made it to the door, it took him a while to get the key in.

He straightened up, inhaled, turned the handle, and entered the kitchen. The light was on, and Marni was munching a salad at the counter, flipping through the new *TV Guide.* She didn't look up.

"Hey, baby," he said.

She still didn't look up. "Hey," she gulped, turning the page and swallowing a chunk of carrot in the same instant. She had long since given up wondering how a man with a Mensa I.Q. couldn't figure out that women hated—and that's hated with a good hissing sound—to be called "baby."

"Look," he said, shoving the bouquet toward her. "Brought you some flowers."

She finally looked up, her hypnotically green eyes only briefly meeting Gavin's. "Oh, yeah, uh . . . thanks," she said, snatching more than receiving them, then hurriedly darting across the floor to find a vase and a knife to cut off the ends and to fuss with the water and the stems and the leaves. "They're beautiful." She admired her arrangement for an instant, before returning to her salad and the *TV Guide*.

Gavin watched as she went about her work. Her long, strawberry blonde hair was pulled back in a ponytail, and she was wearing baggy old sweats.

"So how was your day?" he said, knowing she usually required some warm-up.

"Oh, ah . . . " she looked up from the salad and the Tuesday movie listings once more and falteringly met his brown eyes before darting away again, as rapidly as the brief connection. "Fine. Found out I got a review coming up this Friday."

"Great," Gavin nodded, not really caring but wanting this brief exchange to continue long enough for her to ask him about the golden, pulsating, dream-come-true tape in his hand.

She did not. She went back to the salad and the synopsis of films suitable for prime time.

Gavin sighed again. Better give it one more push. "Are they gonna give you a better title, more bucks, or more flight attendants to supervise, or what?"

"No new title," she said, glancing up again, "but I'll probably get one more crew—and hopefully, a few more dollars."

Gavin began tapping his fingers on the tape—his future, everything he'd always wanted, wrapped up in a black plastic box.

"Here," she said, grabbing a stack of letters and catalogs. "I brought in your mail for you."

Gavin shot her an acidic glare, which missed its mark. He took the pile with his right hand but didn't look through it, since he still clutched the tape with his left. "Anything interesting?" he sneered, wondering if he sounded as sarcastic as he felt about it.

She shook her head. "Mostly bills. And this month's installment from your dad."

Gavin put the pile back down on the counter without looking at it. He sighed. "Good old dad," he mumbled. "What would I do without his check for twenty bucks every month?"

"Imagine you'd starve," she said under her breath, eyes glued to the *Guide*.

All right, he thought. Enough. Enough about flight attendants, and enough about a tired old man who hasn't got a clue. "You wouldn't believe what I've got here," he blurted out like a little kid with an autographed baseball bat. "The intro spot—it's done!"

Marni wrinkled her eyebrows, wanting to be certain she didn't miss the point of all Gavin's excitement, and then smiled a big smile. For an instant, when Gavin saw that smile, he thought he remembered the feeling he had when they first fell for each other, but before he could savor it, he flew back into his moment of glory.

She tossed down the fork and the *TV Guide*, reached over, and playfully pulled the tape from his hand. "Great!" she said. "Can I see it?"

"Can you see it? Hey, you'll be one of the first! The Man hasn't even seen it yet!"

"Well, I'm honored," she said, also feeling a hint of rekindled flame. She ran into the living room with the tape and popped it into the VCR.

Gavin watched the light from the screen reflect onto Marni's face and into her eyes. He wanted to see her reaction, to feel it and sense it, and to know that this was going to be the winner it had to be.

The spot ended, and Marni turned toward Gavin. He looked like a kid who'd just seen some soot fall into the fireplace on Christmas Eve. Her jaw dropped, and there was that smile again.

"Well?" He couldn't wait. He just couldn't.

"It's gonna be as incredible as you thought. Even better," she said. "All your hard work is gonna pay off big time," she said.

"Hard work and brains," he helped her. He winked and pointed to his temple, in all seriousness, and at once she remembered what he sounded like when he called her "baby."

"Yeah, well, great," she said, getting up and heading back to her salad. "You should be very, very pleased," she threw over her shoulder.

But Gavin was too lost in himself to pick up the stiffened body language. He just agreed with her words and talked to himself: "Great! This is gonna be great!"

He skipped off into the kitchen to put together a sandwich for his late dinner. Although the two people occupied the same room, they were in different worlds.

Marni left for her apartment early, not long after dinner. *How come she keeps gunning her engine?* Gavin grumbled, sliding the curtain over enough to catch an eyeful of halogen headlights. He let the curtain fall back into place and wondered for a passing moment why she wasn't more excited about sharing this great victory with him. But that thought quickly passed in his desire to think about how smoothly it all was going to work.

He watched the tape again and again before realizing the day had slipped away to midnight. He started straightening up, and just before flipping the light switch in the kitchen, his eye caught the vase that was still there. He frowned. *Does Marni appreciate anything?* He'd gone to a lot of trouble to get those flowers, after all. He went over to dump them into the trash, but as his fingers slid onto the cool textured glass of the vase he noticed the mail. The handwriting on the top envelope was unmistakable. He let go of the vase, and used his thumb to tear open the flap. A small white sheet of paper with a check for twenty dollars folded inside. As always, a terse note. "Gavin: Buy yourself something you need with this. Dad."

He stared at the check and tossed it on the counter. He crumbled the note and flipped it crisply into the garbage can.

"Dad," he'd argued the last time he was home, some three years earlier, "I don't need you to send me a check every month. Or any month, for that matter. I'm making lots of money, Dad. Six figures."

"You're still my son," Vincent Duke had said resolutely, his arms folded across his chest.

"Dad, look. You're retired now. Money's tighter than you're used to around here. You need it more than I do. Just stop it, okay?"

"I take care of my son," he said stubbornly. "Nothing but the best. You can have everything you want. Not like when I grew up. We didn't have—"

"I know the drill, Dad," Gavin interrupted. "And I appreciate the thought. But the fact is, I just don't need it. And I don't want it."

"You don't want me to be a father to you?"

Don't get me started, Gavin wanted to say, straining to hold back with all his might. *Why would you want to start now?* he thought. *You never were there. Always on the road, always off to another meeting, never there for me. No wonder Mom left. You think some sorry little check can make up for missing ten years of my life! You weren't even there when I graduated, man! Do you have any idea how that feels to an eighteen-year-old kid?*

Gavin cleared his throat. "Yeah, Dad. I appreciate your wanting to be a father to me. But sending me a check every month just isn't—"

"Then there's no more discussion," Vincent Duke announced, standing up and picking up the newspaper, folding it in half and slapping the end table with the classifieds as he turned his back on his son one more time and sauntered from the cold, dim room.

Gavin blinked the memory away and realized his eyes were tired. "You're not here," he muttered out loud. "Get out of my head." He flipped off the kitchen light. "This is my time. My victory." He bounced around the house for another half hour or so before jumping into bed. He stared at the ceiling for almost another hour, punctuated by a toss here and a turn there. "It'll come soon enough," he advised himself. "Just be patient. Your time will come. Your time will come . . . "

Two

The alarm shook Gavin out of a dream—he was running and running toward something but couldn't quite make out what he was after. Exhilaration and frustration, all wrapped up in one great big blur of emotion.

On his way to the office, he rehearsed the presentation he and Carolina would make that afternoon. There would be an audience of only one: The Man.

H. Gary Harperson was president and CEO of First Southern. A great guy but something of a caricature. Almost sixty. Round. Balding and gray at the edges. Wire-rimmed specs. The ultimate company man, with thirty-two years of banker's hours behind him, all at the same bank. *How he hasn't died of boredom*, Gavin mused, *I'll never know.*

Harperson sat on a variety of civic and corporate boards. Knew the President of the United States and owned several congressmen. Yet he was a real-live family man, married only once and serving as the patriarch of several children and even more grandchildren.

Gavin was planning the bank's 150th anniversary campaign a few years earlier when he'd stumbled on a cache of fading black-and-white photos. One showed a skinny, fresh-from-college version of The Man (*The Boy?* Gavin chuckled to himself) with a full head of hair, sitting behind a big black typewriter and a hand-cranked adding machine.

You could also make out an old rotary-dial phone on the desk and a box of what appeared to be carbon paper.

"For such a relic, it's amazing how The Man's mind works," Gavin had told Carolina during a Southern Gold strategy session. "I've seen him make some gutsy decisions for a conservative old banker."

"You two seem to work pretty well together," she observed, "despite being such opposites."

"He doesn't seem to look down on my style," Gavin replied. "And he usually gives me enough freedom to make or break my own career."

"Southern Gold is going to be the ultimate stretch, though," she suggested.

"Indeed," Gavin nodded, remembering the fading photo. "Indeed."

Early on, Gavin and Carolina agreed to play the idea close to the vest before seeking The Man's blessing. All the bugs had to be out before Harperson could know of it. And even then, the presentation itself was delicate. Gavin and Carolina decided the best way to break the ice was over lunch at the country club.

"I think the safest approach is to position the historical aspect first," she'd suggested, and Gavin agreed. She engaged Harperson in a lengthy, heavily-romanced conversation about the lost Confederate gold. Did he think it still existed? Could it be buried somewhere— perhaps nearby? Maybe even right under the fourteenth green!

"No wonder I always get nervous on that approach!" Harperson laughed. Carolina and Gavin tried to share a poker-faced glance, but the eyes gave away their ecstasy. They knew they had him from then on.

Carolina deftly bridged from history to regional pride to the logical tie-ins that would make a modern-day treasure hunt the ideal marketing ploy for a bank of First Southern's prestige. He seemed hesitant at first, understandably—after all, this is a sweepstakes, and First Southern is a venerable institution. But in the end, The Man trusted this pair enough to bless their fleshing out the campaign.

And now, the day had come. The moment H. Gary Harperson could, with a single overly conservative decision, ruin everything.

Gavin felt a sudden chill at the thought—for the first time in a long while it occurred to him that The Man might actually kill it.

Gavin looked out the driver's side window to see the rising sun glistening on the penthouse spire of the Peachtree Tower, where he had seen the commercial for the first time only hours earlier. If anyone could pull this off, it was Carolina. And Gavin, of course. He digested that reassuring thought and quickly recaptured his momentarily shaken confidence.

Gavin's corner office occupied a good chunk of the First Southern building's sixtieth floor. He'd earned it. The view was expansive, and the appointments just shy of the luxurious decor he felt he really deserved—can't have top brass thinking they're paying him too much. Gavin had been described five years earlier by *Business Week* as "a marvelous hybrid, an alchemist's perfect fusion of the adman and the banker" when, at thirty-one, he claimed a vice-presidency at First Southern—no small feat in a world still dominated by gray-headed ol' boys who chomp cigars and still manage to call their assistants "honey."

"Working seven days a week pays off," he told the reporter. "The phones don't ring on Sundays, so I can breeze by the other guys."

Gavin parked the Mercedes and boarded the elevator, his mind a swirl of thoughts.

"Good morning." Ruth looked up as he breezed in. She was always there first, mapping out the day and getting the coffee started.

"Ruth. Ruth! The spot is unbelievable," he blurted to his startled assistant. "Carrie's done it again. C'mon. Take a look at this!"

Ruth Chandler followed Gavin into his office for the private screening. He trusted her enough to show her the spot before The Man would see it, which said a lot for Ruth. Gavin was distrustful to the point of being almost paranoid, and Ruth knew it.

They watched together and, naturally, Ruth loved it. "I'll call Mr. Harperson's office so we can set up the presentation time," she volunteered, knowing that would be the next step.

She buzzed him minutes later: "It's all set. Three o'clock, in the boardroom, you and Ms. Gates and Mr. Harperson. I'll arrange for catering to have some beverages ready."

Gavin dove into some paperwork, knowing the best way to endure the wait would be to stay busy. But time dragged anyway, and he wondered if three o'clock would ever crawl into view.

At ten before three, Carolina made her entrance. "Ready?" she asked.

"Roger," Gavin replied, bouncing out from behind the black marble desk. "Let's go knock The Man dead!"

"Or at least comatose," she retorted with a wry grin.

The meeting felt like a dream to Gavin. Carolina's and Harperson's voices seemed to echo, and his own words felt disembodied. But like clockwork, Carolina Gates delivered the perfect setup and paid it off with the golden spot.

No wonder she's been able to land every hot account in the region, Gavin thought as Carolina nailed point after point. The fact was, Carolina Gates Advertising had—in just ten years—propelled itself to being the largest ad agency based in the Southeast. Her blue-chip client roster was envied even on Madison Avenue: Coca-Cola, Delta Airlines, CNN, and of course, First Southern Bank.

"Thank you, Mr. Harperson," Carolina's crisp voice announced. "That concludes our presentation."

She was finished. She slowly closed her leather folder. And she sat back down.

The Man didn't say a thing at first. Gavin thought about free-falling out his office window if the big thumb went down. He glanced over at Carolina, whose eyes were fixed on Harperson's. Gavin wondered if she was thinking about the big dive too.

The Man cleared his throat. "If I were the marketing director," he drawled, "I wouldn't go with it. Too risky."

Gavin gulped. Carolina didn't flinch.

"But, I don't hire the smartest people I can find to micromanage them. You do it if you think it's the right thing to do. Just remember—it's your necks on the block with this one."

Gavin's heart skipped half a dozen beats, he estimated. But he had finally gotten his go-ahead.

As they rode the elevator down five stories to Gavin's office, the emotional tension was enormous. The long and hard silence snapped as they broke into simultaneous fits of laughter.

Gavin wiped a tear away from each eye and said, "I was picturing a sixty-five-story jump for a minute there."

"I'd have been holding your hand," Carolina said. "Splat!"

The elevator door opened in front of the kid from the mailroom, who didn't quite know what to make of this man and this woman rolling forward in convulsions of laughter.

Three

This was Gavin's favorite table at JohnBarley's.

It was big, round, and strategically located in a corner—tucked away from conspicuous attention during hush-hush meetings, yet providing a sweeping view of everyone who came into—or out of—the place.

JohnBarley's was a popular downtown grill. It was run by John Bently, proprietor, a genuine Brit's Brit who gave up a career in advertising to chase his dream. John made it a point to know the regulars, like Gavin, and to stay on top of things. He was a veritable who's who of Atlanta; Gavin always could catch up on some fascinating business insights when John was around.

But on this night, Gavin was all by himself at the corner table, with papers and pencils and a calculator strewn about, along with the napkins, peanut shells, and dreams of grandeur. Gavin was assembling his thoughts on how Southern Gold would be structured, in his favorite environment—all alone at JohnBarley's.

The campaign would work roughly like this. First Southern would assemble a fortune similar to the lost treasure of the Confederacy—one million dollars worth of gold bars. It would be sealed in a brass and hickory trunk and hidden somewhere in the South.

Roughly, the South was First Southern's market. The bank also had offices in Kentucky and West Virginia. First Southern was a super-regional bank—with $97 billion in assets, it was the fourth largest in the country. Founded in 1842 as the Cotton-Growers' Co-Operative Exchange of Macon, Georgia, it was one of the few banks to survive the Civil War. It prospered through various gestations and ownerships before becoming the gleaming corporation it was today.

But wait, Gavin thought. *That's too unfocused. Too big. Let's make a tighter bull's-eye: The loot will be stashed somewhere in Georgia, First Southern's home state.* It might call more attention to the fact that the bank was based in Atlanta—in case any out-of-town banks wanted to buy the bank out (and make Gavin's stock soar), they could feel comfortable that First Southern was situated in a real metropolis and not a place like Frog Bend, Mississippi. Better still, Gavin could keep tighter reins of control—no regional directors or managers might try to force their way in on anything if it was right under Gavin's nose.

Good. That's settled. Now, back to the good stuff. Current customers would automatically be included, but the real ticket was drawing new customers in. Anyone who opened a new account within ninety days of the program kick-off would begin to get clues as to the treasure's location. Each week, another clue would be mailed out. Current customers, of course, would also get all of the dozen clues. Customers would get them more quickly by having more accounts. For instance, a person who already had a checking account would get three clues in three months. But if he or she added a savings account, there would be three more clues—six in all for that person during the first three weeks. A new customer taking out a car loan would get three clues. Someone with a dozen accounts, theoretically, could get all twelve clues the first week. *No, there has to be a limit. Yeah—a maximum of three clues per week.*

At the end of four months, if nobody had found the treasure, ten lucky customers would get a map with their monthly statement. Nine of the maps would lead to a check for one thousand dollars—not a bad consolation prize. The tenth would point the way to the one million dollars in Southern Gold.

Gavin would personally deliver tnese ten statements. To heighten the drama, none of the maps would indicate whether this was a consolation prize or the real thing. Camera crews would accompany Gavin and the breathless customers.

There were only two things left to do now. The first was to get with Carolina and her people to put everything in place. The second: to bury the treasure.

This problem began to take on enormous complexities as Gavin pondered it more and more. Would The Man really go for hiding a million bucks worth of gold without making a fuss about security? Would he in fact even authorize such an expenditure—after all, even First Southern didn't keep that much lying around in petty cash. Or was this inspired plan now potentially back on the chopping block? Where do you go to get that much gold, anyway—Fort Knox? The Queen Mother? The Emir of Kuwait? How about the Crown Prince of the Pekoe Islands?

And how was Gavin going to figure out where to hide it, or get it there unnoticed? He absentmindedly pulled a coin out of his pants pocket and turned it from side to side. The lights from the bar glistened dimly on the edges as he turned it, over and over again.

This was no ordinary coin. H. Gary Harperson had given it to him a couple of weeks earlier. Gavin was working at his desk late one night when The Man stopped by. He was carrying a tiny manila envelope.

"Hey, Gavin, got a minute?"

"Sure, Gary. Pull up a chair." He motioned with his hand.

"Gavin, I've got a little something for you here, a gift I've given a lot of thought to. I wanted to personally express my gratitude for all you've poured into this Confederate promotion, just from me to you." He held out the envelope. Gavin took it and rolled the coin into his palm. For once, he was speechless.

The Man had managed to get ahold of a rather rare silver half-dollar, one struck from the dies used to make genuine Confederate coinage. Only five hundred of these re-strikes had been minted, more than a century ago, and rare coin dealers sold them for nearly two thousand dollars. Harperson then had it electroplated with fourteen-karat gold.

On the front was an engraving of a female figure representing

Liberty. She wore a flowing, silky gown. Beneath the figure was the year: 1861. The back said "Confederate States of America" and "Half Dol." around the edges. In the center was a shield, with seven stars representing the original seven seceding states. It was beautiful.

Gavin was so touched by the gesture, he decided to carry the coin with him at all times. It's not that he was superstitious or considered it a lucky charm—he believed far too much in himself to feel the need for any such hocus-pocus—he simply considered it a tangible reminder of good things to come as Southern Gold unfolded.

"Gavin!"

John Bently didn't notice the coin. Gavin slid it back into his pocket.

"You look like you're about to give birth to the greatest idea since refrigeration," John said from underneath his dark curly moustache. His endearing British accent helped ease any frustration a marketing VP could feel.

"No lie," Gavin said. "And I've just about got it."

"Shall I have Allie bring you another? Oh, sorry, she just went off shift. Olivia! Tend to this fine man!"

The waitress came over and smiled. "What can I get for you two boys?" she said with a wink.

"How about something clear, sparkling, and sweet," he said, rubbing his chin.

"Number eleven," John said to her, and she darted off before Gavin had a chance to find out just what "number eleven" might be.

"Thanks, my friend," Gavin said.

"Not a problem." He paused. "Well, I can see you're behind the eight-ball here. I'll let you get back at it. I'll see you later on, fair enough?"

"Fair enough," Gavin smiled, and got back to the problem at hand.

Okay, he told himself, *tomorrow morning Ruth can dig around and find out about where we can get the money, about insuring it—yeah, it needs to be insured—and I can drop by legal and see if I can get something that big without creating an uproar upstairs.*

"Done," he said audibly, starting to stack the papers. Gavin was without question a doer and wasn't necessarily comfortable leaving something undone. Nonetheless, he'd learned early on how to pace himself—if there was nothing more that could be done until the next morning, he could close it off, shut it out, and relax.

He flipped his wrist over to glance at his watch. *Almost nine. What can a dashing young man-about-town find to do here while the evening is still young?* He craned his neck over toward the bar as he slid his hand into his pocket. He began to roll the gold half-dollar between his fingers, without taking it out, as he fixed his gaze upon some long golden curls. He began contemplating what he might say to introduce . . .

"Hey, sailor!" a familiar voice broke in.

He looked up. It was Marni. He felt his face grow flush as his eyes met hers, and he heard himself taking a deep breath. "Honey!" he fluttered, about to mutter the obvious remark about wondering what she was doing here, what a coincidence, ad nauseam. He pulled his hand out of his pocket, leaving the coin behind.

"Didn't forget our date, did you?" she purred. She was kidding, but the precision of the joke frightened him.

His gaze darted toward the spot he had last sighted the golden curls, but they had vanished. *Ah, well, back to reality.*

"'Course not, darling," he said, giving her a Hollywood kiss. "Here, I was just clearing the table off for you."

Gavin's timing was better than an all-star hitter's that night; Olivia, the waitress, appeared at that very instant with the effervescent number eleven John Bently had called for a moment ago.

"Er, look—I ordered something for you. I hope you don't mind my being so presumptuous!" He flashed the famous Gavin Duke smile.

"Why, you're so sweet," Marni replied, reaching over to touch his hand as she flashed a smile of her own. "But aren't you going to have something?"

"I've already had a couple—sorry. Been here working for quite a while." He motioned to the papers, which were about to be briefcased.

"No phones, huh?" she asked, taking a little sip. She made a curious face, punctuated with a grin. "Hey, this is good. What is it anyway?"

"'Number eleven,'" Gavin said as though he invented it and personally committed the formula to memory.

"I see," she laughed, sharing again with him the smile he'd noticed twice the night before. Her eyes looked right into his and pierced straight into his soul. For the first time in two weeks, he forgot about the campaign.

He'd had a moment to get his wits about him and remembered setting up the get-together. *She's already had dinner, so don't stick your foot in your mouth with "Where do you want to eat?" or something similarly stupid.* She'd had a meeting in Midtown scheduled that evening, so they'd planned on getting together at his favorite watering hole. From there, they'd decide if they wanted to go dancing, try to find a late show, or plan something else. *Okay*, Gavin thought, *now I can deal with this.*

"Well, what's the plan?" she asked. "Are you into a movie, or how about a play?"

"Are you on your normal hours tomorrow morning?" he asked.

"Yeah," she frowned, resting her chin on her right hand. "I probably ought to get in pretty early." Gavin could hear the background noise of the pub as she paused. "But then again, we haven't seen each other much lately. Maybe I can be a little groggy tomorrow morning, if you've got something really special up your sleeve." She arched her eyebrows and cocked her head expectantly.

"Well . . . " Gavin looked away, hoping once more to catch a glimpse of the golden curls at the bar. He took a breath, straightened himself, and said, "You know, I've been so buried in the new campaign lately, I know I ought to take a break, but I think maybe I just need to catch some shut-eye."

Marni sighed and sank back a little. *Maybe it was for the best*, she reasoned. *Five-thirty always came like a ton of bricks—especially after kicking up my heels. Besides, I'm not sixteen any more. Staying out all night and getting up early isn't any good for an old lady.* Suddenly, she felt like an old lady. She looked across at Gavin, and realized he had already forgotten about her and was patrolling the place with his ever-roving eyes. *Must be quite a looker over my shoulder*, she thought to herself.

"Yeah, maybe you're right," Marni admitted. "Let's call it quits early." She got up, picked up her purse, and started out, making sure to mutter under her breath, "Us old ladies start to creak after nine o'clock anyway," so she could at least enjoy the satisfaction of her own sarcasm. Gavin stuffed his papers in his briefcase and followed close behind.

On the way to her car, a fight ensued. Gavin never did put his finger on what started it or what it ended up being about. They sped their separate ways. He crawled into bed early, but didn't find any sleep until nearly three A.M.

🥮   🥮   🥮

Gavin downed enough coffee to make it out the door before seven the next morning, but he didn't even think about Marni on the way to the office.

It was a smooth trip in, as usual, one of the benefits of beating rush hour. The only delay was just outside his neighborhood. A local church was expanding so one lane was blocked off to allow some underground utility work. "They haven't made any progress in a week," Gavin grumbled to himself, making a mental comparison between a church adding members and a bank adding customers. "If these guys can manage to grow," he decided, "we'd better be able to. Ha! All they offer is hard wooden benches, and we're giving people a chance to become filthy rich!"

At work, he had Ruth follow him into his suite as soon as he arrived. As though only a few seconds had passed from his meeting with himself the night before, he set right out to deliver the marching orders. "By the end of the day today," he began, "I want to know the best place to get ahold of one million dollars in gold bullion. I want to know about insuring it. I need to know what other problems might blindside me about the money. And I need a custom furniture company—the best in town—to make the treasure chest itself. I'll talk to John Merritt, in legal, to see exactly how I can requisition a million dollars without The Man having a coronary."

He looked up to see if Ruth was laughing; she was not. She was writing furiously. He paused long enough for her to catch up. She did, but she still did not laugh. He tapped his fingers on his desktop. "Any questions?"

She finished writing but didn't really look up. "No."

Oh, great, he thought. *First Marni. Now Ruth. Doesn't anybody want to treat me with the respect I deserve? Ah, forget it. Onward.*

"Okay, then, let's go!" he clapped his hands together and swung around in his chair. He grabbed the phone and punched in John Merritt's number. Ruth walked out unnoticed.

John picked up on the first ring. *For a corporate attorney, he's all right,* Gavin thought. *Detail-oriented. Nice guy. Bright. On a fast enough track of his own—department head at thirty-five or so.* Gavin respected him.

"John, what do you call half a dozen attorneys buried up to their necks in sand?" Gavin blurted into the sleek black phone.

"I think you told me this one last week," John offered, good-naturedly trying to get to the point of the call.

"Not enough sand! Pretty great, huh?" Gavin said, not waiting for a laugh or even a groan. "Hey, John, a quick question. Our big new promotion is coming up, and we need—get this—a million in gold bars for the grand prize." He paused to let that sink in, but John just kept listening. The respect was not mutual.

"What I need to know is, what's the best way for me to run the paperwork? How do I get my hands on that much money in a hurry?"

John said, "I've got a couple of ideas, but let me check them out first. I'll have Teresa and Abby check a couple of other paths, then Kelly or I will get back to you. End of the day okay?"

"The sooner the better. And thanks."

The day flew by—not enough hours. At four, John Merritt called. He said there were two ways to handle it. One, negotiate a payment schedule with whoever provides the gold and pay in installments. Surely, anyone must recognize First Southern would be good for the money. Option two, simply requisition it through the ad budget and see if it flies.

"With that one, obviously, I'd need to have a contingency plan set up—what to do if The Man reacts badly," Gavin thought out loud.

"Agreed," said John.

"It's good to know it's that easy," Gavin started to wrap up. "Thanks, John. Good to know I can always count on you. I owe ya one, buddy. A steak dinner some night."

"Thanks," John hurried. "Talk to you later." He hung up before having to actually set up a get-together with Gavin.

Carolina called a few minutes later with a bevy of last-minute details for the agency to handle. "Anything else?" Gavin asked after she'd gone through her checklist.

"Nope. I just need to confirm a few things with Ruth now."

"Is she taking good care of you?"

"Do you even have to ask?"

Gavin chuckled. "No, I guess not. I think *efficiency* is Ruth's middle name. Keeps me from getting buried at my own desk."

Carolina considered her words carefully before she spoke. "Don't you worry about losing her?"

"Nah," Gavin replied, stretching out the word. "She's a sharp girl, sharp enough to stick with the winning program."

"Oh, I see," Carolina nodded into the phone, biting her lower lip. *Lord, open his eyes*, she added silently. She thought back to one of the rare glimpses behind his public face, a time he showed a softer, deeper side. It was the Christmas campaign two years earlier. A disaster in the making—a commercial that had to hit the air on Tuesday morning, but the lawyers had come in on Monday at six with a slew of changes. Gavin and Carolina stayed up all night in the edit suite.

🍩 🍩 🍩

Around 4:30 in the morning, Gavin had leaned back, yawned, sighed, and turned to look at his bleary-eyed counterpart. "Carrie," he'd said. "Do you ever wonder if all this is worth it?"

She'd turned to look at him without a reply, waiting for him to continue this most unusual train of thought.

"I mean, here we are. Top of our careers, both of us. Not rich. Yet. But doing okay, you know?" A pause. "And look at us. Middle of the night, and for what? So we can beat this idiotic deadline, so we can get this blasted spot on the air, and then everybody just gets up and fixes a sandwich when this stupid thing comes on?"

"We simply have to get the job done," she muttered back, fascinated by the depth of his thoughts and not accustomed to them floating to the surface.

He sighed. "Yeah, I guess so." He thought some more and continued. "You know, you're the best," he smiled. "You really are remarkable, Carrie. Sometimes, I wish I could be as settled as you are, happily married and all that. There's something warm and inviting about the way you and Burl live your lives."

Carolina blushed, not sure what to say to anyone who'd pay such a compliment, and certainly caught off-guard to hear words such as these from Gavin Duke. So she watched him; looked as though he was struggling to formulate a profound thought, an idea, a concept that might actually be life-changing. She waited, and he finally broke the silence.

"Besides," he said, an impish grin slowly replacing the wilted expression. "It looks like The Man is planning a pretty hefty bonus for me on this one. Got that from a reliable source." He'd straightened up and clapped his hands together, then rubbed them as though trying to start a fire. "Ten bills," he nodded slowly, winking at Carolina, before turning back to the hapless engineer, tapping him on the shoulder, and bellowing, "C'mon, can't you move a little quicker? Let's see if we can get out of here by sunrise!"

❧   ❧   ❧

"Carrie? Carrie! Anybody in there?" Gavin's impatience flowed through the phone line.

"Oh, I'm sorry, Gavin," Carolina apologized. "Guess I got distracted there for a second."

"Yeah, right. Well, if there's nothing else, I'll talk to you later."

Carolina put the phone down and stared out the window. She knew there was so much more to Gavin Duke than what met the eye. If only God would bring someone into his life who could get beneath the veneer. Someone who could truly make a difference . . .

❧   ❧   ❧

Within the hour, Gavin was starting to drown in the sea of papers that had flooded his desk. Ruth interrupted Gavin's cataclysm by buzzing him and saying she had the preliminary answers he needed.

She entered his office to find him rubbing his eyes and loosening his stiff neck muscles. The strain was starting to show, with all the big plans, the excitement, and the emotion-stuffing he was doing. He wanted someone to share the roller-coaster ride he was taking.

Ruth stopped, and for the first time in a long while saw him as a person instead of just a demanding, egocentric boss. She gazed at him with a measure of sympathy. He looked up, and their eyes met. Gavin was struck with the notion that for this instant, he was connecting with a woman. He studied her face. Hazel eyes. Sandy hair, pulled back tight and clipped. Pursed lips, without any lipstick. Not much makeup at all, in fact. And of course, the obligatory navy blue "uniform."

Ruth was a loyal employee, dedicated to Gavin and to the bank. But whenever she heard Harperson introduce her boss—"Gavin is our finest team player" was Harperson's stock line when introducing his marketing genius—Gavin never saw past the handshakes and the smiles to notice Ruth wince.

She had joined the bank five years earlier, right after Gavin's promotion. A few weeks after she started, the two were working late one night, developing an ad campaign for a new branch opening in a smaller market. Gavin had come up with a campaign based on local residents expressing their frustration with the existing community banks—short hours, limited services, inconvenient locations.

"What if we took a more positive approach?" Ruth wondered aloud. "Do you think maybe they would find that tack more palatable? Instead of voicing complaints about the well-established banks, maybe they could instead more subtly talk about their wish lists for a bank. Which, of course, First Southern could fulfill."

Gavin gave her a swaggering look and said, "Look, honey, don't play amateur psychologist here. People like to gripe a little, especially at banks, so they'll need to get this out of their systems before we can come riding in on a white horse."

She felt as though she'd been punched in the stomach but tried to write it off as Gavin being tired. It was late, after all. And had that been the end of it, she probably would have forgotten it altogether. But the very next day, still feeling slightly stung, she got a dose of Gavin at his worst.

Carolina had come over, along with the rest of the agency's account team that was assigned to the bank. Gavin began to lay out his idea, so the creative director, writer, and art director could prepare the ads. A pensive look crossed over Carolina's face and she said, "Gavin, I do love it. But what if we take the more positive approach and . . . "

Before she could finish—and before Ruth could assemble her emotions of vindication, joy, and relief—Gavin shot a piercing look straight through her and said, "Now, Ruth, I'm gonna have to reprimand you on this one, in front of everybody. Carolina's right— this needs to be more positive and not so whiny. I told you, but you insisted I go with your gut on this one. So I listened to you, and here, what do we have? The brightest, smartest adwoman this side of the Mississippi agrees with me. Maybe next time you'll trust my instincts, huh?"

Ruth was too shocked to cough out a reply, and even if she had been able to overcome the blow, she was too young to realize she could do anything except put up with it and gulp, "Yes, Mr. Duke. I'm sorry." But she did manage to make her first mental note of genuine contempt against Gavin. It would not be the last.

"Sit down, Ruth," Gavin said as he motioned to the chair. He smiled sweetly. "What have you got?"

"Okay," she said, immune to his temporary mood shifts. "Getting the gold is no problem. The best bet is to try the Fed first. In case the red tape is too thick there, I've made a list of the three leading brokers in town. All that's left is for you to negotiate their fees."

"Fees. Give me a break," he said. Still, even in his frustration, he admired Ruth. She always got to the hard stuff before it was a problem.

"Next, insurance. Kathy Jewett can handle that—it's just a minor variation on the cash holdings and safe deposit box holdings the bank maintains every day."

Good, Gavin thought. *Kathy is the best and brightest corporate insurance agent in town. She'll do us good.*

"For the trunk, Ogilvy's can handle that. They're sending a delivery service over with one of their catalogs, which you can take a look at. When you're ready, they can talk about whatever custom options you want. They've got a top designer on the payroll." She handed the catalog across the desk to him.

"Anything else?" he asked.

"I couldn't think of any other potential problems, except keeping it quiet—where we hide it, of course," she told him.

"'We'?" he repeated. She looked down. Silence. She walked out, tired.

Gavin watched her go. He missed Marni, but he just wasn't capable of drumming up the energy to fix things, especially now that the campaign was consuming everything he had. Yet he was tired of being so alone. He gulped and licked his lips.

"Ruth?"

She stopped and turned.

"Maybe I could buy you a drink sometime, after work."

She felt a surge of rage flow up from her stomach, past her neck, coming to a boil behind her eyes. "Sure," she said with as forced a smile as she ever had to make in her life, quickly turning on her high heels and spinning out through the office door.

She tried to shuffle some papers into order once she made it back to her desk, but her hands were shaking too violently. She darted to the bathroom and heaved cold water onto her face, again and again, before clutching the faucet and peering into the mirror. The water was dripping off her hot red cheeks, and the image staring back into her eyes startled her—too much anger, too much fear. She didn't look young any more. She coughed until she nearly gagged, but managed to pour some cool water down her throat, although her hands still trembled.

Gavin stayed late and wasn't aware of Ruth leaving. He finally packed it in around nine to head home and collapse onto the couch. He kept hoping Marni would call, but she didn't. He fell asleep with the TV on before stumbling up after midnight to get into his bed.

❧   ❧   ❧

Across town that night, Ruth spoke softly but with determination as she lay next to her husband. Her head rested lightly on the pillow, and she stared at the darkened ceiling.

"Someday, somehow, I'm gonna get back at him," she said. Ronnie knew about every put-down and snide remark Gavin had dished out, so he knew what she felt. He reached over and touched her arm but found it stiff and unyielding. Ruth was changing, and he wasn't sure if he knew what to expect from her any more. He did know one thing, though—his own anger toward Gavin Duke was growing into a deep, gnawing hatred too. Something was going to have to give. Soon.

Four

The hings were really starting to roll now.

Gavin had his coveted go-ahead from The Man. He had his plan for getting the gold, which he would carry out simultaneously with the agency's preparation of the rest of the campaign. And he had a roomful of people, hanging on his every move and ready to jump through endless hoops at his will.

It was eight A.M., straight up. Ten people were assembled around the marketing department conference table, at the heart of the sixtieth floor. Gavin sat at one head of the table, Carolina at the other. He slowly gazed around the table, relishing the moment; truly this was an assemblage of all-stars, the very best at each specific craft.

At Gavin's left was Ruth. Next to her, Jenny Nicholas, the account executive from the agency. At Jenny's left was Amy Christiansen, the traffic coordinator. Between Amy and Carolina was Beth Forrester, the media director. On Carolina's left was Kelvin Overland, the art director. Next to Kelvin: Gregg Walton, the copywriter. Beside Gregg was Bill Carlton, the producer/director who'd put together the TV spots. Between Bill and Gavin was Ernie Santiago, the agency's creative director.

"Where's Allyn?" Gavin asked. "Not coming?"

"No," Carolina said. "He's in Boston this week, but Ernie can fill him in. Maureen's not here either." Jim Allyn was the agency's direct mail expert, and Maureen Hale headed Carolina's PR division. Gavin and Carolina had already planned to meet separately with Maureen, since her tasks would be based on the ad campaign and would follow a different course of action.

"All right, then, let's get started," Gavin said crisply. "You've all seen the spot Bill produced last week. It's been okayed, and we'll be going back into the edit suite to tighten up a few things here and there. But overall, that's the direction we'll be heading with this." He paused to let his intro sink in.

"You've also seen the marketing plan Carolina and I have put together," he said. Each person had in front of them a copy in a binder of blue and gold, First Southern's colors.

"Let's start with questions about the plan. Anyone?"

"I'll want to get a better idea of how you want to weigh spending in the mid-size and smaller markets," Beth said, flipping back and forth between two pages near the end of the plan.

"Okay," said Gavin, looking over to make sure Ruth was making a note of it. She was.

"Other questions and comments?"

"Let's talk about the groundwork of the creative strategy," Ernie said as he leaned into a sip of hot coffee. "There really are two creative campaigns here, not counting the PR. We've got the tease campaign before the treasure hunt starts, to build the excitement to a crescendo, and the ongoing maintenance campaign. Even that will have to be dynamic, constantly changing, as people come into it and we have to adjust to any close calls, false alarms, or other circumstances."

He paused for another sip. "In fact, this is going to be a pretty unique campaign—it's going to have to act more like a PR campaign than a typical ad campaign, since we will have to be more responsive than usual. We can't just set this one up and let it ride. We've got to be ready to get new executions on the air or in the paper on a moment's notice."

"How's the creative department staffing situation right now?" Gavin asked Carolina.

"Ernie and I were talking about that on the way over this morning.

We've got the regulars in place, and the new business team just wrapped up the pitch on the state tourism account, so they're . . . "

"Congratulations, by the way," Gavin interrupted with a smile. "Great campaign."

"Thanks, Gavin," Carolina smiled, darting a glance at Ernie, "Great job, Ernie." Ernie shrugged a "thanks" of his own, but Gavin didn't notice. He was already well into his next agenda item.

Carolina got back to her thought. "The new business team has two little pitches to start thinking about, but their schedule is clean enough right now that they can act as backup. And of course, we've also got the usual stable of freelancers in case there's a major crunch."

"Bottom line: it's under control," Ernie said to Gavin.

"Great. Other concerns?"

"Not a concern, just an update," Beth said. "I've already talked to the key stations in our top markets. We've got roadblocks set up for G-Day."

Gavin laughed to himself at how that sentence would sound to an outsider. He got a kick out of his bridging two industries—that he could rattle off jargon in both banking-ese and advertising-ese. A roadblock? Ad lingo for the same commercial on more than one station at the exact same time, so the consumer has no choice but to get the message. And G-Day? Ah, G-Day. The result of a late-night planning session at JohnBarley's with Carolina.

"What'll we call the kick-off date?" she'd asked one groggy night.

He said, "How about 'The Dukester's Delight' or 'Carrie's Cash-In'?"

"Maybe 'Harperson's Horrible Nightmare,'" Gavin presented, "because that's when he'll finally figure out he's really giving away one million dollars!"

When they'd gotten their wits more about them, they'd settled on G-Day, for "Gold Day," à la D-Day. It was a good name, appropriate and fun for the agency team to work with.

G-Day was set for May first, now just eight weeks away. A frenetic time frame, even by advertising standards, but not to worry. Gavin and Carolina had handled tasks that made this schedule look like child's play.

"Gregg, Kelvin. Ruth has a background packet for you guys on the logistics. Beth, you'll get the final budget figures over the fax this afternoon. Jenny, Amy, I'll look for the agency wish-list from you two this week—any special P.O. requirements or other routing issues." Everyone scribbled madly, and Gavin enjoyed it. He was hitting stride.

"That should just about do it, unless there's anything else," Carolina said, implying the meeting was over.

No one spoke up, so everyone stood, started the small talk, grabbed some more coffee or a danish, and got ready to head back to their parts in this enormous puzzle.

"Pleased, Mr. Duke?" Carolina appeared before her client as he turned around from saying something to Jenny.

"You don't know how to do it any other way, Carrie," he said, stuffing half a jelly doughnut into his right cheek.

Carolina and Maureen, the PR expert, were already sitting at the table when Gavin arrived for lunch the next day. Maureen, like anyone else who had achieved a key position with Carolina, was superbly talented. She was blessed with a warm nature, an incisive mind, and penetrating, thoughtful eyes. Gavin felt very comfortable with her leading the public relations charge to G-Day and beyond.

"Hey, ladies," he said, pulling up a chair and noticing Carolina looked a little tired today. "How're things?"

"Just great," Carolina said.

"No complaints," Maureen said. "It's good to see you—it's been a while."

"Since the Christmas party last year, wasn't it?" Gavin recalled.

"Yep," Maureen said. "Looks like quite a lot's happened since then."

"That's nothing compared to the next few months!" Gavin added, and he grinned. Carolina grinned too, and shook her head in agreement.

They continued in normal business banter—the small talk that precedes getting down to business. Gavin loved the fact that Carolina and her top hitters needed so little direction, and these two women were prime examples of short and sweet meetings that didn't eat up a lot of his time.

Gavin moved his steak sandwich aside and said, "Did you have any thoughts on the marketing plan?"

Maureen shook her head. "No, it's pretty straightforward. I'm leaving the PR plan with you so you can scope out the details. But the basic outline is this: we'll set the stage with Ernie's teaser campaign—lots of mystery and romance about the Confederate gold—but with no payoff as to the details of the sweeps, only the fact that it's out there, it's been out there for more than a century, it may be right under your feet, and now you've got a chance to be a part of history and cash in."

Gavin listened intently and ate a thick french fry.

"On April fifteenth, two weeks before G-Day, we'll start contacting the media and major support players," she continued. "Like the various law enforcement officials and government agencies, to see if we can get them in on the act. We'll set up the press conference for May first, which will be held in the Grand Ballroom of the Ritz, downtown. Unless . . . "

"Unless what?" Gavin asked.

"We're trying to get clearance to have it right on the steps of the state capitol building, in front of the golden dome. But with all the red tape involved, it's doubtful that'll work."

"It'd be a nice touch, though," Gavin said, looking to Carolina for agreement. She smiled and nodded. It *would* be a nice touch—the Georgia capitol building in Atlanta was crowned by a golden dome, gold mined in the mountains north of the city.

Actually, the first big gold rush in the United States took place in the South, not California or Alaska, in the early 1800s—long before the Civil War, long before there was a Confederacy or any Confederate treasure. The genuine Southern Gold backdrop was the perfect place to kick off the Southern Gold campaign.

"Of course," Carolina pointed out, "it'd be a disaster if a rainstorm came along." She frowned.

Gavin thought for a moment. "That's too big a risk, even though the payoff would be fabulous. Scratch the capitol. Let's do the Ritz."

"The Ritz it is," said Maureen. She continued reading from her notes. "We're trying to talk the governor into being there. By playing the historical angle right, we may be able to get his interest."

"That'd be fabulous," Carolina said.

"You're something else!" Gavin said to Maureen.

She blushed just a little but looked back down at her notes quickly enough that neither Gavin nor Carolina noticed, she hoped. "From there, we start phase two: making a big deal out of every move anybody makes. If somebody claims they find it, we call the TV stations. If new clues go out, we alert the papers. If anybody comes from out of state to look for the gold, we're on the phone or writing an updated press release. In fact, we've got a system in place to fax daily account activity updates to the media—which is highly unusual in the banking industry—to show the frenzy we're creating."

She paused, and the pause became more dramatic as all three realized at once how big a disaster they could be setting themselves up for. What if they threw this really great party and nobody came?

But none of the three articulated that thought. In fact, Gavin quickly dismissed it altogether. Plenty of reporters would pick up every morsel, like that new reporter for the *Atlanta Business Courier* who was replacing Fast Eddie on the bank beat. What was his name? Gavin realized he hadn't heard yet. Surely, whoever it was would be ready to make a splash, and he'd be looking for anything he could get. Gavin returned to his sandwich, and the big pow-wow gently revolved back into the small talk with which they'd started. The meeting ended gracefully, a big success. All the planning, preparation, and excitement pushed the fear of failure aside. Southern Gold was destined to be a big hit.

✎   ✎   ✎

Over the next few weeks, as G-Day approached, it seemed odd to Gavin that First Southern's president didn't appear all too eager for updates. True, H. Gary Harperson took a much more laid-back management approach than his marketing genius, but it seemed oddly unlike him to not be sweating more details—a million dollars' worth of details! Nonetheless, Gavin was pleased and relieved. His nerves were jangling enough as it was, and he certainly didn't need anybody breathing down his neck. Especially the one person in the United States who could cause Gavin career problems at this point.

Time alternately dragged and flew. Gavin had never felt such a roller-coaster ride of emotion before—higher highs and lower lows than ever, often within minutes of one another. Much of this was taken out on Ruth, and although Gavin didn't realize what he was doing, Ruth was keeping track of every cutting and sarcastic remark he made to her.

Ruth's notions of settling the score started simply enough, months earlier, when Ronnie was out of town on business. Too scared by the creaking of the house to sleep, Ruth stayed up late watching lousy old movies. Around 3:30 one morning, she found herself sobbing uncontrollably while watching a film where an innocently wronged girl just couldn't escape her tormentor. She fell asleep with the TV on and dreamed of being tortured by Gavin, calling and calling for help, but no one could hear her. She woke up in a cold sweat.

No, she could never do physical harm to anyone—not even Gavin Duke—but the concept of payback had been firmly ingrained into her thoughts.

They seemed harmless at first. Throwing a drink in his face at an office gathering, or delivering a well-rehearsed, vicious cut at an agency meeting, or leaving a large dent in the driver's side door of his precious Mercedes.

But the cuts from Gavin grew deeper and more frequent. She found herself in tears almost every day—in the ladies' room at work, driving home, and in Ronnie's arms. "Too bad I can't ask Gavin's advice on how to get even," she thought on the way home one night. "Wouldn't that be a wonderful irony? He's so good at chopping human beings to pieces when it fits his agenda, he'd surely devise a wonderful plan for me to carry out!"

"Maybe I just need to quit," she said once over dinner. She continued before Ronnie could point out she'd been saying that for more than a year now. "But it's easier said than done. Gavin doesn't like being crossed, and he'd see my leaving as disloyalty—a major stab in the back after all he thinks he's done for me. He could make all the clichés come true. I'd never work in this town again." She knew that was a box she couldn't afford to fall into because Ronnie's income just didn't make the ends meet yet—not by a long stretch. She pushed her plate away and drummed her fingers.

She hated herself for daring to think about a concept as dark as revenge, and she hated Gavin for driving her to that point. She was a bright, kind person, after all. How could anybody push her into being a basket case like this?

One afternoon, three weeks before G-Day, everything came to a head. It was late, about 8:30 on a Friday night, and she was still at work, no questions asked, because Gavin was still running. She was exhausted and wanted to head home to see her husband, to eat, or just to kick her feet up and let down her hair. Finally, she decided she just had to say, "Look, I've got to go." And she started to—no less than four times. But each time, Gavin interrupted with some other gruff instruction. She'd had it, and she noticed she was starting to shake.

Gavin reached suddenly across his desk to grab a media schedule, and the move surprised Ruth. She jerked her hand out of the way, hitting Gavin's half-empty coffee cup and spilling the contents onto his slacks. He jumped up, more than a bit frayed at this point. "You airhead!" he called out. "Can't you just . . . just . . ." he caught himself, realizing his words might be too strong for the crime, but feeling angry and tired and needing to be in control. He took a long breath and, not hearing her apologize yet—she'd just sat there, motionless—said, "Of course, I'll send you the cleaning bill."

He went into the washroom to clean up as best as he could, and while he was out of the office, Ruth slowly got up and walked out. She didn't say anything about the coffee incident to Ronnie that night. She just muttered "You know Gavin," and curled up in front of the TV with a warm, old blanket.

When she came into work Monday morning—at 8:30 instead of the usual 7:30 or 7:45—she found a yellow slip on her chair. No note, no explanation, just a dry-cleaning bill for $8.25.

Eight dollars and twenty-five cents. This from a man who makes a hundred and fifty grand a year, three thousand a week, six hundred a day, seventy-five an hour, a dollar and a quarter a minute . . . Let's see, that's about six minutes it takes him to make eight and a quarter. And he puts his dry-cleaning bill on my chair, without a note, as if he is the Deity himself, expecting I'll know who it's from and wire it to his Swiss bank account?

That was it. Ruth could keep the smile for a while longer, but from this moment on she would plot her payback in earnest. And bless his cold, black little heart, Gavin gave her the idea himself. It seemed so obvious, so easy, so simple, so divinely appropriate, she thought it funny that she hadn't stumbled over it before. It would zing Gavin right in the career, but no one would be physically hurt. And she would get the payback of all paybacks herself—a life of opulence and luxury, far away from the madman who had reverted her life into one of slavery.

Five

As the jet was beginning its descent into Atlanta, Torrie Wilson squirmed. It was getting hot on the plane, and her blouse was sticking to her back. She reached up to make sure the cool air was blowing at her, and finding it was, she sighed and squirmed some more. The fat man next to her, whose hairy arm kept encroaching her space, wasn't helping any.

She craned her neck to look past the sleeping woman in the window seat to see the skyline out beyond the wing. Torrie could make out both the Peachtree Tower and the First Southern building. She smiled.

She settled back into her seat and closed her eyes to think about her new beginning. It was good to be here, and she was glad she'd be getting settled at last.

"Are you from Atlanta?" the lady in the window seat had asked as they'd fastened themselves in before leaving Indianapolis.

"Oh, not yet!" Torrie laughed. "I'm moving down today, in fact."

"Really?" The lady, handsomely fifty-something, peered around Torrie at the large man. "Is your husband being transferred?"

Torrie shuddered. "Well, no, I'm not . . . He's not my . . . I mean, I'm single. I'm being transferred. Or actually, I'm transferring myself."

The lady looked confused. "Oh, I see. So you two are just, um, living together?"

Torrie took a deep breath. "I'm traveling alone," she smiled. "And no, I'm not living with anyone. Except my cat, that is."

The lady beamed. "Let me show you my kitties," she said, pulling her bag out from beneath the seat in front of her. Her wallet bulged with feline photos. Calicos. Siamese. Persians. Tabbies. Mutts.

"How nice," Torrie said. "So you have about fifty?"

"Oh, no," the lady blushed. "Just twelve." Torrie handed her the wallet back, just as the flight attendant suggested putting the bag back under the seat for takeoff.

"I'm Torrie."

"Oh. I'm Mrs. Melville. Now, tell me, Torrie, what is it you're going to do in Atlanta?"

"I'm a journalist. I'm going to cover banks for the *Atlanta Business Courier*, as a staff reporter."

"A writer! How fascinating! Tell me all about what you've written, dear!"

Torrie described the bumpy path she'd taken, with three job changes in the five years since college. "The newspaper business just isn't as stable as it used to be. I hope this is the last stop for a while. Eventually, I'd like to freelance from home and be a mom. Packing up every time I feel like I'm starting to belong is getting a little old." She paused. "And how about you? Why are you flying to Atlanta?"

Mrs. Melville explained she was visiting her son, who had a very important job with the county.

Torrie took a deep breath. "Mrs. Melville, since I'm new to Atlanta, I don't know about where the good churches are. Do you know if your son likes the church he's going to?"

"Why, I imagine so."

Torrie leaned forward a bit. "Really? Do you know what it's called?"

"Now, let me think," Mrs. Melville replied, bringing her fingers to her lips. "No, I'm afraid not. I'm terribly sorry. I suppose I should ask him once I arrive."

"Which church have you been going to in Indianapolis?"

"I'm afraid I haven't gone in years. Mr. Melville and I, we used to go together when the children were little. But it's been a long time . . . " Her face flushed a little, and she turned away from Torrie to look out the window.

Torrie leaned back. *Help me to know what I should say, Father,* she asked silently. She had become a Christian in college, and she truly wanted to let people know Christianity wasn't heavy and dreary, as many chose to believe. But she realized most people just weren't all that comfortable talking about life and death with a total stranger.

She licked her lips and decided to ask Mrs. Melville if she had any special memories from the times she'd gone to church, but before Torrie could say another word, Mrs. Melville suddenly turned back from the window and pulled out her bag again. "Oh, I can't believe I forgot—I have two more sets of pictures to show you!"

Torrie sighed. *Amazing,* she thought, *how often people become distracted as soon as I drum up the nerve to talk about my faith.* "Two more sets of your cats?"

"Oh, of course not. Only one more set of my kitties. The other set is photos of my grandchildren!"

Torrie had smiled as the jet leaned upward and glided into the sky.

During the rest of the flight, they talked about the cats and the grandkids and what Mr. Melville used to do and Mrs. Melville's civic activities and Torrie's childhood in Rancho Cordova, California, journalism school in Santa Barbara, and her first real job, writing engagement announcements for the *San Diego Union.* But whenever the subject got close to spiritual things, out came more cats.

"So why did you decide to leave Indianapolis for Atlanta?"

"I guess my California genes never knew what 'wind chill' really meant until I went through a winter where it dug right through my skin, past my bones, and into my inner being."

"My gracious," Mrs. Melville gasped. "You really are a writer, aren't you?"

Mrs. Melville eventually dozed off, and Torrie enjoyed the chance to think and pray for a few minutes before the plane's wheels skidded down on the runway. The fat man was gripping the armrest with his fingers while trying to look nonchalant. His knuckles were white, which Torrie found amusing. Mrs. Melville woke up with the bump, and looked around, disoriented for an instant.

"I've enjoyed chatting with you, Mrs. Melville," Torrie said warmly.

"And I certainly hope you find what you're looking for here," Mrs. Melville said, patting her wrist.

They said good-bye, and Torrie hopped on a train at the airport and rode it to the Peachtree Center station, fifteen minutes away. The station was carved out of the granite that held up the skyline, and the escalator ride to street level was a long one. She felt like a kid at Disneyland.

Her job didn't actually start until tomorrow, but Torrie wanted to drop by the *Business Courier* office as her first stop. She didn't really know anyone in Atlanta yet—just a few people she'd interviewed with at the paper—so she decided to treat herself to a little familiarity to get off to a good start.

The *Business Courier* came out once a week, reaching the movers and shakers, the dreamers, and the stars of tomorrow. Torrie liked the style—more spunky and feature-oriented than the conservative approach most dailies tended to take, despite their liberal editorial pages. She could write her own ticket at this paper. If she had an idea for an investigative series, they were open to that. She'd have her assigned beat—financial—but that was about as far as the editorial direction went. The editors assumed their writers knew the basic "five W's" from Journalism 101—who, what, where, when, and why—and that they'd meet their deadlines. After that, the sky was the limit.

The pay was pretty good too, to her surprise. Journalism was not the path paved with gold, unless you were Woodward or Bernstein, and she was pleasantly surprised that the coastal cost of living she'd grown up with had not reached the South—even a major metropolis that was on a roll, hosting a recent Super Bowl and the 1996 Summer Olympics.

She walked past the reception area and into the newsroom. It looked like most any other newsroom, with bright, white, high ceilings and an open floor plan. Desks lined the floor, and piles of paper covered the desks. Phones rang, young men and women with harried looks on their faces and bags under their eyes scurried to and fro, and Torrie Wilson knew she was home.

"Torrie?"

The voice came from behind, to the left. She turned to see Sandy Myers, her editor.

"It is you! I wasn't sure for a minute. I wasn't expecting you today. How was the flight down?"

Torrie smiled at her. *A good boss for a change,* Torrie thought. *She knew her stuff, she was patient and kind, and she would be a friend instead of just an editor.* Torrie liked that idea.

"Not bad," Torrie replied. "I'm just so glad to be here. I hope you don't mind my stopping by today, but I just wanted to feel a little more at home before I went and set up in my apartment."

"Sounds like a smart idea to me," Sandy smiled. "I'd have probably done the same thing, if I'd have thought of it!"

Torrie smiled back. *This was a good decision.*

"Say, I don't know if you're hungry or if they fed you on the plane, but I was gonna run out in about ten minutes and grab a bite. Do you want to join me?" Sandy asked.

The clock on the wall said 12:45. Torrie had been so wrapped up with the newness of everything that she forgot she hadn't eaten since early that morning. All of a sudden, she was famished. "I'd love to," she said.

"Great!" Sandy clapped her hands together. "Give me a few minutes—I've got to do two quick things—and then we'll get out of here."

The ten minutes stretched to twenty, but Torrie didn't mind. She was in a room that felt comfortable, both emotionally and physically. She wondered how journalists—or anybody, for that matter—worked all day in the South before air conditioning came along.

The two headed down the front steps and walked about a block to the Peachtree Tower. "There's a great little deli in here," Sandy said. "It's always good for a quick lunch."

As they worked their way past the thinning but still heavy lunchtime crowd, Torrie nearly bumped into a tall, dark-haired man who spun around quickly. They stopped dead in their tracks, face-to-face, with all of a half inch between their noses. By sheer coincidence, the man was Gavin Duke.

They both chuckled an uneasy "I'm sorry" and went back about their business.

Torrie turned to Sandy and said, "Sure got some real men here."

Sandy said, "Watch out—that one's dangerous."

Torrie laughed. "Don't tell me you know that dressed-for-success rascal?"

"Not really," Sandy grinned. "I don't know him, but I know who he is. You're the one who's gonna know him."

Torrie stopped short. She couldn't let a tease like that slide by easily. "Try me again on that one," she said, putting on her best quizzical look.

"That's your assignment, Torrie Wilson!" Sandy announced. "That's Mr. Gavin Duke, marketing veep for First Southern Bank!"

"Get out of here!" Torrie mocked. "You didn't tell me about the perks!"

Sandy said, "Well, I shouldn't wreck the beautiful picture for you so soon—you're bound to find out for yourself—but Gavin is as vain as he is gorgeous, and he can be as nasty as he is brilliant."

"Hmm. Figures," Torrie said, frowning. "Still, who says a girl can't have a little fun? Living on the edge has its payoff too—so long as I know ahead of time what I'm up against."

Hey, she told herself, *somebody has to share God's truths with this guy. Why not me?*

Sandy smiled, glad to see Torrie was the same person she had seemed to be during her job interview. Sandy's notes had words like *outgoing, energetic,* and *charming.* Torrie had shoulder length brown hair, with a hint of reddish tint, and captivating brown eyes. "I love to work out—waterskiing, swimming, cycling, stuff like that," she had said. Sandy knew from looking through Torrie's clips that she was a natural writer, with an easy, fluid style.

"I'd like to write a novel someday. But not yet. I want to hone my skills on a paper for a few more years."

"Good answer," Sandy laughed. She recommended Torrie as

highly as anyone she'd ever interviewed. She could tell Torrie had a special something extra about her.

Over lunch, Sandy filled her new reporter in, very informally, about the big story that was brewing over at First Southern. The rumor mill was buzzing day and night about some earth-shaking announcement. A merger? A change in top management? Surely they weren't going to fire Carolina Gates Advertising?

"Your job," Sandy said, "will be to try and crack the news before anybody else does. That's a tall order, given the fact that the blood-thirsty TV stations, the daily paper, and everybody else within a hundred miles of here wants to know what's going on. And of course, to make matters worse, you don't have any contacts of your own yet."

"Well, maybe one." Torrie smiled as she twirled her spoon through what remained of her raspberry frozen yogurt. She looked up, and when her eyes met Sandy's, they both laughed.

🐚   🐚   🐚

A few hours later, Torrie flung herself down on the couch in her new living room. She'd had enough of arranging yet-to-be-unpacked boxes for now, and she was going to take a well-deserved breather. A good time to sort through the information overload.

She couldn't believe how she'd almost bumped into her first big story—literally—earlier that day. She really did have to talk with Gavin Duke of First Southern Bank. After all, that's where the story was. The question before her was whether he would remember her from that chance near-meeting or not.

She leaned back and opened her eyes to gaze out the big picture window of her fabulous new apartment. It was in Midtown, a great place for single professionals, complete with manned security, an on-site fitness center, dry cleaning, and a coffee shop. She'd gotten a great deal on a thirty-fifth floor corner unit with two bedrooms—one to sleep in and one to set up as a home office. Writing, she'd learned, was not something to set your clock by.

Casey, her cat, jumped onto her stomach, purring loudly. The stress of travel was catching up with Torrie's old friend. "Hang in there, kid. We're both gonna make some great new friends here!" Casey meowed in agreement and curled up for a nap as Torrie opened the novel she was reading, quickly finding herself swept away to the Channel Islands with a family seeking paradise.

🥐   🥐   🥐

Torrie woke up half an hour before the alarm the next morning, genuinely excited about starting work. She pulled open the curtain to see the morning mist rise over Piedmont Park, laid out gracefully before the downtown skyline. She poured a cup of coffee and took in the view from the best seat in the house, situated just so on the balcony, and had a refreshing quiet time with her daily devotional and the book of Psalms.

At 8:25, still managing to stay ahead of schedule, Torrie walked into the newsroom again. It looked even better to her today. She angled over to her desk, noticing that the buzz of activity from the day before had subsided substantially. On top of her desk, in the center, were three neatly stacked sheets of paper, with a big black headline across the top one: Assignment Sheet.

This was Tuesday morning; the deadline was Thursday noon. Not much time, but not bad. A weekly was actually a breath of fresh air after the pressures of daily deadlines. She didn't know how people lasted thirty years at that.

Her mission was to get an official denial from First Southern about all the rumors that were being bandied about. Two word-processed pages from her, to turn into ten to twelve column inches inside the paper.

She knew from the assignment sheet, as well as the lunch conversation with Sandy the day before, that nobody expected her to come up with a scoop yet. That time would come, but the powers that be at the paper were smart enough to know not to expect miracles after two days on the job.

Beneath the assignment sheet were two other assignments. One was to write a two-inch blurb, summarizing a press release that was paper-clipped to the back of the assignment sheet. The other was to interview the branch manager of a small S&L about the success of their new Saturday hours. This was to be four to five inches long and would be folded into the financial column.

Torrie was hired to cover financial news, which included writing the column. She would write the column starting next week; this week, she'd be allowed to get her feet wet while the retiring writer, Ed Rizzuto, would post a farewell column.

Torrie could almost knock these out in her sleep, but some planning was required. First, she'd call Gavin Duke to set up a meeting, then she'd write the other two pieces (she could interview the S&L manager over the phone). Then she'd meet with Gavin and write up the interview.

She called the First Southern switchboard and asked for Gavin Duke. "Thank you," the operator said, and patched her right through. The phone rang.

This, thought Torrie, *is gonna be cake.*

On the second ring, Ruth Chandler picked up. "Marketing department, Mr. Duke's office."

Rats, Torrie thought. *Should've known.* But always the seasoned journalist, she didn't miss a beat. "Is Gavin around?" she tossed out casually, with the familiarity of a close friend.

"He's not available at the moment." Ruth stonewalled with precise efficiency. "May I take a message, please?"

"Sure. This is Torrie Wilson, with the *Atlanta Business Courier*. I wanted to touch base with him on a couple of things."

"Is there anything I can help you with?" Ruth asked with just a touch of iciness.

"Actually, I just wanted to follow up on a couple of quick questions. When can I talk to him?"

"I'm afraid he'll be tied up in meetings all day," Ruth said. "What's your extension over there?"

Torrie knew two things about the stonewall routine. One, "May I have your number?" without " . . . and have him call you" was a bad sign. And two, a reporter was not generally on anyone's list of calls to return first—and the higher up the person, the shorter the odds of a call-back. *With a guy like Gavin Duke*, Torrie reasoned, *the chances are something along the lines of raising a man from the dead.*

"Sure," Torrie said. "555-2400, and the extension is 755. That's Torrie Wilson, with the *Business Courier*."

"I'll be sure he gets the message." *Click.*

"Yeah, right," Torrie told the phone before setting it down. She thought for a minute and decided to clear the other two stories out of the way before taking another crack at this man who was becoming more and more intriguing to Torrie Wilson.

🐚   🐚   🐚

By early afternoon, she had not only interviewed the S&L manager, but she had written that story as well as the other she'd been assigned. She stuffed them both into her briefcase to proofread at home later that night, a good warm mug of cocoa and her trusty cat Casey at her side.

She picked up the phone, dialed the bank's main number, and asked for Gavin again.

Ruth picked it up on the first hop this time. "Marketing, Mr. Duke's office," she said. She sounded more harried this time, and Torrie imagined a strand of hair having fallen down across her forehead. She wasn't surprised to hear Ruth's voice again, though she had hoped to get Gavin directly this time around.

She quickly hung up. She knew calling back before the first call was returned was suicide—a caller perceived as pesky by the stonewall gang would never get through. She would try again later, hoping Gavin might grab the phone himself. The odds were better after five, when most employees went home for the day.

Torrie made good use of the next few hours, chatting with some of the other reporters and columnists at the paper and getting familiar with the library. And before she knew it, 5:25 had come.

She tried Gavin again. Click. Ring. "Marketing." It was Ruth.

"Yes, this is Torrie Wilson, with the *Business Courier*. I left Gavin a message earlier . . . "

"Yes, he's been tied up in meetings all day."

"Oh. Well, I'm on a deadline, and I just had a couple of quick . . . "

"I thought the deadline down at the *Business Courier* wasn't until Thursday," Ruth said impatiently.

Wow, Torrie thought, *this one's good.* She decided to dodge the issue and push again. "Will he be available this evening? Just for a moment?"

"I'll let him know you called again," Ruth said. "That's the best I can do."

"Thanks," Torrie said, "I appreciate it." She hung up.

She figured the lobby at the First Southern Tower would be locked up by six, so she quickly pulled everything she needed together and headed off toward the bank.

The lobby of the Tower was something to behold. A big black and white checkerboard marble floor, with opulent chandeliers and brass in abundance. Footsteps echo if the heels are hard and it's not too crowded. Torrie walked over to the directory that was served up under glass, and found Marketing. *Okay, sixtieth floor.* Up she went.

The elevator door opened, and the foyer was eerily silent. No receptionist sat behind the desk. *Good—no need to fight through that one.* She peered around a corner and heard voices.

Her eyes took in as much as she could. Signs directed you wherever you wanted to go. Direct Marketing, this way. Telemarketing, that way. Executive Marketing Offices, over there. She slowly went down the hall.

Ruth was working at her desk, just across the hall from Gavin's front door. She looked up. "Can I help you?"

"Just wanted to see if I could catch Gavin before he left for the day," she said sheepishly, motioning toward the door of the mystery man who was now by all appearances her lifelong friend.

"I'm sorry, I didn't catch your name . . . " Ruth's eyes darted over Torrie's outfit. Torrie realized that Ruth was looking for the I.D. badge of someone who worked at the bank and that Ruth was starting to stand up—most likely planning to physically bar her from Gavin's office.

Gavin came charging out his office door, papers in hand, and without looking up said, "Ruth, I . . . "

He stopped. He looked at Ruth, then at Torrie. "Hey, it's you," he smiled. "The vision from the lobby yesterday!"

Ruth frowned, and Torrie breezed by her, as though Ruth were invisible. "I don't believe we've been properly introduced, Mr. Duke," she said sweetly. "Torrie Wilson. And the pleasure is all mine, of course!"

Oh, please, thought Ruth, connecting the voice. *It was "my good buddy Gavin" all day, and now it's "Mr. Duke."*

"Well, you certainly seem to know who I am," Gavin said, mustering as much modesty as he had at any moment since junior high. "How is that?"

"Oh, everyone knows Gavin Duke," she lobbed back. Ruth wondered if she would make it through much more of this.

"Ruth, could you find some coffee for Miss—for Torrie," Gavin said, without removing his eyes from his guest's.

Anything to get out of here before I drown, Ruth thought, ignoring the usual patronizing Gavin garbage. She turned on her heel and marched off toward the break room.

"To what do I owe the pleasure?" Gavin asked.

Out came the sheepish voice again. "Well, I'm not sure you're going to be so pleased when I tell you."

"Uh oh. Got a subpoena for me?" Gavin said, holding his arms out as if to say "don't shoot."

"No, nothing like that," she laughed. "I'm with the *Business Courier,* and I just wanted to ask you two or three questions."

Gavin liked the way she scrunched up her nose when she said it. "Mmm, a reporter? I love a challenge. I suppose I can spare five minutes for a reporter as gracious as you." He put his left hand gently behind her shoulder and directed her into his office, as he slid his right hand into his pocket to make sure the gold Confederate half-dollar was there. "But no more than that. I'm a very busy man."

"I'll be out before you know it," she promised.

She sat down, and Gavin sat in the other visitor's chair, positioning himself in front of his desk instead of behind it. *Good PR,* he thought.

"How come I don't know you, except from the lobby?" he asked. "The *Courier* isn't exactly *Time* magazine. I'm not often surprised like this." He leaned forward. "Unless you're really a spy from First National!"

"I thought I was supposed to be asking the questions," she said, pulling a notepad from her purse. The recorder might be a little too pushy for this first interview. "Actually, this is my first day. Ed Rizzuto is retiring, and I'm taking over the financial page."

Gavin's eyes flew open. "You're the guy—woman—who's replacing Fast Eddie! I must've done something very good today!"

Torrie laughed.

"Don't get me wrong," Gavin said, "I like old Eddie. But he's a funny old guy, a grumpy old trenchcoat-in-hand, fedora-on-the-head kind of newspaperman from ancient history. But you, you're . . . "

Ruth brought the coffee in. "Anything else?"

"No. Thanks, babe," Gavin said. Neither woman showed particular amusement.

"I think I'll be heading home," Ruth said. "Nice meeting you," she tossed toward Torrie.

"Actually, I don't think we did officially meet. Torrie Wilson, with the *Business Courier*." She extended her hand.

"Ruth Chandler." She gave her hand a breezy shake. "Good night!"

"See you tomorrow morning," Gavin said, turning back to Torrie. "Okay, now, where were we?"

"I'm here to find out what the big secret is," she said.

"Big secret? I guess they're keeping it a secret from me too!" he laughed, flashing the Gavin smile.

"Quick. Very quick. I like that," she said. "But no baloney. What's going on that's got the rumor-mongers working overtime? And if you're not going to let the cat out of the bag, at least give me a hint as to when you will!"

"You don't pull any punches, do you, Miss Torrie Wilson?" He noticed the lack of a ring on her finger.

"Are there merger talks?"

"Nobody's told me. But hey, I'm just the marketing guy."

"A shake-up at the top?"

"I'm five whole floors from the top. Wouldn't know about that."

She leaned forward. "Are you going to fire Carolina Gates?"

Gavin's head cocked back with that one—it took him by surprise. "No . . . " And then, realizing the importance of going on with the tease, added " . . . comment!"

Torrie's ears perked up. The way he said it usually meant "Yes, but I can't confirm that yet." Quickly, to avoid creating a bad spill with his friend Carolina, he stopped the dance for a moment.

"No. We're not firing Carolina Gates. We're very happy. No firing, no agency review. Everything is wonderful, and we look forward to a long, mutually prosperous relationship."

"You sound like a press release," she frowned, sensing the feeling of loss a reporter experiences when a big one gets away.

"Anything else you'd like to know?"

"Anything else?" she parroted him. "You haven't told me a single thing."

"Have I told you I'd like to buy you a drink?" he asked, grinning.

"I thought we were talking about what's going on here at the bank," she shot back.

"I had something else in mind altogether."

"I guess you'd better keep it there," she said, flipping the notepad closed and stuffing it back in her purse. She knew how to be friendly to get more information, but she also knew when to cut her losses. This man wasn't thinking about what he could do for her. And while she was unquestionably intrigued by this powerful man, she also had a fair inkling that Prince Charming may have more than a few flaws.

"You've got the number at the paper," she said. "If you think you'd like your side of the story to get some fair play, my deadline is noon Thursday." She took quick steps toward the door, then stopped. She shot him a quick look over her shoulder and vanished.

As Torrie hopped into a cab to go home—it was only a few blocks, but she didn't want to walk alone at dusk before she was more familiar with the lay of the land—she tried to take stock of what had just transpired. A contest of wills, of wits, and who knows what else—and she had held her own with someone who, she was beginning to realize, was much larger than life.

She tipped the driver and walked up the front steps of her

apartment complex. The spring air smelled sweet, and she felt very alive. Coming here was right, and she knew the future would hold surprises she couldn't even begin to imagine this night. And to a woman like Torrie Wilson, that was hopeful material to sleep on.

Six

There are a dozen district Federal Reserve banks across the United States, set up by a government charter in 1914. One is in downtown Atlanta, just a few blocks from First Southern's headquarters.

One of the Fed's many functions is to act as a banker to the banks. On this day, Gavin was taking his banker to lunch.

He sat across the table from Bill Ramey, his primary contact at his friendly neighborhood Fed branch. Bill was a New Yorker, blunt and more direct than many Southerners, and Gavin liked his no-nonsense approach. Bill was a stocky guy, built like a fire hydrant, and an old Navy vet—served on a submarine for months at a time, which seemed unfathomable to Gavin, who needed more contact with the other gender on a more regular basis. Bill had a couple of tattoos on his arms. *Odd*, Gavin thought. *Not a lot of bankers sport tattoos.*

"I must tell you, Gav," Bill said, fingering his coaster, "you guys over at Southern are making life a lot more interesting for everybody these days. We've got about fifty pools going as to what the announcement is really going to be, and when it's gonna hit!"

Gavin smirked. "It's pretty fun being in the driver's seat—I can lead anybody on any kind of goose chase I want, and they'll dive for it hook, line, and sinker. Like the other night—have you seen Fast Ed's replacement over at the paper?"

"No. They get somebody even older—like dead, maybe?"

Gavin leaned way back in his chair and looked across the room. "Hot new item from up north. She asked me if we were gonna fire Carrie—can you believe that one?"

"I'd heard it," Bill said, "but I don't think it's got any serious takers on the pool. Biggest money's on the buyout stuff."

"Amazing, just amazing. I was teasing her a little, and I said, 'No comment' like I ought to be in Washington. But it really spooked me, because she'd print it as though I was making some kind of official, smoke-screen denial. I had to make sure she understood there was no such idea."

"Can't keep your eyes off those press people for a minute," Bill said. "I could tell you some horror stories . . . "

"Don't I know it," Gavin agreed. "But so far, there's been no major damage. The stock's been a little jittery lately, and the volume's been up, but it's nothing to worry about. Especially in a few months. It'll go through the roof." He leaned in and lowered his voice a bit. Bill wondered if this was for effect or if Gavin really was giving him some inside news that would do him some good. "Sock away a few shares over the next few weeks, Billy. You'll thank me for it this fall."

Bill knew Gavin enough to know anything that flew from his mouth needed to be taken with a grain of salt. But still, this one was tempting. The notion of making a killing was always appealing, of course—particularly to someone who's devoted his life to watching millions go by. It made him think the answer was obvious: First Southern had put itself on the block, and some big out-of-town bank wanted to use this super-regional as a piece of its national vision.

"I'll take that to heart," Bill said. "But I imagine your announcing a new career as a stock broker isn't why you wanted to get together today."

"You never miss a trick, do you, William? I'm surprised the president hasn't invited you to take over Greenspan's job by now."

"Maybe I already turned him down," Bill said, unable to keep the laugh back. "Maybe I'd just miss all you wonderful human beings too much, trapped there inside the Beltway."

"Okay, I'm gonna die from all the sarcasm. Stop. Please. I'll tell you my mission. One of our big-bucks, old-money customers got a crazy notion the other day. He wanted to buy some gold. A lot of gold," Gavin lied.

"So what's the big deal?" Bill shrugged, taking a sip of Sprite. "Can't he look up Gold Dealers in the Yellow Pages?"

"He's got a couple of problems with that. First, he doesn't want to create much of a stir. It's an awful lot of the stuff."

"How much? Hundred grand? Two?"

"Try a million." Gavin waited for Bill's reaction.

Bill kept right on eating. "Look, Duke, I see more than that every day. Chump change. Peanuts."

"Well, yeah, maybe to you big-spending government guys," Gavin said defensively. "But that's still a lot for one guy—remember, we're talking a private individual here."

"Granted. But I still don't see why you need me for this."

"As a favor to The Man," Gavin said. "This guy's an old golfing chum. He wants anonymity, but the real reason is the price tag. You know how much those sharks want to broker this kind of deal?"

"I think it's about five percent," Bill said, wiping his mouth with the napkin. "Right?"

"It's trading at $360 an ounce today. The broker wants eighteen more, per ounce, on every ounce. That's fine for a few grand worth, but my guy needs around a hundred and seventy pounds of the stuff, and no one will give him a price break worth mentioning—no quantity discounts. So to get what he needs, he's looking at something like twenty-five grand to the dealer! So you get the idea? The Man's buddy doesn't want to blow that much on a fee. What can we do to help him?"

"If you can guarantee me you can keep it quiet, I can transfer it over to the bank's precious metals department for some token nickel-and-dime stuff—you pay for the delivery, the security, the paperwork. We'll have to shake in a charge of some kind, a transfer fee, but we're talking no more than a hundred bucks for that. Overall, I think we're looking at maybe two hundred dollars. Now keep in mind, that's us getting it to the bank, your cash up front. Whatever you arrange from there, getting it into Mr. Big's hands, that's between you and him—

stuff like extending a line of credit until you pay us, that kind of thing. Plus any fees you charge him. Hey, you're saving the guy twenty-five thousand—I'd think you can still ding him something pretty good but come in way under the going rate."

"Yeah, except this is a buddy of The Man's, the good ol' boy thing. I don't think it's proper Southern etiquette to charge a fee for a favor, even if it's a mega-favor."

"Like I said, that's your problem," Bill reiterated. "But remember—this can blow up in my face if anybody, and that means anybody, gets wind. It's not illegal, since I'm getting it to the bank, but it sure would look pretty bad if some reporter discovered it."

"Bill, you are a pal and a genius, a gentleman and a scholar. Your secret is safe with me. And of course, you also have my infinite gratitude."

"Save it for the judge," Bill laughed, with just a fraction of uneasiness. He knew Gavin was lying through his teeth, but he didn't want to push it. Why should he? Probably better that he didn't really know—kept his hands cleaner. After all, he was just doing his job; he was simply sending legal tender over to a bank.

◐   ◐   ◐

Back at the office, Gavin filled Ruth in on the details from lunch. Three weeks before G-Day, when the big announcement would be made, a million dollars in gold would be delivered to his office, coming from the Fed by armored truck. Ruth would sign for it once it got to the sixtieth floor, to dispel the appearance that it was of any significance beyond computer paper or magnetic tapes for the mainframe, and she would stash it in the department supply room under lock and key.

"But won't the armored truck tip somebody off?" she suggested.

"Not really. It's going into the vault first, where I'll be waiting to repackage it—stuff it into brown cardboard boxes. Even if someone were watching closely, they wouldn't connect the truck delivery with the delivery upstairs."

"Then what?" Ruth asked.

Gavin straightened up with a good measure of self-importance. "I'll take it from there. Don't worry your pretty little . . . "

She refused to listen to the rest of his cliché. She knew Gavin's strengths, and she knew his weaknesses; this time, she would gain her edge by knowing his penchant for being overly concerned with control and secrecy. She was fully aware he would handle hiding the gold himself, and that he would trust no one—not even her—with the location.

"That's good, because the wooden trunk is scheduled for delivery two or three days before that," Ruth said when he'd finished. "I'll keep on top of them to make sure they don't miss the deadline."

"Good work, Ruth." He'd been on the rocks with Marni so long, he felt like he'd been on a submarine. *A woman like Ruth would kill for a crack at a man like me*, he figured. Her eyes stayed with his for a moment, but she couldn't stand it. She looked away, acutely aware of the deafening silence.

Making the poor girl nervous, he thought.

"Anything else?" she asked to break the discomfort.

"That's all," he said, and started to turn and walk away. He stopped, turned to look over his shoulder, and added, "for now." Again, he gazed into her eyes.

Ruth looked away quickly, got up, and didn't say another word. It was a week before the tease campaign would go on the air, just three weeks before G–Day, so Ruth knew she just had to keep her nose to the grindstone for now and that it wouldn't be long before her day would come.

🪙   🪙   🪙

The next day, Torrie called Gavin again. She and Ruth both knew who'd won their war of wits, so Torrie could call and leave a message any time she wanted, and Ruth had to pass it on or connect her to Gavin if he was available.

Gavin picked up the phone with a smile. "Torrie Wilson, I sure enjoyed your first piece. I think I need to take you to lunch to congratulate you on your new job—as a professional courtesy, of course."

"Why, how could I refuse?" she smiled. "When's good for you?"

"I'm really swamped, so how about . . . today?" he teased.

"Got a good place in mind?"

"I sure do," he said. "Is twelve okay?"

"Yeah."

"Great. I'll come by your office and pick you up."

"Great," she said back. "I'll see you then."

"Hey, wait a minute," he broke in. "What was it you called about?"

She knew he'd gotten to her—she realized it in a second. He'd swept her off balance, she'd lapsed on the business at hand, and they both knew it. She came back as quickly as she could.

"Oh, I just figured we'd cover it at lunch," she retorted, dodging the bullet.

"Oh, I see," he beamed. "Got my curiosity aroused. Can't wait. Bye!"

"Bye-bye," she said, and hung up. *Good. If I stay on my toes*, she thought, *maybe I can get to the bottom of the mystery—still a pretty slick accomplishment for week two on the job.*

        ❦   ❦   ❦

As the clock struck noon, Gavin Duke glided into the newsroom. He was wearing a deep navy blue suit, double-breasted, with pin-stripes. Given his dark hair and eyes and his perpetually tan complexion, he looked his best. A flashy banker, bearing a single white rose.

Torrie looked up and felt embarrassed at the rose. Her eyes darted across the room, hoping no one would see. As chance would have it—at the height of lunch hour—there were only a couple of other people there, and they were clear across on the other side.

"Gavin!" she scolded with a smile. "You shouldn't have brought a rose! This is business!"

"Sorry, can't take it back."

"You are incorrigible," she said, grabbing her purse. She decided to leave her satchel, which she used instead of a briefcase. She didn't want to lug it around, but Gavin did notice as she dropped both her notepad and her tape recorder into the purse.

"Shall we, m'lady?"

"Indeed," she said, making her way toward the door. *We match,* she thought—she was also wearing navy pinstripes, and they did make a handsome couple.

"Where're we off to?" she asked when they got to the street. Without a word, he caught her eyes and slowly directed them up the side of a skyscraper just one block away.

"We're having a picnic in a hot air balloon!" she joked.

"Oh, no, something better. And safer!"

She waited for him to continue as they walked along. He didn't. "Well?"

"You want to know where we're going, huh? You just have to wait!"

"Okay," she said. "Always the mystery man."

"You love it."

"What makes you think so?"

"I just have an innate understanding of women," he said. "I have an uncanny knack for knowing what women want."

"I do love humility in a man," she nudged. She did like a little self-confidence. But not too much, and Gavin Duke danced dangerously close to the line.

Just then he said, "Here we are!" and the two went through the revolving door at the entrance of the Westin Peachtree Plaza Hotel.

"Must be a pretty nice restaurant in here," she said.

"Ever heard of the Sun Dial?"

"No."

"You're gonna love it. Just wait and see."

The Sun Dial was a revolving restaurant atop the Westin Peachtree—the world's tallest hotel, checking in at seventy-two cylindrical stories of mirrored glass. The steaks were thick, the desserts were rich, and the view was indescribable. A moving, breathtaking panorama, reaching twenty miles in every direction on a clear day. It was without a doubt the place to be during a sunset, since you'd get to double your pleasure—take in a daytime view as well as the skyline by night, lit up like an overzealous Christmas tree.

Of course, he hadn't told her about the elevator.

A ride up the side of the Westin was a glimpse of Disneyworld, without the price of admission. It wasn't for the faint of heart. Of course, Gavin knew this too, since he'd taken enough ladies up to know you could place money on having her clutch your arm in mock terror as the pavement flew further and further away. True to form, Torrie looked away as they soared skyward, then peeked back out, then closed her eyes and grabbed onto Gavin's waiting and willing forearm.

Once they were safely inside the restaurant, they made small talk for ten or fifteen minutes, but then—after ordering—Torrie pulled out her notepad, a blue pen, and her tape recorder. She unceremoniously placed them in order where her lunch was supposed to go, and looked up to see Gavin's glowing countenance turn downcast, if ever so slightly.

"What's this?" he asked.

"What do you mean?" she replied. "I called to set up an interview. Lunch was your idea." She leaned forward. "Thanks, you didn't have to!" She grinned.

He gave her a good-natured smile. "Okay. Fire away."

"Mind if I use the recorder?" she asked. "Helps with my accuracy." She looked up innocently. "Flunked shorthand."

"How about if we don't this time," he said. "Let's save that for the more in-depth stuff. I think maybe I'll be giving you ideas to go on today, instead of complete sound bites."

She looked as though she wanted to argue the point but thought better of it. She put the recorder back into her purse, picked up the pen, and flipped open the notepad.

"All right. What's the big secret with the bank?"

"Still haven't learned to beat around the bush, have you?"

"I thought we went through this before," she prodded. "I ask the questions, you answer the questions."

Their waiter interrupted with the bread and the drinks. "You really ought to try this honey butter," Gavin said, dodging her question. "Great stuff."

"Mmm-hmm," she said, picking up her butter knife as she bowed her head to give thanks. Once she had established a relationship with someone, she usually asked, "Mind if I pray?" But with Gavin, she felt he might make a snap judgment and write off any credibility she was building. So she decided to pray quietly this time. Gavin didn't notice and forged right ahead.

"I'll bet," he said, sinking his teeth into a thick, warm slice of sourdough, "that you would love for me to stop teasing you every time you try to ask me a question."

"Now that's one I don't mind answering," she replied as she tore off a chunk of fresh bread. She leaned forward. "Yes."

Gavin breathed in slowly, leaned back in his chair, and fixed his gaze somewhere beyond CNN Center, which had just come into view with the continuous turn of the room. Without shifting his gaze toward Torrie—which surprised her a bit, given his playfully pushy nature—he spoke slowly.

"It's out there," he said. "Somewhere."

This guy is beyond compare, she thought. *Could have made it on Broadway, with his flair for the dramatic.*

She waited. And he waited. He would not withdraw his gaze from the undefined spot in the distance. This was poker at its finest, a battle of nerves between two pros.

The waiter, who must have had the table bugged for opportune entrances, brought the salad. A huge wooden bowl, mixed fresh at tableside with freshly ground black pepper and aged Parmesan cheese.

The man in the tux could bring Gavin back, Torrie noticed, musing that the way to any man's heart—even a man who thought of little else besides cold, hard cash—was through his digestive tract.

"Thank you," she said, looking up at the waiter.

"Thank you," Gavin said, looking over at Torrie.

"Fine," she said. "What's 'out there—somewhere'?"

"Did you study much history in school? Civil War history?"

Now she was totally baffled. *What kind of curveball was this? But*, she reasoned, *it was his game. Go with the flow.*

"I grew up in California," she said, "so we studied more about Sir Francis Drake looking for San Francisco Bay than we did about the *Monitor* and the *Merrimac*."

"Did you ever stop to think about how they paid for those gray uniforms, or the cannons, or the battle flags?"

"Well, no, I guess not. I suppose they had a treasury department.

After all, they did set up a provisional government with Jefferson Davis as president. I've seen some of the old Confederate money—script and coins. Funny. I've never thought about rebels filling out their income tax forms before. It's just not an image of the Civil War you got in school!"

She was finding this more amusing now, her curiosity piqued by where this man was taking all this.

"You're exactly right," he said. "They had a government, and a treasury, which consisted mostly of gold bullion—the global currency of all time—to get anything they wanted, when they wanted it, so long as they could afford it."

"Just like every government since governments began," she chimed in.

"Exactly," he said. "But here is the critical question: What happened to the Confederate gold when the war ended?"

"I suppose the Union troops captured it," she guessed. "Didn't they?"

"No one knows, actually. Maybe a renegade Union unit got it and made hay. Maybe the Confederate leadership divvied it up. But for more than a century, legend has it that in the rush to stay ahead of the advancing army, they loaded it onto a train and took it farther and farther south."

Torrie sat forward. This was getting pretty interesting.

"As far as anyone knows," he concluded, "It could be right underneath your office right now, or right below where we're sitting . . . "

The waiter stopped by, on cue. "How is everything?" he grinned, showing every tooth he had.

"Just lovely," she said, hurriedly crunching into a crouton. She realized she'd been so involved in Gavin's story—or Gavin, which was it?—that she hadn't touched her salad.

"What a fabulous story, really. But Gavin, what on earth has that got to do with First Southern?"

Gavin leaned back and smiled as he swallowed a substantial spinach leaf. "Congratulations. You're about to get a lead on the story everybody's been knocking themselves out over for weeks now."

"You're handing me the scoop? How come?"

"Let's get that straight right off. You're not going to walk off with a scoop here today. I'm not going to tell you exactly what's going on. I'm giving you a hint."

She sat back. She'd sort through the difference between a hint and a scoop in a minute; she knew she was getting something here that nobody else had but everybody else wanted. What concerned her more was, why her?

"Why are you doing this?" she asked. "Why are you telling me? You know Eddie—and all the other reporters—a lot better than me. Why am I getting the big Gavin Duke break?"

A loaded question. One that required a deft answer.

Gavin was up to the challenge. "Why not you?" he lobbed back at her.

She paused for air. There was no way to be subtle, so she had to jump right in at the risk of coming off with an attitude. It didn't take a rocket scientist to figure out that Gavin didn't enjoy women who were too strong.

"Do you expect something from me, in gratitude for this important tidbit?" She stared right into his eyes, which was difficult after a loaded question like that one, but she held her own.

"Of course I do," he said, gingerly placing his salad fork down where it belonged. "I expect you'll be smart enough to run with it."

Touché, she thought. Since he wasn't going to come straight out and ask for anything, she felt okay going on. She scribbled onto her pad, "Confederate gold lost in time. Where is it?" She looked up to see him trying to read her notes.

"Can you read upside down?" she asked.

"No comment," he said.

"What's the Confederate gold got to do with the bank?" she continued.

"Here's the big clue—something nobody else knows yet. We're breaking a big teaser campaign on Monday with TV, radio, ads in the paper, and plenty of outdoor."

Outdoor, she remembered from journalism school, was the industry jargon term for billboards.

"We'll be using statement stuffers too, and plenty of point-of-sale materials at all the branches—signs, banners, counter cards, handouts, and buttons for the tellers. And it'll all be nothing but a great big teaser campaign, pointing to what's going to happen on May first."

She was scribbling furiously. This was terrific, meaty stuff. But still, it didn't all quite fit. There was lost Confederate gold, a big teaser campaign about something that was going to happen in a couple of weeks or so . . . She didn't get it.

Her ineptness in shorthand was catching up with her. She felt Gavin watching her as she furiously tried to get everything he'd just said down on paper. She finally finished and looked up.

"You've got to bear with me, Gavin, seeing as I'm the new kid in town. I'm having a hard time putting a thread through all this."

"That, my dear, is precisely the difference between a hint and a scoop." And with that, he excused himself and strolled off to the men's room.

It wasn't hot in the restaurant, but Torrie had to fan herself for a moment. What had just happened here? He told her everything, but he told her nothing. A new ad campaign, to generate interest for the real ad campaign, and something about lost treasure? She realized she was a pawn in all this, of course: her column would hit the newsstands on Saturday, and her minor-league version of a scoop would simply heighten interest in the First Southern tease campaign that would break two days later.

If she went with it, she'd be helping Gavin—acting as his freebie PR arm, in a way—but it was a great story, and quite a coup for the new kid at that. She had to go with it, but she wasn't very comfortable with being used by the big bank, and much worse than that, she wasn't all too pleased with being outsmarted so masterfully. Another woman might resent Gavin for it, but it actually catalyzed Torrie's interest. She was secure enough with herself for that. She liked a smart man, and besides, he really was just doing his job. And doing it very well.

When Gavin came back, Torrie decided to shift gears. "Tell me about your background. How you got into bank marketing."

"I'll have Ruth fax you my bio in the morning. Tell me about your name."

"My name?" She shifted in her seat. *He did it again!*

"Yeah. 'Torrie.' What's that all about?"

"Victoria," she said.

"Victoria. That's pretty." He paused, and she blushed. "So why not 'Vickie'?"

"I don't feel like a 'Vickie.' Do I look like a 'Vickie'?"

"Hmm, suppose not."

"Now, stop. Wait a minute. No more of this turning the tables now. I'm the reporter, okay?"

"As you wish, Miss Victoria Wilson."

"We were talking about your background. Were your parents in marketing or banking?"

"No."

She waited. "Would you care to expand on that?"

He took a sip of ice water. "No."

"What did your dad do then?"

"Sales."

"What'd he sell?"

"Look, he didn't sell banks, okay? So it's not relevant."

Torrie leaned back. "Sorry. Didn't mean to hit a nerve."

"You didn't hit a—" Gavin caught himself before his voice rose any more. He leaned forward and tried to whisper. "You didn't hit a nerve. I just don't want to talk about it, okay? I'd rather talk about you. Or, I'll even talk about me, if you twist my arm. But I don't want to talk about my parents, okay?"

"You're the boss," she said.

"Good. Glad we got that straight."

Make a note of that, Torrie told herself. *If you ever want to get under this guy's skin, you found the button. Wonder what the deal is . . .*

The conversation centered on small talk over the next few courses. Torrie decided to relax and have a good time with a charming, intelligent man. She made it a point to offer up quick prayers two or three times, not only for Gavin but also for herself—since she was definitely in uncharted territory here.

The elevator ride down was a little less nerve-wracking. When they got back to the street level, he asked, "Can I take you back to the office?"

"No, thanks," Torrie said pertly as she darted toward the train station that was just steps away. "Thanks for lunch," she threw over her shoulder, "and for the interview. See ya!"

And with that, she disappeared below the sidewalk on an escalator to the cavern below.

Gavin stood there, not quite stunned but certainly not in total control like he was used to. *Have I met my match?* True, Carolina stood toe-to-toe with him, but that was different. His relationship with Carolina was strictly business; she may as well have been one of the boys. But Torrie . . . this relationship had love-interest all over it. She kept him off balance. *That never happened before*, he thought. He didn't know quite what to do about it, so he just walked off toward the bank. There was something disarmingly different about this girl, but he couldn't quite put his finger on it.

❧   ❧   ❧

When Gavin got home that night, there was a single envelope with his name written on it resting on the kitchen counter. He opened it up and started reading the letter inside.

> *Dear Gavin,*
>
> *This is a difficult note to write, but it can't wait any longer. We are not seeing things the same way any more. I do not feel you are as committed to this relationship as I am, and I don't see any effort to change. I can't last another day. I think we both need to clear our heads. Maybe in a couple of weeks we can get together and try to start working things out. But for now, I just need my space.*
>
> *Marni*

Start working things out? he mocked. *Not in this lifetime, doll.* He crumpled the note, along with the envelope, and shoved it down into the garbage disposal. He turned on a steady stream of water, and ground it into bits. "It's about time I got you off my back," he said into the sink.

He poured himself a glassful of something harsh, mixed to make him forget any pain he wouldn't admit he felt. He drank it in gulps and stared at his gold-gilded fifty-cent piece. As he put the emptied glass onto the kitchen counter, he looked back toward the sink, as if Marni herself lay bleeding there—crushed into tiny bits—and started to say, "And another thing, sweetheart . . . " But he decided against finishing it. He waved his hand down toward the fragmented, wet remnants of Marni's good-bye. He stretched out on the couch in his pinstriped slacks and his $79 monogrammed shirt. The tie was loosened but still laced through the collar. His thoughts drifted back twenty-two years, to an angry, scared kid of fourteen whose world was being torn apart.

"Mom, please. You've gotta stay. You've just got to."

Mrs. Duke shook her head. "You can't possibly understand now," she said sternly to her son Gavin, "and I hope you never do fully understand. But I have to go."

"But why, Mom? Can't you and Dad try harder to work things out?"

She fought back the tears. "There are just some things that can't be forgiven," she said.

"Don't leave me, Mom."

"I'm not leaving you, Gavin. I'm leaving your father."

"You're leaving me too!" The tears were flowing steadily. "Even if you can't stay for him, stay for me!"

"I have to go now, son." She stood up, but her little man clung to her.

"Don't leave me, Mom. Don't."

But Gavin Duke's mother walked out the door, never to return, leaving her son alone with his father.

"Dad, when are you coming back?"

"Dad, how long will you be gone this time?"

"Dad, can I come with you on this trip? I'll keep up with my homework, I promise."

"Dad, don't go. I hate being alone all the time."

"Thanks, Dad. Can I have another five this time so I can get pizza?"

"Say, Dad, can you give me ten more?"

"Dad, since you'll be gone for a whole week, can you give me twenty this time?"

"Dad, gimme twenty-five bucks. Hurry up, okay? I gotta go."

The dream went on all night. Somebody kept leaving Gavin Duke, over and over again. His mother. His father. Marni. *Won't somebody come and stay? Anybody?*

By the next morning, he was over it. Or so he thought. He kept replaying lunch with Torrie again and again in his mind.

A few blocks away, Torrie was dialing another downtown number.

"Good morning, Carolina Gates Advertising!"

"Could you ring her office, please?"

"Certainly."

Torrie remembered playing this sport with Gavin the week before. Somehow, with all she'd heard about Carolina, she felt this contest should be much easier.

"Ms. Gates's office."

"Hi, this is Torrie Wilson, with the *Business Courier*. Is she in?"

"One moment, please."

Torrie bet herself an ice cream sundae that Carolina wouldn't really come on the line.

"This is Carrie Gates."

Shoot. She had been fantasizing about the caramel and the nuts already.

"Oh, hi, Carrie, this is Torrie Wilson, with the *Business Courier*."

"Hi, Torrie!"

"Do you have just a second?"

"That's about all," Carolina laughed. "Really, I'm about to go into a meeting. Is it something quick, or can I call you back later this morning?"

This is a refreshing change after dealing with Gavin, thought Torrie, *the man with ice in his veins.*

"Well, let's try, if you don't mind. It's just one or two questions."

"Have at it!"

"I'm doing a story on what's brewing at First Southern, and I understand you're launching a tease campaign on Monday."

A short silence. For the first time, Carolina's cheerfulness and accessibility ceased to function. "Who told you that?" She was concerned—as far as she knew secrecy and the surprise were still in Gavin's court.

"Actually, Gavin Duke did."

Carolina stopped to think. She knew reporters well enough to worry that this was a ploy or an outright lie. If one of her staffers had let it leak, Carolina might be walking into a trap and Gavin would eat her alive when the story broke.

"Tell you what, Torrie—I'm sorry. I don't have that second after all. I do want to talk to you, though, really. Can I call you back around, say, eleven this morning?"

"That'd be fine," Torrie said, fascinated by the way people turned to Silly Putty when Gavin's name was mentioned.

Carolina called Gavin as soon as she hung up with Torrie. "Gavin, have you met Torrie, uh, Wilson, the reporter for the *Business Courier*?"

"Yeah, but forget it. I got dibs on her," Gavin announced into the phone.

"Did you give her an interview yet?"

"Yeah, I thought she'd be a great way to hype the tease. I told her you'd have a two-week campaign breaking Monday, all media, and that it would all come out on May first. Oh, and that it had something to do with lost Confederate gold."

"I'm surprised," Carolina said. "I mean, it sounds like a great way to get extra mileage out of the tease campaign, but I guess it caught me off guard."

"Caught me off guard too," Gavin said. "Just a spur of the moment thing."

"She wants me to call her back," Carolina said. "What do you want me to tell her?"

"Not much more," Gavin said. "She's got enough to give us some good play. Let's track it from there."

"Gotcha. Thanks, Gav."

"No sweat, Carrie. Later."

Seven

Gavin Duke's own mother wouldn't have recognized him. Not like this. Dressed in shiny brown polyester pants, too tight and too short, a short-sleeved cotton shirt with a white T-shirt visible at the neck, a pocket protector filled with pens, white sweat socks and cheap sneakers, and—the crowning touch—a bent-rimmed ball cap that proudly displayed a "God Bless America" slogan.

He rented a banged-up Ford Econoline and gingerly placed the gold in the back. The gold was in disguise, too, lest anyone stumble upon it before its appointed time. He had managed to assemble together three oil drums marked *Danger: Toxic Waste. Do Not Handle or Incinerate* and had hidden the brass and wooden trunk that housed the gold in the bottom of the middle drum. At the very top, he had set a pan of used motor oil in place, so anyone who did manage to get as far as opening up the drum would see that toxic waste did reside there. Next to the drums, banging against them enough to make him nervous every time he went around a turn, was a pushcart for moving the heavy center drum into place. A million dollars in gold weighed in at close to one hundred and seventy-five pounds, slightly less than Gavin himself. He'd amused himself with being worth his weight in gold just before a farmer in a tractor pulled out in front of the van to make a tight enough squeeze on the road that Gavin's heart jumped before cursing the farmer and swerving violently around the old man.

Gavin came to a four-way intersection, complete with railroad crossing, and stopped to look at the map. Almost there.

The gold was about to be hidden in a remarkably inauspicious, uncharacteristically low-tech manner. *But it's perfect,* Gavin cackled with delight. No one could imagine or suspect a thing. He would do it himself—the last thing anyone would guess, since Gavin was well-known for not wanting to get his hands dirty, both figuratively and literally. His manicured nails were a source of jokes around town, and people kidded him that his hands looked like a surgeon's. No way would Gavin Duke bury a trunkful of metal in the dirt!

He took off the cap, wiped his brow, and pulled out the road map. *Highway 27 at the Old Plantation Road? Yeah, that's right. Just a few more miles, this way.*

Gavin shifted back into gear and headed off with a roar. He'd come a long way to get to this point, dressed in civil servant digs and driving around the back roads of rural Georgia in a beat-up van.

The good thing was, The Man had no clue how earthily Gavin was hiding the treasure. He wouldn't have stood for it, not for a minute. There would have been armed guards, day and night, police blockades, and teams of Dobermans. Gavin had initially considered such measures but grew more and more uneasy over time. *Why not just have searchlights and skywriters?* he thought. *No, no. This had to be completely inauspicious. Heck, even one of those lousy five-dollar-an-hour hicks he'd hire to guard the loot would be smart enough to figure out a way to vanish to a tropical isle with the stuff instead of working ten-hour days for the next forty years of his life to be able to afford a double-wide, at best. Nope, not on your life.* Gavin had to control this one himself, top to bottom. No cops, no dogs, no attention.

Harperson trusted Gavin enough to assume it was under control. Which it was, of course, but just not in a way The Man would approve. So Gavin didn't ask, and he prepared a well-scripted dodge in case it happened to come up. It might go something like this:

"Is security all set for the gold?" Harperson would wonder.

"I can assure you," Gavin would boast, "that the best mind

available is managing security on this." (Gavin even planned chuckling to himself at this point in the imaginary conversation.) And then, the diversion. "Say, I don't recall seeing that tie/those cuff links/that tie tack/suit before. Is it/are they new?"

Gavin Duke. The man of a thousand faces.

Yet for good measure, he did stage a PR ceremony where a sealed envelope identifying the location was stored with the bank's law firm. He neglected to mention he changed the location after the envelope was sealed. "Trust the lawyers?" he asked himself. "Who are we kidding here?"

But he had confided in Carolina—at least a little more—brainstorming for ideas at JohnBarley's early on in the game.

"Where would you hide it?" he asked her.

"I've given that some thought," she replied. "At first, I thought it made good sense to put it near Dahlonega, somewhere up in the mountains, where the gold rush took place in the early 1800s. There are even some old mine pits there. That's where the gold for the state capitol dome came from, and . . . "

"That's no good," he interrupted. "It's too obvious."

"Yeah, that's what I'd concluded too. Then, I thought about Atlanta. Right down in the bank vault, or some other landmark. But that would be too easy for someone to stumble over and too tough to protect without being obvious."

"I agree," he said.

"Another one that came to mind but I scratched as being too blatant was the Golden Isles, along the coast."

"I'm with you."

"Which, of course, leaves everything in between!" she laughed.

"Which is exactly where I am," he shrugged. "That only leaves about two thousand square miles of real estate to cover. Doing anything this weekend? Got yourself a full tank of gas?"

She said, "There must be a way to hone it down some. Have you got any internal criteria for that?"

"No, not really. I thought maybe we could come up with something together, Carrie."

"Okay," she said, pulling out a Mont Blanc pen and sliding a cocktail napkin over. *An interesting irony of materials*, Gavin noted.

"First, outside the metro area."

"Check," she said.

"Not Dahlonega. Not the coast."

"Okay."

Silence. "Maybe we're going about this all wrong," he said. "How about if we just look at a map to see if anything strikes our fancy?"

"Good idea," she said, putting away the pen and setting the napkin under her drink. "I don't suppose you happen to have a map of Georgia handy, do you? Maybe we should ask for one."

"Carrie," he scolded, "don't you know I'm the ultimate boy scout?" as he pulled a map from his briefcase.

"You might always be prepared," she scolded right back, "but you're no boy scout!"

"Watch it, or I'll help you cross the street. Everybody'll be calling you 'Old Lady Gates.'"

"Okay, you win. And by the way, I am impressed at your constant resourcefulness!"

"Thank you, Ms. Gates. Here, pull this flap over to your side."

They unfolded the map and started looking over it.

"I feel like a little kid about to embark on a great treasure hunt," she looked up to say.

"You are," he said. And they looked at the map.

He was amazed that there were actually places called Ball Ground, Enigma, and Faceville. He already knew about Okefenokee, and he thought that was bad enough. But Uvalda? Santa Claus? And Fowlstown?

"Pretty scary," he said. "What if we put it out in the middle of nowhere, only to find we had technically encroached the city limits of a place called Goofstown or something? That would make The Man's day."

"Good point. Silly, but true," she agreed. They went back to the map, but to no avail. Gavin might as well have used the dartboard approach. No place looked better than any other. *There must be a better way*, he thought.

That night at home, Gavin couldn't sleep. He'd gone to the kitchen, made himself a sandwich, and sat down in front of the TV. Not to watch anything, just to have some foreground noise on. *What have we got here? The Country Music Channel, The Family Channel, Channel for the Left-Handed, ESPN. Aha! Late-night rerun of the golf tourney—the video form of supermarket music. Just what I need to unwind.*

One of the commercials that aired during the next break was for a factory outlet shopping center in Columbus, Georgia. Gavin smiled and remembered when First Southern bought out a little regional bank in Columbus a couple of years earlier. A most unusual weekend, hosted by the small town ol' boy bank president and his wife, charming relics of the old South. He and The Man had spent the day there, wading through a thousand details and enjoying a home-cooked meal at the president's aging antebellum mansion.

"What do you do for excitement around here?" Gavin asked, wondering how either Mr. or Mrs. Bailor would field that one and suspecting that the answer would be either hog calling, a pleasant date at the Bijou, or settin' 'round the kettle, watchin' the peanuts boil.

"We were planning on taking you and Mr. Harperson on a sunset cruise," Marcus Bailor replied.

"You'll really enjoy it," his wife, Patricia, added. "We certainly do."

Wait a minute, Gavin had thought, *it may be my imagination, but I don't think I'm in Key West here. A sunset cruise? In Columbus, Georgia? Sorry, folks, but I most definitely did not fall off that turnip truck yesterday.*

H. Gary Harperson asked the question first. "Just where do you pick up a sunset cruise hereabouts?"

"Why, at our dock, of course!"

The Man and the marketing VP exchanged a look as Marcus went on.

"We've got ourselves a boat, a little runabout, moored on the river. It's a terrific place to enjoy a pleasant summer evening."

Gavin feigned a smile. *Hey, it could be worse. At least it's not a hootenanny. Sunset cruise on the river, a refreshing drink in hand? If you have to spend an evening in a small town, that's a welcome diversion.*

The Chattahoochee River drifts past Columbus after its winding jaunt through Atlanta, a couple hours' drive to the northeast. It's not navigable by barges or other ships of commerce—only pleasure craft—and once you get a mile or two past town, its banks are unspoiled, a pristine voyage into the South of Scarlett O'Hara, Rhett Butler, and lost Confederate gold. A picturesque, relaxing couple of hours.

Gavin was expecting a weathered wooden skiff, equipped with a temperamental, loud, smoky outboard engine screwed perilously loose to the back end. He hiked down the steep steps toward the dock, right behind Patricia. In all fairness, she was a lovely woman, treated well by life as a darling of the small society that made up her world.

He made sure his first step on the dock was a careful one—he didn't know if the planks would hold up. Once he felt more secure in his footing, he looked up and saw Patricia stepping into the "skiff."

His jaw dropped.

Here was this lovely Southern Belle, along with her diminutive, gray-headed little husband, stepping into a twenty-five-foot Cigarette boat, the kind drug runners use to lose the Coast Guard. These sleek machines top out at more than eighty miles an hour and can cost as much as a hundred grand. This one was painted bright blue, with thin purple stripes. On the back, in elegant script, was her name, *Daddy's Sweetheart*.

Gavin shook his head as Patricia helped him in. *This is too weird*, he thought.

They untied the ropes and cast off, ever so slowly. *Must be the no wake zone*, Gavin figured. *Any second now, Bailor's gonna let 'er rip*. He sat back, held on, and waited. Marcus got it up to about ten miles an hour and held steady. Gavin waited and adjusted his grip. Nothing. He waited some more. Still nothing. "Hey, captain," he shouted over the din of ninety gazillion horsepower—even at only eight and a half knots, a Cigarette boat lets you know it's coming—"I'm afraid you're going a little too fast for me!"

With a startled look, Marcus waved an acknowledgment, then quickly cut the throttle back to about half speed. He turned and smiled. "How's that? Better?" he asked.

Gavin smiled as graciously as he could and waved back. "Great," he said. After Marcus turned back around to pilot this mighty vessel, Gavin muttered, "Just great."

After what seemed like two days traveling downriver—it was actually seven minutes—Gavin noticed a most unusual rock formation, partially hidden by a clump of sycamore trees, past a bend in the river. It was a cliff, granite or some similar type of stone, jutting up about thirty feet above the flat plain that stretched in both directions from its base.

"What's that?" he asked. Marcus and Patricia looked at each other, hoping for a good answer.

"Don't know," Marcus said. "Just a rock. It doesn't have a name, as far as I know. It marks the spot where the old tank parts factory used to be."

"Tank parts?" Gavin asked, not really interested but so bored that any conversation was a welcome treat.

"Back before World War II, there was an old textile mill up here along the river—what was it called, anyway?"

"Southern Looms," Patricia said.

"That's right. Southern Looms. But during the war, the government came in and took it over and converted it to making fenders, bumpers, things like that, for the tanks they used in Europe and Africa. After the war, they kept it open a couple of years more, but shut it down—must be forty years ago now. The man who ran the mill passed away during the war and left no widow, no children to take over the business, so the government ended up just keeping it. I think they reopened it and used it as a supply depot for a few years during the fifties, but it's been locked tight ever since."

By now, even the slow boat to nowhere had gone past the monolith. Gavin noticed some rusted chain-link fencing topped with barbed wire, defending the area from encroachment by way of the river.

Gavin suddenly flashed forward to the golf rerun on TV. *Odd; I hadn't thought of that "dream getaway" to Columbus in ages, especially not the big, nameless rock, protected by an imposing fence from whatever river rat might want to invade a factory that hadn't been used in four decades.*

He sat up. "That's it," he said to himself. "That's it!" He'd found the spot where the gold would be hidden—buried treasure, under a cliff, near a river bend, in the middle of nowhere! It was perfect. Now, all he had to do was figure out how to get in there—and out again—without creating a stir.

He jumped up, zapped off the TV just as Peter Jacobsen was sinking a thirty-foot putt, and ran to the next room to grab a pencil and some paper. He knew he wouldn't be able to sleep now. Not until the plan was mapped out. Gavin was on a roll.

First, he had to check out the place, by land. Was there anyone in charge of the place who could let him in or was sneaking in the only option? And what would he use as his cover? He certainly couldn't tip anybody off that First Southern was scouting out a place like that—it'd be obvious that something was up, especially in a small town. Time to do a little sleuthing. Under any other circumstances, he'd simply pass the legwork off to Ruth. But not this time. He had to handle it himself.

Ruth was surprised when Gavin had called at five till eight the next day. "I'll be working out of my home office for a few hours this morning," he said. "I'll touch base with you later. Reschedule my appointments, will you?" He'd only worked at home two or three times before, and only when he'd been feeling under the weather. But never on the spur of the moment, and certainly never with a loaded schedule of back-to-back meetings.

Ruth knew something was amiss, but she didn't say a word. If Gavin wanted to let her know, he'd let her know. If he didn't, he'd take her head off for asking.

From his home base, Gavin could make some phone calls without being detected. He dialed information in Columbus and asked for several numbers: chamber of commerce, the county sheriff, the nearest army base, and the county government office that housed deeds and other property records.

He tried the first.

"Muscogee County Chamber of Commerce, please hold."

"Great start," he said. "Guess their phones are ringing off the hook these days!"

"Sorry to keep you waiting, sir. This is Glenn. How may I help you?"

"Why, yes," Gavin said, using his best Southern drawl. "I'm representing a major real estate concern, and I wanted to ask a question. The old tank manufacturing facility, just outside of town? I was wondering if . . . "

"Excuse me, the what?"

"The old mill, south of town, along the river—where they made tank parts years ago?"

"I'm afraid I don't know what you're describing. Please hold while I connect you with Mrs. Moore."

Oh, boy, thought Gavin. *I'm gonna make eight million phone calls, and talk to eight million morons who never went more than five miles from their front door in their whole lives, never bothering to wonder about the huge, fenced-in, shut-down plant that's a three-minute drive from their face.*

"Stella Moore!" The voice came crisply through the line.

"Hey!" Gavin said. "I was hoping you could help me. I am representing a firm which is interested in finding out some more information about the old plant, just south of Columbus. I believe the army once used it to manufacture tank parts?"

"Why, sure!" Stella said. "The old Southern Looms plant!"

"Yes! That's the one!" Gavin liked Stella.

"I'm afraid I can't help you." Gavin hated Stella. "That's in the next county, Stewart. Let me get you the phone number for their chamber."

"Wait!" Gavin wanted to reach through the phone and grab her, since she knew what she was talking about. "I sure appreciate your getting me their number. But before I call, what can you tell me about the mill?"

"Not very much. I do know it's been closed down for years, after the government took it over. Locked up tight."

Music to Gavin's ears.

"Do you know who owns it now? Does the government still maintain it?"

She laughed. "Nobody maintains it. It's all overgrown and falling to pieces. Just makes a good home for squirrels and bluebirds, I suppose!"

"So it probably still belongs to Uncle Sam?"

"I imagine. But they'll be able to help you better over in Stewart County. Ask for Miriam Owenby. Her telephone number is 912-555-8136. Sorry I couldn't be of more help."

"You've been wonderful, believe me. Thanks." He hung up, realizing he'd wasted his time getting all those government numbers in the wrong county and that he'd have to do it all over again. But first, the referral. He punched in the number with lightning speed.

"Stewart County Chamber. This is Bill."

"Could I speak with Miriam, please?"

"Hang on."

The line clicked a few times, and Gavin thought he was going to be cut off.

"Has anyone helped you?" a soft female voice asked.

"I'm trying to get Miriam," he said.

"This is she!"

"Why, hello, Miriam. I'm seeking some information on the old mill south of Columbus, along the river."

"Now, why would anybody be interested in that old place?"

"Actually, I can't tell you just now. I'm representing a real estate concern in Atlanta that may be interested in acquiring some of that land—but if word gets out, they'll back off in a hurry. Can I swear you to secrecy, Miriam?"

"Goodness, it sounds very important. You have my word."

"Good. I just have a couple of quick questions. Does the army still own it?"

"No, as a matter of fact. They arranged to turn it over to the county some years ago."

Fascinating, Gavin thought. *And good news too. Surely a rural county's dump would be more accessible than something the army owned.*

"Is it used for anything at all?"

"Not any more. Once in a while, every two or three years, I think, some of the county offices box up their older documents and they take them out and leave them in one of the warehouses there. I imagine it must be cheaper than finding a place to store it in town."

"How do they get in? Is there someone at the front gate?"

"Oh, no," she laughed. "There's no need to have anyone there, because no one would ever want to go all the way out to an empty factory."

"Then how do they get in when it's time to store the old documents?"

"I suppose Brick lets them in. But why are you so interested in what's stored out there and how they get in?"

Brick lets them in? Can't let that one slide. But first, better make sure she doesn't start getting suspicious. "Well, ma'am, my client may wish to take a look around. You know, see how the terrain looks, see if any of the buildings are worth saving. He may be interested in getting inside to take a look around."

"Oh, I see. Then you would definitely want to talk with Brick."

"And how do I do that?"

"Well, you could try and call him, I suppose. He doesn't really have an office. He works out of the county courthouse."

"Ma'am?"

"Oh, he's the maintenance man. He keeps all the keys to, gracious, just about every lock in Stewart County. He has to keep one for the front gate somewhere. You'll need to reach him."

"Brick. Do you have his number? I mean, the number where I can try to reach him?"

"I believe I can find it. Let me get on my glasses here." He just knew she was lifting a pair of bifocals from a chain that hung around her neck. "Try 555-9077. That's the main reception area at the courthouse, and they should be able to track him down."

"And that's his name—Brick?"

"I suppose it is a bit unusual," she realized. "Yes, his name is Brick McKay. Very nice man."

"Thank you, Mrs. Owenby. I truly appreciate your help."

"You're very welcome, young man. Have a pleasant day."

"Thank you—and you too." Gavin hung up and licked his lips.

Never called anyone named Brick before, he thought, *especially someone who didn't have a phone. This oughta be good.*

"Stewart County Courthouse."

"Yes, I need to speak with, ah, Brick."

"Brick? He's around here somewhere. I can get a message to him."

Gavin was beginning to realize he'd simply need to make a trip to see Brick in the flesh—this wasn't going to work, leaving a message for a man without a phone who probably didn't read much anyway. "That's okay, I . . ."

"Wait, hang on just a sec."

Gavin heard a muffling sound, then some blurred speaking he couldn't make out. Wonderful—the hold button hadn't reached these people yet.

"Hullo?"

A different voice came over the phone. A man with a deep, echoing voice—not young, but not a senior citizen either.

"Yeah, hello," Gavin said, growing impatient. "I was trying to find Brick, but . . ."

"This's Brick."

Gavin froze. He couldn't believe he was actually speaking to Brick—something of a celebrity in Stewart County, it seemed. And what luck. The reclusive Mr. McKay just happened to be strolling through the courthouse lobby at that very moment. "Brick," he said.

"Yup. Who is this I'm talkin' to?"

"This is, um, Michael Jester, with the Environmental Protection Agency. I may be needing you to let me into the front gate of the old Southern Looms mill, where they used to build tank parts, next to the river—"

"Y'all got some boxes to store up there?"

"Yeah," Gavin said, "got some old stuff to store."

"When y'all wantin' to do it?"

No, Gavin thought. *This is too easy. Surely, another bank has bugged my phone, and then planted this guy—some big practical joke, so there will be cameras and lights all over the place when I get there with the gold.*

"When?" Gavin repeated back to Brick.

"Yeah. Like, if you're wantin' to do it this afternoon, I can't help you. But if you're thinkin' about tomorrow . . . "

"Actually, I'm not sure when I'll be. Can I just stop by the courthouse when I'm ready and try to catch up with you?"

"Yeah, that'd be fine."

"Great. Thanks, Brick. I look forward to seeing you in a few days."

"Yep." Click.

Gavin hung up, absolutely stunned. Was it really going to be this ridiculously easy? He'd just drive into Stewart County, find Brick, have him unlock the gate, stash the gold, and be gone?

"You are a genius," Gavin said out loud, quick to turn a remarkably fortuitous string of coincidences into a scenario he could take full credit for, as though he'd planned it for months. He sat back and laughed. *Sorry, Captain and Mrs. Bailor—won't have time to stop by for another rip-roaring boat ride!* he thought. He laughed until his eyes were wet with tears.

☙   ☙   ☙

So here was Gavin, traveling the road less traveled, on his way to the Stewart County courthouse in a city called Lumpkin. He suspected it would prove to be an appropriate name.

Minutes later, Gavin saw a road sign that announced:

LUMPKIN   6
CUTHBERT 26

All right, guys—three touchdowns and a missed extra point. Beat the spread, Gavin thought. He was a funny guy.

He slowed as he went through town, gazing carefully at the old brick and wooden facades, storefronts of an America long forgotten by those who dwell in skyscrapers and neatly-hedged suburban tracts, polka-dotted by the colorful plastic of fast food and convenience stores. As with most small towns that doubled as a county seat, there was a large turn-of-the-century building smack in the center of town. The square. He circled it once, like a famished beast stalking its prey, and pulled the van slowly into an empty parking space.

He hopped out and closed the door carefully, making sure it was locked. *Can't just leave a million dollars in gold unattended for long*, he laughed to himself. Maybe he ought to leave his wallet on the front seat as a decoy, in case a burglar should happen by.

Gavin circled the building again, on foot this time, hardly noticing the stately huge trees and painstakingly beautiful architecture. Gavin was looking for a man named Brick.

He'd hoped to avoid having to call attention to himself by asking for Brick. Ideally, he wouldn't even have to set foot inside the building—no human contact at all, except the trusty maintenance man.

He turned the southeastern corner and gazed across a new view of the grounds. More trees. Another monument or two. Couple of old guys sitting on a bench. *Probably chatting about their wounds from World War I*, Gavin imagined. A squirrel. Some bright sunshine-colored zinnias. A large, messy man picking up some more flowers from a wheelbarrow.

Brick?

Gavin swallowed hard. He walked over toward the man. He was wearing a uniform of sorts—deep green work pants and a shirt that matched, and he was rather filthy from the topsoil and the sweat of his brow. Gavin guessed he was around forty, but it was hard to tell. He had thick, coarse, straight auburn hair and a five o'clock shadow, heavy facial features, and unusually large hands and fingers. He wore steel-toed jet black work boots, and on one of his belt loops was a large round keyring—the kind a jailer in a place like Mayberry might keep. Gavin gazed lovingly at the keys as they jangled gently beside the green pant leg, imagining one as the key to his dreams—or at least to the gate at the old mill.

"Are you Brick?"

Gavin's heart fell as the man kept working, as though not realizing Gavin was speaking to him, because *he* knew he wasn't Brick. Gavin was about to turn and continue his quest when the man spoke.

"Yup."

Gavin turned back around and felt his heart return to its initial location. *Okay, so Brick is slow. I knew that.*

"I'm Brick."

"Brick, Michael Jester, EPA. We spoke on the phone the other day." He extended his hand.

Brick moved methodically, placing flowers into the earth without looking up and not returning the handshake, pleasing Gavin to no end.

Gavin decided monologue was the only way to have an intelligent conversation at this juncture. He cleared his throat and continued. "I was wondering when you might be able to come out and unlock the front gate at the old mill for me, so I can store some materials there."

Brick finally stopped. He wiped a row of sweat from his forehead with his massive right forearm and stared at Gavin.

"You with the government?"

"Yes," said Gavin. "Michael Jester, EPA."

Brick stared some more. "I ain't seen you before."

Gavin thought fast. "I just drove down from Atlanta today. My first time."

Brick went back to his plants. "Awright."

Gavin blinked his eyes several times. "Great. When?"

"When I'm finished here."

Gavin peered into the wheelbarrow. Just two plants left.

"Um, do you have a car to get there . . . "

"Nope. Truck. I'll drive the truck. You can follow me."

I can live with that, Gavin said to himself. He sat down on a concrete bench and waited for Brick to finish. It took all of about three minutes, but it seemed much longer to Gavin.

"Where y'all parked?" Brick asked as he tipped the excess dirt off the wheelbarrow and leaned it against the courthouse. He clapped his hands as clean as Gavin imagined they ever got.

"Right over there," Gavin pointed. "White van."

Brick squinted. "Awful dirty white," he said.

"Speak for yourself," Gavin muttered under his breath.

"I'll get the truck and drive it 'round that side. You can follow me." Brick repeated. Gavin imagined Brick must have taken a public-speaking course, to have such an in-depth knowledge of the value of repetition.

"Right. I'll follow you."

Gavin scurried over, glad to find he had really remembered to lock the door, hopped in, and revved up the engine. *Yahoo*, he thought. He was getting into this.

He followed Brick onto progressively more narrow and less paved roads. Occasionally he caught a glimpse of the river where he had enjoyed the sunset cruise. It was an appropriate memory, given that apparently Brick had learned to drive where the bank president had learned to boat. Brick crept along skittishly, maxing out at twenty-five miles an hour but maintaining a cruising speed of around twenty most of the way. Left on his own, Gavin would be hitting fifty, maybe sixty on this road. And only because of the occasional chuckholes.

Finally, Gavin saw it. The corner of a rusting, rotting fence, concrete-block walls fitted with ridged tin or aluminum sheet metal roofing, the rust from the nails bleeding down profusely, and there, off in the distance, no-name rock.

It was beautiful. A sight to behold.

After what must have been a full quarter mile of fencing, Brick pulled over. For a moment, Gavin regretted seeing *Deliverance*—his freedom flashed before his eyes. But Brick climbed out of his pickup, left the door wide open so Gavin could get a good look at the Stewart County seal, and lumbered over to the fence. A massive gate—big enough to drive a tank through—swayed as Brick fingered the members of his belt-loop key ring, finally picked one, and turned it in the lock. The lock fell open, Brick unwrapped the chain, and swung the gate open. He walked over to Gavin's window.

"Just lock up when you're fixin' to leave," he said before disappearing back into the county truck, making a tornado of gravel dust as he did a 180 and headed slowly back to town. Gavin guessed he'd get there by Tuesday.

Gavin jumped out of his rent-a-van in sheer childlike enthusiasm. He let out a whoop before hopping back into the van and driving past the gate, into this rusting relic of unimportant Georgia history. Unimportant until Gavin Duke came along, that is.

He drove slowly, at Brick's pace, through the compound. There was a main building, plus one, two, three—no, four—smaller ones. And then, straight ahead, the rock.

Gavin stopped the engine and walked toward the giant slab of granite slowly, barely able to contain himself. This was the moment he'd been waiting for.

What little asphalt remained beneath his feet—broken to pieces by decades of wind, rain, hail, the sun's baking, and weeds that cared little where they sprang up—soon gave up its feeble attempt to cover the red Georgia clay that led to the monolith. Step by step, Gavin drew closer to his holy hill, finally reaching his goal and then circling it, as he had circled the county courthouse shortly before.

As he made his way counterclockwise, he got a gift he hadn't expected. There, built right into the foot of the stone, was an old cellar door. It was a big double door, the paint long since peeled off and the wood warping with age, that led into the ground, as if to go underneath the stone. He must be dreaming. Did somebody really dig him a cavern underneath his rock—the perfect place to hide the Southern Gold—so he wouldn't have to lift a single shovelful of mud? This was too good to be true.

He reached toward the handle, only to find it was locked. *Too bad Brick left. He probably has the key to this lock too.* Gavin sprinted back to the van, started the engine again, and burned rubber over to the doors so he'd have the needed excavating equipment nearby.

He flew out, grabbed the crowbar from the back—he'd come prepared for any contingency—and with three good yanks, managed to pry the door open. He grabbed the flashlight he'd packed, flicked it on, and descended the steps.

There weren't many steps, just six. The ceiling was only about five feet high, so Gavin had to hunch over. He came to a landing and a single locked door. Back to the crowbar.

He noticed nervously how the masonry above this door was crumbling, and a few grains of gray dust fell as the door flew open. The rock was solid, he knew, but what about the cavern underneath it? *I'd better hurry.* He darted through the opening, finding himself in a corridor that was maybe ten feet long.

He stopped, stooped over by necessity—the ceiling, such as it was, was still only about five feet from the floor. He flashed the beam through its makeshift-looking rafters, detecting a multitude of lengthy, dusty cobwebs. The rafters themselves were warping, rotting, hand-hewn timbers, barely able to support each other, let alone all the granite up above. He realized he was shuddering and reached subconsciously to feel the gold coin.

It was difficult to move quickly yet carefully, especially since he had to hunch over. *What if my head hits one of the old beams? Will the entire tunnel come crashing down on me?* He reached the far side, glad to finally make it to the room he hoped to find. Gavin straightened up, grateful for an eight-foot ceiling. He gave the chamber a quick once-over with his flashlight, starting with the ceiling support. Not much better in here; in fact, a few beams had cracked and were dangling perilously from each other. The room was maybe twenty feet square, with wooden four-by-fours acting as posts, extending up from the floor to give additional support to the ceiling. There were four posts and lots of empty shelves. *Must have been a storage room. But why here, under the rock? Maybe this was for sensitive materials,* he decided. *Double locked doors, only one way in and one way out. Easy to secure.*

He dared to press his hand against one of the posts but stopped suddenly when it moved. Some dust sprinkled down from the rafters above. He slowly removed his hand from the post, imagining that if he were to accidentally bump into it with one of his barrels, it'd be over in a hurry. He made a mental note to be slower with the pushcart than he would want to be.

The place was empty, so there was ample room for Gavin's three barrels of "toxic waste." He lost no time moving them in, although the one with the gold was more work than he thought, even with the pushcart, given the steps, the low ceilings, and his fear of being crushed to death under a pile of rubble. He began to question the sanity of this exercise—was anything worth the fear he was experiencing at this endless moment? He managed to set the barrels in place, with the one housing the gold in the middle, as planned. He then pulled a big black tarp over the drums and rushed back to the van, glad to have made it out from the chamber and the tunnels two consecutive times but also knowing his work wasn't complete.

Before continuing, he had to stop for a minute and keep himself from hyperventilating. What might have happened in there? What if the pressure or the motion from his footsteps or the weight of the drums created enough of a stir to . . . He snapped out of it. "You're okay, Gav. You're in one piece," he told himself, clapping his hands together twice as if to say, *Let's get on with it.*

He'd brought enough tools to set up a carpentry shop, including plenty of heavy-duty locks, and he paused to give himself a pat on the back, knowing the work wouldn't be complete without this advance planning. Although he didn't have to pass through the narrow corridor or into the chamber again, he still had to head down the steps and secure the second doorway. He stood still and silent at the top of the steps for a minute and a half, convincing himself that if an avalanche were imminent, he would detect some advance warning sign and be able to dart up the steps to safety before the world came crashing down on him. He took a long, slow, deep breath, descended the steps, and set about his work. He fastened two of the locks to the inside door and double-checked that it was sealed. More crumbs of deteriorating mortar, or concrete, or something fell in a steadier stream this time. He licked his lips, and told himself it was nothing major—yet—but he got out in an awful hurry when he knew the door was locked tight.

Back outside for good this time, Gavin stopped to think about a new problem. *Sure, I made it out. But what if the whole thing caves in?* He mulled the notion, before saying "So what?" out loud. *The gold isn't gonna break, and I know where it is. A minor cave-in might be even better—it really would be buried treasure!*

He went about double-locking the outside doors, the ones that looked like cellar doors, and loaded his tools back into the van. He pulled an ice-cold diet Coke out of the cooler, leaned against the hood, and soaked it all in. He realized his heart was still pounding. He practiced breathing slowly, steadily, to bring his pulse down, caressing his gold half-dollar and reminding himself that he was Gavin Duke, God's chosen marketing genius. He was immortal, invincible, and immune to harm.

A gentle breeze helped him relax, tickling the leaves of the mature hardwoods that were nearby. He was getting his wits back about him. "Time to head home," he said at last, looking at his watch. There was some gray-white dust on the face, which he wiped off with his thumb to discover it was 4:30. *Shoot—I never checked back in with Ruth. He'd told her he had some fires to put out and would be away all day but that he'd check in. Ruth will think it odd that I didn't call. Ah, well, no matter—she'll have things under control. I'll head home, take a shower, maybe go to the club for a quick rubdown—those muscles got a workout—then cruise into the office for fifteen minutes to see what piled up today.*

He backed up the van, turned around, and drove past the gate. "Can't disappoint my old buddy Brick," he said to himself, hopping out to loop the chain through the links, double-checking to see that the lock was fastened. He held the lock in his hand, looked upward to see the top of the rock, and smiled.

As Gavin drove off, he didn't see the other rental car hidden off the road, well camouflaged by the overgrown shrubbery in a way that only an efficient, detail-oriented person could.

A solitary figure emerged from the shadows to get a better view of the van speeding down the country road through a pair of high-powered binoculars.

Lowering the binoculars, Ruth Chandler—loyal assistant, trusted right hand, faithful employee—smiled. She knew most of Gavin's other secrets, and now she knew the only one that mattered.

🥐 🥐 🥐

Two days before the tease campaign began, Torrie Wilson's first page-one byline in the *Atlanta Business Courier* appeared:

FIRST SOUTHERN MYSTERY SOLVED —OR DEEPENED?

By Torrie Wilson
Atlanta Business Courier Exclusive
ATLANTA — After weeks of rumors and hometown gossip, First Southern Bank will answer the questions Monday when it unveils a new ad campaign.

Unfortunately, the new campaign may raise as many new questions as it answers.

The multimedia campaign, developed by long-time First Southern agency Carolina Gates Advertising, is designed to be a tease campaign, calling attention to the fact that only on May 1 will bank executives end the mystery.

Top-level sources from both the bank and the agency confirm some link between the legendary lost gold of the Confederate States of America and the pending announcement, but no further details were available at press time.

Gavin, at work on a Saturday—as always—folded the paper in half after reading the story and smiled as he gazed out the window and took in the city below. It was a city he would hold in the palm of his hand for the next several months.

Eight

Thanks to the seed Torrie planted, everyone was buzzing about the tease campaign before it hit the airwaves.

Tami Olson from Channel 2 was the first to call Gavin. She caught him at his office around noon on Saturday.

"Gav," she said. She was a playful, happy-go-lucky young woman, a sharp contrast to the nagging, cynical nature of many of her peers. *Even cheerier than Torrie*, he observed. *And photogenic too, the unstated job requirement for broadcast news.* Tami had not only big Barbie eyes but a brain as well, which was most certainly not a requirement for an anchor slot. And she was dating a local NBA player, the power forward for the Atlanta Hawks.

"Tam," he grinned back over the phone. "How come you're in on Saturday?"

"I took a personal day earlier in the week, so my fair-minded producer decided I needed Saturday duty. Which is a good thing, given the fact that the *Business Courier* burned my fingertips this morning. What's the deal with the new kid? I can't imagine how she got the edge here while all us old timers missed it!" Whatever gift Carolina had for smoothing the edges on what could otherwise be a rough conversation, Tami had the same talent.

"Why, what do you mean?" asked Gavin, innocent as could be.

"Just wondering if you knew where the leak was," Tami prodded. Sweet, but still a journalist. "I'd like to add that person to my unnamed source file!"

"Think nothing of it. She just fell into it," Gavin fibbed.

"Oh, sure. Now, I suppose you're gonna offer me below-prime financing on some repossessed swamp front property in Florida, huh Gav?"

Gavin laughed. "Okay. I know you didn't call just to harangue me. I imagine you have a follow-up or two?"

"I'd love to get you on camera for the weekend report, since I didn't get the big break," she said. "Think the mobile truck could catch up with you before, say, three?"

Gavin looked at his watch. "Tell you what," he offered, "I ought to head downstairs for a sandwich now, anyway. How about if I just leg it on over to the studio for a couple of minutes? That way, if anybody else tries to get me for a video bite, they may not make the evening show. You'll have the TV exclusive!"

"You're a dream, Gav—almost. We'll be ready for you. Thanks!"

"See you in thirty, sugar." Gavin hung up, grabbed his jacket, and headed for the elevator. He wore a suit when he went in on Saturdays, usually because he always managed to run into someone or some situation that made it worthwhile. Today was the perfect example. He couldn't appear on the local ABC affiliate wearing a golf shirt, could he?

He hopped in a cab, where he scarfed down a sub as he took the mile-and-a-half ride to Midtown—it was easier than fighting the multiple ins-and-outs of parking garages. At the front desk, the receptionist told him to go straight back to studio 3-B. He walked in and saw two stools, a backdrop that looked like a lawyer's office—lots of stained mahogany, books, and flowers arranged on the shelves—and the normal lighting and camera gear you'd find in a TV production facility. As he entered from the left, Tami and her producer came in from the right.

"Thanks, Gav," she said, extending her right hand in a hurry. He reached to shake her hand but realized she was instead handing him a clip-on microphone. He put it on and sat down in the position he'd assumed on several occasions before.

"Sound check. How're my levels, Elizabeth?" asked Tami, staring off past the lights as she sat down beside him and fiddled with her mike. She was balancing a clipboard on her lap.

"Gav, give me a level, would you?"

"One, two, one two," he said, knowing the drill.

"Let's do it," she said. "I'll do an audio slate." She looked into the camera and waited until the red light blinked on. "Interview with Gavin Duke, First Southern, Saturday, the fifteenth of April. Three, two . . . " She paused for a couple of seconds, then turned to Gavin.

"Mr. Duke, the *Atlanta Business Courier* reported today that First Southern is planning a major new campaign. Can you tell us more about what's going on?"

"Tami, we're going to launch a program in a few weeks, on May first, that's unlike anything ever attempted in the history of marketing. It's so big, we just have to let people know something's up—which is why we're launching this tease campaign on Monday, as you saw in the paper."

"Can you tell us more about the nature of the campaign? The published report said it had something to do with lost Confederate gold?"

"Oh, did it?" Gavin said, looking genuinely surprised. Tami wondered if a viewer who didn't know this man might actually fall for his faux sincerity.

"Yes, that's what the report said. Anything you can add to that?"

"No, not just now. But I can tell you some of the tease campaign commercials will be airing on your station Monday—I believe they start during the six o'clock news, in fact!"

"Thank you, Mr. Duke." Tami knew when to cut her losses. They both waited for a shout from behind the camera.

"All clear," it came, and they unhooked their mikes and stood up at the same time.

"Get what you needed?" he asked.

"Mmm, maybe half of what I needed," she said with a big broad smile.

"Best I could do today, sweetie."

"Fair enough. Let's grab some lunch one of these days and get caught up," she said. "It's been too long—I haven't gotten with you or Marni in ages."

He decided not to be the bearer of bad news and left the reference to Marni alone. "I'd love it. But after these next few weeks, okay? It's gonna be insane."

"I understand, believe me. And thanks again, Gav." She leaned in, and they shared a Hollywood hug.

Gavin smiled to himself as he walked out of the studio, and he wondered what Torrie was doing at that moment.

Gavin climbed into another cab and pulled his mini-cellular phone from his inside jacket pocket. He called the *Business Courier* office but was told Torrie wasn't there. He dug around to see if he had her card with him and hit paydirt. She'd written her home number on the back, so he punched it in, only to get a busy signal. He tried two more times before the cab brought him back to the First Southern Tower, to no avail.

After being gone for barely more than an hour, he found his voice mail was loaded. Karen Skidmore from Channel 5. Dennis Goode from Channel 11. Cindy Furlong from Channel 46. George Paukstam from the *Journal-Constitution*. Liza Jabobs from *Adweek*. Did the whole world work on Saturday? At least the *Business Courier* people would be happy to see everybody was reading!

He returned the calls, not in the order received but in an arbitrary order based on how much he liked the way they covered the bank. And how they covered him.

By mid-afternoon, he'd gotten several more calls, so it took longer than he'd hoped to return them all. But, he managed to make it through the pile and headed home. He'd gotten too buried to try calling Torrie again, and by the end of the day he was so wrapped up in himself, he didn't have room for anyone else in his thoughts.

🥐   🥐   🥐

Monday evening, when the tease commercials hit the air, Gavin thought JohnBarley's was the best place to be. He'd get instant audience reaction, to provide a clear picture of how the public was going to take all this. One of the problems with being so close to something for so long was that you tended to lose perspective. Mixing in with the masses was a great way to get things back into focus.

He settled into his favorite booth, from which he could see three TV monitors and several people in front of each. The Channel 2 news was on, and Tami was anchoring, after her one-day weekend. At precisely 6:04 P.M., she faded to black as she turned over a sheet of paper. The screen went silent.

The tease campaign was totally different from the series that would break on G-Day. Gavin had just assumed they'd share the same rich, textured feel. He was surprised when Carolina presented it to him, and he didn't like the idea at first. But she and Ernie made an impassioned plea.

"If we bombard everybody with the teasers for two weeks," she'd said, "when the real thing hits, and it looks ninety percent the same, everybody's gonna say 'seen this before,' and we'll have shot ourselves in the foot."

"The tease has to get everybody thinking," Ernie had chimed in, "which will set up the real campaign. Then we can crank up the emotion. The logical foundation has to be in everybody's mind first before they can get immersed in the fantasy. It's like knowing a girl before you can fall in love with her, you know what I mean?"

"I don't know. I can fall in love in about three seconds," Gavin said, playing devil's advocate, "and I do—about twenty times a day."

"Perhaps," said Carolina, "but the average person just doesn't have quite the same level of passion that you do. Most folks require more setup in their brains before their hearts can kick in." She could sell anything to anyone, any time, any place.

Gavin had grudgingly agreed, and as time went by—and the ads came together with Carolina's customary brilliance—he'd been won over. And now, the big night had arrived.

Gavin held his breath and clutched the gold coin as a commercial for a car dealer came on. He exhaled with gusto.

Thirty seconds later, he held his breath again. And this time, he got his wish. Up came the first First Southern spot.

The screen lit up with a close-up of a thirty-something man, listening to the offscreen announcer asking him a question.

"Ever hear of the lost Confederate gold?"

"The what?"

Cut to an older, rounder woman. "I lost a gold ring once."

Cut to a group of construction workers on the back of a pickup truck, looking quizzically at each other.

Cut to woman holding a baby, listening to a new question from the same off-camera announcer.

"Did you know the whole Confederate treasury vanished mysteriously after the Civil War ended—a million dollars in gold?"

Her eyes flew open wide. "And nobody's ever found it?"

Cut to a boy in a little league uniform. "Man! A million dollars?"

Cut to a businesswoman. "Really?"

Cut to a waiter, as the announcer speaks again.

"It could be anywhere. Maybe buried beneath where we're standing right now!"

The waiter's jaw drops, and then he looks straight down.

Cut to a man in a suit. "You got a shovel I can borrow?"

Cut to a golden retriever, digging furiously. The announcer's voice comes back on: "If you could use a million dollars, First Southern has some good news for you. Coming May first—stay tuned."

The bank logo appeared, and the spot faded out.

Gavin realized he'd been holding his breath for the entire thirty seconds. He looked around, quickly covering the room to see if anybody was reacting. He got up to listen in on any conversations the spot had sparked, letting the coin fall loosely back into his pocket.

At the first table, two guys were laughing about something that happened at the office that day. Next.

At the second table, a couple was having a fight over the way he never met her needs. He did a double take to make sure the girl wasn't Marni, or at least her just-as-evil twin. Over to the bar. He came in on a young guy in mid-sentence.

" . . . or maybe some slick little corporal got it, and his great-great-grandkids are still living off it, in some old mansion in Buckhead!"

The guy two stools over, waving a half-filled bottle as he spoke, said, "No way. Somebody would have been suspicious—here comes this twerp, right after the whole place is burned to ashes. And he's luggin' this trunk behind him, and he starts building this ten thousand square foot plantation. Yeah, right!"

The girl between the two guys said, "You really think nobody would have stumbled over it by now? I mean, even if it got hidden back then, wouldn't a bulldozer have knocked into it when they were building a mall or something?"

"How did you manage to turn this around into talking about the mall? That really is your whole life, isn't it?" the first guy kidded, with a bit of an edge. Gavin laughed a little.

"Give it a rest, Gonzo," she said, yanking at his necktie. "I deserve nothing but the best."

"Hey, you two are hogging all the pretzels," said the second guy as he grabbed across the girl for the bowl.

Gavin realized the conversation wasn't going back to the gold, but that was okay. His informal market research told him what he needed. Southern Gold had the mass appeal, the promise of pure greed it needed to capture imaginations and hearts all across the South. He smiled and walked off with an extra skip in his step.

🥏   🥏   🥏

The next day, Gavin was scheduled to have lunch over at the agency. They'd set up some preliminary market research to see how the spots went over, a more scientific sampling than Gavin's barroom poll. It was tough for Gavin to wait until noon, but the reaction around the bank was encouraging. H. Gary Harperson himself stopped by to offer a kind word. He poked his head into Gavin's office, gave the thumbs-up sign, and winked.

"I must've gotten half a dozen calls already this morning," The Man said. "Everybody thinks it's great, and they're all asking me what this is all about. People are talking, and that's what we want!"

"Thanks, chief," Gavin said, pleased that his star was already rising with his brilliant idea—and it was still two weeks from G-Day!

🥏   🥏   🥏

Up in Carolina's office, the steward rolled in a tray containing two fresh pasta salads as Gavin arrived. "You want me to eat this girl food?" Gavin said, seemingly unaware it was impolite to point.

"I guess we could order you a porterhouse steak," Carolina offered. "With some extra cholesterol on the side."

"Nah," Gavin said digging in. "Just giving you a hard time. So what's the word? Are we geniuses or what?"

"The numbers look very, very good," she said, "both from the focus groups and the phone surveys."

The focus groups included three sets of eight adults, who were given a twenty-dollar stipend to sit in a room and watch the six o'clock news on Channel 2. After the half hour was over, a moderator asked some very generic leading questions: "What news stories caught your attention? Did you remember any commercials? Which ones? Why?"

In all three groups, Carolina told Gavin, the bank commercial was the first one mentioned. It had definitely generated interest, and people remembered seeing it as well as the basic idea that there may be a lost treasure. Less dramatic was the connection people made with the bank—it took a little nudging from the moderator or the others in the group before everybody could recall it had something to do with First Southern.

"I don't think that's a real problem," she said. "The point of the teaser is to give credibility to the idea of a lost treasure, so people are excited about it. Two weeks from now, we'll come marching into town as the hero who can help them find the gold."

"I tend to agree," Gavin said, "but let's keep an eye on it. It's still new enough that I'm not concerned. After we blow plenty of bucks on it over the next couple of weeks, that should start to change. But if the numbers don't get better on this one, we may want to add more punch to the bank I.D."

"Good," she said, filling Gavin in on the results of the phone survey. More of the same: very positive feedback.

When she'd finished, he looked straight at her and said, "Methinks we have a winner here."

"Methinks you're right, sir!"

They toasted each other with cans of Coca-Cola.

That afternoon, Torrie called. She was doing a follow-up on her semi-scoop for the next issue.

"Writer's work is never done, is it?" he kidded. "As soon as you make one deadline, up comes the next."

"That's what they tell me," she said. "Can you pass along any feedback you've gotten from the big tease campaign, or is it still too early?"

"We're very, very pleased," he said, launching into corporatespeak. "But if you want something more tangible, give us a couple of days. Carrie's got some overnight numbers right now, but there'll be more by Wednesday."

"People around here are sure buzzing," she said.

"Really?" Gavin sat up, taking his feet off the corner of the desk, the spot where he'd propped them when he knew it was Torrie on the line.

"Why, you sound surprised," she smiled. "Does this mean all the confident talk was just bluster?"

"No, of course not. I just didn't know journalists lowered themselves to 'buzzing' about the goings-on of popular culture," he came back.

"We're just full of surprises," Torrie said.

"I'll bet you are."

She changed direction again, as she'd done before when Gavin started to set the mood. "Okay, then, I'll call you Wednesday to get that quote. Thanks, Gavin. G'bye."

"Uh, bye," he said, once again thrown off balance by this woman. This remarkable, fascinating woman.

Over the next several days, the news got better and better. Media attention intensified, and by the middle of the second week, CNN ran a feature on the precampaign campaign that had everybody wondering. This was global coverage for his bank, on top of the steady stream of local and regional stories and a smattering of national reports over the wire services.

Calls poured in from banks too, as the industry got wind of it.

Gavin never knew how many people he'd met at a convention or a seminar who crawled out of the woodwork to reestablish contact with him. *Half of them are really checking out job opportunities*, he was sure. Nonetheless, everything was rolling along according to plan, if not better.

"Ruth," he barked late one afternoon when he was getting tired enough to be overtly cranky.

"Yes, Gavin?"

"Send these reports over to Mac Abrams at the law firm," he said. He stopped, watching her, and let his unbridled passions get the best of him. "Ruth?"

"Something else?" she asked.

"Yeah. Come here," he smiled.

She walked over to the desk, sat in the chair and leaned forward, waiting for the next instruction, or the next gripe, or whatever else he was about to spew forth.

"Great dress," he said.

She didn't respond.

"Say, I was thinking, you've been working a lot of long hours lately, and I was wondering if maybe, for a break, I could buy you a drink?"

Her mind—and her pulse—raced. She felt bolder now, having learned his great secret. Yet she also felt vulnerable—terrified at the thought of actually making off with a million dollars, not to mention the more common stresses of sixty-hour weeks and working for this man. She sat still and silent.

Gavin didn't notice her struggle. He was way too into himself. " . . . And then, maybe, we could have a quiet dinner, at my place . . . "

Oh, how I hate him! At least he's making my decision about the money easier. Gavin Duke owes me so much, she thought.

He finished his invitation, and the pause between the question and an answer was just crossing the line from acceptable to uncomfortable when H. Gary Harperson stepped in. *Saved by The Man*, Ruth thought.

"Hope I'm not interrupting anything," he apologized. "Gavin, I know you've got a million things going on, but the network TV people from Canada got here a day ahead of schedule, and they're setting up in my office right now. They want to put us on the evening news up there tomorrow night!"

Gavin popped up as if Ruth weren't even in the room. He slapped The Man on the shoulder and started some happy talk as the two left to go upstairs.

Ruth stayed in her chair for about five minutes, motionless, her eyes welling with tears but none quite able to fall onto her cheeks. She wasn't going to last much longer under this strain. And to make matters worse, she still hadn't revealed her plan to her husband or told him she knew where the gold was hidden.

She'd learned a few tricks from Gavin, though. Like setting up your audience. She knew you couldn't just sit down to dinner and say, "Oh, honey, I have this opportunity to steal a million dollars—what do you think? Pass the mashed potatoes, please." She knew she would have to stir Ronnie's own anger, his own hatred of Gavin, to set the stage. And after this afternoon's episode, tonight was the night.

She arrived home first, figuring he'd get there about fifteen minutes later. Typically, she'd change clothes before he arrived and then start dinner. But this time, she just sat down on the couch, still in her dress and heels, and didn't move a muscle. Minutes later, Ronnie came in. He opened the front door, called out, "Hi, hon—" and stopped as he turned to his left and saw Ruth, tense and shaking.

"What's wrong?" he asked, hurrying over. "What happened? Are you okay?"

She turned her head toward him and leaned it down on his shoulder when he sat next to her and put his arm around her. She burst into tears.

"It's okay. It's okay," he soothed.

She tried to catch her breath. "That Gavin! I don't know if I can take it any more . . . "

They'd been through the idea of her quitting her job. But with two cars, the rent, and lingering college loans, they were up to their ears in debt. Both had to work, and even with their combined salaries, there wasn't much left at the end of the month. Money was a constant concern.

"Do you want to talk about it?"

"He asked me if I wanted to have a drink, then he said I should come to his place for a 'quiet dinner.'"

"He *what*?" It was Ronnie's turn to stiffen up.

"He's such a jerk," she said. "He yells at me one minute, and the next he's out to get whatever he can. He's the most arrogant human being I've ever known. He makes me so miserable, I just don't know what to do."

Ronnie knew enough about office politics to realize that saying anything at the bank wouldn't work—Gavin was as teflon-coated as they came, and he'd manage not only to sneak out from under any accusations but to crush his accuser as well. Ruth had filled him in on the horror stories of people who'd crossed Gavin Duke. There was no denying the facts—she was stuck in a bad situation, and there didn't seem to be any way out. It just wasn't fair.

"I wish there was some way I could get back at him," she sniffed.

Ronnie just held on, not knowing if anything he'd say could help. He just let her talk.

"I wish I didn't have to work with him. I wish I could just quit, just for a while, to clear my head, then try and find something else. I'm so sick of not having any money."

"I know. Me too, me too," Ronnie said.

"I sure wish I could get my hands on some of that Southern Gold," she said. "That'd take care of it."

Ronnie knew the basics of the campaign before the general public did. Ruth generally did a good job of keeping work secrets at the office, but she'd let this one slide. She knew Ronnie could keep it to himself until G-Day. And of course, Ronnie knew that as an employee, Ruth wasn't eligible to play.

"Well, maybe we'll just get us a few lottery tickets," he suggested.

"Ronnie?"

"Yeah, what?"

"What if you knew you were gonna win the lottery?" she asked, wiping the straggling tears away. "I mean, if you had some way of knowing, what would you do?"

"I'd sock Gavin Duke in the nose!" he said.

She laughed. "I'm serious. What would you do?"

"Hey, I was serious too. What would I do? First thing, I'd want you to quit your job. Then, let's see . . . I'd wanna take a long, romantic getaway, just the two of us, some place incredible. You know, like Tahiti."

She pictured the lush, green cliffs plunging into deep blue lagoons she'd seen in travel brochures. A million miles away from stress, pressure, and Gavin Duke.

She decided to leave it at that, to let Ronnie think about the end result of having a million or so in spare change.

That night as they were getting ready for bed, she brought it up again. "Ronnie?"

"Yeah, honey?"

"What if I knew where the million dollars was hidden?"

"The what?"

"The gold. The million dollars in gold, for the bank."

He paused. "Gosh, I don't know. I guess I'd assume you would know, wouldn't you? Part of your job, right?"

"Well, no, not really. You know how paranoid Gavin can get. He didn't want to tell anybody."

"Nobody? Not you? Not even Harperson?"

"That's right. But . . . "

"But what?"

"I followed him, Ronnie. I know where he hid it."

"And he doesn't know you know?"

"No. Not a clue."

"So what are you saying? Do you plan to tip somebody off, like maybe the paper or something, to mess up his great campaign?"

"No, not exactly . . . "

"Well, what then?"

She took a long, deep breath. "Ronnie, remember when we were talking before, about what if we had a million dollars?"

"Yeah. So?"

"Ronnie, think about it. No more money problems. No more Gavin. Just you and me, sailing off to Tahiti . . . "

"Are you saying what I think you're saying? You're talking crazy, Ruth. That man has you talking crazy!"

"No, Ronnie, listen to me. Nobody hates him more than you do, right?"

"Ruth, I'm about to go over there and rip the guy's head off."

"Then think about it. This campaign is his ticket—he gets bigger and nastier and richer after it's all over, and think about what that means for me. After all these years of putting up with him, with his tantrums and his harassment, I'd make one tiny mistake one day, get canned, and be blacklisted forever. So if something goes wrong with his brainstorm, it'll bring him down a notch. Plus all our debts'll be gone—no more money problems, ever!"

"I don't believe what you're saying. How could you get at it? Even if you know where it is, that doesn't mean anything. There must be four, five armed guards, alarms, all kinds of security set up day and night to watch all that gold."

Ruth noticed a distinct change in Ronnie's reaction; he'd gone from objecting to the heist to questioning logistics.

"That's what's so great," she egged him on. "Gavin's paranoia! He didn't tell anybody; he doesn't trust anybody! There's no guards, no alarms, no security—just a hole in the ground with a million dollars in it, waiting for somebody to find it."

Ronnie sat and soaked this in. *No alarms? No guards? Just take the money and run?*

"This is nuts, talking like this," he said. "But suppose you could really get in there and get it. Don't you think the bank might figure something's wrong when they open the hole and it's empty? And add to that, you've just quit work and started paying cash for minks and Rolls Royces? Honey, this is crazy."

"After all that rat has put me through," she said, grinding her teeth together, "nothing could ever make up for it."

"But they'd know it was you."

"Maybe. But if we got out early enough, and went far enough away from here—I'm serious, Tahiti makes sense—we could do it."

This was information overload for Ronnie. *Taking a few pencils home from work was one thing,* he thought. *But one million dollars in gold?* Too much for one night. He hoped Ruth's anger was still doing the talking, not Ruth, so that tomorrow he wouldn't have to deal with it any more. They had enough to worry about in real life.

Still, mile-high green cliffs and white sandy beaches, sea breezes and white puffy clouds dancing across a stress-free pale blue sky did have its allure . . .

Book 2

The Plan in Motion

Nine

Gavin awoke with a violent start and sat up quickly in bed. It was the same dream as before. Or was it? He couldn't remember the exact images, just the basic idea—intense feelings of hopelessness and being out of control, like the fabled recurring nightmare of missing finals in school or showing up to work in your pajamas.

He blinked enough times to make out the digital clock on the night stand. As soon as it came into focus, it popped from 4:59 to 5:00.

He slowly rested his head back onto the pillow, not sure whether to try to get a few more winks or just get up and get going. He nervously checked to see that the alarm genuinely was set to go off at six. It was. He decided to catch a quick catnap before attacking this day—which was no ordinary day.

This was G-Day.

He felt himself dozing back into slumber a couple of times, but it was no use. His mind was spinning faster with each passing moment. *The press conference—will the mikes work?* 5:14. *The Q&A session afterward—will The Man be smooth?* 5:23. *The press corps' reaction—hostile, or amused and cooperative?* 5:29. *Torrie! Will she play along or evolve into just another contemptuous reporter?* 5:29 and a half.

Gavin got up. *On a day like this one, you can't be too early.* He lumbered stiffly into the bathroom, thinking he must look a little like

Brick right now. He glanced into the mirror, grumbled at his own image, got undressed, and stepped into the shower. The hot steam felt good.

He shaved and dressed. The gold tie bar, the gold stickpin, and the gold cuff links were important subtle symbols today. He slid on the gold Rolex, plunked his trusty Confederate coin into his pocket, and grabbed his briefcase as he sipped a quick shot of fully-loaded black coffee before dashing out into the predawn air.

Don't subconsciously drive to the office, he reminded himself, enjoying the lighter-than-usual traffic. It was just after six, a good hour or so before the real rush began, but Gavin bristled from the glare of the oncoming headlights. He wasn't 100 percent yet—the caffeine kick was pending.

Go to the hotel, he said, tapping the dash. *The hotel, not the office.*

There are two Ritz-Carlton hotels in Atlanta, one downtown near his office, the other in Buckhead, the Beverly Hills of the Atlanta metro area. The chain was headquartered here, and Gavin was golfing buddies with the Ritzy big shots. The grand ballroom at the downtown location was the perfect place to kick off G-Day—the posh statement of the Ritz and quick access to the office in case anything came up were knockout punches in its favor.

Gavin thought it better to park at the hotel rather than the office, even though he'd be driving home from the bank at the end of the day. He liked the security of having his wheels nearby. He laughed at an embryonic thought of having to clear out of town in a hurry if the press got ugly, but he wasn't in the mood to flesh out the notion, so he pushed it aside.

He pulled up to the side entrance, hopped out, and waved to the all-night valet. "Morning, Mr. Duke. Beautiful morning!"

"Not yet," Gavin muttered, noticing the golden name tag on the man's burgundy uniform. "Keep this for me, would you, Claude?"

"My pleasure, sir, Here's your ticket."

"Thanks." Gavin traded the ticket for a pair of one dollar bills he'd folded together.

"Thank you, Mr. Duke!" Claude tipped his cap.

Gavin pushed through the revolving door and wished to himself that life could be like the Ritz. *Everyone's eager to help you and the rewards of your own success surround you from the entrance all the way up to the penthouse. You even have to ante up ten bucks if you want a hamburger! Kind of a Disneyland for the up-and-up*, he grinned.

He breezed through the lobby and descended to the grand ballroom. It reminded him of his trip downstairs at no-name rock a few days earlier, which caused him to smile, thinking it rather amusing to note that the decor was definitely nicer here than there. But then again there were a million dollars' worth of furnishings at the other spot.

The subterranean grand ballroom at the Ritz-Carlton Hotel/Atlanta, like its unexpected sister location in Stewart County, had been blasted and dug out from underneath existing structures. Gavin laughed at the continuing irony of the comparison. It was partly underneath the Ritz, and partly underneath the adjoining twin towers of the 191 Peachtree building—a column-capped skyline neighbor of both his own bank and Carolina's ad agency.

The grand ballroom was much too big to host this press conference, actually. Many of the adjoining conference rooms made more sense, in terms of seating capacity. But Gavin wanted to make a statement with the Ritz, and he liked the added effect of the high ceiling with the spectacular chandelier. Better still, the open space could make for better acoustics.

He'd arranged—or rather, Ruth had arranged—for the hotel's convention services team to partition off much of the ballroom, so the press conference could be centered under the chandelier. Additional partitions would create something of a dramatic entranceway to the site of the announcement.

Press conferences have been labeled pseudo-events by those who study such things. It's not really news, just manufactured news. A non-event. A drummed-up happening. Anybody can call a press conference at any time—just dial up the papers and the networks and ask them to send Dan Rather out. The issue is whether anybody actually comes or not.

Gavin had been through a few press conferences in his time—one when First Southern bought out the Columbus bank, another when

The Man replaced his predecessor, one when Carolina's campaign swept the local Addy awards and made an impressive showing at the Clios in New York and managed to skip the seas by taking home not one but two Gold Lions at the Cannes Film Festival. A week in the south of France, with the shareholders of First Southern picking up the tab. Life was like the Ritz then.

But those were Mickey Mouse press conferences compared to this. That was typical business page stuff; this would be epic.

He stopped, pleased to see easily visible signs in place, directing reporters to the site. Down the temporary corridor he went, feeling every bit the gladiator about to enter the Colosseum in Rome. *Bring on the lions!* he decided.

The makeshift room came into view. On either side of the center aisle, five rows of six chairs afforded ample legroom. *Sixty seats. Okay. There may be a few more attendees than that, depending on how many of the backwoods weeklies send a roving reporter. That's good; standing room only creates an atmosphere of more excitement, and who cares if the cub reporter from the* Valdosta Daily Times *has to stand up in the back? It's a long drive, and he'll be tired of sitting, anyway.* Behind the chairs and along the sides there was plenty of space for the camera crews to move around. The poles for the TV lights were already set up, waiting for the lights to be attached and clicked on.

Up front, the stage. An oversized screen stood behind the stage, so the audience could get a special sneak preview of the new commercials. He turned around, glad to see the projection unit in place. A podium stood in front of the screen, at the center, bearing the Ritz nameplate for the cameras. At each side of the podium were two chairs, positioned behind small tables. Gavin would sit there, then The Man, and on the other side, Carolina and Maureen Hale. And off to the sides, directly in front of the stage, were the two tables where the campaign would get its additional visual boost: to the left, there would be a small replica of the treasure trunk with spray-painted gold bars spilling out; to the right, a carefully styled setup of the ad materials for the campaign—newspaper ads, magazine ads, brochures, and samples of the in-branch signs, buttons, and posters.

These two tables were empty at the moment, but Gavin wasn't

concerned. It was a little past 6:30, according to the Rolex, and Ruth had told him she'd be there around seven to set up. The press conference wasn't supposed to start until ten. The camera guys and TV reporters usually started filtering in half an hour or so before the show, and the rest of the press generally didn't get there until the last minute. Everything was under control.

Gavin heard a noise from the back of the room and turned to see Ruth strolling in. "Hey, boss," she said, without a smile. "I've got the guys bringing the stuff in." She was wearing a gray flannel suit, consisting of a straight-cut skirt and matching jacket with a crisp white blouse and a burgundy bow in her hair. Very corporate.

Two of the hotel staff followed her in. One was pushing a luggage cart, and the other was sort of steering from the front. Three large boxes rested on the cart. "Here, let me," said self-sufficient Ruth, sliding one onto the floor. "These other two go up front, for those tables. This one over on that side, and the other over there." She gestured appropriately so they'd know which went where.

Gavin strode back to see her. "Got everything?"

"Yep. One hundred press kits," she said, pulling one out from the box she'd just pushed onto the floor. The press kits—the handout packages given to reporters—started with a flat box, printed to look like an old treasure chest. Inside was a videotape of the new campaign's commercials, a chocolate bar wrapped in shiny golden foil and embossed with the First Southern logo, and the required information about the legend of the Confederate gold as well as details about the bank and its new promotion.

"The wolves are gonna love this," he said.

"Hey, anytime we can feed them," Ruth added. "Have you tried the chocolate yet?"

"Yeah. Good stuff. Not Godiva, but close."

They walked to the front to arrange the items from the other boxes onto the tables.

"Nervous?" he asked her.

"A little," she said, lying through her teeth. *"Nervous" doesn't adequately describe a person about to pilfer a million dollars in gold. Nervous? Nah. Positively petrified? Now, that's more like it . . .*

The hotel crew had unloaded the boxes and wheeled the cart away. Ruth started unloading the mini-trunk, the fake gold bars, and the other items from the one box onto its table. She'd put things generally in order, and then Maureen would tidy it up. She carried the box to the back of the room and set it down.

She walked back to the other table as Gavin watched. Ruth took out the ad materials, moved them here and there a little, and repeated the procedure of carrying that box to the entrance. The next time someone from the Ritz came in, he or she could take the emptied boxes out.

It was now a quarter after seven.

"What's next?" she asked, taking a front row seat next to Gavin— almost. He wondered briefly why she left an empty chair between them.

"We wait, I suppose. The agency people will be here in a few minutes. They can finish arranging everything, then we can go through logistics one more time and try a couple of dry runs. By then The Man should be here, and we can have a full-fledged rehearsal or two." He paused. "Had time for breakfast?"

"I grabbed an orange on the way out," she said.

"Let's have them send some sweet rolls and O.J. down," he said, pulling his mini-cellular phone from his coat pocket.

"They'll be bringing a cart later on," she said. "Danish, juice, coffee, and some fruit. I'll wait."

"All right," he said, "so can I. I'm not sure I want to eat anything now anyway. I'm kinda jumpy."

"Jumpy?"

"Yeah. Beneath this cool exterior lies a man whose entire career hinges on this morning," he said.

No, she thought, *that's coming up in a few weeks*. She looked away from him, pretending to be interested in the chandelier.

"Look at this—a couple of customers already," a cheery voice shouted from the back of the room. Carolina Gates, with Maureen alongside.

"Girls!" Gavin hopped up. Ruth stood up, scowling behind her expression at the phrase Gavin had chosen to describe two of the most successful women in the city.

"How aah you, dahling?" Carolina asked in her best mock Hollywood.

"Dashing," Gavin said, providing the best double-cheek kiss he could muster. They shared a laugh as he turned and squeezed Maureen's elbow to greet her.

The four spent the next hour making sure everything was perfect. And it was. Right on schedule, they practiced their parts as best they could before Harperson arrived. When he came, they took their places and, with Ruth acting as the audience, proceeded to put on three flawless dry runs. After the final one, Carolina asked Ruth, "How's our energy level on that last one?"

"Best performance yet," she smiled, giving the high sign. "I'm ready to go out and start digging." H. Gary Harperson laughed broadly, making a mental note to praise Gavin for the way his assistant was coming along.

They stepped down from the stage, leaving the clickers for the slides and the remotes for the video behind. The tension was starting to fill the air. The early-bird camera crews were starting to clunk their heavy equipment into the back of the room. Gavin stroked his lucky coin, still not admitting to himself that he'd come to count on the piece for moral support, as he paced small circles, like a lion on the prowl.

Gavin and the others tried to make the time pass more quickly by making small talk with the reporters they knew, but it was tough. *How can I chat about the weather or the new baseball season when I'm about to send my life, and the lives of tens of thousands of other people, spinning wildly out of control?*

At ten till ten, Torrie Wilson walked in. "Good morning, Mr. Duke," she said coolly, extending her hand. Gavin noticed a glint of chandelier light reflecting off one of her earrings, a tiny gold cross.

"Glad you could join us," said Gavin, pretending to seem disinterested. All business, he quickly excused himself, moved to huddle with Carolina and The Man, and said, "How about if we start getting everybody to their places?"

"Good idea," answered Carolina. "Maureen?" Maureen was chatting with an editor from the *Macon Telegraph* business page.

"Be right there," she said. Ruth came over too, and Gavin asked her to start ushering the reporters to their seats. The four moved to their assigned spots on the stage, and at precisely ten A.M. Eastern Standard Time on Monday, May 1, G-Day began.

Gavin stood at the microphone. He was unaware that he was spinning his gold coin furiously in his pocket, but no matter; safely positioned behind the podium, no one could tell he was anything but the picture of calm. Except H. Gary Harperson, sitting directly to Gavin's right, who could see Gavin's hand was moving about.

The team had rehearsed several dozen times over the past few days, and Gavin had his part down cold. But on that momentous morning, he went through it in something like a daze, not particularly aware of his speech, his inflections, or even his delivery when he launched a few perfectly-timed punch lines, to the delight of the crowd. He loosened everyone up early, paving the way to a press corps that was going to like the campaign.

Gavin's introductory remarks were designed to do just that—soften the crowd—before introducing the bank president. Harperson himself would make the announcement, after which Gavin would then come up and introduce Carolina, who would present the ads. Then, Gavin again, before Maureen would go through the PR tie-ins, the educational programs for school history classes, and the charitable donations the bank would make as part of the program, as Ruth passed out the press kits.

Maureen had managed her coup in getting the governor to agree to appear, but a schedule conflict forced a video version instead. *No great loss*, Gavin thought. *The guy looks better on tape than in person anyway*. His message appeared during Harperson's dignified presentation.

Later, when the commercials showed, Gavin and the others were delighted to hear some soft oohs and aahs at the drama of the spots. The tease had worked—everyone was set up for the campaign, which took them to the next step of personal involvement. These people wanted to go on a treasure hunt! Gavin leaned back in his chair to catch Carolina's eye, and the two shared a meaningful moment without a word.

After Maureen wrapped up, Gavin strode back up to the mike. The hard part was over, unless the question and answer session got off track. That was always a possibility, of course, but with the top-to-bottom excellence of the campaign and the way things had gone so far, Gavin had a good feeling. *Besides, if you were about to be attacked by a frenzied group of testy reporters, who better to have at your side than the team sharing this stage?*

"Carolina and her creative geniuses never cease to amaze me," Gavin said, adjusting the microphone. "I can't imagine anybody could possibly have any unanswered questions after all this, but if anybody does, we'll be taking questions for about fifteen minutes."

"Is the gold already hidden?" came a voice from the back.

Gavin: "Yes."

Another voice came from the same general area. "Where is it?"

Amid the delayed laughter that crept across the room, the more seasoned vets turned around and wondered, "Who was that?" as Gavin went with it and said, "There's always one wise guy in the room! Other questions?"

A woman Gavin didn't recognize stood up from the middle of the pack. "Donna Simonds, NBC," she said with authority, knocking Gavin off balance for a split second. He looked at Carolina and raised his eyebrows. Not the local affiliate—the network. Already!

"Aren't you worried that given the tense racial situation that exists in America today, First Southern is creating a bad example by glorifying not only war in general but a culture that oppressed black men, women, and children into slavery and subhuman conditions, and as a follow-up, I'd like . . . "

The room of mostly local reporters grew strangely quiet as she built her question. Gavin raised his hand and interrupted, "Whoa, hang on—one at a time. Let's tackle the first part, and then we'll go on to the second." As he was speaking, Maureen was already making her way to Gavin's side, a solid example of the depth and preparation Carolina Gates Advertising provided its clients.

"That's a good question, Donna," Maureen said, moving in over Gavin's shoulder, "and here's how we've already addressed that issue. First, we're starting First Southern scholarship funds for students at twelve predominantly black colleges and universities in the South with proceeds from the Southern Gold promotion. Also, we are funding workshops at those schools as well as in . . . "

Gavin stepped behind Maureen and felt his blood pressure coming back down. He'd worked with Carolina and her lieutenants long enough to expect miracles, but sometimes they still managed to surprise him. Here a reporter was just about to derail the whole promotion as a racist overture by a redneck bank, and the brilliant woman speaking into the mike was single-handedly convincing everyone that without this honorable effort of First Southern's, the world as we know it would end tomorrow.

From there, no more curves came from the audience, only gently tossed puffballs from friends like Tami Olson at Channel 2 ("Has anything like this ever been attempted before, or do you believe this promotion is truly unique in the history of marketing?") and Torrie ("Gavin, is it true you're the only person who knows the exact location of the hidden gold?").

With all the other tumultuous events surrounding Southern Gold, this single question, Gavin always felt, did more to shape the course of his life than any other part of the process. For that single question took a remarkable program—and its own growing, churning energy— to the only higher plane that it could possibly occupy. A legend was born with that question, and the legend was Gavin Duke. Every other human being on the face of the earth wanted to know where the gold rested, and Gavin was the only one who did know.

"Yes, as a matter of fact, I am the only person who knows the exact location of the gold." The room was still as the impact sunk in, until a young woman named Alice Burnett, a reporter for the CBS station in Savannah, quipped: "Will you marry me?"

The room went nuts, the foursome on the stage went nuts, and even Ruth, hidden behind the glare of the lights at the back, grinned from ear to ear.

For all the genuinely interesting news that came out of the press conference, that amusing interchange was the most featured clip from the entire hour-long session—locally, regionally, and even nationally. It's the kind of extra that can't be planned. Even the best and brightest marketing minds in the country can do everything right, but magical moments just happen, out of the blue, when they're good and ready to. And this particular moment, like the campaign, was a golden one.

After two or three anticlimactic questions, the conference was adjourned, and the reporters scurried back to file their reports. The four great minds assembled on the stage offered hearty congratulations to each other, instinctively knowing they'd belted the home run of home runs—seventh game, world series, bottom of the ninth, two outs. They'd arranged to reconvene in the bank's executive dining room for a private, quiet lunch, a necessity after the chaos of a busy press conference. Four people, not five. Gavin hadn't thought to lobby for Ruth's getting to share in the celebration, and by now, she was beginning to actually enjoy such lapses instead of resenting them. She relished each time Gavin presented her with the short end of the stick because it stiffened her resolve to take what was coming to her.

📖   📖   📖

Over roast duckling and vegetables prepared so fancily that Gavin really had no idea what they were—but at this point, who cared?—the coronated quartet saturated themselves in the moment.

"To us!" Gavin said.

"To all the new accounts that'll come streaming in," corrected his boss, who had grown more oriented toward the bottom line over the years.

They laughed and carried on like double-dating teenagers after the prom, stretching the lunch hour into three and making the rest of the afternoon as unproductive as possible. But they'd earned it, and there would be plenty of time to hit the grindstone again later. This was their finest hour, and no one could take it away from them.

Ten

The home theater setup in Gavin's house revolved around a seventy-two-inch screen, from which he could watch six channels at the same time—a far cry from growing up in the early sixties, when everybody had one bulky black-and-white TV with a little knob you had to turn to change to one of only three or four available channels. Then a house had one black rotary-dial phone too. Now Gavin had seven, not counting the one he carried in his pocket.

"The wonders of technology," he smiled to himself as he settled in, able to simultaneously watch all three local newscasts at the touch of a button. It was six o'clock, the evening of G-Day, and he wanted to see how the coverage was going to go. It was early for him to be home from the office, but it had been an extraordinary day. He'd driven straight home after the marathon lunch and brought a full briefcase with him, planning on getting back at it again later in relative peace and quiet. He'd had the big screen on for a while already, with the volume down. And he'd only turned it up twice before now, when the First Southern commercials came on—Beth Forrester, the media director at the agency, had faxed Gavin a schedule of when the spots would air that first day. He still loved them, still thought they were rich and warm, even though he had seen them dozens of times.

He didn't have to watch, technically, since one of the agency's services was total media monitoring. The next day, if he so desired, he could watch a tape of all the event coverage from every station while he leafed through all the printed reports from various newspapers. But Gavin was like a kid in a candy store—G-Day had to be experienced live, moment by breathless moment.

Figuring Tami's report might be the most sympathetic, he started off with Channel 2 on the big screen, with the other two network affiliates visible in small boxes at the corners. If one of them came on with some press conference coverage, Gavin could quickly switch that station to the big screen.

"From Georgia's news leader," the resonant voice boomed, "this is Action News at six!" A medium close-up of Tami behind the news desk flashed up, with the First Southern logo over her shoulder. Gavin sat up straight in a hurry, not expecting this, and took his feet down from the coffee table.

"Good evening, I'm Tami Olson. A Georgia tradition is mixing the past with the present today—a great big present for one lucky customer, in fact. First Southern Bank announced a million-dollar treasure hunt that's sure to stir up a lot of interest around the South. Earl Wright joins us with a live report from Birmingham. Earl, what's happening out there?"

Gavin darted his eyes to the other two stations. One was leading with the latest on that crazy billionaire's takeover of a Caribbean nation, but the other was also starting off with the bank story. He couldn't believe his eyes, and quickly decided to stick with Channel 2—he'd wait for the next day's summary for the other report.

The screen filled with Earl Wright, a sportscaster turned investigative journalist, standing in front of a First Southern branch. *Why on earth are they covering from Birmingham,* Gavin wondered, *when everything is centered in Atlanta?*

"Tami, the scene here has been close to bedlam for the last couple of hours, since word started getting out about First Southern's plan to bury—yes, bury—a million dollars worth of gold. More on that in a second, but first, let's pan around beside me here to get a look at what's happening at this First Southern Branch office here in Birmingham. The office hours end at five, which was about one minute ago—we're an hour earlier than you are, of course—but the local branch manager has informed me they'll be keeping the doors open longer, until this crowd thins out. These people have been standing in line here, some for more than an hour already, to open an account."

Gavin stared at the screen in abject disbelief. At least a hundred people must have been in line, trying to crowd in to open a bank account—at just one First Southern branch! He understood why they'd selected Birmingham—its time zone offered a better visual image for the cameras.

Earl continued, "The rush started earlier today. In a press conference in downtown Atlanta, bank officials announced what they call 'Southern Gold,' an ad campaign to do just what you see happening here—to drum up new business." The screen switched to the "Will you marry me?" clip, then back to Earl, wearing a big grin. "Of course, the bank has been running a series of ads the past couple of weeks to try and drum up interest in today's announcement, and by all signs here, Tami, it seems to be working."

Tami asked, "Earl, can you tell us more about this Southern Gold campaign?"

"Tami, it's based on the legend that the Confederate treasury, maybe millions of dollars worth of gold, was hidden after the war and never recovered. The bank is burying a treasure chest, and giving away clues. The catch, of course, is you have to open an account to get the clues, which is why you see this mob here."

"Can you talk with some of the people there, Earl?"

Earl started across the crowded parking lot, pulling his mike with him, as the cameraman bumpily followed along. "We'll sure try, Tami." He shoved the microphone in front of an older man wearing a ball cap, who looked like he hadn't shaved in a few days. "Sir, how come you're willing to wait in line to open an account here?"

"You kiddin'? There's a million dollars out there somewhere, and I wanna take a crack at it."

"Thank you, sir. And you, ma'am?" He pushed the microphone in front of a well-dressed woman, about forty, who looked like she worked in an office.

"I've got to have a checking account anyway, so I may as well have it here—they're offering me a chance at a million dollars!"

Earl pulled the mike back for his wrap-up. "Well, as you can see, Tami, everyone here seems to have their eyes on just one thing—or, should I say, one million things! Reporting live from Birmingham, I'm Earl Wright for Action News 2."

Tami cocked her head as she turned back toward the camera and said, "Can't blame them for that!" After the briefest of pauses, she moved right along to the next story: "A hostage-taking gunman in a . . ."

Snap to it, Gavin told himself, not allowing himself time to be stunned, or shocked, or even ecstatic—he had to track this. All the branches on eastern time had closed an hour earlier and were just closing, or at least supposed to be closing, in the central time zone. Could he try to call one? He darted to the next room, where he had a company directory, and furiously flipped through it. Finding a branch in Birmingham, he punched in the number and got a busy signal. "Better double-check," he told himself before assuming he'd dialed correctly, as he tried again. Still busy.

This seemingly minor fact was significant to Gavin. As a bank, First Southern dedicated itself to a customer-driven approach—lots of smiles in the branches, extended hours, and easy access if a customer had a question. It also meant a specific commitment to installing extra phone lines to keep annoyances like busy signals to a minimum. A quality control team periodically checked such details, so the branch managers had to stay on their toes. A busy signal was rare, and Gavin didn't recall hearing one on a First Southern branch phone in the past year or so—until now. He smiled, finding the excuse in this case easy to forgive.

He tried one more time. Same sound. He tried another branch. Busy. And a third. Also busy. The phones were ringing off their hooks, and network TV stations were opening their broadcasts with live feeds of people crushing into First Southern branches after the bank was supposed to be closed for the day. Gavin walked into the bathroom and splashed cool water on his face, allowing its snap to enliven his tired but thrilled spirit. His phone rang. It was The Man.

"Do you have Channel 11 on?" Harperson asked.

Gavin laughed. "No, actually, I had it on 2. What'd they have?"

"They showed a couple of branches, one in Marietta and one in Sandy Springs, I think, with big crowds of people streaming in and out all afternoon!"

"Fabulous. Channel 2 did a live piece from Birmingham. You wouldn't believe it—people were standing on top of each other, trying to get in, and they're still coming!"

"Gavin, after seeing all this, I can't imagine this is going to be a shooting star. I always had complete confidence in you and Carrie, but this is beyond anything I'd expected . . . "

Gavin sighed. "It's gonna be fun to watch, boss."

"Congratulations, Gavin," The Man said, brimming with pride. If Gavin were to guess, he'd imagine Harperson was feeling like he was his own son right now.

"Thank you, sir."

"I'll see you in the morning, Gavin. Great job. Great job."

Euphoria was setting in, but Gavin wanted Carolina's read on all this first. He tried her at her office, and she grabbed it on the first ring.

"Carrie! Have you seen this mayhem you've wrought?"

"You can never underestimate the raw power of a great idea," she smiled. "The good Lord seems to be with us on this one."

"Unbelievable," he said, dismissing the divine reference as no more than a figure of speech. "Just unbelievable."

"The summary's going to be something," she said. "Maureen and her gang are already well into it."

"Wonderful."

"I've only got one thing yet to nail down," Carolina said with a drop of concern in her voice.

"What's that?" Gavin asked.

"'Will you marry me?'" she uttered, straight-voiced.

"Get out of here, you knucklehead!" he laughed, and she laughed, and they both hung up.

Gavin tapped the outside of his pant leg to make a light drumming sound on the half-dollar, which was pressing through to create a round shape in the fabric. His mind was racing at a million miles an hour.

He realized he hadn't seen the evening edition of the paper. He slipped on a pair of shoes, grabbed his keys, and raced over to the corner gas station. He froze.

There before him on a stack of freshly piled papers, was a full color photo of Gavin with his arm around Harperson at the press conference. The banner headline read, "First Southern kicks off a 'one in a million' treasure hunt."

He wanted to read every word right then and there but decided he would rather do this in private. He plunked a dollar bill down on the counter and didn't wait for his change before racing back through the swinging glass door and into his still-running Mercedes.

As he floored it past the five blocks to his house, he contemplated how unusual it was for a private corporation to get such dominant media coverage. *Yes, this is news—but is it that big, in comparison to wars, the rest of the nation's economy, and other stories? When Coca-Cola changed its formula a few years back, that made page one—but that was Coke, for heaven's sake. When UPS moved its headquarters to Atlanta, the story made page one, but on the bottom half of the page, not a banner headline.* As he pulled into the driveway, he shuddered. *The Man's connections, the board of directors, the governor, the powers that be—am I fooling myself in taking credit for being the rocket behind this wild ride? Could it be that The Man got a little help from his friends in high places, without ever thinking to ask for it? Is there something Carolina isn't telling me, or maybe Maureen is behind it?*

He realized he was sitting right in front of his house, his fingers firmly wrapped around the wheel, instead of running inside to read the paper. He got out of the car, and told himself, *No. Nobody could make all those average people in different cities line up to move their checking accounts. It has to be a genuine, spontaneous reaction. Even if somebody did yank some strings at the paper or a couple of the TV stations, the people are still coming out.* He decided to bury the idea. It didn't matter how or why it was happening. Just that it was happening.

Inside, he cracked the paper open and read the account:

Forget the lottery.
First Southern Bank has announced a cheaper way to try your

hand at taking home a million dollars, with its new "Southern Gold" promotion.

In a press conference at the Ritz ballroom downtown this morning, bank president and CEO H. Gary Harperson unveiled details about a program that's had the city and the region buzzing for weeks now.

"Yes, we've buried a million dollars in gold, somewhere in the South," Harperson, 57, said at the briefing. By opening an account, he said, customers would get clues as to the treasure's location.

Bank marketing whiz Gavin Duke is credited with dreaming up the plan. Duke claimed he's the only person who knows the true location of the gold—which quickly prompted a mock marriage proposal from one journalist in attendance.

Please see SOUTHERN GOLD on page 16, column A

Gavin took a deep breath before turning the page. He did take time to read the caption beneath the photo:

THERE'S SOUTHERN GOLD IN THEM THAR HILLS! First Southern president/CEO H. Gary Harperson, left, and VP/marketing Gavin Duke announced burying $1 million in gold to draw customers.

💿   💿   💿

Several miles away, still in her office, Ruth was holding a copy of the paper, staring at the photo of Gavin with contempt. She was extremely nervous about going home that night and seeing Ronnie and his reaction to the events that had unfolded in the past few hours. *Where is his head in all this? Is he with me or not?*

She still had a good hour's worth of paperwork to clear up, she guesstimated, but looking at Gavin's picture on page one pushed her over the edge. She threw the newspaper into the trash can beside her desk, grabbed her purse, and got up to leave without even straightening up her desktop, which was strewn with Styrofoam cups, pencils, and computer printouts.

Rush hour was on its last legs when she hit the road. Traffic was heavy, but not stop and start by any stretch. As she drove, she took deep, long looks at the people in the other cars, wondering if they had heard about the promotion, and if in fact some of them had already stormed a nearby First Southern branch to open an account. She drove beside a gray-haired woman for a moment, who made her think of her grandmother, and she wondered how this lady might react if she knew there never really would be a legitimate chance to get the gold. Ruth thought it odd that she really didn't feel any guilt or remorse or anxiety anymore. She had grown numb. And she asked herself if she shouldn't be horrified at the very fact that she was numb to such a great criminal act, grand theft of one million dollars, but there was no feeling there, either. She drove on.

Ronnie had beat her home that night and was grilling some chicken on their back patio. May first was fairly early to be cooking out, but it had been a very mild day, sunny and hitting the upper seventies. "Hi, honey," he said, flashing a big toothy grin. *He looks cute in that old apron*, she thought, coming up behind him and cuddling close. "Watch out," he warned good-naturedly. "This is hot!" She enjoyed the moment, feeling far away from Gavin for the first time in a long while.

"I saw the news," he said. "Looks like old nine-lives Gavin keeps on shining, no matter what."

"Well, maybe not," Ruth replied. "It'll come around for him someday."

Ronnie looked into her eyes, feeling her hurt and her pain but not wanting to address the issue yet. He changed the subject.

"I managed to find the marinated chicken," he said. "Teriyaki."

"Mmm, yeah," said Ruth. She looked up to see the other identical apartments in her cramped complex and wondered how long her life would have to be on hold.

The subject of the gold was not bridged again that evening, strangely, since it had dominated Ruth's day. They made some small talk, watched a little TV, and went to bed.

🐟   🐟   🐟

Gavin had intended to be in early the next day, but he'd nearly completed a report and pulled it out to review over breakfast. He decided to quickly wrap it up at home before heading into the office. He got there a few minutes after nine.

The First Southern Tower's lobby housed its flagship bank branch, as is the case with many big city banks. To set the tone for the company, this branch had been decorated exquisitely. In this lobby were no less than fifteen teller's windows, to assure as short a wait as possible to keep the customers happy. Customers of this branch were primarily successful executives who worked downtown, so The Man wanted to be sure this branch was spotless.

Gavin entered the lobby from the parking deck, striding ahead without looking for the first two or three steps until he sensed something was different. He stopped in his tracks and looked up. Gavin gulped. He'd never seen the lobby like this. It looked like the line to Space Mountain at Disney World on a Saturday in the middle of August—people were wrapped up and back, and up and back, and around—all the way out the front doors. He blinked and stared. This lobby the size of a football field was nearly filled to capacity. Surely everyone in downtown Atlanta was standing in this one room and, given the length of the line, would be here for quite some time yet. Gavin had made commerce come to a standstill, except at First Southern.

He edged his way past the pack and snuck out a side door onto Peachtree Street. The lines were spilling outside the bank's doors, just a little, with men and women reading newspapers or chatting with the people next to them in line. Gavin walked up to the end, to become a part of this deliciously wonderful madness.

"What's this all about?" he asked the man in front of him.

"Don't you know?" the man said, implying Gavin must be the only human being in the city who didn't.

"Sorry. Visiting from out of town," Gavin smiled.

The man quickly gave Gavin the once over, head to toe to head again, the way Gavin might look at a woman, and must have decided he was okay. "The bank hid a million dollars in gold—lost Confederate treasure," the man informed Gavin. "Open an account, and you get a chance to find it."

"You mean they'll enter your name in a drawing?" Gavin asked, fascinated by all this.

"No," an older woman interrupted. "They'll give you clues if you open up an account, clues to where you can find it!"

Gavin was thrilled at how well they seemed to understand how it all worked, particularly since it was just the morning after G-Day.

"Where do you think it is?" Gavin asked, not directing the question to anyone in particular, just throwing it out to the crowd, the way a wild animal trainer casually tosses a chunk of raw flesh to the subject inside the cage.

"I bet it's in an old Civil War cemetery," the woman nodded with authority.

"Nah, they wouldn't want to have people digging around an old graveyard." A young man popped up from behind. "That's too ghoulish."

"Go ahead and doubt me," she warned him, "that's fine with me. Then you won't stumble on it first."

"Where are you gonna look?" Gavin asked the first man.

"Me? I'm waiting for the clues. Could be anywhere."

Gavin nodded in agreement, and said, "Too bad I'm just here on business. Wish I had enough with me to open up an account!" He gracefully backed out of his spot in line, to the delight of the half dozen or so more people who had taken a place behind him. "Hope you find it," he said, quickly tossing glances at the man and the woman. The man acknowledged his smile, but the woman was deep in her own world and obviously not pleased that the young man behind her had contradicted her flawless wisdom.

Gavin walked toward the next main entrance, starting to wonder how he might get past all these people and make it back into the lobby without getting lynched for taking cuts. He decided his best bet was to walk back up the parking ramp and once again go through the door where he'd first entered just minutes ago.

All of a sudden, someone grabbed Gavin's arm from behind. It startled him, and he pulled away as he whirled around, quickly clenching his left fist and bringing up his briefcase with the other hand in a defensive posture.

"Hey, relax," smiled a whimsical set of dark brown eyes. It was Torrie, armed with only her satchel and a well-thumbed New Testament.

"Torrie! You scared—" he caught himself, and said, "You never know what can happen in a big crowd. I wasn't expecting to see you out here."

"What? And miss the story of the century?" she kidded.

"Well, how are we doing, in the esteemed opinion of the press?" he asked.

"No opinions. I'm objective, remember?" she grinned. "Since I've got you, do you mind if I ask you a couple of questions? There still seems to be, shall we say, something of a story here."

"Great," he said, "but away from the masses, please. Let's go up to my office, where we can hear ourselves think."

"Really? I'd think you would want to personally shake hands with each and every one of these people," Torrie observed.

"Not yet. C'mon."

"I'll be honest with you," she said as they went up. "I really have no idea what my story's going to be this week. I'm in sort of an unusual position—everybody else beats me to the punch with the announcement itself. But on the other side of the coin, I've got an advantage. I can hang back a little, see what angle everybody else is taking, and go my own direction. And I can go into a little more depth too."

"Oh, I see," Gavin said, trying to formulate his next line, but the elevator quickly filled up so he had to keep it to himself. The bell rang, and the door opened to reveal the sixtieth floor.

"I believe you know the way, my dear," he said, sweeping his hand forward with a slight bow. "After you."

"Thank you, kind sir," she said, stepping down the hallway. "Have you talked to Harperson?" she asked, not yet taking out her notebook. This was a strange place for a reporter, that bridge between small talk and an interview, when you sometimes have to remember something without the privilege of having it in your notes.

"Good morning," said Ruth, but it was obvious she didn't believe it.

"Oh, hi, Ruth," Gavin said. "Grab us some coffee, would you?"

Torrie, more sensitive than Gavin, asked, "How are you today, Ruth? You must be pretty excited at how well everything's turning out!"

"Oh, we're all thrilled," she said.

"I can only imagine," Torrie said as Gavin interrupted.

"Yeah. Well, if you'll excuse us, Ruth, we've got to get started on our interview. Don't worry about knocking with the coffee—just bring it right in."

The two disappeared into Gavin's office as Ruth turned and muttered "Yes, master" under her breath.

Gavin's gaze left Torrie for the first time since they'd bumped into each other. The view from the picture window in his office was spectacular today, with the morning mist dissolving up into the atmosphere. "What a magnificent place to be," he said, leaning so far into the window his breath actually steamed the glass a bit.

"If your name happens to be Gavin Duke," she added.

He turned back to face her. "Yes," he said with a smirk. "So, do I assume that since you haven't discovered your angle yet, you don't have any questions prepared?"

She tilted her head. "Guilty," she said. "But at least I can try to cover the basics." She pulled out the pad. "So how does it feel?"

"How does it feel," he repeated, looking down and rubbing his chin as he walked toward his desk and then leaned against it. He thrust his hands into his pockets and remembered there was a secret coin there.

"It feels great, Torrie!" he said, slipping out of his traditional interview voice—the usual banking image he projected with reporters. "There are people lined up in the streets to catch a piece of a dream, and one of them is going to be a million dollars richer before they know what hits 'em!"

Ruth walked in with the coffee and placed it on the small round conference table without a word.

"Thank you, Ruth," said Torrie.

"Oh, yeah, thanks, honey," Gavin called out, a little late. Torrie wondered if he was just lazy about the way he talked to some people, or if he actually tried to be nasty on occasion. She wanted to believe the best about Gavin Duke, but he made it very hard at times.

They sipped the coffee as she scribbled furiously, trying to catch a pearl as he began a discourse about the social good the promotion was going to do. After filling five pages, she decided she needed to let things settle in some more over the next couple of days before committing herself to a specific approach, since it was only Tuesday morning and her deadline was a lifetime away at the pace things were happening.

"I think I've got what I need for now," she said, sliding the pencil through the spiral rings at the top of the notebook but not shutting it yet. She batted her eyes as she asked, "May I reserve the right to call you again as events progress this week?"

"Nah. But I'll have the agency send you a press release," he teased.

"Okay!" she said, snapping the notepad shut and standing up straight and tall. He quickly moved toward her, but she was out the door before he could catch her. She turned and looked in at him, and said, "Thanks for the coffee. Bye!"

Gavin watched her turn again and walk out. "Soon," he promised himself. Everything else was looking up, so Torrie, he figured, was a sure thing.

As Torrie made her way toward the elevator, she crossed paths with Ruth. "I'd really like to have lunch with you sometime, Ruth," Torrie said. Her sincerity startled Ruth.

"Ah, yes, I'd—I'd like that," Ruth stammered. Torrie smiled and walked away. Ruth wanted to feel touched by the gesture but battled her cynicism. *Torrie's just playing me to get to Gavin*, she decided. But as she sat back down at her desk, she couldn't get the notion out of her head that perhaps, just perhaps, Torrie could have meant it. She pulled out a pencil and pressed it into her electric pencil sharpener, confused at feeling more than just the numbness that had gripped her for a good long time now.

Eleven

Ruth brought the report to Gavin and laid it on his desk.

"What's this?" he asked, looking up from the memo he was holding.

"The numbers from week one," she said matter-of-factly.

"The numbers!" he said, tossing the memo aside and excitedly picking up the report. This was the bottom line, a summary of how many new accounts and lines of credit First Southern had added during the first seven days of the campaign.

"Did you look at them? What did you think?"

"Oh, of course I peeked. But I'll let you decide for yourself . . . "

"Okay. Thanks," said Gavin, diving into the report.

He licked his thumb and flipped past the first few introductory baloney pages to get to the executive summary. There it was:

NEW CHECKING ACCOUNTS:	27,349
NEW SAVINGS ACCOUNTS:	11,057
NEW COMBO ACCOUNTS:	7,645
NEW CERTIFICATES OF DEPOSIT:	3,021
NEW ACCOUNTS/OTHER TYPES:	655
TOTAL NEW ACCOUNTS:	49,727
x AVERAGE NEW BALANCE:	$ 1,056
= TOTAL NEW DEPOSITS:	$52,511,712

NEW MORTGAGE APPLICATIONS:	2,587
NEW HOME EQUITY LOAN APPLICATIONS:	6,223
NEW AUTO LOAN APPLICATIONS:	5,571
NEW CREDIT CARD APPLICATIONS:	8,990
NEW LOAN/CREDIT LINE APPLICATIONS/MISC:	302
TOTAL NEW LOAN/CREDIT LINE APPLICATIONS:	23,673
x AVERAGE CREDIT REQUEST	$18,255
= POTENTIAL NEW CREDIT ISSUED:	$432,150,615

He threw himself back into his big, overstuffed chair and opened his eyes wide in amazement. Fifty million in new deposits? Almost half a billion in new loans? In the first week? He'd just created an entire new bank—and a good-sized one, at that—overnight! He pulled out his calculator and started punching numbers. *If this keeps up at, say, only half this rate for the rest of this quarter, twelve more weeks, we'll have well over a quarter of a billion dollars in new deposits, and over two and a half billion in new loan money out there. All with First Southern's name on it!*

He rushed out to Ruth's desk, and said, "Quick, fax the summary page to Carrie. I'm calling her right now with the news. This is fabulous!" He ran back into his office, not waiting for Ruth to say anything, picked up the phone, and dialed Carolina's office.

"Carrie," he said breathlessly, "I'm faxing you the first week's numbers—they're incredible!"

"How incredible?"

"Fifty-some million in new deposits, almost half a billion in new credit apps. That's just the first week, Carrie!"

"Gosh, sorry the campaign bombed," she said, occasionally a match for Gavin in the sarcasm department.

"Yeah. You're fired," he said.

"Thought you'd never ask," she came back. "Have you heard from The Man yet?"

"He's on the road today, up in D.C."

"Oh, really?"

"Yep. Gotta keep the Feds on their toes."

"He's gonna flip when he sees these," Carrie surmised.

"No kidding. I'll keep you posted."

"Thanks. Bye."

As thrilled as he was, Gavin still felt a spot of nervousness in the pit of his stomach. What if Harperson had been wrong earlier when he said this wasn't going to be a shooting star? There was a chance it was a fad and would fizzle out fast over the next few days. There was no denying the burst of increased business, but one or two hot weeks—even remarkably hot weeks—were certainly no justification for a program of this magnitude. He gazed out the window, looking down as the tiny cars moved along the streets below, and wondered if any of those drivers were hightailing it to their nearby First Southern branch to go for the gold . . .

Over the course of the second week, the resounding level of customer enthusiasm didn't wane but in fact seemed to grow. As did the media coverage, which of course continued to fuel the fire. Each day brought a new sampling of colorful tidbits, like these:

🥨   🥨   🥨

A Louisiana family of nine moved all their earthly possessions to Bibb County, Georgia, and planned on traversing the countryside in search of the gold. Why Bibb County? "I just woke up one morning, and knew that's where it was," Mrs. Maridel Sandberg said. Her husband, Bruce, didn't dispute her intuition and brought Laura, Ruthie, Teddy, Joshua, Daniel, Isaac, and Sparky the dog to live under the stars until they hit their jackpot.

🥨   🥨   🥨

The Anniston, Alabama, chapter of the Daughters of the Confederacy called for a boycott of the bank, complete with pickets, claiming they were entitled to the gold, as descendants of "genuine Southern heroes." Interestingly, business at the branch where they centered their protest outpaced the upswing of typical branches by more than 20 percent.

🥨   🥨   🥨

A man from Galveston, Texas, claimed he found the treasure but wouldn't reveal where he allegedly stumbled upon it, nor would he show anybody the gold. Two days later, he said he'd donated the money to various charities, but wouldn't reveal which ones. Two days after that, he admitted he was just kidding.

🪙   🪙   🪙

By the end of the second week, it was time to prepare for the next big PR burst—the first clue was about to go out. Gavin met with Carolina and Maureen at JohnBarley's to discuss logistics.

"The first insert will go into monthly statements," Carolina said, passing one to Gavin but stopping short. "You have to promise not to tell anybody what the clue is," she said.

"I wrote the clue," he barked, grabbing the tiny slip of paper which, at this moment, was worth its weight in gold.

"Oh, yeah. I forgot," Carolina said as Maureen got a good laugh out of the entire exchange.

Gavin placed the slip on the table in front of him after pushing his coaster and his glass off to the side. The slip was printed on coated paper in the bank's signature blue and gold. It said:

SOUTHERN GOLD CLUE #1:
Where water is, gold hides nearby.

Gavin had spent a lot of time on this one, almost dismissing it as being too obvious. But then, he got to thinking—there are hundreds of rivers, lakes, streams, and ponds in the region, not to mention thousands of miles of shoreline, plus swamps, aquariums, and even swimming pools. This clue revealed almost nothing, except eliminating a couple of acres of a peanut farm near Valdosta, Georgia.

He turned the slip over to find an eloquent vignette the agency had prepared to further romance the Civil War connection, illustrated by an intricate engraving of men in uniform pushing a huge trunk over the side of a wooden riverboat. It read:

STUCK IN THE MUD?

The United States Mint in New Orleans, Louisiana, was busily striking coins of silver and gold when the War Between the States began. What happened to the bullion? Many suspect it was donated to the Confederate treasury, while one southern story-teller imagines it was cast into the murky mud of the Mississippi River by Union loyalists—better there than in the hands of those filthy rebels. No trace of any such jettisoned booty has ever been found. Do you suppose it could still be there?

Gavin looked up to see both women leaning forward, intently staring at him. "Well?" Carolina asked.

"Your creative geniuses have done it again," he said. "What a great idea, playing off the water clue to come up with this beautiful bit about sinking treasure! Brilliant! What a great diversion!"

"Diversion?" Carolina asked, turning to look at Maureen and then back at Gavin again. "Seems you've just tipped your hand for us, Mr. Duke. So the treasure's not submerged near New Orleans, huh?"

"Okay, you nabbed me," he laughed. "That just means you can save your energy on clue number one and kick back while all the river rats go dredging the Mississippi. You can breeze by them on the next clue!"

"Now there's an idea," Carolina said, looking to Maureen again. "Let's remember that."

"Sounds like a plan," said Maureen. She paused. "I hate to bring this up, but there is one potential problem we need to go over."

"What's that?" asked Gavin, feeling immune to any difficulties at this juncture.

"Well, once we start releasing the clues, there's nothing stopping the media from publishing them. Of course, we've contacted every-body and asked them to go along with this, but all it takes is one weekly paper in the middle of nowhere or one five-thousand-watt radio station to realize this is their chance to scoop the whole world, and the stampede is on."

"Any good solutions besides crossing our fingers?" Gavin asked, swirling what was left of his drink in his glass.

"Unfortunately, no," Carolina interjected. "The only viable way around it is to assign chances of winning to people's account numbers, but that'd turn it into a sweepstakes, which we don't want to do. The whole point of this thing, the magic in it, is the fact that it's a treasure hunt."

"I agree with you," he said.

"Now, the obvious downside," Maureen continued, "is the fact that as soon as people can get the clues on TV, or read them in the paper, there's no need to open an account. In a worst-case scenario, the well could dry up in a hurry."

Carolina added, "One thing working in our favor is the issue of perception versus reality. It works the same way as the sweepstakes we have done, where you don't have to buy anything to enter. We can say an entry is an entry is an entry until we're blue in the face, but a lot of people just feel like their odds are better if they buy something. Some of them are simply suspicious of big businesses and think they have to ante up, even though we've told them it's not true. Others are just superstitious. And there's another group that feels like they have to have done something, no matter how small, to have earned it. They figure if they've bought something when they enter, they're more deserving than if they didn't."

"So what you're saying," Gavin asked, "is that you think people will still sign up in droves, even if they can just flip on the TV to get clues?"

"Exactly. Plus, we can help them out a little by implying that customers not only get first crack at the clues but that maybe they'll know about something the press never manages to get ahold of. After all, they'll never know if there's a clue that doesn't get on the tube if they don't have an account."

"Sounds pretty reassuring," Gavin said. "Your research gang sure does their homework."

"What research?" Carolina said with a straight face. "I just made all that up."

"Adwomen," Gavin grumbled, finishing off the last of his drink.

As the next week began, Gavin held his breath every time he turned on the TV or opened the paper, expecting to see clue number one flashed all over the place. But no one seemed to break the story of the clue. The bank seemed to be enjoying the best of both worlds—the promotion and its massive following were still given ample coverage, yet the press seemed to ignore the value of the clues as news items. Perhaps the clues were perceived as just another ad, and the ads themselves weren't the newsmakers—it was the reaction of the people that seemed to matter.

There were, however, several stories about dozens, then hundreds of modern-day prospectors digging around and even under the Mississippi River delta near New Orleans. References were made to the first clue and the short story on the back of the insert, but the clue itself was never mentioned or even implied.

That Thursday morning, around eleven, Torrie called Gavin.

"Little late to be starting your interviews for this week, isn't it?" he said right off. "Isn't your deadline just about an hour away?"

"Actually, I've already filed my story for the week," she said.

"A whole hour ahead of schedule? Goodness, would you like a job here at the bank? I could use a few like you. Hang on while I buzz Personnel and tell them to expect your resumé . . . "

"Oh, stuff a sock in it, Mr. Duke," she said playfully. "I called to see if you had plans for lunch."

"Getting a jump on next week's deadline?" he asked.

"Nope. This is a social call," she announced.

"Social call?" He sat up. "You mean pleasure, not business?"

"Hope that doesn't offend your sensibilities," she said.

"Well, I'll think about it. Sure, I'll be free around one."

"One P.M. it is," she said.

"Do you have a place in mind for this social call?" he asked.

"Yeah. Meet me at Feliccia's. Know where that is?"

"I'll just follow my nose to the best breadsticks this side of Sicily."

"You do know it!"

"One of my favorite little hideaways."

"Glad to hear it. I'll see you there!"

Cool, in-control Gavin was taken slightly aback. The elusive, evasive Torrie called him and invited him to lunch—at a dark and noticeably intimate place, no less—and got right to the point about not wanting to talk business? He paced across the floor, then closed his office door enough to see the mirror that hung on the back. He peered closely at his face, checking the smoothness of the shave and adjusting his necktie below the gold bar that pushed the knot forward. *Perfect*, he thought, opening the door again as he strolled back to his desk.

Gavin was generally too smug to ride the train, but he decided to take it to Midtown this time. Maybe he just wanted a few minutes to relax without fighting the rigors of the lunchtime traffic crowd, maybe he thought he might bump into Torrie on the way up. Even to a macho thinker like Gavin, there was something romantic about taking a train ride with a fascinating woman.

As he reached into his pocket to pull out some change for the fare, he couldn't help but smile when he opened his palm to see the gold-plated half-dollar Harperson had given him. He needed to thank The Man again next time he saw him, to let him know how many moments of pleasure that coin had given him.

The bumpy train ride to Midtown only took about four minutes, and Gavin scrambled up the escalator. He was eager for this meeting because he liked Torrie, obviously, but perhaps even more than that—he was truly intrigued by what she might have in mind. He walked briskly to cover the two blocks from the train station to Feliccia's, glancing back over his shoulder a couple of times to see if perhaps he'd get a glimpse of her, but to no avail.

Ah, here we are. He pushed through the door and allowed a fraction of a second for his eyes to adjust to the dark, wood-paneled foyer that always seemed to be covered with a light coating of airborne oil of some kind, perhaps olive oil, to give it just the right ambience. When the room came into focus, he saw Torrie sitting on the bench right inside the door, looking right at him.

"Hi, Gavin." she smiled, standing and stepping toward him. She was not carrying a briefcase or a satchel, nor a tape recorder or a notepad—just a small handbag.

"You look great," she said to him.

"Thank you," he almost blushed, agreeing but still rather taken by surprise. "You too."

"Why, thanks," she said, walking him to the maitre d's lectern, where a little green light overlooked a plasticized map of the floor plan.

"Table for two, in nonsmoking." Lorenzo nodded and pressed into the seating area.

He must not have seen the smoke rising from my ears, Gavin said to himself as he fell in behind Torrie. They made their way to the table.

Small talk filled the air until after the menus were safely put away, touching ever-so-gingerly on the topic of the promotion but not getting beyond acknowledging that Gavin must be thrilled with the way things were turning out and that Carolina was certainly a brilliant woman.

Torrie decided to wait one more time before bridging the issue of public prayer with Gavin. She bowed her head silently before picking up a breadstick doused with enough garlic butter to make one an outcast. Gavin decided it was time to find firmer footing about this lunch date.

"I must admit," he said, running his finger around the rim of his ice water and stopping long enough to bob the lemon wedge down through the cubes, "that your call took me a little by surprise."

"Oh?" she asked, cool as Gavin usually was. "How so?"

"Well, I just thought you were all business, so I—"

"Whatever gave you that idea?" she cut in, munching into the freshly baked delight.

Gavin was falling further into this conversation than he had wanted to. Surface level was his comfort zone and getting into deep discussions about emotions was not his idea of a fun date.

"Never mind," he said, sipping the water. He looked past her, feigning interest in a still life of grapes and a pitcher that graced the wall behind her head.

Interesting, she thought to herself. A student of human nature, she was fascinated by this man of great personal bluster who, beneath it all, was as vulnerable and afraid as everybody else. The question is, would anyone ever be able to inspire him to reach deep enough to truly feel a great love, a great hurt, or God's best for his life? She was wise enough to know that if she pushed now, she might lay the first bricks of a wall which may never be scaled, so she backed off. She absentmindedly toyed with the tiny silver cross she was wearing.

"Tell me about Ruth," Torrie said, letting go of the cross to reach for another breadstick. "She seems to do a remarkably good job of protecting you from all us pesky reporters!"

Gavin smiled. "She was a diamond in the rough when I got her," he boasted, "but she's coming around. In a few more years, she'll be ready for management."

Torrie realized having a sandwich with Ruth would definitely be a treat, like one of those sitcom episodes where two characters describe the same incident in a comically different way.

"She must take quite a load off your shoulders," Torrie observed, subconsciously mirroring Gavin's gesture on the rim of her own water glass.

Gavin paused. "I guess. She pushes a lot of paperwork, all the gritty details I can't be bothered with. But if she didn't do it, I sure as heck wouldn't. Somebody else would."

She looked deep into his dark eyes as he spoke, wondering about her own motivations. Here she was, offended by his arrogance and sexism, yet strangely drawn toward his ability to project strength and control. She found him hard to resist—even though his flaws were obvious—and that made him very, very dangerous. She struggled with her desire to just be with him, as a woman, and the tug in her heart to tell him about Jesus and how Christ could change his heart. The trouble was, she knew Gavin felt no need to have his heart changed just then.

"But let's not talk about Ruth," he said, bringing her back. "I'd like to talk about you."

"*Moi*?" she said, batting her lashes.

"Yeah, *vous*," he said. "How do you like our big city? Enough going on for a swingin' single?"

"I wouldn't know about that," she said. "I'm not what you'd call much of a swinger. But I do love what I've seen so far. Lots of energy, lots of movers and shakers. There's a neat mix of old and new here—a sense of history and genteel keepers of the old South, like Gary

Harperson, right alongside the skyscrapers and the slick young players."

"If this thing with the paper doesn't work out, sounds like you've got yourself a job writing press releases for the chamber of commerce."

"Cut it out. Don't tell me you don't love being here right now too!"

"Guilty," he pleaded. "I do indeed."

"But what's next for you, Gavin?" she tried to be casual. "New York? Your own arbitrage network? Or a family?" Her head was tilted down, and a few strands of hair fell in front of her eye, which she smoothly rolled up to see Gavin's reaction.

He missed the depth of her sequence, handling it as a goal/objectives question instead of the personal lob Torrie had intended. "This promotion may very well tell the answer to that question," Gavin said, wondering why she was looking at him so coyly. "If it turns out to be the home run it's shaping into, I'll be in a unique position to have just about any option I want. Yeah, New York, or even Tokyo—that's where the real money is, if I wanted to deal with it. Maybe a consultancy—jet into Honolulu for a couple months, clean up a bank there, then off to Germany for a week, answer their questions, then the Caribbean, to tighten up one of the off-shore tax shelter banks . . . "

"Sounds like a wandering spirit underneath that corporate iron man exterior," she interjected. "Just like me."

Gavin remained silent, not yet realizing fully that they had again crossed the line. But he liked the way she said it, and the way she was looking at him.

"How so?" he managed to get out.

"Oh, I don't know," she said, flipping her hair back as she looked at the ceiling. "I love what I'm doing, but I don't know if I want to keep on doing the same thing forever. I feel like people need to reinvent themselves every now and then, to keep the cobwebs from choking the zest out of life."

"'Zest,'" Gavin repeated to himself. He couldn't remember the last time he was with a woman who used the word *zest* in conversation, particularly a conversation about her life, without it sounding corny or contrived. When Torrie said it, it seemed to have a sheen all around it.

"Well, what then, if not the Pulitzer Prize?" he asked, more and more intrigued by this woman as each moment passed.

"Mmm, maybe the Victoria Wilson Prize. I mean, why win an award that's named after somebody else when you can have an award named after you?"

"That's a fascinating way to capture the concept of excellence," Gavin said, amazed at how truly impressed he was with this woman's mind as well as her spirit. *Just what is it that's so different about her, anyway?*

"Maybe I should be a writer," she suggested with a smirk.

"Or maybe have a newspaper named after you!" he said, and they both laughed.

"Do you ever want to write a book? Like a novel?" Gavin asked.

"Every writer fantasizes about writing novels, perched high atop a loft that overlooks some magnificently poetic body of water," she said, as if she'd given that answer some thought before. "And I'm sure I'll try my hand at it some day. But I'm too young inside just yet. There's too much life to live before I have to start living it out through other people on a computer screen. Then again, maybe your ingenious promotion will keep getting more and more out of hand, and I'll write a book about you."

"A book about me, huh?" Gavin sat back and mulled that one. "How would you describe me?"

"Let's see," she said, squinting at him. "Pot-bellied, balding, and wearing old flat slippers around the house with a thirty-year-old sweater on, over a white T-shirt, at all times."

"Got me pegged," he said, willing to let her get away. But she brought it back.

"No. Tall and powerful and dark, projecting a level of confidence that draws a woman near him, not certain exactly what it is, yet unable to turn away when he penetrates her heart with his piercing eyes of steel." She finished, her heart pounding, not sure if she should have uttered such literature.

Gavin had seldom experienced the awkwardness that surged through his very being at that instant. He felt like a teenager, trapped and helpless, not knowing how to react when a woman spoke such words.

Realizing her willingness to dig around was unnerving the man, Torrie broke the tension.

"Not!" she laughed.

He paused, then joined in her laughter, although somewhat cautiously and nervously. The room felt like it was closing in on him. *Strange, I've never felt claustrophobic before. Is it getting hot in here?* He unconsciously tugged at his collar and said, "Excuse me, I think I need to head to the—to powder my nose." He sauntered off, furiously rubbing his gold half-dollar.

She watched him walk away, not really enjoying the fact that she was able to make him squirm. That wasn't what she was after—yes, she wanted to get under his skin, but she knew this relationship had to get below the surface at some point if it was ever going to amount to anything. That was her aim in keeping him off balance. Gavin had his flaws, some pretty major ones, in fact, but he also possessed some remarkable gifts and enormous potential, if he would just come to grips with concepts greater than his own world. Torrie knew she would eventually have to bridge the topic of faith before she could truly commit to anything herself, and she had talked herself into thinking that playing with this particular brand of fire was worth the risk.

Give me wisdom and discernment, she prayed silently as she took another sip of water. *And help me to watch my big mouth!*

      ⚜   ⚜   ⚜

Gavin splashed some cold water onto his face and looked up at himself in the mirror as the refreshing liquid dripped down. He usually toyed with others, or, in rare cases like his frequent head-to-head sessions with Carolina, jousted with the very best on equal footing. But today, he'd definitely been caught off guard. Time to regroup. *Do I want to get involved with Torrie? Yes. Absolutely. Maybe.* He did, but she was making him nervous. *So what's my next move? The obvious one—at the end of the lunch date, ask her to dinner. But what if she says no? No, she won't say no, she's crazy about you—she asked you to lunch, and look at the way she's looking at you. And talking to you!* But she'd teased him before, so he wasn't sure.

"This little pep talk was a lot of help," he said sarcastically, deciding he needed more time. He paced back and forth inside the tiny room and told himself to think about how well the promotion was going. Another man entered the cramped quarters to wash his hands, and he eyed Gavin suspiciously as the flustered banker paced in small circles with his lips fluttering.

Gavin came back to find lunch had been set at the table. *Good—a chance to get back to the small talk.* "Ooh, boy, Feliccia's lasagna," he said, rubbing his hands together.

"Dig in," Torrie said, having decided to follow Gavin's lead in conversation for the rest of their time together.

He talked about baseball and told her an amusing anecdote about the mayor that she hadn't heard. *The second half of lunch,* Gavin found himself thinking, *is going decidedly smoother than the first half.*

When the check came, Torrie reached for it. "Hey, that's mine," Gavin insisted, reaching for the leather-covered folder.

"Nope—I invited you," she corrected him, pulling it away. He wasn't used to this, and he wasn't sure he liked it. "Of course," she added, "you can get the next one."

Gavin leaned into the big red seat and spread his arms across the back of his side of the booth. "Okay," he said, catching the not-par-ticularly-subtle go-ahead.

"Taking the train back?" he asked as they walked out into the sunlight and pulled on their sunglasses. He liked being able to hide his eyes, but he hated not being able to read hers.

"No, I've got an interview over at O&M, with Virginia," she said, motioning up the street.

"I'll walk you up," he offered.

"Come on," she said as she headed north.

When they got to One Midtown Plaza, Torrie's destination, they stopped on the steps, just like in the movies. Her hair was gently blowing in the breeze.

"Uh, thanks for lunch," he said with a chuckle, realizing that was usually someone else's line.

"My pleasure, sir."

"I'd sure like to return the favor. Can I take you to dinner this Saturday?"

"Oh, I'm sorry," she said, as he felt his blood start to boil. "I've got a banquet I've got to cover, and I've got to go with my editor."

Gavin was beginning to decide this was the last time he'd fall for Torrie's teasing games, and that . . .

"But I'm free all afternoon on Sunday!"

His temperature began its descent, and he said, "I'll call you, and we'll think of something."

"I can't wait," she said.

"Me too," he said, starting to back down the steps because he knew a daytime lunch was no opportunity for a kiss, but he was just as uncomfortable with a businesslike handshake.

She gave him a little wave and stood watching him instead of turning and walking through the revolving door, as he expected.

Gavin found himself still walking two blocks past the train station, his mind churning about something besides the gold. *Who is this remarkable woman, and where did she come from?* The *Business Courier*, he realized, and all at once he stopped. "The *Business Courier*," he said out loud. He found himself standing there, waging a bitter internal battle between his paranoia ("She's looking for a scoop") and his ego ("She won't be able to keep her hands off you on Sunday!"). All at once, he realized he didn't have any real friends he could talk to about this struggle. Carolina was a friend, but a business friend, and he certainly couldn't present himself vulnerable before her. It would forever change the nature of their relationship. He started walking again. The man whose fertile mind had dug up a one-hundred-and-thirty-year-old mystery and made it today's headlines, the man who had turned thousands of lives into treasure hunts was absolutely stumped by a woman he hadn't even known a month ago.

He kept on walking, deciding by now he may as well go all the way to the next train station, four or five more blocks down the road. He knew Torrie wasn't going to be on the train this time either, but he found himself scouring the station with his eyes as he made his way toward the platform.

🪙　🪙　🪙

Torrie peered out the window, trying to catch a glimpse of Gavin walking down Peachtree Street. Her appointment was running a few minutes late, so she had a moment or two to think.

Is this crossing the line? she asked herself. *Maybe I need to back off for a while. My heart's getting way in front of my head here. Gavin's not what I'm looking for. I couldn't marry him. No way.* A flock of pigeons down below became alarmed and suddenly fluttered up and over as one before settling back into their head-bobbing routine. *But that's just why he needs me—I can be the one who helps him see the truth.* A police car flashed on his light and zipped past several cars, but didn't flick his siren on. "Oh, shut up! You're just rationalizing! You know that's not the best! You're walking the fence. It's too easy to start compromising in a situation like this, when you're letting go of being in control of your emotions! That's not what . . . "

"Excuse me, did you say something?" The receptionist was giving Torrie a funny look.

Torrie blushed as she looked over her shoulder and then turned away from the window to face the lobby. "Oh, uh, I'm sorry," she mumbled sheepishly. "I guess I was just thinking out loud, maybe a little louder than I wanted to!" They both laughed nervously, and Torrie realized she was wringing her hands. "I think I'll just visit the ladies' room while I'm waiting." She disappeared down the hall in a flash.

🪙　🪙　🪙

When Gavin got back to the office, he found Wink Wiley, a reporter for *Georgia Trend* magazine, waiting for him. *Uh oh—he's been waiting for a three o'clock appointment, and it's nearly four.*

"I'm dreadfully sorry," Gavin said repeatedly, which caught Ruth's attention. She had seldom heard Gavin apologize to anyone, especially with genuine sincerity. She wondered what to make of it.

The reporter emerged an hour later. He seemed pleased that he'd gotten the story he wanted, and Gavin walked him out. As Gavin came back past Ruth's desk toward his office, he stopped. She looked up, waiting for Gavin to reprimand her for not reminding him the reporter was coming that afternoon.

"Ruth," he said softly, "do you think most reporters will do anything to get their story?" She was surprised at the philosophical nature of his question, but it seemed plausible given what was going on and given a reporter had just left Gavin's office. She wondered what Wink Wiley had asked that made Gavin feel that way.

"I guess it depends on the reporter," she said. "Some will, and some won't. Tami Olson probably wouldn't; Fast Eddie probably would." When she said "Fast Eddie" and remembered who replaced him, she realized this had nothing to do with Wink Wiley.

Gavin stood there, contemplating another question.

"Did the *Georgia Trend* interview go okay?" she asked, seeing how he'd handle a chance to tell the truth.

"Huh? Oh, yeah, fine." Another pause. "Ruth, what do you think of that new girl over at the *Business Courier*, the one who replaced Fast Eddie?"

"Torrie Wilson?"

"Yeah."

"What about her?"

"What do you think of her? Is she one of those people who'd do anything to get a story or not?"

Ruth carefully planned her response. "I don't really know her that well . . . "

"But what's your gut say? Surely by now, you've seen me go on my instincts enough to give it a try yourself. Go ahead—what do you think?"

I think I'm going to make you the laughingstock of thirteen states—if not the whole country, she said to herself, once again quickly reminded of how arrogant Gavin could be. "My gut," she said through gritted teeth. She thought quickly. *What do I really think? What does he want to hear? Does it matter—he certainly doesn't want to hear what my gut tells me unless it agrees with his own conclusions.* Having already decided to sell out on her career and her conscience, this decision was a piece of cake—she'd give the answer Gavin wanted, to declaw the beast and make him a little more pleasant to be around. "My gut tells me she's smart and a good reporter but basically honest. I don't think she'd deep-six anybody just to get a good story."

Gavin nodded slowly.

"Any particular reason you're thinking about that?" Ruth asked, interested to see if Gavin would reveal any more.

"Just trying to cover all my bases, Ruth." He walked into his office and shut the door.

"Figures," she muttered, walking back to her desk and settling herself into the chair. It was just before five, and her motivation to stay late was shrinking by the minute. She double-clicked her way out of the document she was working on, popped off the computer when it got to the *c:* prompt, and started to straighten the papers on her desktop. She sat for several minutes, not reading anything or writing anything down or even pretending to get anything done, even as others walked by. Just thinking, wondering how she had gotten to this point and wishing it could come to an end soon. She knew it was as simple as being able to solve the great riddle of the South: "Where water is, gold hides nearby."

Twelve

Sunday afternoon was bright and beautiful, a sun-drenched masterpiece of blue skies with white wispy cirrus clouds high above the world—the perfect day for a drive in the country. Gavin's Mercedes was a convertible, and Torrie looked like she was born to be in a fancy car with the top down.

She kept a jeep in the garage at her complex, which he found surprising for a young single woman who lived in the city, but then again not surprising, knowing her personality. It seemed to fit. She hadn't found as many opportunities to drive since moving to Atlanta, what with getting her feet wet at the paper and being within train-shot of just about anywhere she needed to go. She walked and sometimes rode her bike too—a veritable poster child for youth and fitness.

The two were soaring up State Highway 400, steadily outpacing the speed limit with Gavin's fuzzbuster activated, heading to Forsyth County, due north of the city. *It's a most unusual setting for a date,* he pondered, *but it'll be fun to go with the flow.*

He had called her on Saturday morning. "Anything special you'd like to do?" he asked.

"As a matter of fact, there is," she told him. He wasn't surprised. But what did surprise him was what she said next. He'd figured on an urban activity, like a show or a trip to a museum or, at the most earthy fringe of his imagination, a picnic in Piedmont Park, right there in Midtown—a basket of fruit and cheese, some expensive crackers, and some Godiva chocolates to top it off.

"Let's go horseback riding!"

Gavin had grown up like all other all-American boys in the early sixties, contemplating NASA and the old west as viable career options, but he hadn't been on a horse since, well . . .

"Horseback riding? Or did you say, 'racing'? Strange, you didn't strike me as one who'd like to blow her paycheck betting on the ponies."

"No—horseback riding. Like 'giddyup!'"

"You mean like big, smelly animals who weigh something close to two tons, who could crush me to death if one of them fell on me?"

"Horses don't weigh two tons, silly," she said, "and they're not going to fall on top of you. You get on top of them!"

"That's what worries me," he said.

"C'mon, it'll be fun."

"I'm not sure I know where we could go," he said, putting up one last protest.

"I've got it covered. One of my girlfriends at the paper, Jane Riordan, goes all the time. She's got a great stable she told me about."

"She owns it?"

"On a reporter's salary? Are you kidding? She rides there. But that is where she boards her horse, Missy."

"Missy," Gavin repeated. "Can't wait to meet Missy."

"If you're going to be a grump about this, I'm sure I can find something else to do on Sunday, like wash my hair."

"Hey, I know. Let's go horseback riding," Gavin popped in.

"What time are you gonna come pick me up?" she asked.

"How about two-ish?" he suggested.

"I will see you then. Bye, Gavin. We're gonna have a great time!"

"Okay. Bye." Gavin pushed the "End" button on his portable phone and thought, *I hope so.*

She breathed a sigh of relief, glad that Gavin didn't propose a time that would conflict with church. She didn't think he was quite ready for that topic yet. She was actually looking forward to his surprise when he found out she was one of those born-again fanatics, since she felt stereotype-busting was a powerful tool. Since so many skeptics thought all Christians were rednecks or simpletons, she was happy to prove that being intelligent and being a believer were actually quite compatible.

Thinking about being with Torrie, especially on a real date instead of during the normal downtown daytime routine, had softened Gavin's worries about being hooved to death; by the time Sunday afternoon came around, he was actually looking forward to having a good time.

It surprised him how different she looked in jeans and an old cotton button-down blouse; the Torrie he knew was always dressed for success. Gavin wore jeans and a sport shirt.

"Oh, look, we're almost there!" Torrie said, pointing to a "Welcome to Forsyth County" sign.

"Mmm-hmm," he said wryly. "Funny thing about Georgia. Guess what county Macon's in."

"Aah—Macon County? Burt Reynolds movie, right?"

"Right movie, wrong county. There is a Macon County, but Macon's not in it. Macon's in Bibb County."

"Makes perfect sense to me," she smiled. "But what on earth made you think of that?"

"I'm getting to that. You see, there's also a town called Forsyth, Georgia," he went on. "Guess what county that's in."

"Could be a trick question," she said, rubbing her chin.

"Actually, no matter what the answer is, I think it qualifies for trick question status at this point," he said.

"I believe you're right. I'll guess you're putting your money on a two-for-two here," she said, "so I'll say Forsyth, Georgia, is definitely not in Forsyth County."

"Give that lady a treasure chest laden with a million dollars in gold," he said. "Forsyth is in Monroe County."

"Gosh, where will I spend it all?"

"I'm sure you'll think of something."

"Well, is there ever anything going on in Monroe County?" she asked. "Maybe I could drop a few hundred grand out there."

"I think the old downtown has been restored—lots of antebellum architecture and gift shops, that kind of thing," Gavin said.

"Is it far off?"

"A couple of hours' drive," he said. "Not bad on an afternoon like this, for a day trip—especially if the company's terrific." He looked over at her and smiled.

She smiled back. "Maybe we ought to try that sometime," she said.

"Maybe," he said. "Looks like our exit."

They turned off the highway and looped over the country roads that looked like ribbons resting gently atop the green rolling hillside. After a mile or two of Torrie reading from the handwritten directions, they saw a sign that said "Pritchett Stables 1 1/2 mi." with an arrow pointing to the left.

Three minutes later, they were there, and Gavin turned off the main road onto a gravel drive. The sign out front read "Pritchett Stables, Riding Lessons, Boarding, Tack Shop."

"I think we have arrived," he said, looking out his window with concern that the dust from the gravel would not only coat his beautiful black luxury car but fill the inside as well.

"Ah, let's live on the edge," he said to Torrie, accelerating down the driveway toward the buildings at the top of the hill.

"I knew there was something about you I liked," she said, pushing her hair back.

Gavin wasn't going to get his in-town picnic, but he was going to get one in the country. Torrie pulled a picnic basket from the backseat as they got out, but she wouldn't give him an advance peek.

"How do you plan to bring that along on horseback?" he asked. "Those things don't come equipped with spacious trunks, do they?"

"We'll see if they can rig it up somehow," she suggested, stepping up onto the old wooden front porch. It was rustic, with the red stain fading, and an old Coca-Cola disc sign hung from the wall. They walked inside.

The room was filled with saddles, hats, boots, and a variety of contraptions and devices quite unfamiliar to Gavin's stainless steel and molded plastic world. *It must be rough to be a horse*, he thought. The room smelled good, a bouquet of leather, and Gavin ran his fingers across an enormous saddle that was on display.

"Can I help you?" a man said, walking in from the back. A woman entered alongside the man.

"We're here for our ride," Gavin answered. "I'm Gavin Duke."

"I'm Tim Pritchett," the owner said, reaching out and giving Gavin a hearty handshake, then repeating the gesture for Torrie. Tim's wife, Betsy, also joined in, and everyone got acquainted.

"You look awfully familiar to me," Tim said, eyeing his guest. "But I don't think you've been up here before."

Before Gavin could reply, Betsy provided the answer. "He's the guy from the bank," she said. "The million dollars in gold?"

Tim's eyes flew open wide. "Say, you are, aren't you?"

Gavin was used to being recognized in business circles—the Bank Marketing Association, the Ad Club—but not by real people, as though he were a celebrity. He didn't know how to react. He looked down at the floor, then up at Torrie, who was staring right at him with the biggest grin stretched across her face.

"Well, yeah, I . . . "

"Hey," said Tim, now his best buddy, tapping Gavin on the chest with a big gloved hand. "Y'all didn't bury the treasure on my horse farm here, did you?" He let out a belly laugh that shook the room.

"Silly," Betsy said, good-naturedly swatting her husband's shoulder. Gavin and Torrie could tell these two had a good time together. Not Gavin's idea of a good time, mind you, but a good time nonetheless. "Leave these two people alone—they came out for a ride, not to hear about whatever your crazy imagination wants to cook up." She turned to Torrie. "Come on out back, and we'll fix you up with a pair of horses."

"Sorry, Tim," Gavin shrugged, following Betsy and Torrie out the other door.

"Hey, that's all right," Tim smiled, following along. "We've got three accounts at the bank anyway, so we're puttin' those clues together. Got the second one yesterday. What was it? 'If gold got spun, it'd end up here,' or something like that. Boy, that one's got me all twisted up." He shook his head.

The second clue looked like this:

SOUTHERN GOLD CLUE #2:
If gold were spun, it could be here.

As with the first clue, Gavin initially thought this one was too obvious; based on the fairy-tale concept of gold being spun from a loom, its burial at the old Southern Looms plant was an easy deduction for someone who was paying attention. But he had learned to always do a little research, even if it were quick and informal. He showed the clue to a few people at the office and at the agency, and most got a mental picture of a finished gold bar being spun around—turned quickly—instead of the loom imagery. Virtually everyone thought it was a directional clue, somehow suggesting north or south.

"What I would think after reading these two clues," Carolina had said, "is that the gold is due north of a body of water. But I would also be very uncertain about that, since something doesn't quite seem to fit. But that's the best guess I can do with just this to go on."

Her creative team has done a wonderful job of ingraining the image of gold bars into everyone's mind, Gavin thought, *which is why the direction thing hit first, and nobody figured out another possibility. And if someone does make the loom connection eventually,* he reasoned, *so what? The South is littered with textile mills. There are hundreds; the secret's safe.*

The back of this clue also contained a yarn that Carolina's staff had cooked up:

A WEB OF DECEIT?

Fancy accounting methods aren't new and they may have been used by the keepers of the Confederate gold. Siphoning off a little here and there, some of the more "creative" Rebel bookkeepers may have secretly tucked some away for themselves. But suppose someone who skimmed the loot never made it back to his hidden bounty, entangled by his own cunningly spun webs of betrayal— it was wartime, after all. Could there be several treasures still hidden under the South?

Gavin was intrigued to realize this was the first time the subject of the contest had come up since he'd gone to Torrie's place to pick her up. *Odd, that this investigative reporter wouldn't try to grab some inside info while I'm off guard. Perhaps, just perhaps, she really does care more about me than her story. Or is she just very, very good at this game?* Gavin looked at her as she lovingly stroked an old horse on the nose, and he saw nothing but the purest of motives.

"This looks like a good one for you," Torrie said with a smile. "Her name's Lucy, and she's a gentle old soul."

Gavin walked over to Lucy, looked her straight in the eye, and said, "Be kind to me, dear animal, or I may have to recommend you for duty at the glue factory."

"Gavin!" Torrie nearly shrieked, putting her hands around his neck. "I'm gonna strangle you!"

"Hey, I'm just getting all the facts out up front," he said. "As a reporter, I'd think you would appreciate that!"

Betsy, taking all this in, said to Torrie, "Don't worry, honey. It's genetic. Men can't help it."

"I'm finding that out," she said, moving to the next stall. "So you're going with me?" she asked the horse, whose name was Charlie Brown. Charlie looked at Torrie and flared his nostrils.

Once saddled up, the two went for a quiet ride in the remarkably beautiful countryside. They didn't say much; each seemed to be enjoying the escape from work and pressure and ringing phones. The horses cantered down a slope, orange and yellow wildflowers painting the terrain, toward a trickling creek. The Pritchetts had placed a park bench under a broad old oak tree near a bend in the creek, inviting a stop.

"Good thing Betsy managed to hook the basket to your saddle," Gavin said as he dismounted, amazing even himself at the ease with which he replanted his feet on solid ground.

"Good thing," she smiled, sliding off Charlie Brown so deftly that Gavin felt embarrassed for thinking he'd looked good at it.

"So what's this big secret in the basket?" Gavin asked, pulling at the red and white checkered tablecloth she'd folded over the top.

"Nope—you gotta wait," she said, pulling it away. "You let me set it up."

"All right," he said, backing off. He went over and tied the horses to a post which the Pritchetts had put next to the stream, presumably so the horses could bend down for a drink. Torrie watched him with the horses, relaxed and unpretentious, and was glad to see the other side of Gavin Duke.

Gavin glanced over at her too, as she unpacked lunch. *She looks so right here, out in the open air*, he thought, *yet she also seems to fit just fine in the frenetic world of crowded sidewalks, power lunches, and empire building. What a balanced person*, he concluded, wishing for a moment that he could keep things in perspective as Torrie managed.

"Ready!" she called, looking up with a smile.

"How'd you fit all this stuff into one little basket?" he asked, his eyes feasting on the spread.

"When you move around enough, you learn to pack a pretty mean suitcase," she said. "Allow me to present today's menu: we have a fresh tossed garden salad, three kinds of cheese, sourdough bread, and homemade lasagna!"

"Lasagna! I love lasagna!" he smiled, remembering that's what he'd ordered at Feliccia's the other day and was quite touched that she'd not only remembered but gone to all the trouble of whipping it up herself. He wondered how she'd managed to keep lasagna in a picnic basket.

"So you cook, too, huh?" he teased. "Is there anything you don't do?"

"Needlepoint," she said without missing a beat. "I don't answer to 'hey, bay-bee,' and let's see, what else . . . "

"Uh, excuse me, bay-bee," Gavin said, doing his very best Schwarzenegger, "pass the munchies, will ya?"

The couple laughed and talked under the shade of the friendly oak, eating lasagna and rolls and salad and cheese and fruit and the richest, creamiest chocolate cake Gavin had ever tasted. He thought it odd that she brought soft drinks instead of wine, but the conversation never paused long enough for him to ask. So he didn't.

After a long day that passed all too quickly, Gavin found himself standing at Torrie's front door, his heart pounding like he was a little kid. "Want to come in for a minute?" she invited, pushing the door as she turned the key in the deadbolt lock.

"Yeah, I'd love to."

Casey the cat darted up to check Gavin out, purring as she massaged his leg. Torrie squatted down to rub Casey's long, shedding body.

"You're gonna hate me for this, but I need to call it quits pretty quick," she said, standing up and making a face. "I've got to get up at 3:30 tomorrow morning for a red-eye flight out to Miami."

"Oh," said Gavin, trying not to spill out his disappointment. He understood the rigors of schedules, and he could read the disappointment in her face too. "What's in Miami?"

"Believe it or not, there is some banking news besides First Southern going on. One of the thrifts down that way has been in some talks with one of the mortgage companies up here."

"Yeah, the Peninsula State deal," he said.

She paused, looking at him. "All my sources said it was pretty hush-hush. Seems like you'd make a pretty good reporter, Mr. Duke!"

There was a short pause, long enough to be uncomfortable. "Can I get you some coffee?"

"That's okay," he said, "I'm sure you need to spend some time poring over the paperwork before you go. Frankly, I need to get at some homework too. I'll take a rain check, though."

"That's a promise I'll hold you to," she said. It was time to get a little nervous.

He moved closer without a word and gazed into her eyes. "Torrie, I had such a good time with you today."

She looked up at him, moving her hand until her fingertips rested gently on his shirt. She started toying with a button. "Me, too, Gavin. Thanks for being such a good sport about the horses."

"It was a great idea," he said. "I just enjoy being with you." He seemed to say "you" in slow motion as he slid his arms around her and was about to kiss her good night when the cat suddenly broke them up, darting between the two.

"Casey," she scolded, looking down quickly before returning her gaze to Gavin. They shared a soft laugh, a tension-breaking burst that was sorely needed at that point.

Gavin stood back, and said, "I hope you have a good trip. When will you come back?"

"Tuesday. I'll call you."

"Okay." He gave her hand a light squeeze as he reached for the door handle and walked out without any more conversation between the two. There was nothing more that needed to be said.

She stood there as Casey came back to rub against her blue jeans again, so she bent down and picked her up. "What are we gonna do with this man, kiddo? What are we gonna do?"

Casey, no great judge of human nature, offered no solutions, so Torrie went into the kitchen to pour herself a glass of ice water. She sat on the balcony for a few minutes and lifted up a short prayer for wisdom before pulling out her journal. But after half an hour of trying, she gave up. It was no use. She just couldn't concentrate. She put down her pen, rubbed her eyes, and stared at the phone. "It's Anita time," she told herself, and she punched the auto-dial number for her old college roommate.

They chatted about Anita's kids and her husband David and things around Tahoe, Torrie's job, her search for a church where she felt like she fit, and the sheer joy of being in Atlanta.

"So," Anita said suddenly, "what's the real reason you called?"

Torrie gulped, then laughed. "How can you see through me when you can't even see me?"

Anita laughed too. "What is it, honey?"

"What else—a male."

"Hmm. What kind of male?"

"Unfortunately, the wrong kind."

"Oh?"

Torrie realized Anita couldn't see her nodding, so she described Gavin. "Handsome. Bright as can be. Sophisticated. Charming."

"But . . . ?"

Torrie sighed. "How do I put this? He's, ah . . . It's a faith issue, Anita. Gavin just doesn't . . . " She trailed off. She didn't want to finish, and she knew that with Anita she wouldn't have to.

"Oh. The old 'evangelistic dating' thing."

Torrie realized she was nodding again. "Uh-huh. He just, well, he just couldn't care less about God or about anything spiritual."

"So has he asked you to compromise in any way?"

"It hasn't come up yet," Torrie said.

"*Yet* seems to be a key concept here."

Torrie blushed. "I just don't know, Anita. I mean, we've seen each other enough that it's time we got below the surface or the relationship isn't going to go anywhere. But I'm just afraid that once it gets below the surface, he's going to lose interest, since everything we really believe in is worlds apart."

"And right now, since the relationship's just staying on the surface level, it's okay?"

"More than okay. It's great!"

"So you don't want to let go of him."

"No, I don't want to lose him."

"But the relationship can't stay in the same place much longer," Anita observed. "It's either got to move on, or it'll get stagnant and fizzle out."

"I know that. And that's the whole problem. It's great where it is, but it can't stay here. Yet I'm afraid that it can't survive the move to the next level."

"Hmm. Maybe that's one rationale behind not starting to date guys who don't share your faith in the first place. There's nowhere for it to go, once you get beyond the first layer of the onion."

Torrie sighed. "I guess maybe God wants me to learn that, in case it ever comes up again. But the trouble is, I'm already in too deep."

"You really care about this guy?"

Torrie licked her lips and stroked Casey's fur. Her eyes welled up with tears. "Yeah, Anita. I really do. I've never met anyone quite like him before."

Anita paused, considering her words. "Be careful, Torrie. It sounds like your heart's giving your common sense a good fight here. And you know how dangerous that can be."

Torrie sighed. "I know. And I've been praying about it. A lot."

"It's too bad you haven't found a church you like yet. You sound like you really need that kind of support right now."

"Yeah, I do. I miss it," she said. "The good news is, I've heard lots of good things about the one I'm visiting next week."

"Good. I'll pray about that too."

"Thanks, Anita."

"Hey, what are—just a second, Torrie—Barry! Don't draw on your sister with those markers! Barry! . . . I'm sorry, Torrie, we're having a small riot here, and . . . "

"That's okay. I'll let you go. Thanks for listening. I love you."

"I love you too, sweetie. I'm glad to know what's going on—we can pray for you big time. It's so good to hear your voice!"

Torrie tapped her fingers on the phone after she put it back down. "Big-time prayer. That's what I need, all right. Don't we, Casey?"

🍂   🍂   🍂

On Monday morning, Gavin was back at the grind too. He had to reread the third-week report on new accounts. He couldn't believe his eyes—the huge new account totals from the first week hadn't dropped back, as he'd projected, but had actually increased again. This was better than he'd ever dreamed.

He answered the phone absentmindedly on the third ring, and it took him a second to realize the magnitude of the call.

"Mr. Duke, this is Ray Nichols, calling from Harpo Productions in Chicago. I'm a producer for the Oprah Winfrey show." Ray knew to pause there, because most people, he'd discovered, liked to react. Gavin did not, still flipping pages on the weekly report.

"What can I do for you, Ray?" he asked.

The producer, taken slightly off guard by the casual nature of Gavin's response, went on. "We're interested in booking you to appear on one of our upcoming shows, to talk about this treasure hunt you're leading." He paused again. *Surely this will get a rise out of this character,* he thought.

It sunk in this time. "You want me to be on Oprah?" Gavin asked, setting the report aside.

Satisfied, Ray responded. "We've gotten quite a few press reports from our research staff, as well as some tips from our affiliate stations across the Southeast, that everybody's going bananas down there about this treasure hunt. And we hear you're the guy behind it."

His ego stroked, Gavin got into it. "Well, yeah, I am. When are you thinking of?" he asked, reaching for his calendar.

"I know it's pretty short notice," Ray said, "but we had a cancellation for next Monday. Could you be here then?"

Gavin's ego deflated a bit, imagining his big break on national TV only came about because a dog who spoke three languages couldn't make it to Chicago.

"I can rearrange some things," Gavin said.

"Excellent," said Ray. "I'll have one of our associate producers make the arrangements with your secretary."

"That'll be fine," Gavin said with a grin as they hung up.

Interesting, he thought to himself. *Will this start an avalanche of national attention?* The thought shook him at first, until he remembered the sneak preview of celebrityhood from the day before, when the Pritchetts recognized him at the stables. *Yeah, that felt great. Will this mean I'd attract a crowd wherever I go from now on, having to sign autographs and pose for pictures with folks from Wichita, Kansas, and Tupelo, Mississippi? No, better than that—admiring crowds will be all over me, no matter where I go. Airports, hotel lobbies, restaurants. Yeah.*

Gavin realized he'd better get back at it, since he would have to lose an entire day next week—a day he couldn't really afford to give up—jetting to Chicago and back. He folded the report over, allowing himself one more smile about it, and reached for the next item in his stack. It was the third clue.

SOUTHERN GOLD CLUE #3:
Where weapons add strength, gold rests in peace.

By the time he'd put this one on paper, he recognized that what he thought obvious—the plant had been converted into a tank parts facility—was not. After all, this was based on Civil War imagery, so everyone would either think of a cannon foundry or, more likely, a battle site. The back romanced the idea even more:

A DYNAMITE FIND

Did Confederate soldiers who were supposed to guard Southern Gold betray their breakaway nation? A number of legends tell stories of Rebel enlisted men hiding gold and other valuables in gun barrels, their shoes, and even cannons to send back home. Perhaps some of these artifacts never made it back, or, if they did, were hidden away but never retrieved. So if you happen to be digging somewhere in the South, or remodeling an older structure, keep an eye out for anything that may have once served as a clever hiding place for Southern Gold.

Gavin didn't see Torrie at all that week, since they both had to be out of town a little and were buried beneath mountains of work. But they did manage to catch up with each other on the phone a couple of times.

On the plane to Chicago, Gavin scanned the remaining clues on the list. If anyone solved the riddle on the basis of these clues alone, Gavin figured, he or she would have to be a genius. Yet they were accurate and specific enough that no one could complain about not having a fair shake. Besides, every account holder got the same clues.

SOUTHERN GOLD CLUE #4:
The golden sun of Florida casts no light over hidden gold.
(It's not in Florida.)

SOUTHERN GOLD CLUE #5:
Close to state lines, the gold must rest.
(It's right across the Chattahoochee River,
which acts as the state border from Alabama.)

SOUTHERN GOLD CLUE #6:
A Georgia peach casts a golden tint.
(It's in Georgia.)

SOUTHERN GOLD CLUE #7:
A western sunset brings golden delights.
(It's on the western state line of Georgia.)

SOUTHERN GOLD CLUE #8:
The governor's gold touch falls to the east.
(Lumpkin, Georgia, the county seat of Stewart County, is east of the gold;
the city is named after an early Georgia governor.)

SOUTHERN GOLD CLUE #9:
Think to the mine to dig your gold.
(The gold is hidden in an underground cavern,
carved out of a rock, to create the feel of a mine.)

SOUTHERN GOLD CLUE #10:
A cheap steel cage protects precious gold.
(The old plant is surrounded by a chain-link fence.)

SOUTHERN GOLD CLUE #11:
A base element lies to gold's north.
(Fort Benning, a major U.S. Army training base,
lies just north of the gold's hiding place.)

SOUTHERN GOLD CLUE #12:
By George, I think you've got it.
(A large lake, named after Walter F. George,
lies a few miles south of the spot Gavin hid the gold.)

He looked at all the clues together, combined with the first three (near water, "spun" gold, and near weapons), and he thought an intelligent person could actually conclude he'd see the spot from the river, between the base and the lake, on the Georgia side, inside a fenced area, and buried underground. But it would take a few more weeks for anyone to get all those clues. He felt good about it, glad to be the only one who knew the gold's location.

✥   ✥   ✥

Oprah started off with a brief recap of the promotion, then introduced Gavin by saying that he was the only person who knew the secret—to the delight of the audience—and then she played the "Will you marry me?" segment from the press conference.

"So did you?" Oprah asked him, as laughter ran through the audience.

"No." Gavin gave his best aw-shucks routine.

"So you're still available," Oprah continued.

"Keep your hands off, honey," Torrie said to the screen, watching from her apartment. Daytime talk shows were not her standard TV fare, but one of the perks of being a journalist was she sometimes got paid for doing fun things—like watching Oprah. The best bets, depending on your tastes, were a major league sports beat, theater reviews, restaurant reviews, and, of course, the job Robin Leach created for himself—jet all around the globe to hang out with celebrities at the poshest spots on earth and get paid a million dollars a year for the effort.

Gavin was great on Oprah, handling himself like, well, like Gavin. Which cast the die for the future. Within twenty-four hours, he'd gotten calls from Donahue, Regis & Kathie Lee, Sally Jessy Raphael, Larry King, Montel Williams, the *Today Show, The Tonight Show,* and every news network from CBS to NBC to ABC to CNN to the BBC, Mutual Radio, *The New York Times, The Wall Street Journal, Time, Newsweek,* and *People* magazine.

People actually put his face on the cover, with the teaser "Gavin Duke, Golden Boy: The Man with the Million-Dollar Mind."

Gavin's burst onto the national scene solved Torrie's dilemma—or at least postponed it, since Gavin's media travel schedule pushed their relationship to a long-distance one. They did manage to get together twice over that patience-testing next few weeks, once for a lovely candlelight dinner and once for a glorious afternoon of sailing on Lake Lanier.

"I guess this is the current answer to prayer," she told Anita. "It seems like God wants to show me some more things before Gavin and I come to our crossroads."

"I'll keep praying," Anita promised.

In these brief and highly charged moments together, Torrie saw little of Gavin the egomaniac. And Torrie had cause for hope, she felt—she was pleasantly surprised he didn't object to her saying grace aloud (he even added his own "Amen") during their latest two outings, but she was frustrated that he managed to skillfully deflect any other conversation that drifted toward spiritual matters.

🐾   🐾   🐾

Ruth's thoughts of Gavin were far from benevolent, though.

"It's hard to believe, but he's getting worse," she complained to Ronnie the night NBC did a feature on the campaign.

"I didn't think it was possible," Ronnie snarled.

"This morning, he buzzed and asked me to pull a file for him. But the phone rang as I was taking it in. I was only on for about thirty seconds, but he came storming out and he yanked it from my hand and yelled, 'Wake up, okay!' so loud that the poor woman on the other end of the line heard it—I think she was more flustered than I was."

Ronnie clenched his fists. "I wish I could be there next time he does something like that. I'd . . . "

"Don't worry," she cut him off. "Our payback's gonna be sweeter than that. A lot sweeter."

"I'd just like to get him alone for a few minutes and shove some of his own medicine back down his throat."

"He'll get his. But don't you worry about me. Now that the great Mr. Duke is on his star tour, he's gone more than he's there. And he tends to check in at the same time of day when he's on the road, so I make it a habit of having call forwarding on when he calls."

Ronnie listened intently, fire in his eyes.

"At least I can relax a little and get some work done without having to fear for my sanity," she said.

Ronnie took a deep breath and gathered his thoughts. "Do you really think . . . Is it possible that we could really get in, get the gold, and get away before anybody was onto us?"

Ruth ground her teeth together and began to shake slightly. "I think my biggest worry is that someone else might actually find the gold before we get to it."

Ronnie looked down and sighed. "I don't know. I mean, nobody hates his guts as much as I do. But this . . . this seems so impossible. I'd rather just get him alone some time and show him what I think of his smug face."

Ruth clutched her husband, and they rocked back and forth. "Shh," she soothed, still shaking. "Shh . . . "

She stood in Gavin's quiet office the next morning, enjoying the fact that she could make use of his view while he was away. She looked out over the trees and rooftops below. The unusual calm of the office seemed to strengthen her resolve, and in the quiet her decision to take the gold looked realistic. Without the fear and tension present, the solution seemed to be within reach.

"I'm going to miss this place," she told herself. The phone jolted her back to the moment, and she scurried around Gavin's massive marble desk to return to being the efficient, professional Ruth everyone expected. "Ms. Gates? Why yes, of course. Those forms are on their way right now, via courier . . . " She turned to face out the window again, soaking up the view as she spoke, and let her mind wander to another plane altogether.

Far from Ruth's pensive gaze, two men sat in a bar in rural Georgia, watching one of Gavin's talk show appearances.

"I sure could use that million dollars," one said.

"So could I," said the other.

Thirteen

Walter Dwight sat on his regular stool at the bar, thinking pretty much the same thoughts he always thought there, destructive thoughts that led to a pit that, when a human being has sunk far enough into it and wallowed in it for a long enough period of time, becomes inescapable.

The bar was one of those junked roadside shacks that looked like it should have been condemned years ago, and it probably would have been if the county inspector weren't on the take. Pickup trucks and rusted-out old cars that couldn't fetch five hundred dollars in the classified ads sat on the gravel-topped parking lot, right off the two-lane country highway.

The sign above the door said "The Flying Dutchman's," but everybody called the place Dutchy's. There was no Dutchy; the place was run by a trio of brothers who also had an excavating business on the side.

Dutchy's sat just outside Murrowstown, a town of not more than a few hundred souls. People pass through in a hurry without ever knowing it's there. A little over an hour north of Atlanta, it was at least three decades away.

Murrowstown had been a company town, home to a big locally-based company that made carpet fibers for three generations. Until CM Processing came to town.

CM Processing was a big conglomerate, based up north, and was run by actuaries and accountants and attorneys and computers and shareholders instead of people, so there was no way it could understand the value of a single human life in Murrowstown—let alone the lives of 220 families. That is the number for whom, on a devastating Thursday afternoon, the tenth day of March in 1988, became as ingrained in their minds as a wedding day, a birthday, or the day a loved one died. That was the day the mill abruptly shut down, with no advance notice and no severance pay. Just one hour's warning, from the time the announcement was made at two P.M. until the end of the seven-to-three shift. The out-of-town conglomerate wanted only some machinery, some tax advantages, and a subsidiary of the home-grown company that did some mining and owned ore-rich land in South Carolina. The plant in Murrowstown—and the people who had given their lives to it—were expendable, mere numbers to a pro forma profit and loss statement, and red numbers at that. So they had to go. Quickly.

Walter Dwight was one of those numbers. He'd been a foreman, a seventeen-year man, who not long before that fateful day was promoted to full foreman on the night shift. His body was finally getting adjusted to breakfast at ten P.M., dinner at eight A.M., and seeing his kids for only half an hour each day. He was fast asleep when the announcement was made, dreaming of the vacation he and his wife were planning for sunny sandy beaches in Florida. They never got to go.

He stared into his brew and tried to forget. It would never go away. He hated his life—not being able to provide for his wife and his two sons—and he hated his anger. Walter did not read psychology books or attend seminars or have the money to seek counseling, so he had no idea that his anger was a result of fear and a deep spiritual void in his life. All he knew was that he inwardly burned, a raging bull on the edge of escalating a minor inconvenience into a fistfight, which happened occasionally.

He lived in a small trailer in what might technically be called a mobile home park but was too tightly squeezed for that. The rent for his tiny patch of earth was $58.50 a month, including the water hook-up, and the trailer was paid for—virtually the sole contributing factor to Walter's net worth of approximately five thousand dollars. He'd owned a home once, which, however Spartan, was still a house, fastened to the earth with concrete blocks and mortar instead of radial tires. Like the other families, his had kept up the payments for a time, obviously unable to sell a home in a town with no jobs, before having to turn it over to the bank. Of all the humiliations that can overtake a man, watching someone else come and take away your house—in front of your wife and children—cannot be understood until it has been laid upon you.

They lived on his life savings and whatever odd jobs a handyman can find in a town of 220 handymen and no money. The savings lasted about a year and a half, during which they lost the house, and by that time his settlement in a class action suit against CM—which none of the families really understood—had arrived in an official manila envelope. That took them another two years, not because it was much but because a little goes a long way when your living expenses have been gnawed to the bone. At least it bought the trailer.

Since that time, the number of odd jobs picked up—enough of the families had moved away that the competition to clean gutters or haul a stump had dwindled—and the government checks added enough that they could actually survive. But physical survival and emotional survival are a different matter, particularly to a man of forty-two with no more prospects, no more dreams, and no more hope.

At the next stool was a man named Reg Disney. Reg's face told the same story: nearly two decades at the plant and nothing but pain since. Only his tale was sadder still. For Reg had lost his family that day, or so he had decided since, and his anger and hatred and resentment were even more fully developed.

Reg had married Lily, his high school sweetheart, in a storybook tale of love that never accepted defeat. Her family had moved away just before their senior year, one of the rare long-distance moves in or out of Murrowstown, but Reg and Lily continued to write to each other over time and great distances. Circumstances always seemed to keep her far away, until one morning more than a decade later, when she simply showed up in Murrowstown, telling Reg she knew it was time. They were married after a whirlwind courtship, and had been together again for less than two years when the bomb dropped on the town.

His tragedy was that Lily had developed a bone marrow disorder, polycythemia, typically manageable with ongoing treatment. With no health coverage after the plant closing, and no money soon afterward, the young couple had no choice but to let the insurance lapse. Without regular treatments, a patient's blood pressure can steadily rise, leading to a heart attack. Lily survived the first but not the second, and Reg lost her just three short years after the factory was shut down.

They were married for almost a year when Lily gave birth to a son, a beautiful boy whose gentle spirit was a constant joy to them. He had a smile for everyone, one of those rare babies who gurgled and chirped and laughed but rarely cried. Lily named him Duane after her father, and she loved her son deeply.

But after Lily's death, Reg simply couldn't handle his son. Every time he looked at little Duane, he saw beautiful Lily's eyes, her smile, her cheekbones. Finally, he could simply no longer bear to look.

With no one to care for Duane, the state came in and took him away. He got to start a new life, to enjoy a family whose love and laughter would not end. Reg was left alone in Murrowstown.

Like Walter, he lived in a tiny trailer, and anyone who walked by at night could see Reg through the window, sitting motionless at the kitchen table, holding a framed photograph of a young couple, frozen happily together, far away from the trouble of the world.

Walter and Reg had known each other since they were kids, played high school football together, and worked at the plant together. They talked occasionally at Dutchy's and ate peanuts from the same dish. Walter had gone to Lily's funeral and bought Reg a beer after Duane was taken from him.

A ball game was just wrapping up on the TV—either Harry Caray announcing a Cubs game or Skip Caray calling a Braves game—and a talk show came on, starring none other than Gavin Duke. He was talking about hidden treasure, and the host played the obligatory marriage proposal tape to emphasize that this guest was the only man who knew where the gold was hidden. A brilliant stroke of planning, compliments of Carolina Gates Advertising's media department, had scheduled several of the bank's commercials to run during the show.

"Look at that guy, would ya?" Walter said, pointing at Gavin's face on the screen. "Everybody thinks he so smart, but he's pretty stupid if you ask me."

Reg turned toward Walter, holding his glass in the air, and thought for a moment before asking, "How do you figure that?"

"He knows where the money is, right? And nobody else knows where the money is, right? So why don't he just take it and hightail it out of town?"

"Maybe he's a millionaire already," Reg offered.

Walter pondered that one for a minute, then took a chug. "I still think he's stupid."

Reg hadn't been paying much attention to the TV, but Walter's comment had drawn his interest. He watched the interview for a minute, as members of the audience asked such profound questions as "Won't you tell me where it is?" and "What did you wear when you buried it?" He finally turned to Walter and asked, "What would you do if you found it?"

Walter laughed. "Ain't got no money in the bank, so they ain't sendin' me no clues," he said.

"Yeah, but what if you just happened on it?"

"What, like I just tripped over it on my way home from Dutchy's?"

"Yeah, what if?"

Walter shifted on the bar stool and coughed. "A million, huh? First thing is, I'd buy a round for everybody."

Reg nodded. "Good start. I bet you'd still have a little left over."

"You're probably right," Walter said. He sat and stared at his own face in the mirror across the bar. "This sounds a little corny, but I really think I'd do somethin' to help out around town. Y'know, the folks that got hardest hit. The little kids."

Reg thought of Duane, and of Lily, when Walter mentioned the folks that got hardest hit. *No amount of money in the world would bring them back*, he thought.

"What about you?" Walter asked, startling Reg out of his deep thought.

"Me? Ah—no way."

"What do you mean, no way? I answered you. Just make somethin' up."

No, Reg thought, *you can't buy away old wounds.* But still he lived in a broken-down trailer and had holes in the bottoms of his shoes. Maybe he deserved some temporal pleasures, to distract him from the pain, however momentary the diversion.

"Maybe . . . Maybe I'd get all cleaned up. Shave, new suit. Buy me a brand new car—no, hire me a stretch limousine, and a driver with a cap and a uniform, and drive all over the countryside, just lookin' out the window, safe and protected from everything, with my TV on and a cool one in my hand."

"Where would you go?" Walter asked.

"Go? I'd go out to the finest restaurant in downtown Atlanta, and I'd buy me the biggest, thickest steak you ever seen in your whole life. I'd buy y'all one too, if you want."

"Boy, that'd be somethin', wouldn't it? I haven't had a piece of steak in who knows how long," Walter added.

Leo, the bartender, had been listening in, and like all good barkeeps, felt the need to stop over and interject his two cents' worth.

"Know what I'd do?" Leo asked, leaning on the counter as he ran a rag around a glass mug and savored a toothpick. Leo was one of the last few fully employed people in Murrowstown, holding this job as long as anyone could remember, some twenty years or more. He was short, stout, balding, and wore thick horn-rimmed glasses.

"What's that, Leo?" Walter bit.

"I'd get me a boat. Not a little rowboat like you put out on the lake, but a real boat, two stories tall with dual engines, and I'd hire me a crew. Couple of guys like you two, and pay you a pretty good wage to cook for me and swab the deck when it needed it, and drive the boat when I got tired. But I'd be the captain, mind you, so I'd be at the helm most of the day. And I'd sail off for who knows where, maybe Australia, with a beautiful lady at my side. Yeah, Australia. And New Zealand. I always wanted to see Australia."

"I'd be honored to swab your yacht, Cap'n Leo," Reg said.

"Aye, aye," saluted Walter, and they shared one of the few good laughs the bar had seen in some time.

The three watched the rest of the talk show, as Gavin dodged questions like a pro. Walter looked over at Reg and wondered if Gavin had ever known the deep, unfilled longing he and his friends endured on a daily basis. *Not that pretty boy*, he concluded to himself, deciding to despise Gavin to the same degree that he hated the men who devoured his company, the politicians who let them do it, and anyone else who was no more noble but somehow managed to have a good job, a nice home, a car that worked, and the secure knowledge that supper would be on the table at the end of the day.

As they sauntered out of Dutchy's later that evening, walking the half mile or so along the highway from the bar to the trailer park, Walter let his thoughts escape.

"What do you think of guys like that?"

"Like who? Like Leo?" said Reg, obviously not thinking the same thoughts.

"No, like the guy from the bank—the pretty boy on TV."

"What do I think of 'em? I dunno. I'd like to have the life a guy like that has—everything he wants. Yeah, I'd like to be on TV, like him."

"But what do you think of him?"

"You kiddin'? He's one of those ivory tower wimps who always tries to keep guys like us down. He and his buddies gang up on us and hide behind their big bucks."

"That's exactly right," Walter said. "They keep pushin' us down, further and further, till there's no place left to go."

"Yep," Reg agreed. They continued to walk along silently until he asked, "So what? Why you thinkin' about all that?"

"I dunno," Walter said. "I's just wonderin' what it'd be like to have that million dollars, what I'd do."

"And what, you're just gonna pick up the phone, without no quarter to make the call with, and ask the operator to make a collect call? And you'd call him right up and ask him to tell you where he hid it 'cuz we're down on our luck?"

"Maybe I'll do just that," Walter said defensively.

"You go right ahead," Reg said. "Tell me what he says to you."

The two walked on, without exchanging another word, and each went to his trailer—Walter to his wife and two sons, Reg to the silence.

🌰   🌰   🌰

An hour or so later, Walter found himself still thinking about the gold and about the young smart aleck he'd seen on TV. He didn't understand why he kept coming back to it, since he'd known about sweepstakes and lotteries before and figured nothing good would ever happen to him. He went out for a walk, not necessarily going anywhere, but at least planning on passing Reg's trailer in the hope that Reg was out too.

His feet crunched across the gravel that covered the broken asphalt. From a distance, he could see the thin curtains slipping in and out of Reg's kitchen window in the breeze. The light was on. Walter approached that side, stood up on his toes, and placed his hands on the weathered lower frame of the window. He was about to call Reg's name but stopped after looking inside to see the sad, lonely figure of what once was a man but now only served as a hollow shell of painful memories and bitter defeats.

Reg was in his usual pose—hunched over the tiny table, a picture frame in his hands, not moving a muscle but staring intently at the image before him. In it were two strangers from the past, an attractive young man who looked vaguely familiar to someone who knew Reg now and a pretty young girl. They both wore spontaneous, loving smiles, and she was looking at him as he looked at the camera, as if she happened to get caught by the camera's shutter as she glanced over at the man she loved.

There were no tears in the sunken eyes, Walter noticed. There may have been years earlier, but Reg was all cried out. There was nothing left.

Walter lowered himself, slowly backed away from the window, and walked on into the night. He couldn't imagine how Reg had survived such crushing blows on top of everything else. He admired him, having to be even stronger than the rest of them.

As Walter walked along that night, he found himself being drawn further and further into his own private brawl, a struggle over what a million dollars meant, and why some men—lesser men than most of the guys from the plant, he felt—could sit on a stool and answer questions on TV before retreating to a life of luxury while he and his family and everyone and everything he knew just sat and rotted away.

"It ain't fair," he said several times as he walked along, oblivious to the cars whizzing by on the country highway. Walter had long since given up, like everyone else in Murrowstown, but this night he once again felt a spark he had not known in years. This was his last chance, his last hope. He had to search for that hidden gold. And maybe getting it wouldn't even matter—after all, he knew it was an impossible quest. Maybe this wasn't about money. Maybe it was about him, about being a man, and about living life instead of being a walking corpse, propped up and wandering around an endless maze of days that all ran together.

✍   ✍   ✍

Walter tossed and turned that night, unable to sleep. He had faced sleepless nights before but not in a long time. He used to square off in angry encounters with the visiting bosses of CM Processing, the robber barons that ruined his life and the lives of so many others. As many times as he fought that fight, there was no relief; the men returned night after night, and he always left them bloodied and begging for mercy. But the anger and the tension never seemed to fade. No justice was served. At the coaxing of his wife, who had more common sense than almost anyone else Walter had ever known, he decided to push the thoughts out of his head instead of replaying them in hopes of finally beating enough fairness back into the situation.

In the morning, Walter decided he needed a plan. He did not know what his objectives were, whether he wanted to search for the treasure or go to Washington or just let out a good long scream, but he knew he had to make one last grasp at living.

He walked over to Reg's again and knocked at the door. "Reg? You in there?"

"Yeah, what is it?"

"It's me, Walter. We gotta talk." They stood in the doorway.

"Reg, do you ever think about gettin' out of here?"

Reg stopped, and looked at Walter, and didn't say a word.

"I need to know somethin', Reg. Tell me if you think I'm crazy, but I think I gotta do somethin'."

"What exactly is it you think you gotta do?"

"That's just it. I dunno. But I can't stop thinkin' about this million dollars, the gold, and I want to do somethin'."

"Like, what, go dig for it?"

"Maybe. Maybe somethin' else."

"Well, what else you think you can do but go and get yourself a shovel?" Reg paused. "May not be a bad idea—got nothin' else to do all day long."

Walter's eyes lit up. "Let's go pay a visit to the pretty boy," he said.

"What for?" Reg laughed at him. "Like I said yesterday, he ain't gonna just hand you money 'cuz you ask him to."

"Maybe we won't ask. Maybe we can tell him to."

Reg looked straight at Walter. "What are you talkin' about?"

Walter breathed in and out, in a deep sigh. "We're just sittin' around here, waitin' to die," he said with such honesty he was surprised to hear himself uttering the words. Reg didn't seem surprised, as if the thought were familiar to him. "Maybe it's time to take one last chance at, I dunno, at gettin' out of this trap." He felt emptier having said those words and sighed again, not sure how Reg might reply.

Reg stepped silently over to the picture on the table and touched the glass that covered the image. "I don't know if I can get out of my trap," Reg said, as defeated as Walter had ever seen.

"Well, we ain't gonna find out sittin' around here, or over at Dutchy's, starin' at the TV, or at some old . . . "

Reg looked up quickly and glared at Walter to stop him from invading his private nightmare. The stare was uncomfortable, and it didn't take Reg long to melt, his eyes falling to the floor, then rising back to the photo, and finally to Walter again, without the glimmer of passion.

"How can we just tell him he's gonna give us the million dollars? He works at a bank. You want us to go and rob a bank?"

Walter shrugged.

"Well, what then?" Reg raised his voice and his arms. He was right—they couldn't just waltz into a First Southern branch, à la Butch Cassidy and the Sundance Kid, stick a Colt .45 in Gavin's ribs, and demand the loot. But Gavin, all by himself, was just one person, and he didn't live at the bank . . .

"Maybe we can follow the pretty boy home, and get him when he's alone, and make him tell us."

"Like one of them car-jackings on the news?" Reg asked.

"Maybe. Or maybe we'd just get him at his house."

"You talkin' prison here, man," Reg said. "You don't just go stick a sawed-off in somebody's face and get away with it. He'd call the cops the second we left, and we'd be busted before we'd ever lay eyes on any money. Besides, even as much as all them big company boys've done to us, I don't wanna hurt nobody."

"I don't wanna hurt nobody neither," Walter said quickly, "but I can't go on like this forever. I gotta do somethin'. We gotta do somethin'."

"Well, you just lemme know if you come up with a great idea," Reg said, walking into the bathroom and closing the door to end the conversation.

Walter looked down, the daily feeling of defeat returning to his tired body. He walked out and went back home.

＊＊＊

That night, as Walter began to replay his conversation with Reg, things started to fall into place. *Make the pretty boy tell us where it is. Catch him alone. But he'll call the cops. Okay, tie him up long enough so they'd have time to get the money and get away. But what if he lives with somebody, or somebody comes by? Okay, take him away. Take him away. Take him away!* Walter sat up in bed. *It's late,* he thought. *I can't believe I'm thinking of this. We kidnap the pretty boy, tuck him away somewhere around here—nobody'd ever come looking up here—heck, those people don't even know we exist. We make him tell us where it is and split. A million bucks? We can go anywhere we want. We can do Leo's thing, get a yacht and have our own world, or . . . Who knows? Who cares? We'd have the money, so the sky's the limit. And we won't hurt him—no, no. Just tie him up, muss up his pretty hair a little, and let him go when it's all over. Nobody gets hurt, and we get out of this dump.*

Morning took forever to come. Walter headed back over to Reg's.

"Reg, listen to me. You know how they took our jobs, and they said it's nobody's fault, it's just a business decision?"

"Yeah," frowned Reg. He didn't need to hear this again.

"If we took the money, but nobody got hurt—it'd be the same, right? Nobody's money, nobody has to go hungry. Just some pencil-pusher's problem."

Reg was starting to pay attention now. Crazy as it was, there was some sense to what Walter was saying.

"It's not like takin' it from anybody. Heck, it'd be our own way of settlin' the score a little, wouldn't it? Spittin' in the eye of some great big company, the little guy havin' the upper hand for once."

Reg didn't know exactly where Walter was going with all this excitement, but he liked the words so far.

"We can do it, Reg. We can make the pretty boy tell us where it is, and nobody gets hurt," he said again, working hard to convince himself it was possible.

Reg finally spoke. "How we gonna do that?"

"We grab him on his way home or somethin', and bring him up here, and hide him away where nobody'll find him. We make him tell us where he hid it, where he hid the gold, and we keep him here under wraps while we go get it. That's it."

Reg soaked it in. "You mean, we tie him up, and gag him, and keep him here? We just go dig up the gold, where he tells us he hid it? Then we let him go?"

Walter hadn't thought through that part. "I guess we let him go. Or we just figure somebody'll find him, after we're gone. I dunno. I haven't thought of everythin' yet."

"Man, they could send us to jail," Reg said.

"So what? So what! Maybe jail'd be better than this! At least I'd know there'll be food on the table."

Reg looked over and saw the picture on the table and dropped his head. What if Lily and Duane had seen him like this, a man so desperate that jail looked good and kidnapping a man looked even better?

"I have to think about it some," Reg said, not sure how much resistance he could muster in his broken spirit.

"Yeah, me too," Walter said, also looking toward the floor. And with that, he walked outside, squinting against the bright morning sun, torn between feeling the anger he thought he had managed to hide away and the long lost feeling of hope, a sensation he never knew he would be able to recapture.

Fourteen

Gavin was starting to get fan mail now.

Women sent him photos from all over the country and from places as diverse as the Philippines and Russia. "What am I, the Department of Immigration and Naturalization?" Thanks to CNN and the *International Herald-Tribune*, he had become the global symbol of the rich American. Purists wrote and condemned him for promoting greed and avarice. *They do have a point*, he thought. *After all, we are promoting greed and avarice.* Where they parted ways was that Gavin didn't think there was anything wrong with that. College kids sent their resumés, wanting to be associated with the happening bank, and many decided buttering up to Gavin for how brilliant he was would be a good place to start. School children wrote, asking for more information on the Civil War connection. Eager prospectors wrote asking for guidance on their interpretations of the latest clues. And fellow admen from around the country dropped him short notes on how brilliant a scheme he had developed.

There were also handwritten notes from Marni—twice—congratulating Gavin on the success of Southern Gold and tap-dancing around the idea of getting together after work some night. But neither note ever received an answer after being rapidly wadded up and chucked into Gavin's kitchen garbage can.

People were asking for his autograph too. One afternoon, as he was taking a two-block walk to lunch with Torrie, three individuals stopped and asked him to sign something—one woman had a copy of *People* magazine, which she dug out of her big canvas bag. Torrie was amused to see how patiently he waited while the lady rummaged through her belongings, in search of her collectors-item-to-be.

"We've had a chance to get together a little more often lately," Torrie told her friend Nancy, from the singles group at her church. She still called Anita from time to time, drawing great strength from the friendship, but she enjoyed having some Christian friends closer to home.

"You don't sound all that happy about it though," Nancy said, puckering her lips and blowing to cool a spoonful of soup.

Torrie crunched into a spinach leaf. "I think God's showing me what I need to do," she said slowly.

"Which is . . . ?"

Torrie took a sip of her diet Coke and stared at the plant across the room. "I love the way Gavin's mind works," she said, not quite ready to admit her conclusion to Nancy—or to herself. "He's so quick, and he sees things like nobody else does."

"I've noticed that, the few times I've seen him on those talk shows."

"And he's funny, and polite to me, and so romantic—I never knew a girl could get so many flowers."

"But," Nancy said.

"But he seems to treat everybody else, well, differently."

"How?"

"The other night we were out at dinner, and they got his order wrong. He called the waiter stupid, right to his face."

Nancy just listened.

"And at the office the other day, I had just come in and he didn't know I was there yet. I was talking to Ruth, and he came flying out the door, yelling at her, but when he saw me he stopped and pretended he was just kidding, and he went to put his arm around Ruth, like it's some inside joke and they're best buddies or something."

"How did Ruth react? I mean, is there a chance he was telling the truth?"

Torrie just looked down.

"So, what do you think God's trying to tell you?"

"I think it's time I . . . we . . . "

"You think you need to break up with him?"

"It's not that simple. I mean, I have to see him almost every day—for the paper. He's my assignment, you know."

"That does complicate things."

"And even then, I don't know. I mean, when we're together, I've had some opportunities to drop some hints."

"Hints?"

"Yeah. Things like saying how much God has blessed me lately, and a couple of times I've been able to quote part of a psalm or two. Just the other day, we were talking about one of the big charities, and I brought up the parable about the widow and her two pennies."

"And how does he react?"

Torrie sighed. "He seems to let everything fly by."

"Have you invited him to church yet?"

"Almost. A couple of times, it seemed the conversation was getting there, but we always seem to get sidetracked. I guess I just need to make it happen."

"I think that'll be a turning point for your relationship," Nancy said.

"I'm afraid so," Torrie agreed. "One way or another. And I think I know which way it's gonna go."

"When will you see him next?"

"Lunch. Tomorrow."

"I can't wait to hear about it."

It was late, and Gavin was tired. He eased the Mercedes into the driveway after a sixteen-hour day, loosening his tie as he killed the headlights. Dawn flight to New York. Makeup. Same old interview for the nine thousandth time. Traffic jam back to LaGuardia. Swallow a chili dog whole at the airport for lunch. Puddle-jump to Philly. More makeup. Repeat interview. Repeat traffic jam to airport. Repeat lunch for dinner. Home.

He sifted through the mail, glad that none of the stuff from work managed to find him while he was off-duty. But it was time for his monthly check from his dad.

Gavin tossed the rest of the mail on the kitchen counter and fingered the envelope. No need to open it—he knew what was inside. He stared at the postmark, crinkling the paper between his fingers. "I don't need this," he said out loud. "I don't need this at all. And I sure don't need you in my face all the time."

He picked up the letter opener and skewered the envelope, right through the heart. "Take a hike, old man," he said, withdrawing the dagger and laying it back down on the countertop. He stuck his thumb through the small hole and tore the envelope and its contents in half.

"Good night, Dad," he sneered as he flipped the letter and the check into the trash. He lumbered from the room without turning out the light and fell into bed.

❧   ❧   ❧

"Have you gotten any indication that anyone's coming close to the gold?" Torrie asked Gavin, assuming a pose that in no way resembled the way a reporter was supposed to look on an interview. She leaned near him over their cozy table at a breezy outdoor cafe, her gaze melting his heart.

"We keep having to sift through the pile of crank letters and crank calls, because some seem to make sense," he told her. Even though this was Torrie, he still couldn't give her any solid hints as to where the treasure was hidden, which meant he couldn't let her in on the message he got last week: "Can you confirm for me that the gold is hidden on the Chattahoochee, along the Georgia-Alabama border?" The day before that, Ruth showed him a letter that asked, "Please write back and tell me if I'm right. I think it's hidden in the Chattahoochee, but I have no idea how to look for it there. What do I do if I know where it is but can't afford to hire a dredging company to bring it up? Can you help me with this? You don't have to tell me exactly where it's sunken, but please just tell me if it's in the river and how to handle this."

"My greatest joy in all this," he said with his mouth full, "is that the genuine level of interest has crossed all socio-economic lines. Everybody is talking about it and thinking about it all the time."

Torrie cleared her throat as Gavin tore off another bite. "Listen, I was thinking. This weekend, this Sunday, in fact, I . . . "

Gavin's portable phone rang from inside his jacket pocket. He raised his finger up in the air, chewed faster, wiped his mouth with his napkin, and washed everything down with a quick gulp. "Just a second," he blurted out as he reached for the phone and yanked it to his ear.

"They *what?*" Gavin's face turned beet red. "Those idiots! How can any human being be so pathetically stupid? No, I'll be right there."

Torrie fell back into her chair and sighed. *No wonder they call it spiritual warfare*, she thought.

He shoved the phone back into his pocket and threw a twenty on the table. "Look, Torrie, I'm sorry, there's a major fire I've gotta go douse. I'll have Ruth give you a buzz and let you know when we can finish the interview, okay?"

"Well, actually, I think I've pretty much covered all the . . ."

"Later," he said, pecking her on the cheek as he careened away.

"Yeah. Bye," she mumbled, toying with her fork. "See you later."

🌑   🌑   🌑

Two men in Murrowstown were thinking about Gavin Duke and the gold too.

Reg and Walter sat on the back steps of Dutchy's, talking over their plan.

"Would it really change our lives? I mean, yeah, we wouldn't be stuck here any more. But who's to say bein' stuck someplace else is gonna be any better? We'll never be able to come back, even if we wanted. We'd have to be lookin' over our shoulders for the rest of our lives."

"I don't think I'd worry too much about comin' back," Walter snapped. "I think once we got out of this place, and I mean really got out, we wouldn't ever wanna see it again."

"Fine. So we don't come back. But like I said, how do you know it's gonna be better anyplace else?"

"All I know's one thing," Walter said, staring off toward the trees. "It can't be worse."

"That's for sure," sighed Reg. The breeze blew through the heavy, aging limbs and branches as they paused to consider their immediate future.

"Have you been thinkin' about where we'd go?" Reg asked.

"Yeah, I been thinkin' about it. I got an idea. I dunno if you'll like it or not. I think I do, but I ain't sure yet."

"What's that?"

"Mexico. They can't touch us there. We'd be safe. Weather's good—warm and sunny, not much rain."

"Oh, and you know how to speak Spanish?" Reg asked.

"No, I don't speak no Spanish. But we won't need to. I saw an ad in the back of some magazine, where lots of Americans are movin' down there. Don't even have to be rich ones. Just regular folks, like you and me. They're puttin' up neighborhoods, only American, so you don't have to know no Spanish. Places for folks to retire where it's warm and nice."

Walter had figured out that they couldn't really live high on the hog after splitting the million dollars. They'd have to live off their share for the rest of their lives. Walter figured he'd pay cash for a nice enough house—a hundred grand would buy a place that'd feel like a mansion to him—which left another $400,000. Without a house payment, he figured they'd live like royalty for about twenty grand a year. That meant the money would last exactly twenty years, if it wasn't drawing any interest. He had no idea how to calculate compounding interest, so he just guessed it'd end up adding about five more years. That bought him twenty-five years in paradise, with no worries, no work, and no pain.

He and Reg had talked about the numbers, and Reg felt even better about his share. He didn't need a house, just a one-bedroom apartment, so he wouldn't lose a hundred thou at the outset. And being single now, his expenses would be less. He planned on being able to travel more, spending his ill-gotten gain on riding jumbo jets to distant lands.

The more Reg thought about Mexico, the more comfortable the

plan became. The perfect getaway, far from U.S. agents, and far from Murrowstown.

"You been thinkin' about where we gonna keep the pretty boy after we go find the gold?" Reg asked the mastermind.

"I got a couple ideas. We could stash him at the plant."

Reg looked up from the spot on the ground where he had fixed his gaze. Even if the plant had been the perfect spot, he never wanted to set foot there again. Not even for this, his sweet revenge.

"Kids go in there and fool around all the time, don't they?" he asked, hoping to eliminate the option before his true feelings had to be made known.

"You mean like high school kids and their girlyfriends? Yeah, I think you're right. Somebody'd find him."

"What's your other idea?"

"Old huntin' cabin, out in the woods."

"Where's that?"

"You know. Ol' Man Steinbeck's place, near Wahoo Creek."

"He's been gone for a long time," Reg said.

"Yeah, and ain't nobody's bought it. It's settin' up there with nobody for miles around."

"How do you know?" Reg asked. "When's the last time you been up there?"

"I dunno, not too long," the ringleader said sheepishly. "But I bet nobody's been there."

"Maybe we better check it out," Reg said.

"That's not a bad idea," Walter perked up, feeling the life being breathed back into his idea.

"When you wanna go?"

Walter paused. "How about now?"

Reg got up. No planes to catch, no calls to make. The two walked off. Neither owned a car any more. Why have a car when there's no place to go? Besides, they didn't have the money to sink into one, even the $300 specials parked outside Dutchy's. They didn't even have a dollar for a gallon of gas.

🥔   🥔   🥔

Old Man Steinbeck's cabin was a good four- or five-mile hike into the hills. It was a heavily wooded area, so the going wasn't easy for the last half mile, after they hopped the old gate at the side of the road and plunged into the thick forest. The driveway was never more than a pair of ruts which matched the width of the axle on Steinbeck's pickup, and since his death, the weeds and vines and saplings had reclaimed the path in the name of nature. He'd passed away right inside the cabin, a victim more of old age and crankiness than anything else, to the best of anyone's guess. He'd been there for more than a week before anyone found him; the mail piled up long enough at his house that the mailman called the sheriff, who discovered Steinbeck hunched over the table inside the cabin, apparently succumbing as he loaded shells into his shotgun. An appropriate end for a man whose greatest joy was filling an amply antlered buck with lead.

"Are you sure we're still on the path?" Reg complained after what seemed like an inordinately long and frustrating battle through the overgrown kudzu vines.

"Yeah, look, I can still see the ridge between the tire ruts," Walter fussed back. "Let's keep movin', we's almost there."

The woods were so thick that even on a sultry day, it felt cool in here. That was the only redeeming factor in their mission as they continued to stumble along. A squirrel darted up a tree, just inches from the two, startling them as much as they had surprised the animal. "Wish I had me a pea-shooter," Walter said, but Reg didn't hear him. He'd just looked up and seen the edge of a roofline.

"That's it," Reg shouted. Walter looked up and smiled a rare smile.

It was a nondescript little brown building, really a shack, with a rusted tin roof. The cabin was a perfect square, only one room, maybe twelve feet by twelve. There was an old capped-off pipe that acted as a chimney of sorts, jutting up from the roof. In front, there was a door and one window. There was another window around the back, and that was all that interrupted the long-ago stained plywood boards Steinbeck had used as facing. They were now rotting and starting to pop off. The cabin was tiny and ugly, but to Walter and Reg, it may as well have been the Taj Mahal.

"Well, looky here," said Walter, walking a circle around it, as Reg followed. They came to the door again. There was no knob, just a latch—the kind a man might put on a tool kit, where a padlock would go. There was no lock on it, so Walter pushed the door open and entered the tiny, dark room. In the center was the table, the table where Steinbeck had died, and the hard wooden chair where he'd been sitting. Behind the chair was a small cupboard, and across the room, in the corner, was the old cast-iron stove he used to heat the place and cook some venison from time to time. A pipe shot straight up from the stove through the ceiling, leading out to the metal chimney he'd seen from the outside. There were no curtains or shades and no pictures hanging on the walls, no hooks or evidence that there ever had been any, no electric outlets, and no sign of running water.

The two took it all in quietly. Reg was the first to speak.

"Shoot, this is perfect," he said.

"Nobody'd ever find the pretty boy out here," Walter said.

"Nobody'd ever come lookin'," Reg agreed.

"We'd need to fix it up a little," Walter suggested. "Need to board them windows shut. Bring in a couple more chairs, so we can watch him. Maybe a radio, so there would be somethin' to do. And some food and water." He went over to the cupboard, a crude box about the size of a medicine cabinet, and swung the door open. There were three shelves, relatively evenly spaced. On the top shelf there was an empty box that once held shotgun ammunition.

Reg sat down in the chair, tired from the long walk. He wiped his forehead with his sleeve. Walter sat up on the table and wiped his brow with a stained old handkerchief he had pulled from his pocket.

"How we gonna get him here?" Reg wondered.

That was a good question. And a big problem. Besides the fact that they had no car, they had no idea how, when, or where they could capture Gavin. Worse still, they had to get all the way to Atlanta and back.

Walter stared hard at the wall, as if hoping to see the answer written there. He tried to put things together as best as he could. "How about Dutchy's van?" he offered. A beat-up van sat behind Dutchy's, which Leo used on occasion to haul supplies to and from the bar. It belonged to the three brothers who owned the place, but they left it there because they had enough vehicles of their own, compliments of guys like Reg and Walter and a hundred others who spent what little money they had at Dutchy's.

Dutchy's van is a great idea, Reg thought. *We could make up some story to Leo, about getting work in the next county, and vanish with it for a day or two. Leo won't bat an eyelash—he'd help us out in a heartbeat. And between the two of us, we could manage to scrape together twenty bucks for a full tank of gas. The government check will cover that, and it doesn't matter that losing the extra ten apiece will mean we won't make it to the end of the month—by the end of the month, we'll have a million dollars in gold!*

That still left the problem of finding their target. Where was the bank? Where did the pretty boy live? When could they grab him unnoticed? There was no way around it. They simply had to go to Atlanta before knowing the rest of their plan, and they'd have to wing it.

"Where'd we stay?" Reg asked, as they made their way back through the woods toward the road.

Walter thought a minute, then answered. "Big cities always got places you can sleep—big churches downtown got cots and places like that for homeless people." The word *homeless* caught him off guard. Was it possible that he was actually better off than someone else? He quickly erased the idea. "But I ain't sure we're gonna have to stay the night there. We might get a break and get it done in a hurry."

Reg wasn't sure if he wanted to laugh or cry when Walter suggested they might get "lucky." Luck was not a commodity either man had ever experienced.

"We need a shotgun or something for this?" Reg wondered.

"Probably not, if we catch the pretty boy at home. But I guess it can't hurt. Shotgun apiece, and maybe a good hunting knife."

That was perhaps the easiest part of the plan to execute. Each still kept his trusty shotgun—it was a potential source of food as well as a badge of manhood, so selling it was not an option. And between them, they also had three good knives.

Over the next few days, they made all the final preparations. Another grueling trip to Steinbeck's cabin, to stock up on bottled water as well as some canned food, crackers, a can opener, three spoons, matches and wood for the stove, some old blankets to sleep on, a flashlight, the extra chair, and a padlock for the door. They boarded up the windows good and tight, not so much fearful of anyone seeing Gavin inside or hearing his cries for help but to make his escape more difficult.

Reg snuck up one more item as well. He may have been embarrassed if he'd have thought about Walter's possible reaction, but he decided to not worry about Walter. Reg brought the photo of himself and Lily on their honeymoon, the one he stared into at night. Wrenching as that photograph was to him, it was his only source of stability, of security in a frighteningly insecure and unstable world. He wanted it to be here when they arrived with Gavin, immediately after the traumatic event that would free him from his present life.

Once the cabin was set, they approached Leo about the van. "No problem," he said, glad for them that they had found both work and the desire to take it. "Except you don't have a license any more, do you?" Both Walter and Reg froze. He was right; they'd both let their driver's licenses expire.

"'Course I have my license," Walter lied. *After all*, he thought, *what's the big deal?*

"Okay," Leo said slowly, not sure he believed him but not wanting any trouble. "When do you want it?"

Walter and Reg looked at each other. "Tomorrow. Tomorrow afternoon," Walter said, having to work up the courage to answer.

"All right. I've gotta get some napkins and a few other things from the distributor over in the next county," Leo said, "so I'll take care of that this afternoon. Just come by tomorrow, and it'll be all yours."

"Thanks, Leo. Thanks a million," Walter said, missing the irony of his words. The two started to walk out when Leo called after them. "Come here, guys."

They nervously walked back to the bar, not having the faintest idea what to expect.

"I'll fill up the tank for you," he said under the din of the jukebox. "The boys'll never know. Just keep it between us, okay?"

"You're the best, Leo. The best," Reg said.

"You're a good one, Leo," Walter added. Both made a mental note to make sure at least one gold bar fell Leo's way.

🐚   🐚   🐚

Both men had restless nights. Walter had told his wife the same story he'd made up for Leo—a good job in the next county, a day or maybe two, for him and Reg. He'd be back with a good-sized roll of money. He felt the decision to not tell her was an obvious one, and Reg agreed immediately when they'd discussed it. No need to get her all upset, or risk having one of the boys hear, or having her try and talk them out of doing it.

"Why are you taking your shotgun?" she asked that morning, startling him from behind as he pulled it from under the bed and tried to unwrap it carefully from the fabric to give it one last check before putting it in the van.

"Uh, might get some huntin' in tonight, after work. Small game."

"You're gonna use that big ol' thing to go after small game?" she asked, more astute and suspicious than he'd expected.

"It's the only gun I got, okay?" he shot back. She left it at that and went into the other room, back to another talk show that had asked Gavin to be the guest.

Now why couldn't I have bagged me a man like that? she wished to herself.

Walter sped out, not really saying good-bye, and stopped at Reg's trailer. "Set?" he said, poking his head in.

"Let's roll," Reg said, sounding as though he'd seen one too many action-adventure films but genuinely meaning it from the heart.

They loaded the guns into the van, carrying the knives with them. "How much money we got?" asked Walter.

Reg pulled out a few small bills from his pocket. He'd kept a stash at home, inside an old ragged envelope that was taped to the bottom of the war-torn sofa. It had thirty-three dollars in it, safely tucked away for an emergency. That, along with what he'd had already in his pocket, came to $38.47.

"And I got twenty in change," Walter said, "so that makes almost sixty between us. That should be more than enough to last as long as we need."

"Hope this don't take long," Reg sneered.

They pushed through the back door of Dutchy's, since the place wasn't opened yet, to get the keys from Leo. It was only around eleven, and Leo wasn't normally there this early, but he'd agreed to do a favor for the guys, and Leo always kept his word.

"Good luck, fellas," was all he said.

🔹 🔹 🔹

Walter drove, being careful to stay with the flow of traffic, since being pulled over without a license in a van that belonged to someone else—someone who didn't know he was driving it—with two shotguns wrapped up in the back and carrying a concealed knife might lead to trouble. He was extremely nervous, not having driven at all during the past few years, and not being used to the excessive speeds one finds on the ten-lane highways that feed into Atlanta.

They pulled off at a coffee shop as the country vanished into suburbs. There was work to be done; they had to get a paper and check the phone book, so they'd know the pretty boy's name for sure as well as the location of the bank. Walter ordered a cup of coffee, black, and Reg asked for an ice water. They sat at the counter, and Reg looked over the paper as Walter made carefully planned small talk with the waitress.

"Gavin Duke. Gavin Duke," Reg repeated to himself, so as to be certain he wouldn't forget, gleaning the needed information from an article about a false alarm in Augusta—a couple of teenagers, fishing in the ponds near the fairgrounds, got a line caught at the bottom. One jumped in and nearly panicked when he realized the line was caught on a large crate, which he naturally assumed was the treasure. His friend had to rescue him from drowning, and when they finally got themselves calmed down enough and pulled it up, it turned out to be nothing more than a big wooden box filled with sludge, rusting scrap metal, and a collection of stripped gears from some old engines. Still, the story made the papers and the teens got their fifteen minutes of fame, if not their treasure, and their toothy grins were plastered all over every newspaper in the state.

As Reg was catching up on all this, Walter asked the waitress, "Been lookin' for the gold?"

At any other time, such a question might have been met with a quizzical look, but not here and definitely not now. She looked up at Walter, smiled a big smile, and sweetly said, "Been thinkin' about it."

"Where do folks around here think it is?"

"Most everybody I talk to says it's probably underwater some- where," she said, "but I don't know. They keep talkin' about it being buried treasure, not sunken treasure, and besides, if they put it in the mud instead of some old hole in the ground, how are they gonna be sure it's still gonna be there when somebody goes to pull it up?" She was obviously too smart to be pouring coffee for a living, and Walter wondered if this was just a temporary job for her, or if life had played a cruel joke on this woman and stuck her in a place she didn't want to be, like so many of the people back in Murrowstown.

"You sure convinced me," Walter smiled, feeling the warmth of the coffee on the outside of the cup. "But a lot of the ladies I've talked to think the real treasure is this bank fella—the one who's on all them TV shows."

"Ooh, Gavin!" she swooned, all of a sudden looking more like a teenager than a mature young woman. She flattened her hand across her heart and rolled her eyes to the ceiling.

"What's the story on him, anyway? What do y'all know about him?"

"He's gorgeous and rich and successful . . . "

" . . . and he's the only one who knows where the gold is, right?" Walter finished the sentence for her.

"I'd sure like a try at gettin' it out of him," she laughed.

Walter laughed too, and thought, *Yeah, so would I.* "He's here in Atlanta, ain't he?"

"Oh, yeah, except when he's off on TV somewhere. One of the papers just said he was the most eligible bachelor in town. Whoo-ee!" She fanned herself with the little pad she used for taking orders.

"Where's he live? What part of town?" Walter pushed, eager to know more.

"What's with all the questions?" she asked, putting her hands on her skinny hips. "You planning on paying Gavin Duke a visit?"

"You might say that," Walter answered, feeling newfound strength just by being away from the oppressive air of Murrowstown.

"I don't know where he lives," she said, "probably some big ol' mansion with white pillars somewhere."

Reg had put down the paper by now and was ready to go. He nodded at Walter, indicating he'd found out what he wanted. Walter put enough change on the counter to pay for the coffee, plus a quarter for a tip, thanked the waitress, and the two went back to the van.

"The name's Gavin Duke, and he's the vice president at First Southern Bank," Reg reported. He pulled out a wrinkled chunk of paper, which he'd torn from the phone book on his way to the bathroom. It was the white pages listing for First Southern, complete with phone numbers and the bank's address: First Southern Tower. "I think if we just head straight downtown, we'll be there," he said, so Walter backed up the van, turned it around, and got back onto the highway, being careful not to arouse the suspicion of any cops.

The drive into downtown Atlanta is a marvelous experience for anyone not bored by gleaming skylines. The cityscape blends varying styles of architecture, highlighted by several masterpieces of modern construction, including the First Southern Tower. Neither Reg nor Walter wanted to sound like little wide-eyed kids, so they both kept their awe to themselves. It had been so long since either had been here, and with the city's rapid growth, it looked completely different. Neither of them had seen a building more than three stories tall in several years, so the experience took them somewhat by surprise.

Walter took the exit that seemed to make the most sense and circled the streets that looped between the tall buildings, hoping to see a First Southern sign. No such luck. They finally rolled down the window and asked for help, learning they were only two blocks away. They edged up the street, and the massive entryway finally came into view. There it was, in big golden letters, above the revolving doors: First Southern Bank.

They circled the block, realizing now they had to find a parking space. Walter was amazed that all the parking garages wanted six dollars, eight dollars, or more—after all, the two men only had sixty dollars between them—but he decided he had no choice. Anyway, this time tomorrow, they would have their hands on one million dollars in cold, hard gold.

They parked on the fifth deck of the garage and worked their way back to street level. The traffic noise, the sounds of the crowd, all those people and cars, and the massive buildings as far as the eye could see—it was almost too much for them. They looked up the street, then back down the other way, before Reg recognized the side of the Tower's ground floor, pointed it out to Walter, and started off in that direction.

The initial part of the plan was simple—scope the place out. Get a feel for it. See if they could determine exactly where Gavin worked, and try and find out where he might be going.

They wandered from one end of the lobby to another, trying not to look too suspicious, especially since they had seen plenty of security guards—two standing inside the bank lobby itself and another sitting behind a big raised desk that blocked the way to the elevators. There was a massive building directory on the wall, white lettering on a black background, under glass. "Let's go take a look at that," Walter pointed.

Under First Southern, the listings were massive and confusing. Comptroller, Fiduciary, Municipal and Treasury Bonds—this was all gibberish to them. It was time for a bold step. Walter strode over to the security man behind the oversized desk.

"May I help you?" the man asked.

"We're lookin' for Gavin Duke's office, at the bank," Walter said, sounding as important as he could. But he may as well have said he was looking for the President of the United States while carrying a bazooka in each hand, given the reaction he got.

The security guard stiffened up and he reached for a black phone that was behind the desk but that Walter had not noticed before. "Do you have an appointment?"

Uh-oh, both Reg and Walter thought, *we're not the first to want to talk to Gavin Duke.*

"No, uh, no appointment. We're just a couple of old friends from out of town, and we thought we'd stop in to say hello while we was passin' through."

The guard put the phone back in its place. "Friends of his, huh? Yeah, sure. And the gold is buried in my backyard. I'll tell you what, that man's got more friends than anybody I've ever known. Sorry, guys, if you want to see Mr. Duke, you'd better call his office and make an appointment. Then, I can let you in."

Walter and Reg exchanged a glance and walked off without a word.

"What're we gonna do now?" Reg asked.

"Hope we can figure that out," Walter told him.

But there was nothing left to figure out. Here were two guys, complete strangers in a major metropolis, with no money to speak of, no connections, and no way to go about smoking out this man.

Having been well versed in dropping hope over the years, they just seemed to give up and decided to wander around downtown. It was a unique diversion for them, almost like a vacation. "It ain't like Ol' Man Steinbeck's cabin in the woods," Reg finally observed, and Walter nodded his assent as they turned another corner, filled with awe at the difference between this place and their place.

They settled into a bar, not like Dutchy's, of course, but a place they could rest their weary legs and their heavy hearts over a cold drink and maybe snag some nuts and pretzels too. It was dark inside, and air conditioned, unlike their regular hangout. A bevy of waitresses scurried about the floor.

The snack food was both lunch and dinner that afternoon. They'd wait a while and maybe buy a hot dog or a sandwich later, still pinching pennies, despite the dream of carrying home a lost treasure.

They emptied their drinks, just one each, and paid the tab but didn't leave a tip. They walked back onto the street to find the sun beginning its descent. They were about three blocks from the bank, so they started back in that direction, still not sure what to do.

"Maybe that security guard had to go home," Walter said.

"Yeah," Reg piped in. "Maybe they got shifts, like they had at the plant, or maybe they just send him home, and don't keep nobody there after the bankers' hours end."

"Let's go find out," Walter said.

They pushed through the revolving doors of the lobby and made their way toward the elevators. The man behind the desk was new—the evening shift—so Reg and Walter tried one more time.

"Hey, we just stopped by to see Gavin Duke for a second."

The evening guy, who apparently didn't get as many cranks looking for Gavin as the daytime guard, had a different attitude altogether. "Sorry, you just missed him."

They couldn't believe their ears. Walter froze. "Just missed him?" Reg managed to blurt out.

"Yeah," the helpful security man said. "Couldn't have been more than a minute or two ago—he was over in the bank lobby, walked right across here and into the parking garage. Too bad—a couple of minutes earlier, and you might have run right into him. Guess you'll just have to try tomorrow."

"Thanks," said Reg, not sure if this was agonizing or wonderful.

They walked out into the street, each contemplating the same dilemma, and started to head back to the van, knowing the adventure was over for this day.

Then it happened.

They were on the sidewalk, where the mouth of the First Southern parking garage empties into the street. Without warning, a big black Mercedes, headlights glaring, screeched around the last bend of the garage and came flying over the sidewalk and onto the street. Reg yanked Walter out of the way as the corner of the car's rear bumper came within an inch or two of Walter's pant leg. They whirled to curse the car and its driver, when both saw the license plate at the same time. It was a vanity plate, the letters on the plate as clear as day. It said, *GAVIN.*

Their hearts still racing from the near-accident, they took off down Peachtree Street, knowing they couldn't outrun a maniac in a turbo-powered Mercedes but hoping against hope to at least catch a glimpse of his face if he hit a stoplight in the next block or two.

At the next corner, the intersection of Peachtree and Luckie Street—of all streets—Gavin did indeed hit a red light. The two panting men reached the corner just as the light changed to green and

Gavin, first in line, took off like lightning. But he was there long enough for them to make out two distinct figures—a beautiful brunette in the passenger seat, with shoulder length hair, laughing as they spoke, and next to her, the man they had seen on TV in Dutchy's a few fateful nights earlier. The Gavin who owned the license plate and the car was none other than Gavin Duke.

The rest of the traffic followed Gavin's Mercedes into the evening, leaving the two men gasping for air at the street corner. They looked at each other as they caught their wind, still without exchanging a word over the events of the last few frenetic moments.

"Tomorrow's our day," Reg said.

They walked a couple blocks to the McDonald's they had seen earlier that afternoon. The pretzels and nuts hadn't been enough, so they each got a Big Mac, some fries, and a Coke. They sat down in a corner booth and talked through their rapidly developing circumstances.

"We just gotta follow him out when he leaves tomorrow, and see where he lives. It's that simple," Walter said.

"No, it ain't that easy," Reg corrected. "We don't know when he's gonna leave, and we can't just sit in the street all day, waitin' for him to come out."

"Shoot, you're right."

"We need to park inside that garage, instead of the one we're in," Reg suggested, "right near where the pretty boy parks. We can stay in the van there and watch for him. When he pulls out, we can follow him."

"That means we gotta follow him in, too, tomorrow morning—and that's the same problem," Walter said. "We can't just wait for him to come in to see where he parks."

Reg thought for a moment. "Remember at the plant, Mr. Rosenblum, the general manager? He had a private parking space that nobody else could park in."

"You think the pretty boy has his own space?"

"We gotta find out."

They wolfed down the rest of their food and walked back to the bank parking garage. They looped in and out of row after row of spaces, mostly empty now. They found the ones nearest the elevator entrances were the ones marked "Reserved," so they stayed over in that part of the building. They were elated to see individuals' names on some of the spots instead of just "Reserved for First Southern Bank."

On the third floor, they hit the jackpot—two spaces from the elevator door, a small plaque on the wall said, "Reserved for Gavin Duke, First Southern Bank. All others will be towed."

They gave each other a high five and threw their arms around each other—it was the first hug of any kind Reg had experienced since the funeral, and the first time in many more years since he'd truly enjoyed a big moment.

They scouted that level. Plenty of empty spaces were available, and they were careful to notice which way a car might leave—so they could park the van facing out, and as close as possible to Gavin's spot, but behind it so they could follow him.

They rushed to the other parking garage, where they had left the van before, and drove to the First Southern Garage. They didn't mind the fact that they'd have to blow another six or eight bucks, and they decided to spend the night in the van, to be there when Gavin arrived, so it was a pretty cheap hotel.

Ironically, Walter slept better that night than he had for a long time. His snoring didn't seem to bother Reg, who was also exhausted from this emotional roller coaster of a day.

⬬   ⬬   ⬬

The next morning, Walter stirred first. He didn't have a watch any more, another sacrifice of the life he'd inherited. He looked over at Reg, who was wearing one. Strange, he'd never noticed that before. Reg was starting to stretch, so he thought he could wait a minute or two to find out what time it was.

Reg rolled over and looked at Walter. "Morning."

"Hey," Walter tossed his head back. "What time you got?"

Reg rolled his wrist. "Just after six."

"I need some coffee."

"Let's head back over to McDonald's. I bet they're open."

"What if we miss pretty boy?" Walter asked.

"All he'll do is come in."

"I guess you're right. Let's go."

They returned at 6:30 with a paper. It was going to be a long day, and although they doubted Gavin would leave early, they couldn't take a chance on being out of the van if he did. They also realized they risked losing their spot if they followed him out for a meeting and he came back instead of going home, but they decided that would only be a minor inconvenience and not a total disaster—they might be able to find another empty spot, or stay in one of the other reserved spots, since they'd be in the van and didn't have to worry about being towed. Or maybe they could just park behind a couple of other cars—they wouldn't block anybody's way, except for maybe a second or two, since they could move the van. Most likely he'd work late again, so if they did lose their spot, some spaces would become available before he left, and they could just pull into one of those.

They climbed into the van, noticing Gavin had not come to work yet. "Do we say anythin' to him when he gets out?" Reg wondered.

"Nah, no need to. We'd just make him suspicious. We need to stay invisible all day."

Twenty minutes later, Gavin pulled in, carelessly screeching his tires as he did as sharp a turn into his space as either of the two onlookers had ever seen. He climbed out of his car, slammed the door shut with authority, and vanished into the corridor that housed the elevator.

"Stinkin' pretty boy," Walter snorted.

He's right, Reg thought. *That's the kind that killed Lily. Settling the score will be sweet.*

Fifteen

Time has an uncanny knack for expanding or contracting to fill any given situation, often in such a way that is diametrically opposed to the situation. Time slows for terrifying events, like automobile accidents, and speeds up when filled with sheer joy, like rare moments with a loved one. Walter and Reg had been trained by the last several years of their lives to ignore time, which served to speed its passage over periods where nothing eventful seemed to occur. Yet this day, condemned to being caged in a dirty old van in a dark parking garage, whose air seemed always wisped with exhaust, time threatened to stop altogether.

Walter read the newspaper twice. Reg wished he'd brought the photo of Lily, beautiful Lily, to gaze at so he could at least pass the time in familiar pain. He had kept the press clipping of her death notice in his wallet, folded neatly, but he seldom looked at it—usually just on special dates, like their anniversary, her birthday, holidays, the anniversary of the factory being shut down, and the anniversary of her death. This day, he pulled it out and looked at it so many times he lost count, so he finally took it out for good and placed it gingerly on the dash, pressing his thumb along the edge where it had been folded in half in order that he might look at the entire article at once.

They had discussed taking turns leaving, watching in shifts, but the problem was what to do if Gavin left while one of the two was gone. But they decided this was too important; there would be no lunch today, and no bathroom breaks. They could climb out of the van and walk around in the immediate vicinity to stretch their legs and break the tedium, but that was the extent of it. They were as chained to this van as they were to Murrowstown. No matter what happened with Gavin, each was deciding independently—without any discussion about it—that going back to Murrowstown and living out life in that hypnotic daze was not going to be possible.

At shortly after three in the afternoon, the tension splintered—Gavin walked out to his car. Walter saw him first. He sat up straight from reclining in the front seat and hurriedly turned around and waved at Reg, who was lying on the floor in the back, next to the shotguns, with his feet kicked up on the front passenger seat. He jumped up onto his knees in a hurry, and peered out the side window, his heart palpitating almost through his shirt.

Gavin walked around to the back of the car and popped open the trunk. He leaned over and shuffled papers from one or two portfolios for a minute or two, prompting Reg to say, "Maybe he's got it hidden in there!"

Walter said, "Shh!" and went back to watching.

Gavin picked up some of the items he'd been fiddling with, slipped them under his arm, slammed the trunk shut, and went back into the building.

"Thought he had us there for a minute," Reg said.

Walter laughed, the only way he knew how to break the tension. The wait resumed.

Cars started leaving steadily around five, and of the spaces they could see—which were pretty much all taken for the entire day—about half were empty by six.

"Is that sucker ever gonna come out?" Walter said, not so much looking for a response from Reg, just wanting to vent his weariness.

"Soon," Reg said. "He's gotta come out soon."

The next half hour dragged by slowly, but the moment finally came. The windows were partially rolled down in the van, so they could hear the voices, first a young woman's, then a man's, echoing in the nearly emptied garage. *It's the girl from the car last night,* Walter thought as he saw Torrie emerge from the corridor that led to the elevator. Gavin came in right next to her, and as they got to the car, she didn't go around to get in, and he didn't circle around to open the passenger door; instead Gavin leaned back against the driver's side door, and she stood right in front of him, as they continued to talk.

Oh, no, Walter thought, *she's gonna go home with him, or they're gonna go out, and this is gonna be a problem.*

But Reg, noticing the fact that they both stood at his side of the car, answered, "She just walked him out, I bet. We're gonna get our man alone here in a second."

The sound of their voices bounced and echoed all around the cavernous concrete vault, so it was difficult to make out what they were saying. There was lots of laughter and steady conversation, but after a few minutes, they stopped talking, and she moved close.

Walter watched, but Reg, slightly embarrassed for Gavin and for Torrie, would have looked away even if it had not been for his scarred old heart. He simply couldn't look at youth in love, and he turned not only his eyes away but also his entire head and upper body, and he covered his face with his hands.

Walter was certain Gavin or Torrie would turn and look straight at him, aware that they were being watched. But the darkness of the garage jumped in the way, and the boys' secret vantage point was safe.

Torrie started to back away, turned, and vanished back down the corridor. Gavin turned around to face the van for the first time since coming in, and Walter could see he had a good solid smirk on his face. *Good for you, boy,* Walter thought. *I'd have that look too, if I had me a girlyfriend like that.*

Gavin went to the trunk again but finished his work quickly this time—he just tossed a briefcase in, shut the top, opened his door, hung his jacket above the side window, got in, and stepped on the brake lights.

Reg sat up again and crawled into the passenger seat. Walter had his hand on the key, already in the ignition, ready to turn it once Gavin had made his move. They had discussed the procedure during the agonizingly long day: wait until he backs out and accelerates forward.

Then start the van and pull out slowly, without turning the lights on. Reg will have the garage ticket and the money ready, which he'll pass to Walter just before they get there. Follow Gavin close enough so as not to lose him, but not so close it's obvious they're on his tail.

Everything went as smooth as silk until they got to the gate. Gavin veered off to the right, down the "monthly pass" lane, but Walter and Reg were stuck going through a different gate. "Hurry," Reg said, passing him the ticket and the cash. Walter bounced in his seat as the large woman sitting inside the tiny booth took an eternity to lift the gate, and then he peeled out to get into the street.

His heart skipped through his throat as he rolled onto Peachtree Street. Gavin's car was not visible. He tore off to the right, which was a quick bend in the road, to see the traffic light of their salvation from the night before. Red once again, and a big black Mercedes with the GAVIN plates rumbling in anticipation. Walter sank into the seat, his heart galloping at a mile a minute, and rolled the van gently behind Gavin. He could see Gavin's eyes in the rearview mirror, gazing straight ahead. Walter wasn't sure if he wanted Gavin to cast a quick glance back, so their eyes might meet; ordinarily, that might have seemed a crazy wish, but Walter's adrenaline was pumping now, and he felt young and healthy and excited. The only adrenaline rushes he had felt since the plant shut down were the times he got into fistfights, usually at Dutchy's. But this was different.

The light turned green, and it took everything Walter had to keep from taking off and tailgating Gavin. Actually, it was hard to keep up with the young turk, who liked to go double the speed limit and weave in and around cars, especially since Walter was trying to not look like a tail. But he managed to do it, focusing intently on the driving but still noticing out of the corner of his eye that Reg was clinging to the door handle with one hand and the dash with the other. His press clipping about Lily had fallen to the floor, but Reg didn't notice.

Gavin's dart through the surface street traffic quickly led to a ramp for the interstate. If he was pushing it before, he decided to go into overdrive now. Walter saw a brief puff of exhaust come out of Gavin's tailpipe as they merged onto the ramp, and just like that, Gavin was gone.

Both men were sweating profusely now, not very pleasant after they had both spent the night in the van. They didn't know if this old hunk of junk could go as fast as Gavin's import, but they had to try. And try Walter did, coaxing and pleading and talking to his trusty steed, and somehow, he made up the lost ground and was three cars behind Gavin, in the same lane—the fast lane—but it was okay, because he was hauling. The remnants of rush hour had made all the difference, because the traffic was still thick enough that Gavin had to settle in at a cruising speed of about sixty-five instead of the eighty or so he'd driven out of the chute.

They had no idea where he was taking them, but they didn't care. As long as they could keep up with him, they were in good shape. It was getting a little tougher, as cars started dropping off and the pace picked up. Gavin was now humming along at seventy-plus, and the van was rattling apprehensively. "Stay with us," Walter pleaded.

Reg was getting his wits back about him, and he picked up the news clipping that had fallen to the floor earlier. He fingered it lovingly for a moment, then abruptly folded it in half and stuck it back into his wallet. Not a word was spoken.

It must have been fifteen minutes on the interstate, maybe twenty, when Gavin started easing over to the slower lanes. "Looks like he's gettin' ready to take an exit," Reg said.

"Looks like," said Walter, rubbing his sweaty palms against the wheel.

Within a couple of minutes, Gavin jerked the Mercedes onto an exit ramp—without signaling—and Walter had to cut off a couple of angry commuters to keep up. Once again, neither man noticed the name or the number of the exit—keeping up with Gavin took all their concentration.

Gavin rolled to a stop once he'd made it off the exit, and Walter pulled up behind him at the light. He could see Gavin's eyes in the rear view mirror again, but after that ride had lost some of his nerve, so he looked away before Gavin could look up. The light changed, and he reminded himself to stay back—which could backfire, if Gavin got a yellow light and decided to gun it. But out of the blue, Gavin wheeled left into a parking lot, again without a turn signal, and Walter knew he had to think fast. *Turn in a hurry, and you might catch his attention*, he told himself, *so keep an eye on him and turn into another entrance, a few yards down the road.*

"Didn't you see him turn?" shouted Reg, but before Walter answered, Reg realized what his partner was up to. He took a left and rolled into the parking lot. It was a strip mall, and Gavin took a space that was clearly marked for handicapped drivers only. He got out and went into an Eckerd drugstore.

"Where can we go that we won't look like a sore thumb when he comes out?" Walter wondered.

"He's probably not goin' back the way he came, so . . . " Reg looked around. "Why not get into that gas station, up there at the corner, and be ready to pull out after him?"

It made sense. The gas station was on the same road that Gavin had been driving, and it was a couple of hundred yards ahead. Clearly, if Gavin was going in that direction, they could casually pull out behind him without him seeing them follow all the way across the parking lot.

Gavin was back out in a flash, carrying a small bag. *Must've forgotten some aspirin or something*, Reg thought. He hopped back into the Mercedes.

"This is it," Walter said, as Gavin turned his headlights on. Gavin started to move forward, and got back on the same street, in the same direction he'd been heading before. The boys waited for him to go by, then casually rolled out into the roadway, several car lengths behind him. The gamble had paid off.

Two or three blocks later—it was hard to tell, given how winding and dark and tree-lined the streets were—Gavin again turned abruptly, with his characteristic lack of a signal, onto a side street. As they went by, Reg could see the street sign clearly: Kinghurst Drive.

They were close enough now that they could relax and notice the surroundings. And what magnificent surroundings, with manicured large lawns that looked more like parks, with BMWs and Saabs and Acuras boastfully parked out front of houses that looked large enough to hold the entire remaining population of Murrowstown.

The Mercedes passed one lazy intersection, then another, and then swung to the right. Gavin parked the car halfway on the drive, and still halfway on the street, to reach out and grab the mail. The garage door began to move open as Gavin's car idled, and there he stayed, sifting through the bills and the catalogs, as a van drove slowly by.

"It's 4752," Reg said. "He lives at 4752 Kinghurst Drive, and there's no other cars there."

"No brunette," Walter added. They swung around and made a U-turn at the next intersection, and as they drove back toward Gavin's place, they saw him pull into the garage. By the time they were right in front of the house, the garage door was starting to lower itself, sealing the owner and the Mercedes inside for any kidnappers who might happen along that night.

They continued along slowly and turned the next corner. Walter parked the car. "When do we do it?" he turned to ask Reg.

"I think if we wait, I'm not gonna make it."

"All right. Do we park right in front, to get him out in a hurry, or down the street, so he don't hear us comin'?"

Reg stared out through the windshield for a minute, then came up with an insightful reply. "This ain't like no trailer park, where every rig that comes down the highway shakes it up. No, these people don't hear all the traffic goin' by. Let's go right into his driveway, so we can get him out in a hurry, in case one of these women comes by walkin' her poodle. He won't hear us—just kill the lights so the glare don't tip him off."

Walter had once seriously considered doing this all alone, but at this moment he was glad he'd teamed up with Reg. It would be a lot easier with the extra set of hands, of course, but Reg added more to the picture than just that—he was smart, and that helped Walter feel more at ease about something going terribly wrong.

So Walter cranked the van up again and rolled it smoothly around, back onto Kinghurst Drive. He took it slow and easy and killed the lights just before Gavin's house, making sure no one was visible on the street at the moment. He parked the van on Gavin Duke's driveway.

"Do we knock?" Walter asked, knowing it sounded like a silly question but, forgive him, this was his first kidnapping.

"Sounds good to me," Reg answered.

They climbed out, careful not to slam the doors, leaving the guns but taking the knives, and they took the sidewalk past the blue hydrangea bush to the pretentious front entrance. They climbed up on the brick step, and Walter pushed the bell.

A low thumping sound, probably Gavin's footsteps, then an impatient voice: "Who is it?"

They both swallowed hard. Walter, absorbing some of Reg's keen thinking, said, "Delivery for Mr. Duke."

Reg's eyes opened wide. *Brilliant*, he thought, trying to lower his heart from his throat.

They heard a click, probably the deadbolt, and saw the knob turn. The door swung open, and there he was. The TV star. The lady's man. The pretty boy who stood for all the pretty boys who sat in boardrooms and made decisions and trimmed budgets and traded in the lives and souls of men like Walter and Reg.

Gavin looked into Walter's eyes, then Reg's, apparently surprised to see two of them. Then his gaze darted to Walter's hands—where a package was supposed to be. Reg and Walter saw a look of fear rush into Gavin's eyes, the fear they'd seen in a deer before shooting it when they'd gotten close and the woods were still and quiet.

"Well?" Gavin snapped. "Where is it, stupid?"

Walter pushed into Gavin, forcing him back into the foyer, as Reg came close behind and shut the door so none of the neighbors could hear Gavin scream.

"What are you people doing? You can't treat me like this! I'm Gavin Duke! What is it you want?"

Interesting, Reg noticed. *The guy who was so cool on TV, surrounded by nice people wearing nice clothes and smiling at him, is different when his life is danger.* The payback had begun.

"Nobody's gonna hurt you, Mr. Duke," Walter said. "Just keep yourself quiet, and nobody's gonna get hurt."

Gavin darted his eyes furiously between the two, as if trying to place them. *Disgruntled employees? Jealous competitors? Some sick sort of practical joke? If not that, who?*

"Go sit on the couch," Reg directed, finding it strange that he was actually enjoying this. Another adrenaline rush.

"What do you mean, 'sit on the couch'? Who are you people? What—"

Walter grabbed Gavin by the wrists and pulled him toward him, right into his face. "Go sit on the couch!" Walter said, his nose nearly touching Gavin's. Gavin's mind churned, thinking how he'd better cooperate—for now—to see what these two wanted. He would plan for his break later.

Walter slowly lowered his hands and let go of Gavin's wrists. Gavin backed off and walked over to the couch. He lowered himself onto it.

Reg moved to Gavin's left. Walter stepped forward to the right.

"We ain't goin' to hurt you," Reg repeated Walter's words.

"We just need to find somethin' out from you," Walter told Gavin, gaining strength as he went. He paused, as Gavin looked up at him. He could almost hear Gavin shouting, "Well, *what*?!"

"We want you to tell us where the gold is."

Gavin's eyes were a study of emotions. He stared blankly at Walter, processing everything under this cloak of terror, and then, suddenly, the light went on, and his eyes filled with bitter contempt and utter hatred. *No,* Gavin told himself, *no. It can't end like this—my brilliant scheme—at the hands of hooligans. I have to think fast. Surely, I can outsmart these hicks, and have them behind bars within a day, another great human interest story that would further seal my image as a heroic figure. Yeah,* he thought, *and I can give the scoop to Torrie . . .*

"Hey, pretty boy, I said, tell us where the gold is."

Gavin thought of all the junked options, particularly the most obvious ones, that he could toss out like a crumb to these ravenous dogs who would dare to violate his home. *I'd better toy with them, though, so they won't get suspicious,* he thought, realizing they couldn't have gotten this far if they were completely stupid.

"What happens if I don't?" he asked.

Not prepared for such arrogance, Walter's head jerked back, as though rabbit punched, and he couldn't think to say a word. But Reg, who was quicker, moved toward Gavin and, as though by magic, slowly produced a large hunting knife that he twisted in the air in front of Gavin's face. He said slowly, "You like the brunette, don't you?"

There are moments by which a life is defined, instants that forever change a person's way of thinking, for better or for worse, and color every other moment thereafter. For these two men, the announcement of the plant closing was just such a moment. For Gavin Duke, *this* was such a moment. He was young, and strong, and swift, knew no tragedy, and held no thought of death and thus no fear of death until this very moment in time. This instant, which Gavin Duke would never forget, would mark every step, every breath he would take from now until his last.

He lost his train of deceptive thought—all he knew was fear, a kind of fear he had never touched before. Gavin was well-known as caring about himself above all else, but that was mere ego. This was now self-preservation—the crazed man with the knife threatened Torrie, not Gavin, but he understood the principle just the same. If they could hurt Torrie just to get what they wanted from him, they could hurt him too.

"What are you gonna do to me?" he whispered hoarsely.

"Nothin', pretty boy. Just tell us where you hid the gold."

"Gold?" Gavin whispered again. *Am I interested in trading my life for a million dollars in gold? Fine, take the gold. Just leave me in one piece.* Then the next blow came—but this time, it did not come with Reg's words, but with Gavin's own realization. *These two will promise not to harm me, until they get the gold. But then, I'm of no use to them! I'm just a witness—someone who can identify them.*

He looked at Walter, then at Reg, peering at him with contempt and hatred. *They're gonna take the gold, and then decide to stuff me into the oil drum, and bury me there!*

He jumped up, knowing Reg had a knife a foot long and imagining Walter's was equally horrifying, but realizing his only chance was here and now—not out in the middle of Stewart County, where the only human within a ten-mile radius was Brick. He grabbed for the lamp on the end table as he made it to his feet, the element of surprise on his side, thinking to swing at Reg first, since his knife was already drawn, and then, as Reg was reeling, he could floor Walter, which would give him enough time to bolt for the door, sprint outside, and find someone who could help him.

But in the terror of the moment, Gavin lost his balance as he stood and reached and swung all at once, and he ended up lunging at Walter, who—instead of striking a blow at Gavin—pushed him away, back toward the couch.

Gavin's fall, his lunge, and Walter's push all served to throw Gavin headfirst into the edge of the coffee table. His head caught the corner, and he toppled downward into a heap. He couldn't fall flat on the floor, being lodged between the sofa and the end table and the coffee table, so he actually formed a contorted shape, leaning this way and that, with his right arm sunken into the lampshade, his left arm bent in front of him and pressed against his chest, his right leg sticking out straight, and his left leg bent and pushing up against the underside of the coffee table. His head was tilted back in response to his banging it severely on the coffee table, and his perfectly groomed hair, for once, was headed in every direction.

Walter and Reg looked at him, then at each other, then back at the pretty boy—not so pretty just now—expecting him to tilt his head back up at them to either launch a new verbal assault, or perhaps a better planned physical assault this time, or maybe just to give it up and tell them what they wanted to know.

But he didn't move. *Possum,* Reg thought. *He's playin' possum, and he's waitin' to try and surprise us again.* But Reg looked at Gavin's twisted wreckage, and realized no man, no matter how athletic, could spring out of a position like that with any effectiveness.

He moved over to Gavin, slowly, carefully, until he leaned directly above him. He put his hand behind Gavin's neck, and tilted it up slowly.

Gavin's scalp was dripping with blood.

"What've we done?" Reg asked, looking to Walter for an answer he would not get.

"He musta hit his head on the table there," Walter said.

"Oh, no, he can't be dead," Reg gasped.

"Check his pulse," Walter said.

Reg leaned over to feel Gavin's jugular, and said, "Listen!"

Walter bent forward too, and turned his head to listen. Gavin's breathing was steady and deep and slow, almost like he was snoring.

"We didn't kill him," Walter sighed, stepping back to get a better look at the blood on Gavin's forehead, which was still flowing and had made a substantial puddle on the sofa cushion already.

"Not yet, anyway," Reg said, "But it's gonna be a different story if we don't get him to stop from bleedin' to death." He grabbed a pillow from the couch and pressed it onto the wound. "Go in his kitchen, an' see if you can bring a bucket of ice in here."

Walter ran into the next room, the dining room, stopped to get his bearings, then darted through to the kitchen. He tore open the freezer door and yanked out the ice bucket. Fortunately, it was nearly full. He sprinted back into the living room just as Reg was lifting the pillow off Gavin's forehead to see what the gash looked like.

The cut was about two inches long, and the skin was definitely split open enough that under normal circumstances, it would warrant getting some stitches. But ice, pressure, and bandages would have to do.

Having spent so many years working in a factory with large machinery, these men had seen enough injuries to qualify for Saturday night duty at an inner-city emergency room. Gavin's wound was child's play. Just ice it and press it, then push it together and wrap it up tight.

Reg got the bleeding slowed to a trickle and applied the gauze Walter had managed to find in the medicine cabinet. Gavin was a mess, but he was gonna be okay.

They propped him up on the sofa, kicked his feet up on the coffee table that started it all, and looked at the room. Blood and puddles of water were everywhere, a lamp had crashed to the floor—it looked like a murder had been committed here.

"You ever get busted for any of them brawls y'all got in outside Dutchy's?" Reg asked Walter.

"Yeah, couple of times. Why?"

"They ever take your prints?"

"Once, yeah."

"Quick, before we get out of here, go rub off anything you touched."

Walter darted off, retracing his steps, once again reminding himself how glad he was Reg was along. Freezer door, bathroom door, medicine cabinet . . . anything else? He polished away any evidence and came back to the living room.

"I think we can move him out to the van now," Reg said. They pushed and pulled and tugged and carried, doing everything they could not to rattle Gavin's head around, and finally got him to the van. They swung the back doors open, and loaded him in, as if he were a case of cocktail napkins or a table coming back from being repaired after a barroom brawl.

Walter wove his way back to the interstate, amazed that he was able to find it. Reg stayed in the back with Gavin, propping his head up and holding him in place, so the swaying of the van wouldn't reopen his wound.

The drive took forever, at night on the highway with all the trucks and the headlights, Reg and Walter knowing that at any moment a blue flashing light could go off for any number of reasons.

Reg's thoughts were slightly more practical: how were they gonna carry this sack of lead through the woods at night, when they barely made it through in broad daylight? But he was in too deep to have any second thoughts. "Just get him there, get him to tell us what we want to know in the morning, and kiss Murrowstown good-bye."

The moon was darting along beside the van, hiding behind the trees and then jumping out again, as Walter sped past Dutchy's. *Pretty funny*, he thought, *with Leo and the rest of the boys in there right now, and me flying by in the company car!*

He rolled to a stop at the entrance to Steinbeck's property. He got out, then unlatched the back door as Reg slid out, glad to be able to finally stretch his legs again. It was pretty cramped back there with all that dead weight.

They agreed to leave the shotguns for now—it would be impossible to carry them and the pretty boy, who Reg was now beginning to think of as the fat boy. They decided to tie him up here, in case he woke up and decided to get feisty on the way down and because it'd make him easier to carry.

Gavin got heavier and heavier as the path wore on; Reg and Walter thought they'd never make it. It was cooler at night, thankfully, but the sweat still rolled down their cheeks and dripped regularly on their arms, onto Gavin, and onto the path as well, as the crickets and the june bugs and every other insect screeched louder as they plodded down the path.

They finally made it to Steinbeck's place. Reg pushed the door open, and they rolled Gavin onto the floor. He must've lost a lot of blood, to still be out cold after all that. Reg picked up one of the milk jugs he'd filled with water and gulped it down. He passed it to Walter, who did the same as they fell to the floor, the door still open to let a hint of the evening breeze in.

Reg clicked on the flashlight and focused it on Gavin's face. No reaction. He squatted down, peeled back the tape and the gauze, and saw the thick black evidence of coagulation. He hoped it wouldn't get infected, but decided that was no major problem—Gavin could get all the medical attention money could buy within a day or two.

Reg straightened up and turned the flashlight to face the table. There, jumping out to hit him right between the eyes, was the picture of him next to Lily on their honeymoon. He sat down in the chair, put the flashlight on the table, and picked up the photo to hold in both hands, in the same pose he struck every other night he spent in Murrowstown. *Lily*, he reminded himself, *did not get all the medical attention money could buy*.

Walter watched the scene, having known it before, and hoped that somehow, all that was happening might finally release Reg from his unending nightmare.

Torrie left the sliding glass door to her balcony open—not many bugs up this high. She didn't talk to Gavin on the phone every night, but once every week or so she would call him late, or he would call her late, and they'd chat for half an hour or more, the kind of conversation that would be sickeningly sweet and extremely embarrassing should anyone else be listening in. She had decided that the phone was not the way to invite him to church. It would be easier—but that was the problem. "It is the chicken's way out," her friend Nancy had observed. "And it'd be easier for him to say no."

Torrie took her iced tea and her cat outside, where she sat in a cushy chair, kicked her feet up on the railing, looked at the moon, and watched the way the city lights twinkled off in the distance. She remembered back to that afternoon, when she bumped into him—an unexpected surprise for both of them—and they shared about five minutes together when she walked him out to his car.

Stupid schedules, she thought. *He's free tonight, taking the normal amount of paperwork home but definitely available, and I had to beg off because of a banquet I had to cover.* She couldn't stop thinking of him as she gazed at the moon and fretted about missing out on a great evening. She sat up resolutely and made up her mind—this was going to be one of those intimate little phone conversation nights. She went inside, and the cat followed, but Torrie came right back out with the cordless phone, confusing Casey terribly.

It was only ten o'clock, so it was plenty early to call. She punched in one, which had become Gavin's number on her auto-dialer. She wondered if she'd ever told him that; it was definitely the kind of personal tidbit that'd be a kick for him to know.

Gavin's phone rang, and Torrie felt her body tense up a little in anticipation of hearing his voice. It rang again. And a third time. After the fourth, the answering machine came on. Odd. She knew he was going to be home. Maybe he was just monitoring calls—surely, he'd pick it up when he heard her voice. And who knows? Ten isn't all that late—maybe they'd still get together that night.

"You've reached 555-0004. Please leave a message at the tone."

The machine beeped, and Torrie spoke slowly and clearly, always the good journalist.

"Hi, it's me. I'm surprised you're not there. I was just looking out at the moon, and Casey was snuggling up next to me, and it just wasn't the same as being with you, so I was thinking about you. Call me if you catch this in the next hour or so, I'd love to hear your voice. Bye."

She was disappointed he didn't come running in; she really did want to talk. *Oh well, tomorrow.* Casey purred and jumped up into Torrie's lap, and the two sat quietly and enjoyed the evening.

Book
3

Operation Haywire

Sixteen

HGary Harperson looked at his wristwatch again and sniffed. It wasn't like Gavin to be late, let alone to miss a meeting altogether. They had scheduled a breakfast get-together at the Swissotel, in Buckhead, to go over the follow-up marketing for the promotion. Harperson wanted to know more about logistics. The Swissotel was a good spot to meet for an occasional business breakfast or lunch. With so many other excellent hotels and restaurants in Buckhead, Midtown, and downtown, it generally offered a quieter, less crowded atmosphere—a good place to relax a little without having to worry about who might be at the next table.

The meeting was set for seven sharp, and it was now twenty after. Harperson slid out from behind the table, strode to the front entrance of the restaurant, and asked for a phone. The attendant in the crisp uniform pointed him to the bar, where the phone sat next to the cash register. Harperson keyed in Gavin's home number, feeling his impatience grow by the fourth ring, before the answering machine clicked on. He hung up and tried Gavin's office. Ruth answered.

"Ruth, this is Gary Harperson. Have you seen Gavin?" He was too agitated to be impressed that she was in at 7:20 A.M.

"Why, no," she said slowly, "I thought he had a breakfast meeting with you."

"I thought so too," Harperson said gruffly. "Would you check his calendar for me, please, to see if perhaps we had the time or the place mixed up?"

"I'll do it right now," she said, clicking a few keys on her PC to call up Gavin's calendar. She used her pencil to point to the screen as she read the words: "Tuesday morning, Mr. Harperson. Breakfast at the Swissotel, seven A.M."

As she was doing so, she had time to think about how differently Harperson and her boss related to people and difficult situations and—most important—how they talked to her. Harperson was obviously rankled, but he still seemed able to be polite, to ask for what he wanted instead of demanding, and to even use the simple word *please*—a word which did not often occupy Mr. Duke's vocabulary. She hoped he would notice her early start at the office though.

Harperson sniffed again. Ruth quickly said, "I'm sorry, Mr. Harperson, I haven't heard from him. But the minute I do, I'll have you paged so you'll know what's going on."

"Thank you, Ruth. I appreciate it."

Ruth put the phone back into the cradle and thought how sorry she was to have to hurt Mr. Harperson by ruining his campaign. She genuinely liked and respected him and—for a moment—tempted herself to think that if she had worked directly for him, instead of Gavin, she might not be planning this caper. But guilt or second thoughts were not productive at this point, she realized, so she pushed them away. She had to be focused, because she was going to go and get what she deserved in just a few short days.

Harperson paced into the lobby, giving the room a good once-over to see if he could spot Gavin before doing a big circle and returning to his table at the restaurant. "Ten more minutes," he told himself as he sat down and picked up his copy of *The Wall Street Journal.*

🥐   🥐   🥐

Gavin felt the sensation of needing to wake up but being too tired to preempt the alarm. He could tell his eyes were closed, but he avoided opening them. Gaining consciousness at an accelerated pace now, he realized something was wrong. He was extremely uncomfortable, and heavy, and not in his bed. The surface was hard, and there was a smell, a different smell, most certainly not his home—a dusty, humid smell he did not know.

His eyes flew open, but he had to blink hard several times to get a clear view. It was a small, dark room, and he was lying on the floor.

"Hey, Walter, look who's finally wakin' up!"

Walter, who'd been standing right outside the door, quickly moved inside. The two figures stared straight down at Gavin Duke.

Gavin's head throbbed, and he went to reach his hand toward it in the meaningless gesture that people with headaches make—as though the pain can be rubbed away—but his hand wouldn't move. He looked down quizzically, and to his amazement and horror found that one arm was tied to the other.

His look shot up at the two men, silhouetted against the dark walls behind them, trying to make out the nature of his nightmare. But this was no mere nightmare—this was his life.

He looked down to see his feet tied together too. It appeared there were splotches on his pant legs, as though a thick liquid had been spilled there.

"Good mornin', Mr. Duke," Reg said.

Gavin did not answer. He did not want to answer, and he did not have to.

"How's your head there?" Reg asked, coming closer for a look. Gavin heaved himself back against the wall, as best as he possibly could with no usable limbs to propel his body. This too, like trying to reach for his forehead, was a useless gesture, but pain and terror tend to erase portions of logical thought.

"Hey, settle down, I just wanna take a look beneath your bandage there." He reached out toward Gavin's wound.

"Bandage?" Gavin said. "What bandage? What's happened to me? And who are you two . . . "

Gavin stopped retreating, not so much because he wanted to do so but because he was worried and curious about the nature and the extent of his injury.

Reg peeled back the tape and saw the wound had not reopened. "Good," he muttered and put the covering back in place.

Gavin felt some sense of relief, inferring the wound was not serious. *Of course not, it couldn't be, or I wouldn't be able to think so clearly.*

That rational thought seemed to awaken Gavin. He realized he needed to know what all this was about. What could he remember? Nothing. He couldn't bring anything into focus.

He looked around at the room again, his eyes adjusted a bit by now but his left eye still slightly blurred and itching, feeling an unfamiliar discomfort. He did not realize it was encrusted with dried blood, which had dripped around it and into it the night before.

He could make out the table and two chairs, and a boarded-up window. Something sat upon the table, but he couldn't make out what it was. To his immediate left was an old cast-iron stove. There was a door, left wide open, and the two men.

Realizing his memory was betraying him, he decided there was no other viable option for getting any answers than to talk to these two.

"Where am I?" he demanded. "And who are you?"

Reg stood up from the crouch he had assumed next to Gavin and walked over to the table, where he sat in a chair. Walter was still standing close to the door.

"You remember anythin' from last night?" Reg asked.

Gavin tried again, but to no avail. "No, I can't. What happened?"

"Let's just say you had a little accident," Reg said, looking again to Walter, who produced a half smile.

"Then why am I here? And who are you people?" Gavin winced from a shooting pain in his very stiff neck.

"You're here for safekeepin'," Walter said, swinging his leg over onto the other chair.

"Safekeeping? What are you talking about?"

"We wanna make sure you're safe from anybody who might be lookin' to harm you to find out where the gold is."

"Gold?" Gavin winced again. "What gold? What are you talking about?" he barked impatiently.

Walter and Reg stared at Gavin, both realizing there may be a chance this was no ploy. Their hearts sank in their chests. After all they'd been through, was there a chance everything was once again going terribly haywire?

✺   ✺   ✺

Harperson stormed off the elevator and strode down the hall, slowing as he approached Ruth's desk. She looked up.

"Have you heard anything yet?" he asked. She could tell he was working at not taking his frustration out on her. This was a man whose time was too valuable to be wasted.

"No, sir, I'm awfully sorry. I keep trying him at home, but all I get is his machine, and there's no answer on his car phone or his portable. I called the agency, but the switchboard's not open yet so I haven't been able to get Carolina or Ernie. No one's seen him."

Ruth's calmness seemed to work a positive influence on Harperson, and he began to settle down a bit. "Thank you, Ruth," he said. "I appreciate your efficiency, as always. Just let me know when you hear anything, okay?"

He rumbled off, and Ruth cast a glance at the digital clock on the corner of her desk. Five after eight. With anyone else, she might write it off as nothing to worry about. But she knew Gavin, and she knew this wasn't his style. She wondered if Torrie had something to do with it—the charms of a femme fatale might explain it. Ruth called the *Business Courier* and wasn't surprised to find Torrie wasn't in yet either, which fueled Ruth's speculation that Gavin had been smitten into this lapse. But to miss a meeting with Harperson? It just didn't make sense.

✺   ✺   ✺

"What do you mean, 'what gold'?" Walter managed to get out. "We's talkin' about the Southern Gold—you know, what you been all over the TV talkin' about."

Gavin listened carefully. Southern gold. TV. It was there, almost, like a word you know but can't quite stretch to your tongue from your mind.

"Southern Gold?" he stammered. His head hurt, his neck ached, his back was bruised, and he was hungry too. "Can I get something to eat?"

Reg resisted the desire to pursue the gold issue as he realized Gavin just needed some food to rush up to his brain. After all, he'd been out cold through a long night, probably without having any dinner, and he'd lost all that blood.

"Yeah, I'll get you somethin'," Reg said, standing up and reaching over toward the little cupboard.

"What're you doin'?" Walter said suddenly, grabbing Reg's arm. "Wait a minute. He's gotta answer us first!"

"What're you gonna do, starve the man to death?" Reg said, pulling his arm away and once again reaching for the cabinet door. "He needs some food. He took a nasty spill on his head there, and he needs somethin' inside him to make sense."

Walter shrugged and backed off. Reg pulled out a box of graham crackers and brought them over along with one of the gallon jugs of water.

"Now, I'm gonna untie your hands in a minute, but no funny stuff, or I'll tie you right back up, and you ain't gettin' nothin' to eat. Understand?"

Gavin nodded. Of course he didn't mind being untied to eat. *Get on with it*, he told Reg in his thoughts.

He stuffed the crackers into his mouth as fast as he could. *Never*, Gavin imagined, *have graham crackers tasted so good*. He swallowed hard and after plunging four more crackers in, he grabbed the water to wash the first round down. He ate half a dozen more, took another drink, and then reached for the box again—just as Reg took it away.

"That's good enough for now," he said, with his back turned to Gavin. "Just enough to get your head runnin' straight." He put the box back on the shelf and placed the water bottle down on the floor in its spot in the corner.

Gavin wanted more but decided against pressing his luck. He sat still as his eyes darted from one man to the other.

"Well, let's try again," Walter said.

Reg had a bad feeling he wanted to clear up. "You know your own name, son?" he asked Gavin.

Gavin was about to answer. *Of course I know my own name, what kind of idiotic question is that?* He took a breath and opened his mouth, but nothing came out. It was as though he had run into an acquaintance after a long time, in a place where the face was out of context, and he had to dash through his memory to stumble upon the name.

Reg and Walter exchanged nervous glances until Gavin finally blurted it out. "Gavin Duke! I'm Gavin Duke!" It was clear it had scared him to have lost control of his own identity, even if only for an instant.

"Good, Mr. Duke," Walter said. "Now, think if you can remember where you hid that million dollars worth of gold, all right?"

Gavin tried to capture that thought too, but as he did, the room began to spin. He blinked his eyes to try to stop it. But he couldn't. His system, shocked from the events of the last twelve hours, was rushing extra blood to his digestive system and for an instant didn't have enough for his brain too. He blacked out, and his head fell limply to his chest.

🐺   🐺   🐺

Carolina returned Ruth's message around eleven. She'd been at a local production company that morning, enjoying a bright new jingle that was being recorded for the Rico's Pizza account.

"What do you mean, no one's heard from Gavin all morning?" Carolina asked, her eyebrows pressing downward as she looked out her window.

"No one's seen him today. He was supposed to meet Mr. Harperson for breakfast and never showed up. He hasn't called or checked in with anyone."

"Have you tried Torrie?"

"I've left messages, but I haven't caught up with her yet," Ruth replied. "It wouldn't surprise me if they're together, but it's just not like Gavin to miss an important meeting without checking in. And on a busy day like today too."

"Mmm, you're right," Carolina agreed, thumbing through her calendar. "You two are supposed to be here around three, aren't you?"

"That's right," Ruth said, as her line beeped. "That may be Gavin," she said. "Let me grab it, and I'll let you know."

"All right, I will too," said Carolina. She hung up and continued to stare out the window, suppressing an anxious feeling.

Ruth pressed the right sequence of buttons and answered crisply. "Ruth Chandler."

"Ruth, this is Torrie. I got your message. Has Gavin popped up yet?"

Ruth was taken by surprise, expecting it to be Gavin. "No, he hasn't," she said. "In fact, I thought your call was him. Did he give you any idea what he was planning for this morning?"

"Not at all," Torrie said, the concern in her voice apparent. "I called him about ten last night, and I was surprised he didn't pick up. I left him a message, and I haven't heard back from him yet."

Ruth shifted nervously in her chair. Gavin stood up both Harperson and Torrie? Something wasn't right. She decided not to fuel Torrie's concern by mentioning Gavin had missed a meeting with the president of the bank.

"Well, let's keep each other posted when he shows up," Ruth said, and Torrie agreed.

At quarter to three, Ruth started pulling together the files she needed for the meeting at Carolina Gates Advertising. Gavin or no Gavin, the meeting had to go on. She took the elevator down, immersed in her thoughts. *Is there any possibility that Gavin decided to pull a fast one on everybody? Might his fiendish mind have concluded that a million in gold was an easier ticket than his fast track to the top? Has he had the idea in mind the whole time, as he developed the promotion? No way, she kept telling herself, no way. Gavin's net worth is closing in on a million already, and after another few months, his salary is going to hit the stratosphere. He's already brought several billion dollars in new assets to the bank, so his future is certain. But what if he really hadn't expected all this? What if he panicked and decided to cash in? No, it's not possible. Gavin Duke simply would not, could not think his brainchild would fail. Not on your life. But then again . . . He is quite an actor. And if he did take it, that means my plans have gone up in smoke. After putting up with all that garbage, that's just too much.*

The elevator doors parted, and she was jolted back to her day. She took a deep breath, scurried across the lobby, and headed for the ad agency.

She was half expecting Gavin to be in Carolina's office when she arrived, but all she found was Carolina, looking surprised to see Ruth entering alone.

"Still no word?" Carolina asked. Ruth admired Carolina's ability to keep cool under pressure, so she was touched to see a genuinely helpless look in those successful blue eyes.

"No, I thought maybe he'd be here."

"No." She paused. "Can I get you some coffee or something? I'm sure he'll come bounding in the door any second now."

"I'm sure he will. But no, thanks, I just had a cup over at the bank."

The two made some small talk, and after about fifteen minutes decided to go ahead with the meeting. They didn't discuss Gavin's disappearance, or their feelings about it, but forged ahead as though everything were in its place.

🕮   🕮   🕮

"He ever gonna wake up?" Walter said to Reg.

"Maybe it's time we helped him," Reg offered. He took some water, put it on a rag, and patted it on Gavin's face.

Gavin shook his head as he opened his eyes. "Who's . . . what . . . stop it . . . "

"Wish you'd thought of that a couple hours ago," Walter said.

Gavin looked up and saw them. "Oh no," he said, a sign that encouraged the two men.

"Glad to have ya back, Mr. Duke," Reg said.

Gavin, waking up more quickly this time, tried to straighten himself. He had more success this time, since his hands were still untied.

"Hope you can think straighter now," Walter said to him, "so we can finish this up quick-like."

"So what'll it be, Mr. Duke? You gonna be able to help us find that gold?"

The gold, Gavin thought. *They're after the gold.* He reached up to touch his throbbing head and felt the gauze. "What happened to me?" he asked, his voice sounding frantic.

"Just a little cut, nothin' to worry about," Reg said.

Gavin pushed himself further up, sliding back against the wall, and for the first time since this ordeal began, he thought about the gold coin in his pocket. He reached in, worrying the two men might have already taken it—but he was cautious, so that if they hadn't, they would not take it now.

His heart skipped a beat when he touched the edge, and he quickly clutched the piece, not wanting to let go, as though it contained some magic power that could transport him from this wretched place and into a beautiful sunny meadow, orange and yellow flowers everywhere, holding onto Torrie, who was wearing a flowing white dress and a big-brimmed floppy hat.

"You gonna help us or not?" Walter blurted out, his patience and his nerves worn thin by now.

It's hot and uncomfortable in this little box of a room, Gavin thought as he clutched the coin tighter still.

"You want me to tell you where the gold is," Gavin said slowly, "and you won't hurt me."

The two men looked at each other and smiled. Walter tasted it; he knew Gavin was about to give them the answer, but Reg remained a skeptic—they had already come this far, last night, and look where it had gotten them.

"That's it exactly," Walter said.

Images flooded Gavin's head. Carolina. Harperson. His office. Torrie. The trouble is, everything seemed so far away. *The gold? Where is the gold?*

"I hid the gold," Gavin said, sounding childlike. "Everybody wants to find it, but I hid it."

Walter, growing exasperated, raised his voice. "We know you hid it. Everybody knows you hid it. But where, man? Where'd ya hide it?"

Gavin's eyes glazed over as he tried to remember. He pushed his mind as fast as it could go, but he felt as though he were having a bad dream, trying to run faster but somehow unable.

He loosened his grip on the gold half-dollar, turning it between his fingers, but stopping suddenly when he realized the men might see the motion. He wanted to pull his hand out of his pocket, but he had to keep touching the coin. He grabbed it tight once again.

"I can't remember," he said at last.

Exhaustion had tempered Walter's natural tendency to jump into a barroom brawl, so he surprised Reg by not attacking Gavin on the spot. "You believe him?" he asked his partner.

"I dunno," Reg answered, eyeing Gavin. "He's a clever one, this one." He paused to bend down and take a closer look into Gavin's eyes. "He's clever enough to save his skin if he could."

This blow to my head must have taken my memory, Gavin realized. He had absolutely no idea where he'd hidden the gold.

Reg didn't say another word but moved over to the cupboard, pulled out a loaf of bread, and prepared Gavin a Spam sandwich. *They were smart in bringing the food up,* he told himself, *because this might have to last a while.*

Walter had returned the van to Dutchy's during Gavin's after-breakfast blackout. He hid the shotguns in the woods before driving it back. He parked it in the lot, left the keys in the ignition, then hurried back to Steinbeck's cabin without trying to find Leo or stopping in at home—he was in no mood to answer any questions. He was surprised to find there were no blood stains on the floor of the van; apparently, he and Reg had done a pretty good job of stopping the flow in Gavin's house.

Once back to the woods, he had unearthed the guns and trudged through the underbrush that was getting all too familiar. He had placed the guns on the floor, in front of the small cupboard, and Reg had to step over them to get the bread and the Spam.

Gavin hungrily ate the sandwich, not knowing or caring if he had eaten Spam since he was a kid. He washed it down with some of the water and realized he had wolfed it down so quickly that he was out of breath when he was done.

Reg gave him a few minutes, then tried again. "You sure you can't remember where you stashed it? The sooner you can recall, the quicker we'll be out of here."

"Out of here," Gavin repeated the sweet words. But he couldn't get his mind to cooperate, and even the weightiest of motivations wasn't going to help. He looked up to see the two men staring at him. "No, I can't," he said. "I'm sorry, I can't help you."

"He'll remember," Reg said quickly to Walter. "Jus' give him some more time."

"Time, I got plenty of," Walter said, throwing his arms up into the air, almost hitting the low ceiling of the shack.

The two men sat down. Reg had been playing solitaire, so Walter assembled the cards into a deck and said, "Let's play some draw." The two men began passing the afternoon in a round of poker without wagers or antes crossing the table.

Gavin listened in as they chatted, and he came to realize that these men had no jobs, no goals, no hope for much of anything—except his million dollars, of course. They were far from hardened criminals but were rather hard-luck stories, slapped around by life. There was no forgiving what they had done to him—tying him up and imprisoning him in this vile shack—and he would settle that score one day. But right now, they were neither harming him nor bothering him, and he saw only two blue-collar dregs of society, the very people to whom he was directing a good part of his campaign.

"What are your names?"

The two looked up at him, surprised at such a comment coming out of the blue.

"Look, boy, we'll ask the—" Walter started off, but Reg interrupted him.

"Aw, he don't mean no harm. My name's Reg. This here's Walter."

Gavin nodded slowly, not having touched lives like these before. He was insulated from much of the world, surrounded by glass and steel and people who jumped when he snapped his fingers, by fine clothes and fine dining and beautiful women. He only knew of these people as angry fists holding signs on the news, when their union had called yet another strike to demand more—never flesh and bones, with voices and hearts and now, for the first time, names.

"Have you contacted anyone yet—about having me, I mean?" Gavin asked.

The card game stopped again. *There's no ransom, so we don't need to call anyone,* Reg thought. Besides, how could they call anyone—there wasn't a phone for miles. And who would they call?

"Nope," he said. "No need to call nobody. You the only one that knows where the loot is."

Interesting, Gavin thought to himself. *A different kind of kidnapping. But it was appropriate, since this was a unique situation; I'm not a millionaire's kid, and the bank certainly won't pay a million dollars for my safe return. Would they? If only I could remember . . .*

Harperson called Carolina around 5:30.

"Has anybody heard anything?" he said, obviously agitated.

"No. Nothing," she said.

"Carolina, you have to tell me the truth. This isn't some publicity stunt, part of the campaign, is it?"

"No, it's not. I wish it were."

"I just don't want the press to get wind of this and turn a little misunderstanding into a mess. Everything's been perfect so far, and I don't want anybody implying there's been any impropriety on the part of anyone involved in this."

Carolina was stunned. "Who said anything about impropriety?"

"No one has—yet," he said, "but do you realize how this might look if it goes on much longer? The one person who knows where the gold is just happens to disappear, and we're all looking like a bunch of idiots?"

Although Carolina certainly deserved her reputation for covering all the bases, she simply had not considered that Gavin might run off with the gold or that Harperson would think such a thing. She had been much more concerned about Gavin's safety—had he been in an accident, or might someone have taken him hostage? Or perhaps it was as simple and awful as a stroke in his house?

"Does anyone else know he's been missing all day?" Harperson asked her.

"Well, no, just Ruth," Carolina said, not pleased with The Man's attitude. And then, remembering, she added, "and Torrie."

"Torrie?" Harperson repeated.

"Yes, Torrie. Torrie Wilson, of the *Business Courier.*"

There was a pause large enough to drive a truck through. "How on earth does someone from the newspaper know? Is she going to print anything?"

"Why, no," Carolina said, realizing the bank president did not keep tabs on his employees' love lives. "He's been seeing her, um, socially, so . . . "

"Gavin's been dating a reporter? The reporter who covers the bank? What else is going on that I don't know about?" he demanded.

"I'll personally call her right now to remind her of the difference between her personal life and her professional life," Carolina offered, not liking this day one bit.

"None of this can get to the papers," he said. "Do you realize what it would do to the bank's image?"

"Yes, sir. I need to let you go, so I can call Torrie. I'll keep you posted."

"Very well," he said, as he hung up.

Carolina dug into her Rolodex for Torrie's number. She felt compelled to call, not so much for Harperson's reasons, but because she thought Torrie might offer some shred of a clue as to what had become of Gavin.

"Torrie Wilson."

"Torrie, this is Carolina Gates."

"Carolina, hi . . . " Torrie was getting rattled.

"I'd like to see you, if you've got a minute," Carolina said.

"Uh, okay," Torrie said, getting more nervous. Given that Carolina was as close to Gavin as anyone else, her call might mean some news, probably bad. "Do you want me to come over to your office?"

"Maybe a neutral site, like JohnBarley's?" Carolina suggested.

The phrase "neutral site" was not well chosen, given the tension that already occupied the air and the potentially adversarial role that often exists between journalists and newsmakers. Torrie agreed, though, since her curiosity was aroused and she was concerned about Gavin.

Torrie sat by the door, instead of going to a table, and she stood up at once when Carolina entered, only about a minute behind her. "I appreciate your seeing me on such short notice," Carolina said as they made their way to the bar. *Funny,* Torrie thought, *I've been here several times but never sat at the bar—always at a table with Gavin or, on one or two other occasions, with a group of reporters at a bigger booth.* She wasn't completely comfortable hanging out at a bar, but she had decided long ago a reporter had to go where the sources were. She had made a personal commitment not to compromise her principles, all the while well aware Jesus made a point of spending time with tax collectors and drunkards—and that He was widely criticized for it.

"I've talked to Ruth, and to Gary Harperson, about why Gavin hasn't shown up today," Carolina began without taking time for a breath, "and none of us has the faintest idea what he's up to." She paused, looking right into Torrie's eyes. "Do you?"

Torrie was taken off guard by Carolina's abruptness, since she had been the picture of Southern graciousness and charm the other times they had seen each other.

"No, and it worries me," she said.

"Have you seen him today at all?" Carolina pushed on.

"No, I haven't—I didn't think anybody had. I saw him just before he went home last night, around six, but then I had a story to cover."

Carolina said, "I've known him for years, and he never ceases to amaze me, but I can't quite figure out today—he hasn't called anyone, and he missed some pretty important meetings." She knew Harperson would hit the roof if he knew she was sharing her concern with a reporter this way, and her own instincts were a bit shaky—she was setting up a potentially bad story, she realized—but Carolina Gates was, if anything, a compassionate human being first and a shrewd businesswoman second. She occasionally let her heart get ahead of her logical side, which may have been one reason she was so successful in a world where too many men and women think cutting throats for a buck is the surest way to the top.

Torrie was sharp enough herself to realize Carolina was taking a mighty big risk right now. She was touched to know such a powerful woman's apparent compassion was genuine.

"Did he give you any hint at all about this sudden . . . change in plans?" Carolina asked.

"I've been over everything in my mind a hundred times already," Torrie said, "and I keep coming up with nothing."

"So the last time you saw him was at six?"

"Yeah, but I tried to call him later, around ten, I think, and I was surprised when his answering machine came on."

Carolina mulled that one over. *Had he already gone somewhere? Surely, he hadn't gone to bed yet—and then missed a breakfast meeting. It doesn't make sense.*

"Do you have a key to his place?" Carolina asked her.

Torrie was shocked at the forward nature of the question, especially considering Carolina's conservative persona. She had actually wondered if perhaps Carolina were a Christian too, but she had no solid basis for such a conclusion. They had only chatted a couple of times before, always briefly, so the subject had not come up. Torrie was a bit embarrassed too, thinking Carolina must not have ever picked up on Torrie's faith. But her concern for Gavin overshadowed any other issues at that moment. She said no, she didn't, and quickly added, "Maybe Ruth does!"

"Ruth?" Carolina said, making an association she couldn't imagine—Gavin having a secret relationship with Ruth.

Torrie, sensing Carolina's surprise, laughed—which helped to ease her nerves—and said, "He's always sending her over to his house to pick something up, drop something off, that kind of thing. He may have given her a key at one time or another."

Carolina pulled out her portable phone and called Ruth.

"Ruth, do you have a key to Gavin's house?"

Ruth was as taken aback by the question as Torrie had been but immediately understood. "I know where one is," she said.

Gavin's need for control didn't allow him to actually entrust Ruth with a key, but he had realized his demands required her to have constant access to his home office. He kept it locked in his desk drawer, a drawer to which only he and Ruth had a key.

"Can I get it from you?" Carolina asked.

Ruth paused. If this turned out to be a false alarm, it might cost Ruth her job. But if it was serious, the key was critical. She stopped. *So what if I get canned? I'm just a few days away from paradise!* She felt a pang of guilt, wondering if perhaps Gavin was indeed in trouble. "Yes, do you want me to bring it over to the agency?"

"Thanks, I'll come pick it up. I'll see you in five minutes."

She rushed back over to Torrie and laid a few bills on the bar. "She's got one, and I'm going over to pick it up."

"And you're planning on heading straight to Gavin's from there?" Torrie asked.

"Yes, I am," she said. "Will you join me, please?"

Torrie wanted to give Carolina a great big hug for the way she had asked. "Of course I will."

"Good," said Carolina, as the two women darted out the door.

Ruth didn't say a word as Carolina and Torrie came to collect the key except to wish them luck as they flew back down the hall.

Carolina raced up the highway. Torrie could see the digital speedometer pushing past eighty, then eighty-five, despite being in roughly the same density of late rush-hour traffic that Gavin had experienced on his last trip home. She prayed silently the entire way.

As they pulled into the driveway, Torrie got out and ran to the front door. They could see the roof of the Mercedes through the windows of the garage. Carolina pulled out the key, but as she put her hand on the knob, she realized it wasn't locked. She turned the handle, and both women darted into the living room.

They froze and their jaws dropped in horror. The lamp was lying on the floor, the couch was a bloody mess, and Gavin Duke was nowhere to be seen.

Seventeen

The sun was setting, but it was hard to tell in woods so deep and thick. There was merely a gradual graying, but before you knew it you were straining to see. Reg and Walter had decided to untie Gavin's legs too, feeling compassion for him as well as being a bit more pragmatic—if he could move around, get some exercise, maybe his head would clear up and he could tell them where he put the gold. There wasn't much space for him to walk, so he paced back and forth in front of Steinbeck's shack. But any movement was a gift to him, after being cramped inside that hard, dirty room.

Gavin had been alternating between feeling anger and trying to feel relaxed throughout the day. The anger came easily, brewing in an instant and threatening not just to bubble over but explode in a rage, not unlike the temper tantrum of a small spoiled child. But the feeling of calm did not come easy. He had to work at it, the way a man works at building a wooden structure with heavy planks and massive steel spikes, lifting and pulling and shoving and reminding himself he can't quit, that he is driven as if by some great unseen force. Gavin realized that his anger only fed itself and made the situation harder to bear, but the quieter times—adapting to the circumstances if only for a moment—allowed the time to pass more easily. It was the same lesson the other two men had learned a thousand times on a thousand different days.

Gavin was stepping around the "grounds" in front of the cabin, as he had named the area to amuse himself. It was flat and looked like a place where someone parked a truck, but small, hardy weeds were beginning to make their way through the dead earth to once again enliven and enrich it. It wasn't thriving like the rest of the path from the road, so Gavin could walk around.

He peered through the woods carefully, trying to see something besides tree trunks and vines and thick underbrush. *Where am I?* he asked himself repeatedly, recognizing the foliage as decidedly southern and assuming he was somewhere in rural Georgia or Alabama. *Wouldn't it be ironic,* he thought, *if I'm only a few miles from where I hid the treasure?* The irony was compounded by the fact that he had no blessed idea where that might be!

"Dinnertime, Mr. Duke!"

He turned and saw Walter standing at the door. Reg had been outside with him, guarding him, even though he would have no idea as to which direction to run.

Gavin went in and was surprised to find what looked like a crude place setting at the table—a tin pie plate, some silverware, one of the water jugs, and a cloth that would serve as a napkin. He peered onto the plate to find it was filled with beans, what looked like a can of pork and beans, with two slices of bread leaning against the side. Reg's photograph had been temporarily displaced to a corner of the floor.

There was only the one place set up, which prompted Gavin to ask, "Aren't you two eating?"

"Yeah, I'm makin' ours now. We just thought it'd be easier to let you get started, since there's only two chairs, then we can eat at the table here after y'all finish."

Gavin didn't say a word—he was too amazed. "Somethin' wrong?" Reg asked.

Gavin looked up. Walter was standing right in front of Gavin. "Ain't you hungry? Why're you just standin' there, starin' like that? You got an important meetin' to go to or somethin'?" Walter and Reg shared a good laugh. "Sit yourself down and eat your supper."

The beans hadn't been heated—they were just room temperature, poured straight from the can. But as far as Gavin was concerned, it was Beluga caviar. He had to keep reminding himself to slow down. He washed it down with the water and soaked up the sauce with the bread. *Strange*, he thought, *but in a way, this Spartan meal was as satisfying as any I've ever had at any of the posh resorts and world-class restaurants.*

As Gavin finished, Walter moved the two plates he'd assembled for himself and Reg into place. Gavin got up and Reg directed him to sit down on the floor where he'd been before, so they could eat in peace without worrying about him darting off into the woods.

He sat down and nearly jumped when he realized his wallet was still in his right hip pocket. Without thinking, he immediately pulled it out and looked through it, surprised to find everything in its place—credit cards, driver's license, and money. Gavin always carried a substantial amount of cash, as much as a thousand dollars or so, not so much for convenience but as a personal symbol of success. He'd never miss a grand if his wallet were lost or stolen, so he felt the risk was worth the rewards. And he carried most of it in big bills too; as he thumbed through, he found four hundreds, two fifties, and an assortment of twenties, tens, and fives. He reached into his front pocket to touch the coin, which he already knew was still there, and stared up at the two men who were so busy eating a good meal that they did not notice Gavin's discovery.

He watched them eat, astounded that they hadn't picked his pocket. "Why didn't you take my wallet?" he blurted out, not realizing how stupid the question sounded.

They both stopped and looked up. "Guess we didn't think of it," Reg said, putting another spoonful of beans in his mouth. He and Walter laughed.

"I guess we may as well," Walter said. "You got any cash money in there?"

Gavin didn't know what to make of this. *Here are two men who must have cooked up a fairly elaborate plan to kidnap me, yet they didn't think to take my money, my credit cards, my gold coin? These are clearly not common thieves. But what then? Average men, driven to desperation? Could a normal man, beaten down enough by wrenching circumstances, be driven to do things he would never have imagined otherwise?*

"You can just lay it right there, on the table," Walter said, gesturing and wearing a broad smile that reflected his sudden good fortune.

Gavin pulled out the cash and did as he was directed. *These two don't appear to be particularly creditworthy,* Gavin told himself, *so they might not catch the fact that I'm keeping the credit cards.* He folded the wallet up and slid it back into his pocket as Walter grabbed the cash.

"Whoo-ee, would you look at this," Walter shouted with glee, fingering the bills. "One hundred, two hundred, three hundred, four hundred . . . man, there's more than five hundred dollars here!"

Reg reached over to take it. It was more than either had seen at one time since they'd received their settlements from the lawsuit. It was glorious and sweet and a telling hint of their future.

It was chump change to Gavin, and he watched as these two men fondled the cash as though it were the treasure of the Sierra Madre. *Five hundred lousy bucks? Even a laborer pulls that in a week,* Gavin thought. But they were acting as if they had never seen that much before.

Gavin's emotions were spinning. He had to know who these men were, these men who appeared so simple at first but were becoming enormous complexities and contradictions. They could steal a million dollars in gold but didn't think to take his wallet? They could kidnap a man but honestly didn't want to hurt him? They could deprive a man his freedom yet serve him dinner—before they ate? He needed answers.

"How long have you been out of work?" he asked.

Walter, still looking at the cash as though it were the best poker hand he'd ever been dealt, didn't look up. "Seven years now, it's been."

Reg nodded. "Seven years."

Gavin stopped. *Seven years?* A few weeks, he could understand. At worst, a couple of months. But seven years?

"I mean, we get odd jobs and that, but seven years since the plant shut down."

"Why did the plant shut down?" Gavin asked.

"Some big company out of town bought it and figured they didn't need us," Walter said. "So they just sent us home."

Gavin felt his face flush. First Southern had been involved in several mergers and buyouts. At the bank in Columbus, about forty jobs had been eliminated—redundancies, they were called—people like the marketing director, who obviously wasn't needed as Gavin was already firmly entrenched in the Tower. He recalled that press conference, when a local reporter had asked about "all those displaced families," and being impressed at how smoothly Harperson had assured the world that First Southern held as its first priority providing placement services for those employees, and job counseling, blah blah blah. But the harsh reality was that those people were just numbers. No names, no faces—just forty records on a computer.

"How have you been able to support your families?"

Reg's head dropped, but he kept on eating. Walter, knowing Reg's pain, just said, "It's been tough."

"It's been tough," Gavin found himself repeating out loud. He slipped back into his thoughts, trying to make sense of anything that had happened to him in the last twenty-four hours. Suddenly, a memory from long ago became vivid again.

"Dad, I've got a big tennis match this weekend. League finals."

"This weekend? Sorry, Gavin. Can't make it." He pulled the newspaper back up.

"But Dad, you haven't been to a single match all year. This one's really important."

The paper didn't budge.

"Dad! You promised three times to come watch and you never have."

Gavin's father slowly lowered the paper and spoke with a voice of restrained anger. "*It's been tough*, Gavin. I need to close a few more deals." The paper went back up.

"Dad, listen to me! It's just one lousy weekend. Dad!" He stormed across the room and swiped his hand through the page, tearing it in half. His father's eyes glowered, and almost as a reflex he backhanded his son across the face.

"Don't you ever do anything like that to me again!" Mr. Duke bellowed. "I'm doing the best I can. It's not easy to support a family these days. It's tough. Real tough." He crumpled the paper and threw it down onto the carpet before storming out of the room.

Torrie and Carolina sat on Gavin's back porch as the detective tried to calm them enough to ask a few questions. The officer's name was David Lee. He was young, not yet forty, and had a kindness about him that made a nightmarish situation easier. Inside the house, a team of police technicians gathered evidence and searched for additional clues.

They had called 911 immediately—there was simply no other option—although they knew there would be major ramifications. Harperson was going to explode, even though he would have to agree there was no choice; Gavin's life was more important than squeaky clean PR.

Torrie was shaking and sobbing, going through tissue after tissue as Carolina slowly stroked her back.

They told Detective Lee all they could, although they were interrupted frequently as another officer would come in to fill him in on some scrap of evidence. He nodded slowly as the two women spoke, and he took copious notes.

When they were finished, he gave them each his card. "Call me anytime," he assured them. "If I'm not in, Terry can help you."

They thanked him, suppressing the tears, and Carolina asked if the police had any idea what might have happened.

"I don't think I can tell you anything you don't already know, at this point," he said. "It appears to be an abduction, plain and simple, and we don't know yet if it's related to the contest or not. We haven't found a note or received any demands so far."

"Can you tell when it happened? And is that Gavin's blood for sure?" Carolina pursued.

"We'll know the specific answers to those questions later, once everything's been through the lab. My guess is that the blood's been there for a while. But that's the best I can do now."

"So you think maybe this may have happened last night?" Torrie managed to get out.

"Again, we'll know for certain later. But in my opinion, I'd say that's probably correct."

She shuddered. What if she had gone over to Gavin's after the banquet? She might have been there. Carolina, sensing Torrie needed a change of scenery, said, "Come on, honey, it's time to go." She led her out, and they stood in the driveway as Detective Lee authorized enough vehicles to move around so they could back Carolina's car out.

Carolina's mind raced as they got onto the highway. *The idea of Gavin running off with the money was far-fetched enough as it was, but this? He couldn't have planned this elaborate a scheme—bleeding all over his own house just to make it look like an abduction. He really has been the victim of foul play. But was it random—did he stumble upon a burglar in his home perhaps—or does this have something to do with the money?*

Torrie wept. *Was there something I could have done that might have prevented this from happening? If I'd been there, maybe the kidnappers would have fled, surprised by the addition of another person to the puzzle. Or what if they decided to take me hostage, too?* She was frightened, too frightened to spend the night in her apartment, alone. *What if they know about me too? Is there a chance I'm in danger? Danger—what about death? With all that blood, is there a chance Gavin is already dead?* She tried to pray but couldn't concentrate.

"Carolina." She spoke faintly.

"Yes, what are you thinking?"

"I hope this doesn't seem, well, crazy to you, but . . . "

"Tell me, what is it?"

"I'm feeling a little afraid, and I'm not sure I'd do too well spending tonight alone. Do you think it would be possible for me to spend the night at your house?"

Carolina breathed a sigh of relief. "Of course. I need to call my husband and let him know. Goodness, I need to call him anyway! Let's stop by your place first, so you can pick some things up, all right?"

"That would be wonderful," Torrie almost smiled. "Thank you, Carolina. I don't know what I'd have done without you tonight."

"We all need each other right now," Carolina said, picking up her cellular phone.

❦   ❦   ❦

Reg had suspended a flashlight from the top rafter, so its beam would shine onto the table. The dinner plates had long since been cleared, so he had lovingly placed his photograph back onto the center of the table. He sat down and began his ritual, oblivious to Walter and Gavin. Gavin was sitting on the floor, and Walter was seated at the table next to Reg. But when Walter realized what Reg was doing, he got up and went out the door, not wanting to see this scene again.

Gavin watched all this, still not knowing what Reg was looking at. After a few minutes, grasping the fact that Reg wasn't planning on doing anything but stare into the photo, Gavin got up, went over to the side of the table, and saw what was in his captor's hands. *The young girl is pretty,* he thought, *and the young man—is that Reg?* His eyes went from the photo to Reg and back again, not understanding this scene in the least. He slowly moved to the door and, seeing Reg wasn't about to stop him, walked out into the night air and approached Walter.

"What's that all about?" Gavin asked.

"Lost his wife and kid," Walter said.

"Oh. Just recently?"

"Few years ago."

"A few years?" Gavin asked. "And he still stares into her picture like that?"

"Got nothin' else to do," Walter said stiffly.

"How did it happen? An accident?"

"Well, in Reg's mind, it's the company's fault. And I ain't so sure I'd disagree with him."

"The company? I don't understand."

"Lily took sick, and Reg couldn't pay for no insurance. Simple as that. Doctors told him they might have saved her if she'd been able to afford the medicine."

Gavin looked down at the ground. "But surely, with government health programs and clinics—something—she should have been able to get the medicine she needed."

"That what you rich boys really think goes on out here? That what they tell you? Ain't so, mister. There's you, and there's us. Y'all get everythin' you need, no matter what, but when you ain't got no job, no money—forget it."

"What about his kid?"

Walter just looked at him a minute. "After Lily died, Reg couldn't take care of Duane anymore. So they came and took him away."

Gavin was stunned. Not only had the man lost his job—and probably a terrible one at that—but he lost his family as well. And he didn't even lose the job because of anything wrong he did, it was just business. A buyout. He was just a statistic, like the numbers Gavin crunched every day on his calculator. He turned to look through the opened door and saw the pathetic figure hunched over a dead memory, dying minute by minute.

"That gold ain't gonna bring her back," Walter said, regaining Gavin's attention. "But at least it'll get ol' Reg out of here. And that's his only chance now, I think."

The gold, Gavin remembered. *That's why I'm here in this mess. These two want to know where I hid it. What did I do with it? Think hard, it may be coming now. Underground vault. Chain link fence. Big rock. Collapsing ceilings. The images are there, but they don't make any sense.* It wasn't coming together—not yet, anyway.

🌰 🌰 🌰

From Torrie's apartment, Carolina called Harperson. She thought he ought to know early on, and as she was dialing she realized this was probably the most unpleasant phone call she would ever have to make.

Harperson had two homes. One was in the city, in Buckhead, where he spent his weeks, and the other, his "cottage" on Lake Lanier, about forty-five minutes north of the city. It was ten thousand square feet of luxury, designed as a Cape Cod home with blue stained cedar shake shingles as siding and filled with artifacts and accessories of the sea. Had he not been a bank president, Carolina imagined, he'd probably have become a ship's captain. Ironically, the lakefront home was less than ten miles from Murrowstown.

She could feel her body tensing up as he came to the phone. "Carolina?"

"Yes, Gary. I have some news."

"I hope it's good," he said.

"I'm afraid not—not yet, anyway. We don't know where Gavin is right now, but I did go to his house and—Gary, apparently he's been kidnapped."

Harperson gulped, feeling a chill. As a highly visible bank president worth millions, he had been well aware that he, his wife, and children, were plausible targets for kidnappers. He'd met with security consultants in the past, but they assured him normal measures would suffice, augmented by a few extra strategically placed panic buttons around the houses. But Gavin—now Gavin was a target.

"Gary? Are you there? Are you all right?"

"Yeah, I'm . . . What happened?"

"All we know so far is there was a struggle in his living room, and he's gone. There was some blood."

"Blood? Oh, no."

"But there hasn't been a note—the police didn't find one and haven't heard anything yet."

"The police!" Harperson exclaimed, realizing the personal tragedy was a business nightmare as well. "We have to meet. Tonight," he said.

She paused to think. She understood his point—the media was going to be all over this, and they needed to ignore their emotions long enough to plan for damage control. Still . . .

"I need you to bring Maureen too. Can you come to the house?"

She bit her lip. "Okay. I'll be there as soon as I can." She hung up, quickly called Maureen's number and made the arrangements. Torrie listened in and spoke when Carolina finished with Maureen.

"Life's just like that, isn't it? A man is missing, someone we care about, but commerce has to march on."

Carolina whirled around. "Torrie, I'm sorry. It's the last thing—"

"No, don't apologize. It's something you've got to do," she said, wiping a tear from each eye. She laughed. "I'm going to have to do the same thing too. I've got to write a story about it. But I can't deal with it tonight. Tomorrow, maybe."

"Are you gonna be okay at my house if I'm not there for a while?"

"Actually, I think I'll just stay here instead," Torrie said, having lost most of her fear—a combination of sheer exhaustion and the prayers she managed to piece together.

"Are you sure?" Carolina prodded. "You're more than welcome."

"Thanks, Carolina. Really." She came up and rubbed Carolina's arm. "I'll be okay. I'll just curl up with my cat and wait by the phone."

"Okay. But call me if you need anything, okay?"

"I promise," Torrie smiled. "Thanks, Carolina." They embraced, and Torrie asked, "Will you pray for me, Carolina?"

"Why, how sweet," Carolina said. "Of course I will." She surprised Torrie by praying aloud right then and there.

"Father," she began, "be with Gavin tonight. Wherever he is. And protect Torrie's heart and comfort her. Amen."

"Amen," Torrie agreed, warmed by Carolina's prayer.

"Good night, Torrie," Carolina said, pulling the door open and walking back toward one of the longest days of her life, which still had quite a ways to go.

❦   ❦   ❦

Carolina, Maureen, and Harperson began their meeting around eleven that night. The agenda was long.

They agreed a press conference would be premature, and they certainly didn't want to generate more news. Maureen would begin to prepare official bank replies to allegations that Gavin might have disappeared with the gold. And the promotion itself would continue without skipping a beat.

"What if people start to think that either Gavin or the kidnappers have already made off with the gold?" Maureen said. "The influx of new accounts would stop, and it's possible a lot of angry people would actually close down their accounts, feeling like we took advantage of them."

Carolina noticed Harperson tightening his fists as the meeting progressed.

"You don't think assuring everyone that the gold is safe and sound would be enough?" Harperson asked.

"We could develop some new ads that promise that's the case, if need be," Carolina offered.

"What if there's evidence that someone has made off with it?"

Carolina paused. "If you're willing to, we could hide another million," she said. "I know that's an outrageous commitment, but in light of what all the new deposits and loans are worth, I suspect you'd lose more than that if everyone pulled their accounts at once."

He sat back in his chair. "Which would you rather do, lose ten million in profits or one million in gold?" he asked rhetorically. "Sounds like a no-win deal."

"Let's just hope it doesn't come to that," she said.

The meeting droned on, and Carolina grew frustrated at Harperson's callous attitude about Gavin's welfare. By midnight, she allowed herself to counter by suggesting prayer would be the best weapon. It seemed to have at least a little impact; Harperson, exhausted, leaned back and recalled a few anecdotes from his childhood Sunday school memories. *Ah, well,* Carolina consoled herself, *at least he's not thinking about his portfolio for a minute.* But the minute ended all too quickly, and The Man grumpily resumed his calculations.

❧　❧　❧

The next morning's headlines screamed scandal. The banner read, "Bank golden boy vanishes." But worse still, in a gray box off to the left, was this headline: "Customers Wonder: Kidnapping or Con Job?"

H. Gary Harperson folded the paper down and wept for the first time since his youngest daughter's wedding.

❧　❧　❧

Ruth read the paper at the breakfast table. She read about the blood, the bent lamp shade, and the self-proclaimed experts who decided Gavin Duke—a man they'd never met—might have taken the money and run.

Ronnie looked lovingly at her. "What's going through your mind?" he asked her.

She put the paper down, stood up, walked over, and threw her arms around him. "I'm so confused," she said. "I've hated Gavin so long, but now—when something might have happened to him—I'm actually worried about him."

"Wouldn't you be worried a little about yourself if you didn't feel some sympathy for another human being in trouble?" Ronnie asked. "Even if it is a guy like Gavin Duke?"

"I suppose," she said. "But I'm worrying about something else too. What if this really is one of his clever schemes? What if the struggle, the blood was all a diversion? What if he's halfway to Tahiti by now—to our island?"

Ronnie, not having worked with Gavin and feeling no admiration at all for the workings of his brilliant mind, said, "No way. This is yours. Your chance. Don't let Gavin Duke cheat you out of another thing, you hear me?"

"Okay," she said, as she buried her head into his neck, not wanting him to realize she had tears in her eyes.

🪙　🪙　🪙

The radio Walter had brought along wasn't working well. The thick woods interfered with the signal, and besides, there weren't that many stations up toward Murrowstown. He decided to go up and get a paper the next morning. It was a long walk, but he was getting bored all cooped up in that tiny room with two other men.

The closest newsstand was an old gas station along the highway. As he drew near, he noticed an unusually large headline, and it stopped him dead in his tracks. He fumbled for the correct change and tore the paper out of the box. The world was onto them, he saw, beads of perspiration forming on his forehead. He looked around nervously, fearing someone was watching him, and quickly folded the paper in half, stuck it inside his shirt so no one would read the headline, and darted back toward Steinbeck's cabin.

Gavin read the paper with horror. *How could anyone accuse me of faking this tragedy and of jettisoning my career to become a thief? I have to get word out somehow. I have to clear my reputation. The world has to know the truth.*

Between the knives and the shotguns and Walter and Reg and the jungle, Gavin knew escape was not an option at this point. He had to think of something else. He looked at Reg and Walter as they tried to decide if they were elated or horrified at the stir they had created, and he got an idea.

"Walter. Reg."

They looked over at him. "With all that blood, lots of people are convinced you intended to seriously hurt me—or may have already," he said, trying not to accept the fact that he was talking about his own well-being. "I think you'd be smart to let the world know I'm okay, that you're treating me well."

There was an uncomfortable silence, which Walter broke. "What do you think we should do?"

"Let me send a message out, saying I'm okay," he said.

"What kinda message? Like a note in a bottle?"

Gavin mulled that one over, his mind still not functioning well—if it had been, he'd remember where the gold was and get out of this mess.

"I could write a note, or . . . you could send a videotape of me."

"A videotape? You see any movie cameras round here?" Walter asked sarcastically, waving his hand around the empty cabin.

Gavin paused again to think about it. "You could get one with the money I had in my wallet," he suggested.

The idea seemed farfetched at first, but neither Walter or Reg wanted to be the first to say so, and the more each thought of it, the more they liked it.

"It'd be a good way to make people realize you're not abusing me out here," he said. "In case you ever get caught, it may help you out." Gavin was not concerned with the court's leniency on these two as much as he wanted to unsully his tarnished reputation. But still, it made sense.

"I could head up to the Ross Repair Shop, down old Orchard Road," Reg suggested. "They got some movie cameras up there."

"How much's that gonna cost?" Walter wondered.

"Ain't got no idea. What do you think, Mr. Duke?"

Gavin said, "Take three hundred to be safe."

The boys shared a look and a shrug. Reg peeled off three of the hundreds, and left. He trudged up the path, hitched a ride to Ross', and bought a used video camera for $159. Mr. Ross reminded him he'd want a tape too.

"Shootin' some home movies?" he asked.

"You might say that," Reg said.

🪙   🪙   🪙

Torrie sat at her desk. Fortunately for her, she wasn't on deadline, so she didn't have to do any writing today. It was a good thing, because she wasn't at her best. She was badly shaken from the scene at Gavin's house, and then to see in the paper today that people actually thought he might have just been a con man—that was too much.

Now that the exhaustion and the initial shock were wearing off, she had time to think about Carolina's prayer. Was it possible that this remarkable woman was a Christian too? She decided to call and find out, and to get herself a little pep talk.

"How're you doing?" Carolina asked, doing her best to keep steady herself.

"I've been better," Torrie said.

"Can we have lunch today?" Carolina suggested.

"Do you have time?"

"I'll make the time."

"I'd love to," Torrie said. She realized she had made a friend in Carolina. It wasn't going to be the kind of relationship she was used to, being young and single while Carolina was older and married with kids. But it was going to be warm, and deep, and good.

When they met for lunch, Torrie didn't mince any words. As soon as they sat down, Torrie asked, "Carolina, how long have you been a Christian?"

Carolina looked slightly startled but broke into a warm smile. "I realized I needed Christ when I was a little girl, about ten years old. And you?"

"I was in college," Torrie said. "Some friends showed me you can't work your way into Heaven."

Carolina's smile glowed. She reached out and grabbed Torrie's hand. "I'm so glad to know that," she said.

With the ice now broken, Torrie and Carolina flew past the small talk and opened their hearts. Torrie talked about her relationship with Gavin and wrestling with her conflicting emotions, and Carolina told her about some of the issues she and her husband had worked through—and were still working through—over the years.

"It's all right for you to let yourself experience your sorrow, you know," Carolina said. She paused. "In fact, I'll let you in on a secret of mine, just between friends. I don't tell many people this, but . . . "

Torrie listened intently, not losing sight of the fact that not only was Carolina opening up to her, but that she didn't make a point of swearing her to secrecy, given the fact that she was a reporter.

"Burl and I lost a child several years ago." She paused again, obviously getting choked up. "It is a pain that never goes away."

Torrie looked at Carolina in awe, realizing that you could know a person, work with them, see someone who looks all together and focused and strong, and not know the hidden hurts and trials and scars that are carried within that heart.

"I fell completely apart. I was useless for months. But over time, with Burl's support and many, many people praying for us, we got through it. We went on."

Both women fought back the tears, but the tears came anyway.

"I'm sure Gavin's fine. Everything will work out all right. But in the meantime, it's okay to feel, to allow yourself to really feel the emotions. David cried out in the psalms—wrenching pain and worry and fear and mountaintop joys. And that was just fine with God."

Torrie nodded and burst into tears. "Okay!" she bellowed, and they laughed and cried together for two hours.

Gavin was startled to see Reg return with a video camera. He had half suspected, from Reg's reaction to the money, that he'd decide to cash in for three hundred dollars and not come back.

As he showed these two how to use the camera, he took a mental break to realize how bizarre this scene was: Gavin Duke, big time bank marketing vice president, in the middle of the woods, showing two unemployed factory workers how to operate a video camera so they can tape his saying he was, in fact, neither dead nor a thief. "Maybe," Gavin said to himself, "I will learn to take life less seriously if I ever get out of this mess." A fleeting memory of Torrie telling him God had a sense of humor flew through his thoughts.

Instead of using the cabin as a backdrop, Reg and Walter agreed the woods would be seen behind Gavin. There was a possibility, no matter how remote, that someone might recognize part of the structure. But woods are woods, from Florida to Louisiana.

Reg held the camera and taped Gavin as he said:

This is Gavin Duke. It is Wednesday the nineteenth, two days after I was taken from my home. The blood was from this cut on my forehead, which I sustained in an accidental fall. Otherwise, I am healthy. I am being well treated, fed regularly, and am allowed to sleep inside. I am not being tortured or beaten. I have seen today's paper which says some people think I have disappeared with the gold. This could not be further from the truth. Anyone who has ever known me or worked with me can confirm that I am honest, fair, and my primary loyalty is to First Southern. I am generous, not the kind of person who would take anything that did not belong to me, and not the kind of person who would intentionally hurt another. I am, in fact, the picture of loyalty. I have often wished I could find people to work for me who were even half as loyal as I am.

Gavin finished, and Reg stopped recording. "You're really worried about people thinkin' you pinched the gold, ain't you?" he asked. "You kinda went on and on about it."

"Let's just get the tape out, okay?" Gavin said. It was so funny, the scope of the ironies he was experiencing here. He had made television commercials with some of the biggest names in Hollywood, films that had cost more than a hundred thousand dollars to produce before winning armloads of awards worldwide, yet this homegrown spot in the woods, taped on a used camera that cost all of a hundred and fifty-nine bucks, was far and away the most important production session of his life.

"What're we supposed to do with it from here?" Walter asked.

Gavin instructed them to send it to Torrie and gave them her address at the paper, which he was surprised he could remember. He tried again to think of where he hid the gold and was pleased to get an image of Brick and the county courthouse this time—but no more.

Now, the question was how to get the tape from here to there. Dropping it in the mail would be too slow, and delivery services didn't make stops in the woods. They certainly couldn't risk another trip into Atlanta. Then Gavin got his brainstorm.

"Is there a landmark up around here somewhere, something that everybody knows about?" He still had no idea what part of Georgia he was in, if he was actually in Georgia at all.

"What do you mean?" Walter asked.

"We're going to leave the tape somewhere and call the paper to let them know where they can pick it up. If we leave it in an ordinary place, like a gas station or a field, they'll be convinced I'm being held nearby. But if it's at a landmark, especially a Civil War landmark, you might be able to convince everybody we're just about anywhere."

Made sense, the two agreed. *Landmarks? Sure.* "There's an old gold minin' site a few miles away—big old historical marker."

"Perfect," Gavin said, "they'll think you put it there because of the promotion and not because we're around here." He also made a mental note: *we're not far from Dahlonega, where the gold rush took place.* He was glad he'd done his homework before the campaign began, and he was glad his memory was coming back.

That night, as Reg stared into the past, Walter snuck off and hid the tape behind the brass marker that was set back a few yards from a seldom-used country highway. On the way back to the cabin, he called the number for the *Business Courier* that Gavin had given him. As Gavin had promised, a recording came on, and Walter left the message for

Torrie that Gavin had written: "Torrie, there's somethin' for you from Gavin. He's okay, and he wanted to let you and everybody else know. It's a tape, and it's hidden behind a state historical marker." He gave the directions, hung up, and made his way back to the cabin as quickly as he could.

Eighteen

Roger Frederichs scurried down the hallway. He was late for the meeting—which was bad enough—but to make matters worse, he'd called the meeting.

He fiddled with one of the buttons on his sweater as he noticed the sound of his wing-tip shoes clacking against the hard slippery tile, the kind of floor you'd expect to find in a government building. He looked out the series of windows as he darted along. "It's a beautiful day," he said to himself, wishing he could get out and about a little more. He used to do more field work. He still got to do some, but now that he had climbed the civil service ladder, he spent most of his time going from building to building, looking at maps and aerial photos of places that were outside.

Roger was a supervisor for the Georgia Department of Transportation, DOT for short. He was meeting this morning with officials of his own agency as well as its sister agency, the Alabama Highway Department, the Georgia Department of Natural Resources, and the U.S. Army Corps of Engineers. *A pretty big meeting for such a little bridge,* he thought with a huff.

The door made the resoundingly loud sound a door makes when you walk into a room late, and everyone turned to look up at him. "Good golly, Miz Molly. I'm finally here," he said. "Sorry to keep you on pins and needles. Couldn't get away from the commissioner."

Everyone nodded or shrugged, having been in the same boat a number of times themselves, and they shuffled papers and took sips of coffee or ice water from paper cups with swirly designs on them.

"Alley oop, then. Let's forge away," he said. "You all have the updated game plan in front of you. The geological surveys have been completed, and you can see from the appendices why we've shifted the ramp location from the site where it was originally planned."

"What's that going to do to our budget?" one of the Alabama officials asked.

Roger smirked. "Hoots and guffaws, Daryl. You're gonna love this one. It won't change yours a penny, because the significant changes are all on the Georgia side of the river. The only difference on the Alabama side is that the pavement shifts direction by about thirty feet."

Roger cleared his throat, pulled out a small pair of nail clippers, and began fiddling with them. "Our cost factors, on the other hand, will take the hit. But believe it or not, it won't be that much. The detonation cost is minimal, and the greater expense—breaking the stone into pieces—will pretty much be offset by the income from the raw materials. You can see in appendix, uh, I think it's appendix four-dash-three, that it's just a matter of the company that got the low bid coming in and clearing it out for us." He didn't look up as he spoke but squinted in concentration, trying feverishly to dislodge some speck that had gotten underneath his left thumbnail. "Gadzooks," he mumbled, prying up and down with the end of the tiny nail file that was attached to the clippers. "Aha!"

He turned to his assistant and pointed to a large map that was rolled up like a window shade on the wall. "Is this the immediate site map or the area map?"

"The area map," the man muttered, sounding as though the coffee hadn't done any good at all.

With a smile, Roger folded the file back into the clippers and dropped them into his sweater pocket. He popped up, darted to the map, and rolled it down to reveal a view of Stewart County, Georgia, where the Chattahoochee River acted as a natural border with

Alabama. "Is everyone set on the orientation?" He pointed to a spot on the river. "The old base—or manufacturing facility, I guess—is here. The Corps has already begun grading on the Alabama side of the river, over here. The bridge will link the two, due to the frequency of material hauling that is planned."

He looked to his assistant again. "Which one is the site map?"

The assistant, with no more energy than before, pointed lazily at another rolled-up map, hanging to the right of the first. "Right there," he said.

Roger pulled down a close-up map of the river that showed roads and buildings and dashed lines to indicate several proposed roads and the bridge. "As I mentioned, the bridge site has been re-routed, as well as portions of the feeder road, obviously, based on the report of the geological survey. While it may seem to be a lot of wasted effort to move a bridge from a flat site to a site where we have to 'move a mountain,' so to speak, the fact is that with the heavy trucks the army is planning on running back and forth along that bridge all day long, the soil conditions along other parts of the riverbank aren't stable enough for that kind of load bearing."

He stopped in mid-thought and chuckled as if he had discovered a great revelation. "To make it simple, think of the rock as the peak to an underground mountain range. The granite itself juts up there, providing a solid base, but in the immediate vicinity, the rock is far below the surface. The soil that makes up the surface upriver and downriver from the rock just isn't solid enough to carry the bridge." He began digging behind a tooth with his tongue as though something were lodged there too.

"So when it comes down to it," the colonel from the Army Corps asked, "you're going to blow up the rock to make way for the bridge."

"In effect, yes," Roger said, sitting down as he searched himself for a matchbook. "We'll only detonate some of the underside of the rock—just loosen it up a bit—and then the excavation company will come in and break the rest up before they haul it away." He paused and grinned as he pulled a matchbook from his pants pocket. "Aha!" He glanced down and inspected it. "But when it comes down to it, that's right. We're going to blow up the rock so we can put the bridge there." He unfolded the matchbook and began to use one corner as a piece of dental floss.

"I love it," the colonel smiled. "Blow the rock out of the way for the bridge. Just the way the army would do it!"

Everyone laughed.

🌰　🌰　🌰

If Torrie had been glad about anything this week, it was that Thursday was finally here. It was deadline day for her, and she wanted to get her story about the kidnapping filed. It was important to her, both personally and professionally, to be able to make it through this story. Lunch with Carolina the day before had given her the boost she needed, and that afternoon she'd gotten the bulk of her work done at the office. This morning, she'd be able to finish up before the noon cutoff.

She got in early, around 7:30, and was surprised to see a message on her voice mail, since she'd stayed until past six on Wednesday. She pushed the playback button as she took her purse from her shoulder and wound the strap around it to slide it in her desk drawer. She froze when she heard Walter's message. She played it again and, cool as she could be, pulled her purse back out and found Dave Lee's card. She hoped he was true to his word, that "anytime day or night" meant just that.

"Detective Lee."

"This is Torrie Wilson. I've gotten a message about Gavin."

"What kind of message?"

"It's on my answering machine. You'd better hear it."

"I'm on my way."

She quickly booted up her computer and left an E-Mail message for Sandy, her editor—she'd most likely have to miss her deadline because she'd be taken out of town to get the tape with the police, but here's where to find her notes, and she'll be checking in throughout the morning. She pressed the Send key, which activated a blinking red light on Sandy's computer for her to find when she arrived. She sat down, closed her eyes tight, and prayed until the detective arrived.

Within minutes, Dave was there, along with a pair of agents from the Georgia Bureau of Investigation, GBI. They listened to the message and asked Torrie if she would come with them, as she expected.

Instead of taking her all the way to the monument, they decided to bring her to the Gainesville office, while other agents would retrieve the tape and meet them there. It saves time—a critical element in an abduction case, they informed her, since things could take unexpected turns at any moment.

How reassuring, she thought, speeding up the highway in a car with a flashing blue light on top and a siren screaming the entire way. She was glad they wanted to move quickly but was unnerved in understanding the reasons why.

The trip took about forty-five minutes—an eternity by the standards of passion, worry, and fear. She was struggling to remember the calm she had worked toward after meeting with Carolina but was having only a modicum of success at it just now.

She was taken to a small, sterile room, where a good-sized color TV and VCR had been placed on a cart. She was introduced to several more GBI agents, who were all polite to her but whose names she did not remember, despite being a reporter covering this story. She really felt like a woman who was hurting for the man she cared about.

They watched the tape—which was difficult because Reg's camera handling skills were shaky at best and positively dizzying at worst—but Torrie was relieved to see Gavin lucid and coherent, if not a little slower than usual, and that the source of all that awful blood was now reduced to a small length of tape-covered gauze above his left eye. She found herself taking several deep sighs and asked if she could visit the bathroom to splash some cool water on her face.

For the next hour or so, the agents made her watch the tape several more times—instructing her to see if she could discern any clues, any code words, that might point them to a location. "No, sorry, I wish I could pick something up, but there's nothing, nothing."

They let her call Sandy and provide some information over the phone for the story Torrie wasn't going to write. They also informed her that they were releasing the tape to all the media, in hopes that someone somewhere may be able to provide some leads that could point them in the right direction.

By eleven she was finished, so the three officers who'd brought her up loaded her back into the car and took off for Atlanta.

"We'll find him," Dave assured her, and his warmth and strength encouraged her that everything was going to turn out all right.

⬬   ⬬   ⬬

H. Gary Harperson was having a meeting of his own, and no more pleasant than Torrie's. He and his top management were huddled in the boardroom with representatives of the Federal Deposit Insurance Corporation. The FDIC had called the meeting to discuss options the bank may have to exercise if the mass exodus of deposits that began the day before continued. If everyone who opened a new checking or savings account decided the promotion was a sham and came asking to close down their accounts, the bank's reserves might not cover all the new outstanding loans to the degree that the government required. In a worse-case scenario, the Feds could temporarily shut the bank down.

Harperson was having a hard time believing this. Just a few short hours after riding high on the most successful new-business campaign in the history of the banking industry, there was serious talk—legitimate talk—of the bank being closed by regulators.

This meeting was no worse than the one late yesterday afternoon, with key executives from the leading brokerage firms. Wall Street had done him a favor by delaying trading of First Southern shares, but the hemorrhaging came anyway: The price per share plummeted $7.25 in one black day, from $25.50 all the way down to $18.25, a dip of more than 28 percent. Harperson personally lost more than two million dollars (on paper, anyway), since he held in excess of three hundred thousand shares, but he'd been around the bend long enough to know the markets were prone to panic and his fortune was secure. What he was worried about was his scalp, since shareholders are not so accommodating. The fact was he could lose a few million dollars, find his bank shut down by the U.S. government, lose the reputation he'd spent thirty-two years cultivating, and end up fired unceremoniously in the very prime of his career—all because of this.

But everything changed when news started to leak out about the tape. The local TV stations cut into the soaps and game shows to break the story, and the exodus of accounts slowed significantly. Customers reasoned Gavin really was kidnapped, and not off on a beach with their money. And while the fear that the kidnappers might get the money was still very real, that was a different scenario altogether—especially since Carolina and Maureen had made sure their contacts in the media knew that a stolen treasure would be replaced by the bank, so everyone's chances were still alive to get their million in Southern Gold.

Gavin woke up that morning and shifted around. He was fully aware of his surroundings now, no longer startled to find himself in a shack. He was also beginning to feel some of the psychological attachment to his captors that hostages have been known to develop—he counted on them for his survival, so he was growing ever so slightly dependent on them emotionally. Of course, the fact that they treated him well contributed to this process, as well as the fact that he truly felt sorry for these two and the cruel circumstances that had befallen them. He wondered why they had been chosen to be so unlucky, and he startled himself by asking God why He allowed such tragedies. Gavin wondered if Carrie had a good answer for that one. Or Torrie. *Somehow, I imagine they do*, he thought.

Reg poured him a cup of hot black coffee for breakfast, and he got to eat a bowl of corn flakes too—dry, since there was no refrigerator to keep milk cold.

"If you end up with the money, Reg, what are you going to do with it?" Gavin asked, surprising himself and Reg with the question. Walter was outside.

"I'm gonna get out of this place," he said without having to think about it. "Far away as I can."

"Do you know where?"

"Nope. Just far away. Walter's been talking about a tropical kinda place, and that'd be fine. Just away from here."

"Is it really that important to get far away?"

"Well, we need to get out of here 'cuz everybody's gonna be lookin' for us," Reg said, "but this town'll kill a man, y'know what I mean?"

"No, not really," Gavin said, seriously trying to understand. "What do you mean?"

"Can't explain it unless a man's been through it," Reg answered. "If you been in a place where you gave everything you had and still got nothin', and no way you'd ever get nothin', and had everything important you loved taken away from you, I guess there's just a time a man decides he needs to get away."

That's the saddest encapsulation of a man's life I've ever heard, Gavin thought. He couldn't help but wonder about Reg's lost family. "Are you going to try to get your son back?"

The question surprised Reg. His head jerked back suddenly and then dropped. "He probably don't even remember me," he said sullenly.

"He's your son! He needs you. How can you just leave him like that?"

Reg stared across the table at Gavin. "My boy deserves a better life than what I can give him. He don't need to be stuck with me."

Gavin still refused to understand. "But you're his father!"

"I'm just a man, Mr. Duke. It was Lily that was raisin' him up good. Now that she's gone . . . " He let his voice trail off. "He's better off where he is now." He stood up and walked silently toward the door just as Walter came in.

"I bet they got your tape by now," he said.

"I hope so," Gavin said.

"You havin' any better luck rememberin' where y'all put that gold today?" he asked.

"Just as far as I got yesterday," Gavin said. "I remember a man named Brick, an old county courthouse, a fenced-in area near a river—or a creek—and an underground tunnel."

"But not where all that is, huh?"

"Maybe I'll get it today," he said. He didn't know when he'd developed a cooperative attitude, but he did know he wasn't as stubborn as he had been before. *So what if they get the gold? At least I'd have my freedom back. And besides, unloading a million dollars in gold isn't simply a matter of heading over to your neighborhood First Southern branch and asking, "Could you change this for me, please? In unmarked small bills?" No, Walter and Reg will get caught, but who knows? If their goal is to get out of the small town they're trapped in, maybe the state prison will probably be a welcome change of pace. Heck, they'll be out in a few years on good behavior, since they're good men at heart and not genuine criminals, and with their share of the book and movie deals, they might just end up living high on the hog anyway.*

Gavin spent the rest of the morning exercising on the grounds, and after lunch he needed a nap—he was still under stress and on the mend from losing all that blood. But flashes of conversations with Torrie kept popping into his head, random bits and pieces about letting God be in control and all things working out for good. Out here, out of control for the first time in his life, or so he thought, there was no choice other than to let God be in control. But as for all things working out for the best, well, he was having a tougher time with that one.

"But there's so much more to life than just getting richer," Torrie had said once.

"That's not what my dad taught me," Gavin had answered.

"But was he really happy?" she asked.

"Let's go get some ice cream," he said, and the topic never came back.

🍪   🍪   🍪

By this time, everyone had seen the Gavin tape on TV, yet the debate raged on. One woman, interviewed at the mall for Channel 11, said, "That poor boy. I hope they find him okay," while the next man who appeared on the screen said, "I'm still pretty skeptical—I mean, if he could fake the kidnapping, and the blood and all, he could fake this too. I think he's in Central America by now."

Ruth had seen the tape too. And Gavin's closing words were not lost on her: "I am, in fact, the picture of loyalty. I have often wished I could find people to work for me who were even half as loyal as I am."

Cooler heads would put the words into context—the man was being falsely accused of gross disloyalty, he had suffered a blow to the head and was under severe stress, perhaps with guns leveled at his head as he spoke. But Ruth was not necessarily thinking logically—she was at the end of her rope, and all she heard was Gavin Duke wishing people like Ruth Chandler could be as loyal and good and virtuous as he.

She stood right up and left the office before lunch, without leaving word with anyone. "Enough of this," she muttered under her breath. She was going home to relax for the rest of the afternoon, and when Ronnie came home after work, they could watch the Gavin tape on the news together, and then they were going to win the lottery.

🌰　🌰　🌰

"What's the schedule for demolition?" one of the Alabama high-waymen asked Roger.

"First thing Saturday morning," Roger said. "Dawn, in fact." He lowered the matchbook and twitched with his tongue again.

"Dawn Saturday?" one off the others piped up. "Whatever happened to weekdays—or daylight?" Two or three others grumbled in unison.

"Tut-tut, now," Roger said, waving his hand. "We've a schedule to keep. But please, don't kill the messenger. I'm only following orders."

"What about overtime costs?"

Roger dropped the matchbook into his sweater pocket, alongside the clippers. "The powers that be have decided that's okeydokey with them. Any other concerns?"

"What kind of prep work has been done to date?"

"Very little has been needed, fortunately. On both sides of the river, the areas in question have been fenced off and secured for years, so there's minimal chance of anyone being in the area. We did a spot check the other day, and it looked secure. The area around the rock is locked up tight, and river access is virtually impossible. I understand the geology team set off some small caps around the base of the rock last week, to get a sense of how much TNT they'll need to get the demolition started, and they were pleased with the results. The report includes their summary, and there's mention of some measurable seismic activity created by their small test explosions." Roger searched himself again, and came up with his pocket calendar. Flipping through the pages, he whistled softly. "Bingo. I'll be heading down that way tomorrow, personally, to make some last-minute checks."

He paused and looked around the room. "Any other questions?" The others at the table looked around, or doodled, or took another sip. "Toot sweet, then," he said. "Thanks for coming this morning."

The others assembled their papers and began to clear out of the room, making small talk about the weather and baseball and plans for the weekend and of course, the gold contest and the kidnapping.

Torrie was feeling hopeful again as she got back to the office, having seen Gavin on the tape. She chided herself for wishing he had mentioned her, or sent a private message to her, knowing it would have cast the spotlight onto her too—the last thing she needed at this point.

It wasn't noon yet, but the deadline was meaningless to her now since the story had been passed onto someone else. Torrie found Sandy in the newsroom, scurrying around to cover all the bases since the editor wasn't excused from deadlines this day.

"Can we have lunch today," Sandy asked her, "after all this madness has died down? How about something more like one, or one-thirty?"

"Sure, I'd love to," Torrie smiled. She walked over to see how the bank story was coming. It was a tough one to handle, since the news was changing by the minute and the *Business Courier* was not intended as a daily paper or a TV station that could do live remotes. The paper's angle would focus on how the kidnapping was affecting business at First Southern and other banks. She'd known that all along, but after seeing the tape of Gavin and being through the rigors of the morning, she bristled. *It seems so cold, so distant, so wrong to make this a story about stock prices and account closings and how much H. Gary Harperson's net worth fluctuated over the past two days.*

She found an empty workstation and called up the story as she looked up at the clock on the wall to find it was quarter to noon. The story was virtually complete, so what she was reading was pretty much what would appear in the paper.

Hmm, The Man is down two mil. Too bad. And what's this about the FDIC? That was new. Let's see, what else . . . bank may bury another million . . . gold was insured by Lloyd's of London . . . Carolina Gates Advertising preparing new ads in case public gets nasty . . . everything seems to be in order. She powered down the computer and decided to take a walk outside to kill some time until her lunch date with Sandy.

As she walked down Peachtree Street, not going anywhere in particular, her thoughts wandered to all that had happened in the past few weeks. It seemed like a million years ago that she flew into Atlanta, not knowing a soul, when Sandy was so nice to her and she bumped into Gavin—literally—before meeting him. And oh yes, Ruth. Getting through, around, under, and past Ruth. That had been quite a challenge.

Ruth! Torrie had spent time with Carolina since the insanity had begun a few days ago, but she hadn't talked to Ruth since the very beginning—when everyone was going from curious to worried when Gavin had been absent all day. Torrie wondered how she was doing. She stopped to get her bearings—she was so deep in thought she really wasn't paying attention to where she was walking. She turned and saw she'd passed the First Southern Tower about three blocks back. She started walking again but this time had a destination in mind. She looked at her watch—just after noon. *Hope Ruth's not at lunch already*, she thought.

As Torrie made her way toward the bank, she realized she hadn't given much thought lately to the nature of Gavin's relationship with Ruth. She knew she had at first imagined they had a strong working chemistry, given the way Ruth did such a masterful job of protecting Gavin from the press—like Torrie. But over time she observed a distinct tension in the air, more often on Ruth's part than on Gavin's, which Torrie decided was because of the condescending, sexist, and sometimes rude way he treated those below him on the corporate ladder. Gavin seemed to like her but was mean to her; Ruth, on the other hand, seemed to harbor some deep resentments, if not downright hostility, toward her boss. Torrie wondered for the first time if there had been something more between them once—or more likely, whether there had been some feelings on Ruth's part that were not reciprocated by Gavin. Perhaps she never even expressed them, since she was married, but Torrie didn't know if that marriage had come before or after the working relationship began. *Interesting*, Torrie thought. *Maybe Ruth's reaction to Gavin's abduction will reveal more answers.*

She boarded the elevator and stepped off at the sixtieth floor. "Rats," she said, finding Ruth's desk covered with papers and the computer on but no Ruth. Torrie assumed she was at lunch and went back downstairs, realizing it was close enough to one o'clock to head back to the paper and pick Sandy up for lunch.

Sandy seemed much more serious than usual as they left the building. *Must be the stress of the bank story and the deadlines*, Torrie thought. *Good thing she'll be able to get out for a while.*

They found a hotel restaurant, which was quieter than most of the more traditional business lunch spots. Sandy asked for a corner table. *Wow, she really does want to get away from it*, Torrie thought.

But when they were seated, Sandy laid her cards on the table.

"I'm a little disturbed—no, let's say concerned—about a few things," the editor said to the reporter.

Torrie, thinking she meant some things about Gavin's case had loose ends, hopped right in. "Me, too. Like the fact that—"

"Hang on, Torrie," Sandy interrupted. "I think we're talking about two different subjects."

"Okay . . . " said Torrie, a bit confused.

"Do you know why the kidnapper called you about the tape?"

Torrie was really confused now. "I don't know exactly what you mean. They wanted everyone to see Gavin was okay, and . . . "

"No, I mean, why did they call *you* instead of one of the other reporters, especially one of the TV people—after all, it was a videotape he sent, not a statement."

"I'm still not sure I understand. I guess he wanted the *Business Courier* to get the story first," she said.

"Perhaps so," said the editor, "but if you think about it, that doesn't make a lot of sense. As I said before, TV was the logical first choice. Then a daily paper. Or the police. But a weekly paper? We can't break anything. And besides, we cover the business angle; from a purely journalistic standpoint, the tape was of little value to our reporting."

"So? He's not thinking through all that . . . They're not thinking through all that. What're you getting at?" Torrie asked, with growing exasperation.

"The point is, I think Gavin sent you that tape for personal reasons rather than professional reasons," Sandy said, looking straight at her.

Torrie shrank back into her seat. "Well, even if that really is the case, why is that a problem?"

"I'm not sure I'm totally comfortable with the ethics of it," Sandy said pointedly. "But more than that, it's a matter of how it's perceived—by our peers, by the people at the bank, by anybody on the outside looking in who sees the bank marketing director dating the *Business Courier*'s finance reporter, just days after she gets into town, when he's being accused in some corners of—"

"Now, wait just a minute!" Torrie said, thrown by this barrage from a person she thought was on her side. "I haven't done a thing wrong, or unethical, and I certainly haven't compromised my principles in any way. I resent the implication!" Her nerves were frazzled enough—she certainly didn't need this.

Sandy, realizing she may have gotten a little carried away, said, "Look, Torrie, I'm sorry. I didn't mean to accuse you of anything. I'm just trying to lay out the facts, so you can see how others may perceive the situation."

"Others? What are you saying?"

"I'm saying . . . I have to reassign you from the bank beat to the general assignment desk." She let out a deep breath when she finished, as though it were a lot of work to get the line out.

"Is this some kind of demotion?" Torrie asked, absolutely astounded.

"No, not at all. And it's not necessarily even permanent. Just until this First Southern ordeal blows over. Then we can reevaluate things."

"But I'm a good reporter. I can handle this," she said.

"Torrie, I had to have someone else cover for you this morning—

you missed your deadline because you were identifying Gavin on the tape, because he had it sent to you! You may be able to handle it, but the paper can't."

Torrie nodded, understanding where Sandy was coming from. "Okay, I've got it, chief."

"Good," Sandy said as their salads arrived. "I hope this doesn't change things between us. We've had a good start, and I'd like to keep things headed in that direction."

"You got yourself a deal," Torrie said, but at this moment she didn't know if she was going to stay in Atlanta after waking from this nightmare.

Harperson was watching the stock ticker in his office. The share price for First Southern had stabilized, and had in fact come back two points since yesterday's free fall. Customers and investors were accepting the fact that this was not an inside job and that the worst possible outcome was the need for a replacement million to make up for the original, if it were stolen by the kidnappers. No company likes to take a million-dollar hit, but that wasn't enough to mess up the bank's balance sheet—especially with all those new accounts and the fact that the gold was insured anyway. The real issue was keeping a lid on customers bailing out.

He was constantly on the phone with the men and women who made up the bank's board of directors. "Andrew," he began, pacing, "we're getting more and more reports from branches in every state that confirm our earlier optimism. Once word of the tape got out, the steady stream of customers demanding their accounts be closed fell to a mere trickle. This whole thing will be completely under control before we know it."

"Just think," he told Carolina and Maureen when they arrived, "when Gavin is freed, this is going through the roof again."

Carolina found herself nodding, still finding something rather distasteful about Gavin Duke's release from captivity being entered in the Public Relations Society of America's annual awards competition as the best PR campaign of the year. She told herself again that The

Man was genuinely concerned about Gavin, as she hid her disappointment at how easily he alternated from tragedy to business.

🥮 🥮 🥮

Gavin awoke from his nap and quickly became aware that he had no real concept of what time it was. He knew he'd eaten lunch, and he could see that it was still light out, so he felt pretty sure it was mid-afternoon.

He looked around the room. Neither of the men could be seen. But through the opened door, he could hear both of their voices outside. He tiptoed over toward the opening, hugging the wall to stay out of sight.

They were talking about hunting squirrels, a notion alien to Gavin. Was that like skeet shooting or something, where it's a challenge because it's a moving target? He didn't realize hungry men had to feed squirrel meat to their families from time to time, when there was no more money and no more food on the shelf.

He was about to go out, to stretch his legs and get some fresh air, but there was a lull in the conversation. He decided to wait for a moment more, to see if the conversation took a new direction. It did.

"I think he's gonna be able to tell us where the gold is by tomorrow," one said. He thought it was Walter.

"I hope you're right," said the other. Definitely Reg.

"Wonder how ol' Gavin's gonna cope with havin' to face all his big-shot buddies, after the money's long gone."

"I'll tell you what," Reg theorized, "you and I know that kind. That's the kind that did us in, and all our friends 'round here. All they care 'bout? Stayin' rich."

"Can't argue with that," Walter agreed. "They'll write ol' Gavin off quicker than you can say Jack Flash."

"Yep. Too bad, too. He ain't such a bad fella, for one of them."

"Yep."

The lull returned, but Gavin decided he didn't need to hear any more. He went back over to his spot on the floor and sat down in the dust. *Could there be some truth, some wisdom to the words of these men who had never been to college, never made an executive decision, never gotten in the trenches of corporate politics? Will my friends shun me? Will there always be a grain of doubt, a subtle suspicion that I fabricated the whole thing and hid the gold in some offshore bank? Will Harperson turn his back on me? Will Carrie? Will Torrie?*

As Gavin reflected on what he heard, he tried to imagine how he would perceive someone else in the same situation. *Would I believe someone—anyone—in a case like this?* He looked inside himself and decided, *Probably not. I wouldn't want to associate with the supposedly-kidnapped-but-now-freed-and-heroic peer. No way. Too weird. Yes, it's true, as the boys said. People will write me off. I'll lose my job, my life, everything.*

As that cold, hard reality started to set in, Gavin's sense of sarcasm retaliated. *At least I'll have those checks from ol' Dad to keep me going!*

Startled by that thought, Gavin sat back, pressing his back against the chair. *Dad. Wonder what he's doing, if he knows I'm here. If he's worried.*

Gavin started to think back about growing up, about the times he spent with his father and the times he didn't spend with his father. As the memories came crashing in on him, Reg's words echoed in Gavin's mind: "I'm just a man . . . just a man . . . " He tried to turn it off, but the words refused to go away. He finally drifted back into a light sleep, waking with a start when he heard his captors coming back in the shack.

Reg came in first, with Walter close behind, and they kidded him about his nap before preparing dinner. As Gavin sat against the wall, watching them, he was certain of one thing—he did not hate these men. He was beginning to think he respected them more than most of the people he had known during his career. Including himself.

🐚   🐚   🐚

Ronnie Chandler arrived home at 5:30, early for him, and was surprised to find Ruth had beat him to it.

He walked inside and saw she had prepared cold sandwiches—a most unusual dinner, but she was a woman in a hurry.

"What's going on?" he asked.

"Have you seen the tape?"

"Well, I haven't actually seen it," he said, "but I've heard it on the radio."

"Do you believe what that man said about me?" Ruth demanded, her eyes filling with fire.

"About you? I didn't hear the part with your name—"

"No, he didn't use my name. Of course not. He wouldn't stoop to that. But what he said about wishing he had loyal people, like him."

"Yeah, I couldn't believe that," Ronnie agreed. "What a jerk."

"Well, this is it, Ronnie. Tonight's the night. Grab yourself a sandwich, and as soon as we're finished, we're going for a little ride."

Ronnie's face lit up with a remarkable combination of excitement and terror all at once. "You want us to go prospecting tonight?"

"Yep."

He took a deep breath. They'd been planning it for weeks, but this was different. The reality frightened him. "But we need to wrap some things up first," he pleaded. "Got to empty out the checking account, and cash advance the credit card. And besides, we have to pack."

She sighed a deep, heavy sigh. "I guess you're right." Her shoulders dropped as his straightened up.

"Tomorrow night, then," he said. "We can tie everything up on Friday."

They embraced hard, their hearts racing, before walking into the kitchen to eat one of their last meals as paupers.

Nineteen

Gavin awoke this fourth morning—Friday—to find his hand lodged in his pocket clutching the coin. He didn't know how long it had been in that position, but it must have been quite a while since his knuckles were tight and sore.

Walter was sitting at the table, reading a newspaper by the light that filtered in through the opened door. Reg must have been outside. Gavin shifted and Walter looked up at him.

"Almost noon—that's one good night's sleep," Walter teased him.

"Noon?" Gavin grumbled. Either his body must be working overtime to heal itself, he thought, or he must be dying.

"I don't think they's any coffee left," Walter told him. "I guess if you really want some, we can put another pot on."

"No, thanks," Gavin squinted, trying to make his fingers nimble, but the hand wasn't ready yet. He imagined it would eventually thaw out. He stood up and stumbled toward the door to find a suitable restroom outside, but he stood up too quickly and slid down suddenly, falling into a sitting position on the floor, barely managing to avoid passing out.

Walter stood up. "You okay?"

Gavin saw stars flashing and heard a buzzing sound. He took a couple of deep breaths and said, "Maybe I'll take that coffee after all."

Walter moved over to help him up, then went over to restoke the fire and brew some coffee for his light-headed prisoner.

"Ah, breakfast in the country," Gavin said out loud as he sat down to yet another bowl of dry corn flakes and black coffee, the morning paper spread before him. "Well, what are they saying about me today—that I'm a mass murderer, perhaps?"

He looked into a grainy photo of his own face, straight from the tape, blown up right there on page one. He had an advanced case of five o'clock shadow, a big chunk of gauze on his forehead, and his hair—his beautiful thick hair—looked more like a porcupine's.

I'm ruined, he thought sarcastically, surprising himself with how well he was adapting to his nightmare. The headline made him feel a little better: "Tape shows Gavin's okay!"

Glad we're on a first name basis again, he smiled to himself. He pored over the article and all the side stories about how the mini-run at the bank had been calmed, how Carolina and her troops were adjusting to the situation, and how Harperson had taken a big hit with his stock holdings. Gavin, who held quite a few shares himself but also was savvy enough to know the price would come back, said, "Two million, huh? Bet The Man's gonna have to go and have himself a garage sale!"

Gavin finished breakfast and the paper. He sat back, recapping where the last few days had taken him. The cut on his forehead was still scabbed over—and quite heavily at that—but amazingly had not become infected, and the bruise around the cut didn't hurt unless he pressed against it. He had taken to leaving the gauze off, finding that it itched, especially as it became caked with the dust and moisture that surrounded the cabin. Plus, the absence of the dressing helped him to forget he even had a gash most of the time.

Walter and Reg were outside. *Walter and Reg. Two amazing men. Tough as nails—tough enough to withstand blows that would have knocked other men out of the box, yet going on with a day at a time, until one day they decide they've had enough and kidnap a man with the intent of stealing a million dollars.* Gavin felt fortunate when he thought of these two—not imagining for a moment that he would ever stoop to such tactics, even under the most obscene of circumstances, but blessed because he simply was not a victim of such cruel testings. Especially Reg, having lost so much. *But he keeps going on*, thought Gavin.

And with that, a light went on for Gavin. He stood up, unable to contain such revelations. "I'm just a man," Gavin said. And he realized at last that his father, too, was just a man. All those years Gavin spent resenting him, all the anger he felt—it all came down to that one phrase: "Just a man."

🍪   🍪   🍪

Ruth showed up late Friday morning, relishing her defiance, and she grinned to herself as she ignored the flashing light on her answering machine. She gingerly picked up a few personal items and stashed them into a small box, glancing up every few seconds to make sure no one came by even though she'd rehearsed a complete set of explanations.

"Finished!" she congratulated herself after about ten minutes. She looked around to see if there was anything else. Nope. Unless . . .

Her eyes darted to Gavin's closed door, and she stared a hole in it. "Why not?" she said out loud. "Why not?"

She booted up her computer and carefully planned her words as it sputtered and buzzed awake. She toggled into E-Mail and decided simplest was best. "Important memo for Gavin," she said to herself. "Urgent!" Her fingernails clicked on the familiar keypad, but she slowed when she came to the message itself. One letter at a time, she slowly savored the feeling. "SURPRISE!" she wrote, and she laughed out loud when she hit the Send key. She snatched the box and walked hurriedly out the door, her heart pounding so hard she thought the other people in the elevator would hear it.

🍪   🍪   🍪

That afternoon, Torrie was finishing up a small insert for the following week's paper. There were often stories like this which weren't time sensitive, and it was good to get them out of the way because you never knew what might hit around deadline time.

She saved the text and sent it electronically across the newsroom to Sandy's desk. Sandy was editing a feature and noticed the red light came on. She looked up and around the room to see who'd transmitted something to her, and then saw Torrie, smiling as their eyes met. The reporter got up and walked over to the editor's desk. "There's the brief on the credit union," she said. "All done."

Sandy shot a glance at the clock on the wall. It was a little after three. She leaned back and said, "Why don't you take off? You need a head start on your weekend."

"Thanks, Sandy. I think I'll take you up on that."

"Got any plans?"

"I don't know," Torrie said, shifting her gaze to nowhere in particular. "I think I just need to get out—you know, take a drive in the country or something."

"Hey, maybe you could head up to the stables with Jane. I know she's planning on riding this weekend."

"No, I don't think so." She remembered her time with Gavin there, and it was warm and rich and beautiful. "I think I just want to be alone tomorrow. And being in church Sunday should give me a lift."

"Fair enough," Sandy smiled. "Now, you get yourself out of here!"

"I'm already gone," Torrie said, turning and heading back to pick up her purse and turn off the computer.

She started off down Peachtree Street, fully intending to go straight to her apartment, but she was overcome by a certain uneasiness, a feeling she couldn't put her finger on. True, she needed to get away this weekend, to be alone, but she wanted one more shared moment of human contact before closing the door. She headed to Carolina Gates Advertising, knowing she could benefit from Carolina's reassuring steadiness and faith.

She didn't stop to realize you don't just burst in on a busy woman like Carolina Gates—especially during a week when she and her staff were burning the midnight oil, doing damage control for one of their key accounts. All she knew was she needed to see her, to feel connected with someone who also knew how to turn to the Lord.

She got off the elevator that took her straight to Carolina's office, having made a mental note before that using the main entrance, two stories below, only meant a potentially lengthy wait in the front reception area. She made her way down the hall, past a small conference room that was two doors away from the corner office.

"Torrie!"

She stopped and took two steps back to peer into the doorway where Carolina and three others were gathered around some TV storyboards.

"Oh, hi, Carrie, I was just . . . " she stopped in mid-sentence, embarrassed to realize that Carolina might just be tied up right now.

"Were you looking for me?" Carolina asked, as the others stared at Torrie, making her even more uncomfortable.

"Well, yes, but, it's not . . . "

Carolina stood up and said, "Give me five minutes," to the group as she moved into the hallway and touched Torrie's arm.

"Is everything all right? Is there more news?"

"Oh, no more news. I was just—" she paused, knowing she sounded a little silly—"I was just in the neighborhood, and I wanted to see you before the weekend."

"Was there something you wanted to talk about?" Carolina asked, with a look of concern in her eyes. "Come on, let's go to my office."

"There's really nothing in particular I wanted to say," Torrie said as they slowly stepped down the hall. "I was just planning on getting away this weekend, out to the country, and before I left I just wanted to thank you again for being so supportive."

Carolina stopped right in front of the double doors that led to her suite and smiled. "You've been through a lot. We've all been through a lot. But you'll make it. We'll have our Gavin back before we know it, and he'll be marching up and down these halls, ranting and raving about why we didn't start a 'Guess where Gavin's hidden' sweepstakes."

Torrie laughed. "Thanks, Carrie. You're such a blessing to me. I'm glad to have a friend like you."

"And Gavin ought to be grateful to have someone like you."

They looked into each other's eyes, both welling up with tears, and they gave each other a hug and laughed at the same time, not imagining for a minute they should be uncomfortable as business associates, in a business setting, displaying such a show of affection.

"Come on, I'll walk you out," Carolina said, wiping her eyes. "I'll bet my mascara's history," she added, and the two laughed again. Carolina poked her head in the door where the meeting was still going on. "Give me thirty more seconds, gang."

She pushed the button for Torrie when they got to the elevator. "Remember, you're in my prayers. Call if you need anything," she said.

"I will."

The bell rang, and the door opened. Torrie stepped on and said, "Thanks again," as Carolina gave her one last reassuring smile and headed off to fix her eye makeup before returning to talk about storyboards.

Torrie felt as though a load had been lifted. She walked briskly down Peachtree Street, planning to walk all the way home. It was a beautiful day, and she wanted to take in the sunny air.

She got home, played with Casey for a few minutes, then decided to go for a swim. When she got back, she showered, changed, and decided it was time to plan her Saturday. She popped in an Amy Grant CD, plunked down on the couch with a map, and unfolded it.

"Wanna go for a ride in the country tomorrow, sweetie?" she asked, stroking Casey's back. Casey pressed her eyes closed. "It'd be nice to get away for a while, wouldn't it?"

Torrie stared out the window. "Then again, maybe I'll just stay in bed all day."

Casey jumped down and darted into the kitchen.

"I don't know what to expect any more," Torrie sighed to herself. "Who knows what tomorrow will bring? Guess I'll just take it when it comes . . . "

☙   ☙   ☙

Roger Frederichs adjusted his yellow hard hat and his ski patrol sunglasses, placed his hands on his hips, and surveyed the scene.

"Yessiree, Bob, lookin' good," he muttered, nodding to himself.

Everything was in place for the predawn blast that would nuke that old rock into oblivion.

He shut the door to the state truck and walked carefully toward the rock, studying his clipboard as he went until he stepped on a sharp golfball-sized chunk of gravel which cost him his balance for an instant. "Joe Palooka!" he sputtered, looking down to see his black wing tips had become coated with a thin dusting of fine white-gray powder. "Aw, what a mess. Not in the little holes too!" he whined. "That'll be impossible to get out."

He heaved a sigh and continued his circle around the rock, checking flags and markers and stakes, making sure the blasting caps would be situated in just the right places.

"Dandy work, boys," he said as he tapped the clipboard, although the boys had already left. He was all alone now, so he could take his time. He went back over to the truck and poured himself a cup of coffee from the large-mouth Thermos bottle, scanning the clipboard one final time.

"Oopsey," he frowned. "Missed number eleven." He strolled over toward the steps that went down beneath the rock and realized some prewired copper cable had come loose. He set down his coffee and his checklist to examine the situation.

"No problem!" he chattered to himself. "Nothing a little splicing won't help." He stood up, but the edge of one step shook as though about to give way. He instinctively thrust his hand onto the door to keep from falling. The door shifted a fraction of an inch, and Roger took a deep breath.

"Good thing you're locked up, or I might've taken a tumble there," he said out loud, as a man might do when all alone more than he'd prefer. He walked back to the truck to retrieve his tools.

    ✿ ✿ ✿

Walter and Reg were talking outside as Gavin took another catnap.

"I'm about out of patience," Walter said. "I can't keep up with this for much longer. It's drivin' me crazy, and besides, I told my wife it'd be a couple days, and she's gonna start worryin' and maybe do somethin' stupid, like call the cops so they'll come lookin' for me."

"Me too," said Reg, "but if he can't remember where he hid the gold, what're we gonna do?"

"I dunno. Give it up, maybe."

"You mean, forget the gold?"

"Don't look like we have no choice, do we? If he can't remember, that's that!"

"But what'll we do with him?"

Walter had to stop and think. "I guess we can just leave him here. He'll get out, sooner or later."

"Yeah, and what next? What's gonna happen to us? He knows our names. He knows about the plant shuttin' down. The cops'll find us quicker than anything."

"Not if we take off."

"Now, how're we supposed to take off if we ain't got no million dollars?" Reg said, obviously agitated at how things weren't working out.

"We still got his five hundred," Walter said. "That'll get us pretty far."

"No we don't—spent a big chunk on that camera there. And besides, we'll lose out on our government checks," Reg protested.

"They can have it. We'll go someplace else, and we'll get us jobs again, so we won't need no government money. We just got to get out of Murrowstown."

Reg digested this. It was true; he had to get out of Murrowstown, no matter what. And if they weren't going to get the gold, they may as well stop wasting their time—even risk being caught—and make a move.

"Okay," he said. "By noon tomorrow, if he can't remember, we'll tie him up and take off. We'll be long gone, across the state line, before he can get out of here."

"I'm with you," Walter said.

🪙   🪙   🪙

After dinner, the three were sitting outside, where there was a gentle breeze, watching the fire die down. They'd cooked hot dogs, a special treat Walter had gone to pick up at the gas station out of sheer boredom.

"Know where I'd like to be right now?" Reg said, watching the flames lick the bark and transform it into a hot glowing orange coal.

"Where's that?" Walter responded, feeling more relaxed than he had in days.

"Out on a boat, pretendin' to fish."

Walter laughed. "Yeah, I know what you mean. Just kickin' back, out in the sun, with nothin' pressin' . . . "

Gavin, not one to enjoy activities that revolved around accomplishing nothing at all, listened intently.

"When's the last time you went?" Reg asked.

"Oh, couple months. Too long. You?"

"Yeah, about a month or so ago. Went out on Jay Dusenberry's boat."

Gavin imagined what kind of boat it must be. Tiny wooden tub, with oars but no motor, patched all over but still leaking here and there. Yet to these men, he imagined, it may as well have been the Queen Mary, providing an exotic getaway to tranquil waters, miles offshore from the din of everyday life in their sorrowful little town.

"Catch anythin'?" Walter wondered.

"Caught us a pair of good bass," he smiled.

Gavin had never eaten bass or catfish. He wondered if it would be good.

"Nothin' like a fresh catch of bass, grilled right in an iron skillet over a fire by the side of the lake," Reg continued.

"Mmm, yeah," said Walter, closing his eyes and savoring the aroma, the flavor, the day in the boat.

Gavin went to sleep early, around eight. He flattened the heavy blanket below him, trying to get as comfortable as he could on the hard plank floor of the cabin.

He tossed and turned, his mind working overtime to make up for lost days. He dreamed images and sounds, images of loud city streets and peaceful lakes and huge rocks and crumbling ceilings and faces—angry faces—staring at him and mocking him, and back to quiet lakes and rivers and boats, small wooden boats and a fast boat, a blue speedboat with purple stripes and a bend in the river and . . .

Gavin threw himself forward, sitting up. He was drenched in sweat, gasping for breath. "The gold!" he shouted into the darkness.

Walter and Reg woke up. Walter flew over to Gavin's side as Reg stumbled for the flashlight. He managed to click it on, noisily clanging into the metal dishes and knocking his beloved photograph over, leaving it flat on the table.

"You okay? Just a dream. It's all right," Walter told Gavin. "Get him some water, would you?" he asked Reg.

Reg brought the jug over, and the two men helped Gavin take a drink. His breathing became more regular, and in the dim light of the shack, he looked into the faces of the two men.

"What time is it?" he asked.

Reg tilted his arm toward the light. "Couple minutes to midnight," he said. "Still got most of the night left—you can get yourself some more sleep. And so can we," he said, starting to get back up.

"Wait," Gavin said. Reg paused. Walter stayed in the same spot, crouched next to Gavin.

The stillness of the night was deafening as Gavin cleared his throat.

"I know where the gold is," he said.

Twenty

Walter's jaw dropped. Reg's jaw dropped. Gavin took another deep breath.

"I can remember now," Gavin said. "I can remember hiding the gold, and getting there—I know where it is." His defiant thoughts from before, when he was first accosted by these two men, had fled in his desire to get out and, strangely, as he had become more sympathetic toward them.

They helped him up and sat him in one of the chairs at the table. Walter grabbed the pencil that was resting on a shelf inside the cupboard and a scrap of paper and stared at Gavin, without a word.

Reg asked the million-dollar question: "Where is it?"

Gavin licked his lips and took another chug of water from the plastic container. "It's in Stewart County, about two hours southwest of Atlanta," he began, "Just a little below Columbus."

Walter looked at Reg. "You ever been down that way?"

"Just a couple times, a long time ago. I don't know it from nothin'."

"Me neither," Walter said, writing Stewart County on the paper.

Gavin took another drink and continued. "Right along the Chattahoochee River, there's a huge rock that juts out of the ground," he said. "But you can't get there from the water. You have to drive. Take Interstate 85 south out of Atlanta, which branches off onto 185, to go through Columbus. You'll get onto, let's see, I think it's 280 and go past Fort Benning once you get south of town, then onto, uh, 27 south into Lumpkin."

Walter was writing furiously, and Gavin was spinning the coin in his pocket.

"From there, take the county highway that goes due west, toward Alabama. I can't remember the number, but everybody knows it. Just look for the signs."

Walter and Reg looked at each other nervously. *Don't start losing details now*, they thought.

"Just before you get to the river, take a right onto the only place you can turn. Head up that road for a few miles until you get to an old manufacturing facility that's been shut down."

The two other men looked at each other again, chilled with the mental picture of a factory, locked up tight.

"You'll have to bust in somehow, since it's chained up and locked pretty good, and the fence goes all around. Once you make it through the main gate, drive past the buildings and you'll be heading straight for the rock. Around to the left, there are some double doors that look like cellar doors, heading right down under the rock. You'll have to bust into those too, and another set of doors inside."

"And that's where the gold is?" Walter said, feeling his palms grow sweaty.

"Yeah. There are three big oil drums, marked toxic waste, which I covered with a big tarp. The two on the outside are empty, but the one in the middle is where the gold is. There's a pan of used motor oil inside the barrel, on top, but don't worry—it's just motor oil. Lift it out and dig through the stuffing, and you'll find your gold."

The words were like a song to Reg and Walter, music to the ears of men who had not heard a sound in ages.

Gavin let out a deep breath when he finished, as though an enormous burden had been removed from him. He sank back into the chair.

"How we gonna get there?" Walter asked, not wanting to waste another minute.

Reg thought a minute, also wanting to get moving and realizing the darkness would help them. "We could wire Dutchy's van," he said, his eyes lighting up.

"Won't they call the cops when they see it's gone?" Walter asked.

"We can leave Leo a note and one of them twenty-dollar bills we got, and tell him we needed it back one more time to finish up the job we're doin' in the next county. We'll be back right quick, anyhow."

"Okay," Walter said. "And we can pick up some tools by the shed, out back, to bust into that old gate with."

"Let's get us a map too, just to make sure we don't end up in Macon or somethin'," Reg said. "We can get that at the gas station. One of them along the highway'll be open—they're open all night."

"What we gonna do about him?" Walter asked, nodding in Gavin's direction.

"We can keep him tied up here, till we get back, in case we don't find no gold and need to make sure we got the directions right."

"Think we oughta take him with us?"

Gavin, hearing his fate discussed openly, felt his stomach knot up.

Reg stared at the table, then said, "No. Too much of a risk. He'll still be here when we get back. We'll just be gone a few hours, so he'll be okay."

"Then what're we waitin' for?" Walter asked. He stood up and looked at Gavin.

"Sorry, Mr. Duke, but we gotta tie you up again. But don't worry, like we said. We'll be back for you later on, so we can let you go after we got our gold."

"Where you plannin' on puttin' him?" Reg asked.

"How about we tie him to the chair here, so he can sit up and not have to be on the floor."

"Good," Reg said, standing Gavin up and moving him over against the wall, putting the chair in place, and setting him down on it.

Gavin remained silent, not knowing whether to be elated or miserable—at last, it was almost over, but an entirely new set of disasters was falling into place. His campaign, his perfect promotion, was crashing to the ground, while he and his bank would end up with egg all over their faces, outsmarted by a couple of small-town yokels with nothing but a pair of shotguns and a ramshackle cabin in the woods.

Walter and Reg worked quickly, each taking a leg and then a wrist, fastening them securely to the chair with thick cords of rope, knotted with enough overkill to secure an elephant in place. *Don't worry*, Gavin thought, *I'll never get out of here. Your secret is safe with me.*

The two straightened up as Walter took the flashlight down. Reg stopped, looking into the photo. *A poignant scene*, Gavin thought, as Reg lifted the photo and for the first time, as far as he knew, Reg spoke into it.

"I'll be back for you, Lily," he said softly as he gently placed it back in the center of the old wooden table, facing Gavin.

Walter darted out the door, shouting, "C'mon, Reg," and his partner followed.

"Bye, guys. Drive carefully," Gavin said, treating himself to some of that old Gavin Duke sarcasm to console himself.

Reg and Walter fought their way through the woods, needing the beam from the flashlight to cut through the thick darkness. The anticipation drove them, a feeling they could not describe because they had never sensed anything like it before. They had known the hopelessness, the despair, the oppressiveness of being trapped—but this was intoxicating, this promise of freedom and wealth and a new start, unencumbered by the ghosts of Murrowstown and their bitter past. They reached the road and took off running toward Dutchy's, the van, and the tool shed.

The road was strangely silent at this hour, although it never was a major artery. Walter and Reg were too out of breath to converse or to continue galloping, so they slowed to a walk. "If a truck or somethin' comes along," Reg said between gasps, "you think we oughta take it?"

"No question in my mind," Walter said. "We can get a ride to Dutchy's."

"And what'll we say to the driver? He's bound to ask us what we're doin' out here at this time of night."

"We can just tell him we was out huntin' and got lost in the woods." They were, after all, carrying shotguns.

"Maybe nobody'd pick us up with—with these guns and all."

"Then I figure we'll just have to walk," Walter said.

Two trucks did drive by, but neither showed the least sign of slowing. Walter and Reg trudged on to Dutchy's.

"You can write the note for Leo, and I can wire the van," Reg said. Walter finished first, so he used the barrel of his shotgun as a crowbar to pry open the doors to the shed. He picked up a real crowbar, a shovel, and a pair of small wire cutters. He wished there were bolt cutters too, but no such luck. He took a quick look around and, not seeing anything else that might be of use, closed the door. As he walked over to the van, he heard the roar of the engine, and saw Reg inside the cab, giving him both thumbs up. He opened the side door, threw his gun alongside Reg's on the floor, and put the tools in next. He slammed the door shut and jumped in the passenger side.

"Mind if I drive this time?" Reg asked.

"All yours," Walter said, recalling the battle of nerves it was to navigate the van without a license.

They made it to the highway in about fifteen minutes, stopping at the exit to grab a map and some coffee at the twenty-four-hour gas station. They were on their way, hopeful they'd be able to complete their task before dawn.

Torrie had found no sleep yet, so she decided to get up and fix herself a cup of hot tea. "Surprised to see me, Casey?" she asked. Casey purred and curled up on Torrie's lap. "Is this ever gonna end, my love?" she asked the cat who, if she had the answer, certainly was not sharing it.

Too late to call anybody here—but wait! It's three hours earlier on the West Coast, only about nine. She called Anita.

"I was about to dump him," she exploded in tears. "How could I have been so cold! How could I have been thinking such a thing when I never had the guts to share the truth with him?"

"It's okay, honey. It's okay," Anita soothed.

"No, it's not. He needed me. He needed me to show him God's love—to tell him about God's love for him. That's all he really needed—someone to step out and tell him! And it was supposed to be me!"

"Now, hold on, Torrie. You—"

"That was my responsibility!" Torrie interrupted. "That's why God brought him into my life. And now, maybe he's . . . Maybe he never got a chance to hear the truth! What if he . . . Oh, Anita! Why didn't I care enough to do what I was supposed to do? Why didn't I ever bring it up?"

"Well, you said you tried several times, but he . . . "

"I was such a coward. I was too busy thinking about myself and how good it felt to be with him. And now, I might never get a second chance . . . "

Anita prayed softly before she was able to get a word in. "Torrie, listen to me. You've got to shut off all those destructive thoughts. You know where they're coming from! Besides, you can't do a thing about the past now, and even if you could, I think you're being way too hard on yourself."

"But it's all true, Anita!"

Anita took a deep breath. "Torrie, stop. Gavin's responsible for Gavin, okay? Gavin and God. You can commit to being bolder in the future, if that's what's best. But Gavin has had plenty of opportunities, and he has to make his own choices. You can't make his choices for him, right?"

"I guess. It's just . . . "

"You need to hold on to the truth, Torrie. And the truth is, the Lord's in control." Torrie paused, pierced by the truth. "Even when it doesn't feel like it," Anita added. "And I know it doesn't feel like it right now."

"No, it doesn't," Torrie answered sheepishly. "But that doesn't change the truth." She sighed. "I guess I just need to focus on that right now."

"Good plan," Anita smiled.

"What would I do without you?" Torrie asked through the tears.

"You'd pay smaller phone bills," Anita smiled. "C'mon, let me pray with you, and then you can get some shut-eye."

They prayed together, and when Torrie hung up she realized how exhausted she was. She scooted Casey back to her pad, turned out the light, slid back into bed, and fell asleep sobbing softly.

🌰　🌰　🌰

"All set?" Ronnie asked Ruth as he picked up the last suitcase. It was one A.M. She took a long, deep breath and nodded. "Then let's go get rich quick!" he laughed. She didn't laugh but grinned. They stepped into the night.

🌰　🌰　🌰

Gavin wriggled his hands and feet, only to find the knots snug and secure and immovable. The ropes were thick cords, twisted hemp a half inch or more in diameter. Like the rope, the darkness was cutting into his very being. His left calf cramped with a tightness he had never before known. Unable to move his limbs, he was helpless and had to let it work itself out. He winced and gritted his teeth. He felt hungry too, but he couldn't move. He looked around the room again. At least no animals had come in to feed on him.

"They'll be back soon enough," he told himself. "Then they'll let me go." He stopped and thought. "Unless there's some kind of trouble." He decided to go through all the possibilities, one at a time.

What if they get into an accident? That's doubtful, and even if they do, at least one of them would be able to talk. Wouldn't they realize the jig was up and tell someone where I am? But what if they're both killed? It's a long drive, after all. Okay, that's possible—but still doubtful.

Arrested, maybe? For what? No, they're being too careful. But if they spend a night in some small county tank, they might not return for a long time. Yet that's unlikely too.

What if they decide to just run off with the gold without coming back? Impossible. This picture means more to Reg than all the gold on earth. After all, he brought it to the shack, didn't he? No, he wouldn't leave it behind. They will come back for the photo, without question—once they find the gold.

But what if they never make it to the gold? Could they have misunderstood the directions? Perhaps. But after a while, they would come back to get better directions.

Or what if they get there but the gold is already gone? Impossible. Sure, everybody and their brother is looking for it, but the news media would have been all over it if someone had gotten there. I've seen Friday's paper, and they left at midnight. What if somebody got it Friday? Highly unlikely that it would have occurred within that small window of time—but plausible. No, wait a minute. Even if I haven't heard the news, Walter and Reg will. They'll hightail it back so Reg can pick up his picture before they blow town.

What else? They make it into the cave, find the gold, and bring it out. Tough to navigate, with those old posts in the way and those low ceilings and those crumbling rafters . . .

Gavin gasped. That unstable roof had left Gavin petrified. *What if Reg and Walter make a big ruckus as they unearth the gold, or what if they did bang into one of those beams? There might be a cave-in right on top of them, and even a million dollars in gold can't save them from that. Walter and Reg might be crushed to death beneath the weight of that great rock, or perhaps injured severely but trapped, or maybe not necessarily even hurt at all but still sealed in a tomb by a cave-in of that little hallway at the entrance.*

He caught himself and shook his head. *No, they can't be dead*, he thought. *Even if the room collapses, there are still several support beams and rafters in the ceiling. No, the whole boulder isn't going to come crashing down on top of them; they may be struck by falling debris, but they're certainly alive in there!*

"No, no, no," Gavin said. "They're fine. They'll get the gold and be fine. Unless they had an accident. Or got lost. Or hurt at the plant." His mind spun. Plenty of things could go wrong—probably a lot more than he could think of in this state. He couldn't just sit there. He had to get out. And he had to be there—just in case. "Torrie," he said, longing for familiar names and faces and sensations. "Carolina. Gary. Ruth." He yanked and twisted and gritted his teeth and he tugged and tugged and tugged some more, leaving his wrists little more than masses of bloodied flesh. The pain was sharp and searing, as he was tearing at his nerve endings, and he realized he had better stop—he knew all too well how a loss of blood can weaken the mind and body, and he would need all his faculties as he planned an alternate method of escape.

He tried shouting next, calling out at regular intervals, in the hopes that eventually a hunter or a hiker or a young couple on a secluded picnic would hear his calls and help him rescue Walter and Reg. *In the middle of the night? Forget it.* He wished he could feel his coin, to be sure it was still tucked safely into his pocket, but he could not.

His inability to reckon time was frustrating him all the more. He yelled and yelled, only to be heard by the wind. He was growing hoarse, and his wrists were still moist and bloody. His ankles were sore too, and his stomach had been suffering a continuous cramp since he had begun calling out. He was feeling light-headed and desperately depressed about the fate of these two men for whom he felt responsible.

He stared toward the spot where the picture was sitting on the table. "I'm sorry, Reg. I'm so sorry." He began to sob. He shifted his wrists—they felt awful. He lifted his eyes again and all at once remembered the multiple tragedies of Reg and Walter's lives—the plant shutdown, Lily's death, Duane's being taken away—*Duane. Little Duane will never know his father,* Gavin thought. *Like I never really knew mine. I just wish I could change that . . .*

Gavin felt rage surging through his body so fully and overwhelmingly that he could only scream. He lunged upward, shouting "Noooo!" and bouncing the chair up and down with the flow of adrenaline, taking such a violent hop that the chair did not land straight on its four feet but caught one leg at an angle. It made an audible cracking sound as it landed.

The cracking sound slapped Gavin back to reality—just as a man blinks if he sees an object heading toward his face, a man stops jumping up and down if the box or the floor or the chair that is supporting him indicates it is about to surrender. He stopped bouncing and cut his primordial yell short, tripped up by his self-preservation instinct.

Gavin's eyes flew open wide. "Yes! Idiot! Why didn't you think of this before?" He smiled—now he had a plan. He practiced jumping the chair, swinging his body to create an uneven landing. Every third or fourth attempt, he caused a cracking sound. Eventually, this chair was going to be kindling, and Gavin Duke—as well as Walter and Reg—would be free.

He bounced and shook and rammed the old wooden chair into the wall, finding that it was much more sturdy than he thought. But after several good heaves, he had managed to crack off two legs, and then an arm, and that was all he needed. From there, it was easy—he slipped his ankles out and moved around, and with greater control of his feet, kicked the rest of the chair apart. He maneuvered the ropes off his ankles and wrists, and he was free.

The door was his escape hatch, and he was about to run away but stopped. "I'd better eat something," he told himself, the adrenaline having caused him to forget his gnawing hunger for a few moments. He felt around the walls and opened the cupboard door to find some corn flakes and crackers—all that was left. He stuffed his mouth, washing it all down with the water that remained in the jug on the floor, and got up, stuffing the remaining crackers inside his shirt. It was time to go. He stood at the door, almost afraid to leave, when he remembered the photo. He turned and grabbed it, staring into it under the moonlight the way Reg did every night. Except this night.

"I'd better take this to him," Gavin said, not realizing he was smearing the frame with blood as he clutched it in his right hand and ran into the woods.

Gavin fought through the foliage, not sure whether to try to run or walk, but really neither was an option—stumbling was the best a man could do in the dark, with heavy ground cover and infinite young trees and fallen logs and pits and gullies, and an occasional rock, jagged and hidden beneath leaves and pine straw beds that concealed them enough to fool you into thinking you were on solid ground until your ankle turned.

He was still wearing his dress shoes. He'd taken them off occasionally in the cabin, to stretch his instep and his calf and to wiggle his toes, and he had removed them to sleep, of course, but he was wearing them now, and they were tight and constricting and slippery on the bottom, an acceptable sole for a stroll along the sidewalk with Torrie but not for a sprint through woods that were growing darker with each passing step. They frequently slipped on the pine straw or the leaves of a shiny little plant. He found that by adjusting his stride, he gained a firmer footing. *Higher knees, higher steps, straight down, solid, plunk, plant it, plunk, no slipping, oops, less slipping, plunk, plant it, plunk.*

He was moving too quickly and, with the unevenness of the terrain and the darkness, much too unsteadily to risk shoving his hand into his pocket to touch the coin, to feel its ridged edge and its smooth surface. Besides, he needed both hands out front to avoid smacking into a tree. But he knew the coin was there, golden and rich in history, representing the promise of great success.

He slipped and had to reach out with his right hand to steady himself against a tree, but he had to use his fist instead of his palm because he was still holding the photograph of Reg and Lily.

Even if Reg gets out with his share of the gold, Gavin thought, *it won't bring Lily and Duane back.* And as far away as Reg might go, knocking the dust of Murrowstown off his feet, starting a new life and perhaps even being able someday to find a new love, he would never be able to forget the pain. No, money wouldn't buy happiness for Reg. And what about for Walter? He too had taken his share of licks and could benefit from getting away. But as a fugitive for the rest of his life, always wondering who was coming up from behind, when the hammer would fall? Gavin knew enough about human nature and from observing Walter to know that he might gain some immediate joy from his great escape from his past, but eventually the truth and the stress would catch up with him.

But what about me? I still have time—lots of time. I can still change things! Gavin pushed away from the tree, realizing his joints were getting stiff from clutching the picture frame, and he switched it over to his left hand. He exercised the fingers that had been wrapped around his precious cargo and took off.

He realized he could hear himself breathing—panting, actually—a frightened sound, near panic, of a man stepping around hot coals who all of a sudden realizes he can no longer see his path. The darkness had turned to black, as deep and as dark a black as Gavin had ever known. There were no stars visible, and no moon through the thick growth, and certainly no lights to guide his trek. Each step could bring him into a tree, as vines and low hanging branches from the smaller trees whacked him in the face. And the holes and rocks became larger now, magnified and intensified by the unknown that surrounded them.

"Stop," he said aloud. He stood silently for a moment, still hearing himself breathe, but the rhythm slowed as he tried to take deep breaths to steady his shattered nerves. "Get your bearings, get a grip," he told himself. Yes, it was dark. He held up his right hand directly in front of his face to confirm that he couldn't see a thing. Yes, he was alone, but no packs of ravenous wolves were prowling these woods, watching him with luminescent eyes and frothing at the mouth and drooling, waiting to sink their fangs into his flesh. In fact, animals were afraid of him and, with their superior night vision and keener senses of smell and hearing, would flee long before he came upon them. He was headed in one direction, not going in circles, so eventually, he would run into a road or a building or a stream he could follow. He was going to make it out. Not at the speed he wanted, but sooner or later. *Who knows? Maybe there's a road or a house just a hundred yards ahead—I'll be there in no time. Nothing to fear, but just keep moving, Gavin. Keep on moving.*

He put the picture down for a second, standing it on its end between his bruised and battered ankles, and he massaged his hands together. He finally reached into his pocket to slide his fingers across the face of the coin, but the torn flesh from the rope burns stung as it met the fabric, and he winced and heard himself saying, "Ow . . . ow," before he reached the coin. But reach it he did, touching it but for a brief moment of emptiness, wondering exactly why he felt the need to touch a coin while lost in the woods in the pitch blackness.

He pulled his hand out, more careful this time to not scratch the torn skin of his wrists. Sighing and picking up the photo, he marched on, once again carrying it in his right hand and leading his way with the left.

His hand mostly bumped branches, as he slowly waved it back and forth in a sweeping motion, but occasionally it did meet a substantial tree trunk. Most were coarse and thick, with ridges of bark moving up and down them, but some were dripping sap, and his hands became encrusted with a sticky substance, or a combination of sticky substances.

"Please, God, help me," he begged, no longer surprised that he could call out to God. "Help me, please."

Once again he became acutely aware of the sounds of the night. The noise level created by the insects chirping and making their mating calls rose to a feverish pitch, as it had those nights in the cabin, and would not abate. He made a mental note about how the thin walls of the shack muffled the din significantly, even though the door was open, as opposed to this direct assault on his eardrums. "Quiet," he cried two different times, thinking perhaps the sound of man might cause their natural survival instinct to still their wings, or their legs, or whatever made the screaming sounds, but there was no break in the intensity of their feverish song. He stopped at one point, once again placing the photo in an upright position between his ankles, and clapped his hands, but this new sound also carried no effect. He grabbed the picture angrily, blowing out two good lungfulls of frustration. "Shut up!" he screamed into the night. "Shut up!" He plodded ahead.

His hand thumped into a tree trunk, a massive one, which he pulled himself against, leaning forward into it, not caring that his face was pressed against the bark. "I've got to stop," he said, spent from this intense workout but having no idea how long he had been at it. All he knew was that his legs ached, his feet throbbed, his ankles were itching, his hands were feeling arthritic from carrying Reg's photo, and he was drenched with dew and sweat, which he couldn't quite wipe from his eyes because of the pitch that had accumulated on his hands and the torn flesh that covered his wrists. His heart was pounding, and his chest was heaving. He fell to the ground, reaching back for the tree trunk, and sat against it, leaning as comfortably as he could.

I'm sorry, Reg, he thought. *I'm sorry, Walter. I can't go on. I just can't go on.* He wept for a moment, then caught himself with a deep sigh. "No, I've got to keep going. And I've got to get home. Got to see Torrie again." He rose to his feet, a little wobbly, and remembered his quest. "Walter and Reg—they might be in danger," he told himself. He felt compelled to pick right up where he had left off, marching through the woods to free them from their captivity. *Wait—only go in one direction. But which way?* He had no idea from which direction he'd come. He remembered stashing the leftover crackers in his shirt, and he pulled them out to find a small crushed package of crumbs. "Good enough," he said, pouring the crumbs into his mouth as he wished he could find some water—he was parched.

He took off again. The terrain had been relatively flat, although rolling, and remained so for the first few hundred yards, but Gavin realized he was scaling a rise and he felt a rush of excitement when he made it over the crest and found himself standing beside a road illuminated by moonlight.

I can stop the first motorist who comes along and hitch a ride toward I-85—if I'm right about where I am. I can find a phone there and call the police, who could rescue Walter and Reg. That's what I'll do.

But Gavin's mind, twisted from nearly a week imprisoned in the woods, being malnourished and suffering from sleep-deprivation and jolted into rethinking everything he had stood for during the course of his life, sought another path. The police would detain Gavin and want to question him and send a team of doctors and nurses to examine him and prod him and poke him, while some Stewart County sheriff would be responsible for saving Reg and Walter. Only Gavin knew the route, where the van might have broken down or rammed into a tree, and only he knew that treacherous cavern, and only he would be able to direct the rescue. He couldn't bear the thought of sitting on a cold examination table and getting word that the one-man county sheriff's department wasn't able to do anything for the two men. *No, I have to get there straightaway; there will be time for police debriefings and complete physicals later. All I have to do is get home, so I can drive to the rock.* There would be no police—not yet. Because not only would they delay him, their involvement would bring the media, and scores of bloodthirsty reporters crowding around Gavin and around the rock, painting Reg and Walter as heartless kidnappers and calculating thieves, objects of scorn and hatred by everyone who looked at them as trying to cheat all the others out of the gold. He had to not only get to the men first—he had to let them get away.

It would be hard to wait several more hours to see Torrie, but a man had to do what he had to do. He wanted to hold her in his arms, to feel her holding onto him, both of them safe at last from the week that had caused them so much pain. *How has she coped?* he wondered. *She's tough,* he smiled to himself, knowing in his heart that she'd be all right. He recalled some of her many subtle—and not-so-subtle—references to trusting God, and he had no doubt she'd be trusting enough for both of them.

And then, he heard it. The first sound of civilization his ears had detected since he couldn't even remember. A roaring, sputtering engine. He spun to see the far-off headlamps of an aging pickup truck, probably thirty years old or more, chugging its way into his path.

Gavin leaped up and down, waving his arms like a madman, right in front of the truck. He wasn't off to the side of the road, hoping the driver would stop—he was either going to get a ride, or get run over.

The driver, a kindhearted country man, pulled over. Gavin rushed up to his open window.

"Please, there's an emergency south of here. I've got to get to 85. Are you going in that direction?"

The man eyed Gavin through his bifocals, curious at his dress shoes and slacks being so soiled and damp, wondering what Gavin was doing out here in the middle of the night, and wondering what he was carrying in his hands. But he was a trusting sort, so he overlooked Gavin's stubby beard and let him in; he'd seen much scruffier characters in this neck of the woods.

"Sure am," the man said. Gavin was ecstatic to realize he knew basically where he was.

The man drove along for a mile or two before speaking—which pleasantly surprised Gavin. He didn't want to get into any explanations. He carefully placed the photo on the cramped floor between his feet, upside down, with the edges of his toes holding the frame in place.

"Are you headed anywhere in particular or just to the highway?" he asked.

"Just the interstate would be fine, thanks," Gavin said. "I can hitch a ride toward Atlanta from there."

The man nodded, once again scanning Gavin's appearance.

"How long will that take—to get to the highway?" Gavin asked.

"Oh, about fifteen minutes," the man said. Gavin was waiting for a question, or a series of questions, like "What were you doing out on the road so early?" or "What's the emergency?" but he had been gifted with a quiet man, the sort of man who played life with the cards given him without asking much else.

They continued past Dutchy's, over Lake Lanier, across Thompson Bridge, and then through Gainesville, and Gavin smiled, knowing precisely where he was. He had crossed this bridge many times before, on the way to Harperson's lake home. *Unbelievable!* he thought, *I was only a few miles from Gary's house!*

The highway was not far, and he could soon begin the next leg of his journey. Hopefully, he could hop an eighteen-wheeler, but would he be so fortunate the next time? What if the operator of the rig recognized Gavin from the paper or the videotape? *One problem at a time*, Gavin reminded himself. *Don't worry about that yet.*

The driver of the pickup truck pulled over just before the overpass and let Gavin out. "Thanks," Gavin waved through the passenger window, as the man nodded politely, smiled, and drove off without so much as a word.

Gavin walked quickly along the overpass and onto the highway, his feet still aching. He kept walking as he hitchhiked, figuring every little bit would help. He realized he'd forgotten to ask the man what time it was. He only knew it was very late.

Several big trucks whizzed by. Most of the traffic at this hour was trucker traffic, drivers rushing their cargo to market. The sound was deafening, even compared to the crickets, as they sent gale force winds against his clothes and his body.

But eventually one of the big trucks pulled over. Gavin ran up to climb aboard, noticing as he ran by that it looked like it was a tanker carrying liquid, perhaps milk or gasoline.

"Thanks," Gavin yelled over the idling diesel engine as he lifted himself into the cab. He looked into the eyes of the driver, a bearded man wearing a ball cap and a flannel shirt.

"Where you headed?" the man asked.

"I'm going to Atlanta," Gavin asked. "Am I on the right train?"

"We'll get you there," the man promised, managing the levers and gears that made the loud sound trucks like these make when they start and stop.

Gavin held his breath, hoping this man was also as disinterested in the news as his previous driver.

"My name's Willie," he said.

Gavin paused. "I'm—Mike," he said, hoping the diversion would keep from tipping Willie off.

"Pleased to meet you, Mike," Willie said, looking straight ahead. Gavin settled back into his seat, feeling more relaxed. *This is great, lucking out twice in a row.* He felt for the coin, ignoring the pain shooting from his wrist, and held on.

"Want some coffee?" Willie asked, reminding Gavin how thirsty he was.

"Great. Thanks," he said, serving himself a cup from the oversized Thermos lodged along the center of the seat.

Willie proved to be as accommodating as the man with the pickup truck—Gavin finally realized he'd never gotten his name at all—not a word was spoken over the next hour. Gavin's eyes scoured the roadside, hoping not to see wreckage beside the road. Once again, the photo was on the floor. The truck driver seemed not to notice.

Maybe I can see Torrie first, he thought. *Just for a minute. But will she understand? She doesn't know Reg and Walter. She'll want them arrested and she'll drag me to the hospital before I can go to the cave. No, it won't work.* As much as he longed to be next to her, to look into her eyes, it had to wait. Calling Torrie first would ruin everything.

"I need to stop up here at the next exit for some gas," Willie informed Gavin as they approached Atlanta. "Hope that's all right with you."

The exit was just two away from the exit that led to Gavin's house—and his car. *Could be worse,* he thought. "No problem. I can catch a ride from here."

"Fair enough," Willie replied, maneuvering the big rig up the ramp.

Gavin had two options. He could try to walk, but he estimated it would be about two miles and an impossible task, given his physical condition at the moment. Or he could call a cab. But he didn't have any money for the fare. *Think, think . . . wait! The cab would take me home, where I have more than enough.* He bummed a quarter off Willie, and made a beeline toward the pay phones.

The cab arrived within five minutes, another arduously long five minutes in a week that threatened never to end. The cabbie followed Gavin's instructions and before Gavin knew it, he was home.

Home. The word was delicious, and he savored it—but not for long. He had to keep moving.

Unfortunately, he had lost his keys somewhere along the way. Or maybe he never had them—probably still lying on the kitchen counter. How was he going to get in? He never was one for keeping a spare under the mat, so he realized he had no other choice—he had to bust a window. Who would have believed it—Gavin Duke, breaking and entering, even if it was his own house.

But the cabbie was watching, so he realized he had to sneak around back instead of doing a number on a front window. He circled behind the garage, peeking through the window of the garage door to steal a look at the Mercedes, and headed for the sliding patio door. He stopped. *What about the alarm? Oh, no. I can deactivate it after I get inside, but the damage will be done as soon as the glass shatters. But what else can I do? I have to take a chance.* The alarm fed directly into his security service but did not have sirens—he had refused to go for sirens. *So if I hurry, I can get rid of the cab and take off before the cops can wind their way here. I'll have to skip a change of clothes or a shower or a better breakfast than cracker crumbs in the woods, but I can live with that—I'll stop at the next convenience store along the way, once I'm safely out of the house, and grab a cup of coffee and a danish. Or two. Or three.*

This was the moment of truth. He put Reg's picture down and picked up the big planter that stood just outside the door. He turned away slightly to avoid the chance of flying shards striking him in the face, and he heaved the pot through the glass. The window shattered into a thousand fragments, and he reached right in, unlatched it, and slid the door open. He ran through the kitchen, finding his keys on the counter, frozen in time next to last Monday's mail. He grabbed them without stopping, darted into the master bedroom, and tore open his sock drawer. He lifted the paper lining, and pulled out a white envelope. He took an instant to glance inside and, safely reassured he now had a few hundred in cash, ran out through the front door and tossed the driver a twenty—the smallest bill he had.

"Keep it!" he shouted on the run, sprinting back up the driveway to outrun the cops.

"Thanks, pal!" the cabbie called out, glad to start the weekend with a fifteen-dollar tip.

Gavin ran in through the front door, which he'd left open, and stopped. There was the bloodied sofa. He reached up to touch his forehead, feeling the gritty scar. His heart skipped a beat.

"No time for this," he reminded himself, as he dashed out into the garage, pressing the automatic door opener as he went. He climbed into the driver's seat and lovingly placed the photo onto the passenger seat before starting the engine. He backed out quickly, reminding himself to close the garage door so that the cops wouldn't realize his car was missing. Getting pulled over on the way to Columbus for driving a stolen car only to be recognized and detained wasn't going to do Reg and Walter any good.

He sped through the neighborhood and smiled to see a patrol cruiser fly by him as he was about to get onto the highway. *Guess the old alarm's working pretty well*, he thought.

He decided to get through town first before stopping for the coffee and danish, even though his head was pounding and his stomach was tight. *No, be patient*, he warned himself. *Get through the city, and then you can relax and eat on the way. Time is running out on Walter and Reg.*

He pulled off at a gas station, hardly losing a minute. The warm coffee was soothing, and the danish were as good as the beans and the hot dogs Reg and Walter had fed him.

He kept his radar detector running and moved along between eighty and ninety, still studying the horizon for a wrecked van. He knew this stretch of highway fairly well and figured there wouldn't be any cops waiting with their radar guns pulled at this hour. His hand kept reaching for the car phone, knowing Torrie's voice was only seconds away.

"No," he told himself again. *Besides, she's out cold. She'll never hear the phone, and I don't want to talk to the machine.*

Still he longed to connect with her, to let her know he was safe, and to feel her emotions—lovingly focused on him, only him.

He shook his head and blinked away the sleep. And he rocketed on.

Twenty-One

By five o'clock, Walter and Reg were hitting the northern out-skirts of Columbus. The two had not conversed much, each trying to process his own emotions.

"How's the gas doin'?" Walter asked.

"We got about a quarter tank left," Reg answered. "Think we oughta pull over and get some?"

"Well, I wanna keep movin', but I guess we oughta have it filled up now so we don't get run out when we got the gold sittin' in the back."

They were just ahead of an exit, so Reg pulled off at a gas station. They were on their way again in minutes, and Walter checked the map to make sure the next stages of the journey didn't trip them up. It had been smooth sailing until now—pretty much staying on the same interstate—but the country roads would provide a challenge.

As they drove along, Reg started thinking about Gavin, and what was next for him. "What's gonna happen to ol' Gavin, once he gets back to the bank?" Reg asked.

"Hard to say," Walter said. "You think they're gonna fire him, maybe?"

"That'd be too bad," Reg said, remembering all too well what that was like.

"He'll bounce back though," Walter said. "He's not like us, stuck in Murrowstown."

"Yeah, he's probably got some rich friends over at the other bank, who'd give him some other great job."

"Probably."

They drove on through Columbus and past Fort Benning. The Stewart County sign in the weak headlights was a sight to behold.

"Almost there," Reg said.

"Almost," Walter nodded.

They went through a small town called Louvale, where a sign told them Lumpkin was now ten miles ahead. From there they would change direction and cut due west toward the river.

They made a half circle around the county courthouse in Lumpkin, where Brick worked, and got onto county road 39C—the number Gavin couldn't recall. This road took them past Providence Canyon State Park to the north and Eufaula National Wildlife Refuge to the south, an excruciatingly long fourteen miles before they realized they were right by the river. The glimpses of the meandering waters in the headlights were welcome, for they knew their quest was nearing an end.

They took a right, driving down a single-lane road that was hidden by the mature hardwood trees whose branches created a tunnel over the surface. Reg wanted to drive quickly, but the potholes demanded a more careful approach.

Suddenly a pair of headlights flew out from behind a bend, startling both men. A small car skidded by the van, missing by a fraction of an inch as the red tail lights vanished into the night.

"What's goin' on?" Walter demanded, but Reg just put his hand to his chest.

"We better keep movin'," Reg finally replied. He had slammed on the brakes, so he pried his foot from the pedal and moved it back to the gas.

They went around the bend, and then they saw it—the first corner of that rusting chain-link fence, wrapping its way around the closed-up factory and the treasure which rested inside, hidden to all but them.

The fence followed the road, and finally the gate appeared. Reg pulled over and put the van in park.

"I imagine we oughta bust open the gate first, then drive in so we can load the gold right in," Walter said.

"I ain't so sure," said Reg, rubbing his chin. "Gavin didn't say there was anybody guardin' the gold, but you never know. I think we oughta check it out first, you know, since we can move faster on foot if there's any trouble. Let's make sure ain't nobody in there first. Why don't we stash the van in the woods over here, just up ahead, till we know what's goin' on in there. If somebody should happen along, or if somebody's already in there, we can hide out till they're gone, or sneak out and get to the van. But if we drive on in, we may be in for some trouble."

"All right," grumbled Walter, agreeing in principle but wanting to get on with it.

They rolled up the road a few yards, and Reg parked the van in the woods. Walter carried the flashlight, crowbar, and wire cutters. Reg brought the shovel and his shotgun. Each was still packing a hunting knife.

They spotted a section of the fence that appeared to be particularly twisted and rusty, and Walter pulled it up enough for Reg to slide underneath. Once Reg and all the equipment were inside, he pulled the fence in the other direction while Walter slid under. They dusted themselves off and gazed at the silent moonlit grounds. It was a chilling reminder of the plant where they had worked. They picked up their things and trudged ahead.

It was just as Gavin had described—a collection of boxy metal huts and, at the end of the path, the rock. They didn't notice the small series of red flags stuck in the ground, markers that pointed the way to explosives that would be detonated within the hour. All they saw was the rock, the double doors, and a million dollars' worth of promises at the end of their arduous tunnel.

They each yanked a door open wide, slamming them into a puff of dust as rock and plaster fell into the first chamber. They coughed and waited for the dust to settle before plunging down the steps, observing how odd it was for the ceiling to be so low. They attacked the second door, creating an eruption of dust and falling mortar significantly more stifling than the first.

They entered the room. Neither man studied the structure as Gavin had, for these two had already lived and died and held no fear of death. Walter directed his beam straight ahead, seeing the pile of tarp Gavin had used to cover the oil drums. The tarp was littered with dust and debris, pieces of fallen rock and plaster and wood beams from the ceiling, and it was crumpled in a heap in front of the drums. Walter held the flashlight in one hand as he swept it out of the way, as Reg tugged furiously from the other end. Away it went in a heap, and both men stood staring at the three barrels marked *Danger. Toxic Waste. Do Not Burn or Incinerate.*

🏈   🏈   🏈

Behind the buildings that littered the compound, two other men sat in a state government truck and waited.

"When's that twerp Frederichs gonna get here?" one demanded, looking at his watch for the fifth time in five minutes.

"I dunno," said the other. He took a sip of coffee. "Wanna go look back around the grounds?"

"Again? What for? Everything's secure. There's nobody for two hundred miles. We locked up behind ourselves, remember?"

"Just thought it might kill the time."

"Go if you want. I think I'll stay right here."

"Ah, that's okay. Mind if I get the radio on?"

"Go ahead. I doubt you'll find any stations around here, especially at quarter to six in the morning."

The other man flicked the dial and rolled it to the right until a country station's familiar twang filled the cab of the truck.

🏈   🏈   🏈

Reg and Walter looked at each other before pushing the right and left barrels out of the way. They stood on either side of the center barrel. Walter continued to hold the light as Reg looked inside. There was no lid, as Gavin had told them, and no motor oil. Walter's light revealed that there was packing material, though—wadded up paper and foam, deeper inside the barrel. Reg began furiously tossing the material out of the oil drum, until he reached the bottom.

There was no gold.

"We musta heard him wrong," Walter bellowed, angry at being cheated from this moment by life once again, yet still thinking there was gold in this room. They turned the other drums over, looked beneath the tarp, and went for the shelves, their anger intensifying with each passing second, until they were heaving the oil drums and pounding the shelves off the very walls, screaming not words but groans and sounds of a wild animal caught in a trap and unable to escape.

And then it began. The unstable walls and ceiling—farther deteriorated by the test blasting of the last few days—finally gave in, and with a rumbling sound louder than either had ever heard, the room started echoing and shaking and filling it with fine white-gray powder. Rocks began to fall as beams broke into splinters, one knocking the flashlight from Walter's hand and fracturing it into darkness. The two men dove toward the exit but were forced to collapse to the floor, pummeled on their way down by still more falling debris.

The rumbling abated, followed by silence, darkness, and stillness. Walter could feel himself breathing, his chest heavy and pounding, and he could hear Reg moaning across the chamber.

"You hear something?" one of the men in the truck asked the other.

"Just Hank Junior," he said, pointing to the radio.

🐚　🐚　🐚

Walter and Reg were in pain, great pain, but were unable to isolate the sources because there were so many bruises and cuts. The air was thick with dust and it was pitch-black. Both men fought to dig and claw and scrape their way out. Had either man stopped to consider what was on the other side of the rubble—life without the gold but with more scars and bitter blows—they might have decided to lie down in defeat and make this cavern their grave. But survival is less attached to the brain than to the spirit, and their hands dug at the rocks.

"Stay with me, Walter," Reg gasped.

"I'm comin', Reg, I'm comin'."

🥔　🥔　🥔

Gavin breathed heavily as he headed into Columbus, knowing he was getting close, and keenly aware that the roads would soon get narrower and smaller and bumpier. The clock on the dash said it was 5:41. He had made good time, whatever that means, given he didn't know how much time Reg or Walter had anymore. He hoped they'd already found the gold and gotten away.

He moved steadily through Stewart County, relieved to see the county courthouse in Lumpkin. He turned onto 39C, remembering that it was exactly fourteen miles to the river and just a few more from there to the rock.

He didn't know how fast to go on this nerve-frazzling stretch of country highway. Was there a speed trap ahead? He couldn't risk being pulled over now, so close to saving Walter and Reg. The posted speed was forty-five, so he tried to keep it between forty-five and fifty, but it was tough to keep it from creeping up and tougher still to let up enough to get back below that. "Forget it," he finally sputtered. "There aren't gonna be any country cops around here right before dawn." He hit the overdrive and took it to eighty, ignoring the curves and the bumps.

Gavin raced up the road, letting out a whoop when he saw the first corner of the fence, flooring it up to the main entrance. He didn't notice the government vehicle parked around the far side of the main building, safely shielded from any flying debris that might result from the explosions. He jumped out of the car, the engine still running and the door wide open and the photograph of Reg and Lily forgotten but safely in its place, still covered with dried blood and sap. He scaled the ten-foot gate, oblivious by now to physical pain, and hopped into the complex as the first hints of sunlight flittered onto the grounds. He sprinted toward the rock, grunting and heaving as he started to call out, "Walter! Reg! Here I come! Here I come!"

📀　📀　📀

"It's a quarter after six," the man in the truck complained. "Frederichs told us to be here at five sharp, and he's still a no-show."

"Let's just go ahead and get it done, so we can get out of here."

"Aw, let's give him ten more minutes. The DJ said they're gonna do three in a row from Alabama. Let's wait'll that's done."

"You got yourself a deal."

📀　📀　📀

Gavin shuddered when he saw the rubble blocking the doors. His worst fears had come true. He started digging at the rocks, pawing at them, ignoring the fact that his hands were already bloodied. Fortunately, only about two feet of debris had piled up in front of the doors, so he was quickly able to open the first pair.

He cautiously peered inside, realizing that he too could become engulfed in a landslide. He tried to let his eyes adjust, but there simply wasn't enough daylight yet.

"Walter? Reg?"

He listened then tried again. "Walter? Reg?" Nothing. He inhaled slowly, wincing as the dust filled his lungs, and he resolutely set out to walk in. But before he took the first step, he heard a faint sound. He stopped and waited. Nothing. He swallowed and listened to his heart pound against his eardrums. *Maybe they made it out in time,* he thought. *Please. Please.* The air was still.

"Ooohh," he heard arising from the rubble.

"Walter! Reg!"

Gavin crept forward, feeling his way as he had in the woods. "Can you hear me? Are you both here?"

Another moan. Reg groggily lifted his head. "What?" he managed.

"Reg! It's me, Gavin. Talk to me, man. Where are you? Where's Walter?"

Reg lifted his head. "Gav . . . Gavin."

Gavin listened carefully, trying to place the sound. He reached out, hoping to find Reg. After fumbling frantically his hand hit Reg's leg. "Reg! Come on. Can you get up?"

"Um, ah, yeah, I . . . What's goin' on?"

"Must have been a cave-in. Come on, I have to get you out of here before it gets worse. Where's Walter?"

"Walter? Walter . . . He was right behind me." Gavin helped Reg sit up, and then he crept further into the darkness. His hands felt sharp stones and fallen timbers and finally Walter. He patted Walter's cheeks. "Come on, Walter. Wake up. You can do it."

Walter twitched but didn't respond. "Walter!" Gavin raised his voice, slapping Walter's face with vigor. Walter shook his head and mumbled.

"We've got to get you two out of here. Now! Help me with Walter, Reg!"

"Reg," Walter said weakly.

"Good," Gavin said. "Come on, up you go."

The three stumbled out, and Gavin took them to the closest building. He leaned them against the wall so they could get some fresh air and regain their bearings.

"Where's it hurt, guys?" he asked. "Any broken bones?"

"Just my head," Reg said.

"I'm okay," Walter muttered after a pause.

"How'd you get here?" Reg asked Gavin. "How'd you get out, and how'd you . . . "

"Don't worry about that," Gavin said. "You guys just better be glad you're alive. I thought you were goners there for a minute."

"Me too," Walter agreed.

Gavin studied their faces. "I think you'd better get back home," he said. "I've gotta call the cops and tell them I'm okay, and I think you'd better be gone by the time they get here."

Reg and Walter looked at each other. "What for?" Walter asked. "So they can come and arrest us once we get home? Why don't we just wait here instead of goin' to all that trouble?"

Gavin looked at him through wet eyes. "What makes you think they'll find out where you live?"

"Aren't you gonna tell them, after all we did to you?"

Gavin slowly shook his head. He looked down and swallowed hard. "I think you two have been through enough. Just go home, okay?"

"You mean, just like that?" Reg asked. "You ain't gonna turn us in or nothin'?"

"Shut up," Walter barked, fighting to his feet. "You heard the man. Let's get out of here!"

The three stood up and stared at each other. There was nothing more to be said, so Reg and Walter limped to the fence where they'd crawled in. They made their way out to find the van and take it back to Dutchy's.

✎   ✎   ✎

The last chord faded away, and the third Alabama song was over.

"Still no Roger. I say let's do this and go home."

A sigh. "Sure." They slid out of the truck and walked over to the detonator, which was resting on the ground.

"Do you want the honors?" The man held up the two wires.

"Be my guest," said the other.

✎   ✎   ✎

Gavin watched Reg and Walter scurry down the road to the spot where they'd hidden the van. They disappeared from view, and Gavin listened to the crickets and the cicadas chirp before a rickety engine roared to life and slowly vanished into the early morning air.

He turned to look across the compound at the rock, impressed at how beautiful it was with the sun sidelighting it so dramatically from the east. He sighed and blinked. *The gold. The gold! Reg and Walter don't have the gold! It's still in there—underneath a pile of rubble, no doubt, but still in there!* He started across the grounds toward the rock, knowing he wouldn't venture too far inside, but wanting to take a look anyway, now that it was getting light out.

His steps crunched into the gravel and he smiled, oddly amused that despite all the insanity, he hadn't lost the gold. Suddenly, out of nowhere, a white light flashed and a sound so loud it felt like a train rammed him in the chest and picked him up as though he were a rag doll and pounded him into the ground. He bounced on his back and felt his head snap forward before his skull bounced again and he landed solidly on the bleached asphalt pathway.

Twenty-Two

Reg and Walter didn't speak as they slowly made their way home, although one or the other occasionally groaned as a particular ache or pain got to be too much.

Walter drove and got lost and, even though he knew he was lost, he refused to ask Reg for help or suggest he needed any. They'd eventually find Atlanta and then Murrowstown. For the first time in ages, there was a sense of "home" attached to Murrowstown.

They came around a bend and saw a car pulled off to the side of the road with the hood up. A man and a woman stood outside the car. Walter sighed and slowed to see if they needed help, but the woman's eyes flared with such anger that Walter's foot quickly pressed back down onto the accelerator.

"Jerks!" Ruth Chandler said. "Couldn't they see we needed help?"

"Shut up," Ronnie snapped back.

"You shut up," she hissed. "You're the only man in the United States who doesn't know how to fix a car engine."

"I told you, it overheated. We just have to wait for the radiator to cool down a little more."

"But it wouldn't have overheated in the first place if you had a clue!"

"I said I'm sorry, okay?" he shouted. "I apologize for not checking the water and the antifreeze, your highness! Give it a rest."

"Give it a rest," she mocked bitterly. "Give it a rest. What a brilliant reply."

Ronnie kicked at the dirt beside the road and cursed her under his breath. "Nothing is worth putting up with this," he said to himself. "Nothing."

Ruth looked out into the woods, grinding her teeth together.

🥮　🥮　🥮

The rain began to fall on Gavin, first a sprinkling of pebbles, then a torrent of small stones and sand, pelting him like pinpricks. He squinted to protect his eyes but the squinting exposed his teeth, so he had to concentrate on both keeping his eyes and his lips tightly shut until the deluge had ended.

He sat up, which was difficult but not so bad because the bruises on his back and legs hadn't begun to swell yet. All he could hear was the ringing in his ears, which was not so much ringing but a long and steady "Eeeeeee" that was much worse than the noise from the insects in the woods.

He looked up, trying to blink away the dust from his eyelids and the lingering images from the flash to see a smoldering carnage, a pile of boulders strewn to and fro, in front of a rock that did not look quite the same as it had just seconds ago. He tried to stand, rolling over onto his hands and knees before pushing himself up. He steadied himself and stumbled ahead to the mass of shattered rock.

The dust was clearing enough so the two engineers could see this solitary figure trudging across the grounds.

"What's he doing? Is that Frederichs? Hey! You! Stop! Get away from there!"

They waved their arms and yelled but Gavin heard none of this. He strode resolutely up to the edge of the blast site, but the path strewn with rubble became impassable so he stopped. His eyes scanned the ground in front of his feet, taking in the boulders, large and small, dusted with pebbles and gravel and powder, white and black and gray. He tilted his head up, toward the rock, and realized there was no way to tell where the double doors were, the old cellar doors, because they no longer existed

The demolition team caught up with Gavin and one grabbed at Gavin's elbow to turn him around. Gavin gently tugged it away and, with one motion, reached into his pocket and produced his gold-plated coin. He turned the coin over, taking one last look at both sides, as the engineers stopped to watch this scene, too puzzled to demand any answers but strangely content to watch as it played out. Gavin sighed and looked down. With a tear creating a clean path through the dust that covered each cheek, he tossed the coin onto the rubble, where it bounced off the edge of a jagged rock with a bright *ping!* before slipping through a crack and out of sight.

🥨 🥨 🥨

Torrie stepped into the room, a private room at Northside Hospital. She was nervous and scared, like a teenager coming down a winding staircase for her first date, but smiling the biggest smile of her life. She had been holding her tears back, but the instant she saw him, the dam burst.

He climbed out of bed, amazingly in the room more for rest and observation than any serious injuries, and they embraced without a word. They eventually loosened their grip to look at each other, and she ran her hand up to touch the scar above his eye.

"We have so much to talk about," he said.

She laughed, from both the tension and the magnitude of the understatement. "Yes, I guess we do," she said, her eyes studying his face. She desperately wanted to ask him what had happened to him, what he went through, to share his ordeal. All she knew from the police reports was that he had been kidnapped. She wanted to know everything, but common sense and compassion made her think it better to wait—a tough call for a reporter.

There was a pause, a good pause, while they looked at each other. "Have you had many visitors?" she asked.

It was his turn to laugh. "Every reporter who ever had a deadline has been trying to get in here," he said. "Can you imagine how good it feels not to return Sam Donaldson's phone calls?"

"Seems like you made an exception in my case," she smiled.

"Guess I did," he said. "Maybe I'll let you write the book."

There was another pause, as she looked into his eyes again, cherishing the moment she was starting to think may never come.

"Carrie's stopping by later this afternoon, I think," he said, finally getting to her question. He looked down and smiled. "What a good friend she is."

Torrie looked at him and listened, intrigued by his referring to Carolina's friendship rather than her business skills.

"She's really religious too," Gavin went on. "Quite a remarkable person."

Torrie was soaking all this in, but Gavin quickly moved on before she could sort everything through. "Harperson sent some flowers, but I don't think he's going to make it, somehow," he said, walking over to the credenza and pulling out the card from a magnificent bouquet, one of several that filled the room. "'Gavin: Best wishes for a speedy recovery. Gary.' Not exactly a ticker-tape parade," he said, but Torrie noticed he didn't seem too concerned. A bit hurt, maybe, but not tense about the ramifications regarding his stellar career.

"Have you heard from Ruth?" she asked.

"No," he said. "No, I haven't." He really looked hurt, and she understood.

"But," he continued, "I can understand why, maybe. I was pretty crummy to her, especially as things heated up. I think I've got some fence-mending to do." He paused and bit his lower lip. "She deserves so much more than I ever gave her. I'm surprised she managed to put up with me sometimes."

Torrie peered intently into this man's face, wondering if she could believe her ears. Could it be that the selfishness that ruled his heart had begun to melt? His mean streak, his preoccupation with success and power and fame and gold, loosened now? She recalled several instances where she'd winced, repulsed by the way he had treated Ruth, always so condescending and arrogant. She understood his actions were merely a symptom of a deeper problem—the spiritual void in his life. But this was a shock. *Just what*, she wondered, *what happened to Gavin Duke during that week he was out there?*

"I'm sure she'll pop in any minute now," Torrie said, not only believing it but genuinely wanting it to happen, for both Gavin and for Ruth.

"Yeah, I hope you're right."

Sensing his sadness, she quickly changed the subject to one more upbeat. "So when are you going to get out?" she asked.

"They want to keep me here one more day," he said, "but I may just ask if I can stay a little longer. I mean, I could sure use the rest. How's this: 'Ow, Doc, my leg, it's killing me! And my arm! Aah! And my chest! Ooh!'"

She giggled. "I would say Tom Cruise is losing sleep tonight."

"You mean I can't play myself in the made-for-TV movie?"

"I'll have my agent call your agent, and they'll do lunch," she said, repeating a joke they'd shared before.

He had worked his way back across the room and was standing right in front of her. He looked into her eyes and said, "It's good to be near you again. I missed you so much, so very much. I thought about you when I was . . . "

"Shhh," she said, touching her fingers softly to his lips. "Not yet. You need to deprogram for a while first and get some rest."

"Okay, doctor," he smirked. They gazed into each others' eyes. He slid his arms around her, remembering how good it felt to hug Torrie.

"I've got to go back to work," she said, pulling away and turning her head so he wouldn't see the tears forming again. She grabbed a tissue from her purse and tried to wipe them dry.

He watched her, touched by how deep and true her emotions were, realizing he wasn't sure if he had truly appreciated and understood this side of her before. He knew he had been attracted to her looks, her feisty streak, and the way her mind worked—and of course he had been aware that she was soft and loving and caring, but he couldn't remember noticing it quite like this before. For the first time, he wondered if it was her faith, like Carrie's, that caused this magnetic facet of her personality.

"Thanks for stopping by," he said softly. "When can you come again?"

She turned back toward him, still slightly embarrassed and sneaking a glance at his eyes before looking away at the floor. "Um, I don't know when visiting hours end . . . "

"I'll tell them you're my physical therapist," he kidded. "You can come any time you want."

"Okay," she smiled. "I've got a couple of interviews stacked up this afternoon, so I'll come over when I've gotten those out of the way—probably around six. How's that?"

"Perfect," he said. They shared one last look, and she started to turn to the door.

"Torrie?"

She turned back to face him, her fingers sliding gently from the handle.

"Thanks for . . . " He stopped. This time, he was the one holding back the tears. "Thanks for visiting me."

She smiled. "I'll see you," she said, and she was gone.

She brushed the tears away as she darted down the hall, almost skipping, praising God for touching Gavin's heart during his ordeal. She sensed in her spirit that soon, once Gavin had gotten settled back into his life, she'd be able to look him square in the eyes and challenge him with the truth about eternity he needed to hear—that God loves Gavin Duke, died and rose for him, and had bigger and better things in store than mere million-dollar contests.

Gavin watched from the window, hoping to be able to see her as she left the building, but his view of the parking lot was limited. He eventually walked over and sat on the edge of the bed, then climbed in, reclining in a comfortable place for the first time in a week.

His mind filled with thoughts about his future and about his past. A swirl of emotions colored each impression, and he realized he had no idea how Carolina, or the bank, would handle the bad PR about losing the gold.

He wondered how he might have reacted if he and Torrie had met Walter or Reg on a Sunday drive to the mountains a few weekends ago—he couldn't imagine where he might have met them. Certainly not at an antique shop or on a rafting trip. Perhaps if they'd stopped at a gas station, or pulled over to view a monument marking some historical event. He wondered about the monument where his tape had been hidden and realized he never found out what it was supposed to mark. Maybe they'd have run into Reg and Walter there. He knew how Torrie might have reacted, smiling and liking them, even if they'd been wearing dirty, threadbare work clothes. She'd have said hello and started talking about how pretty it was in the country, asking them if they lived nearby and making their day a little brighter. But Gavin probably would have ignored them, impatiently going back to the car and pretending to be interested in something off in the distance, tapping his fingers on the steering wheel until Torrie got the hint and climbed back in, leaving the men with smiles on their faces, gladdened to have had a friendly young girl add some sunshine to their lives, if only for a moment.

Gavin turned his head toward the credenza, where a photograph behind a cracked piece of glass stood partially hidden by fresh flowers. He gazed at the long-lost image with a tear in each eye—one for Walter and one for Reg, two men he knew and cared about. He thought about the tragedy of Lily's death and about where Duane might be now. And he thought about his own father, the man he had finally come to forgive, and Gavin smiled.

I hope Carrie stops by soon, he thought, knowing that she too was the kind of person who could brighten your whole day with a well-placed word. *Maybe Ruth and Gary will come along too. Yeah, that'd be nice.*

He rolled over, feeling a nap coming on, and soon slipped into sleep, dreaming of a future with a girl in a big white floppy hat and a pretty cotton dress blowing in the breeze, on a picnic in a field flecked with orange and yellow flowers.

Epilogue

The warm Caribbean sunshine danced across the water and the breeze gently rocked the yacht, which was anchored offshore within a small round cove. The white sandy beach was dotted with swaying palms, and a family of ivory gulls floated overhead.

The cabin boy hurriedly arranged some fruit atop a polished silver platter. A crystal dish rattled softly against the tray as he made his way up the narrow steps.

"Will there be anything else, sir?" he asked with a slight bow.

The man in the deck chair looked up. He tilted his straw hat and pulled up one of his black socks, which went past the calf but not quite to the baggy plaid clam-diggers. He tapped his black wing-tip shoes against the railing, not aware of the fact that the cabin boy was considering how pasty white this fussy man's legs looked.

"Tut-tut, man," he said. "I don't see any apples there. I specifically requested some apples, did I not?"

"My apologies, Mister Frederichs. I will bring up two fine apples." He scurried down below.

"Toot-sweet, now," he said. "Make it snappy, will you?"

Roger Frederichs gazed out over the horizon. He sighed deeply and frowned. "Wonder where the next stop will be," he muttered, picking at his nails. "Hope it's nicer than this one." He plucked a grape from the stem and tossed it out into the water.

AUTHOR'S AFTERTHOUGHTS

My friend Virginia was heading to England for the summer—a lengthy family vacation in a quaint coastal village.

"Why don't you write a book while you're there," I suggested.

"What would I write about?" she asked.

I outlined the basic plot for *Southern Gold*, which had been rattling around my mind for nearly a decade but never found its way to a sheet of paper.

"Nah," she said. "I don't want to write a book—I want to sit under a tree and *read* a book. It's your idea, anyway. Why don't *you* write it?"

So I did.

Thanks, Virginia—you are a Santa Claus. For you gave me a simple yet profound gift that day, wise counsel that set this novel in motion.

Plenty of others deserve a special note of thanks, as well:

Kathy, I couldn't have done it without your support, encouragement, and love.

And Marie Hearn. Without your faithfulness, this would not have come to pass. You two too, Bruce and Maridel.

Wm. Brock and Bodie, whose boots I am not worthy to buff: We all owe you an immeasurable debt . . . for elevating the very standard of an entire industry.

For the whole gang at K. Jewett & Associates, three cheers for being the best in the business.

To Victoria and K.C. James, many thanks for always being there.

To David Ogilvy, Sig Rosenblum, Bill Jayme, and the enduring memory of Ernest Hemingway, I give boundless thanks for teaching the rhythm of great writing to wide-eyed readers. And to Bernie Taupin and Sylvester Stallone, I send infinite gratitude for showing us how to infuse passion into the written word.

Mike Russell, Caryl ("The Boss") Myers, Mom, and Dad: the words of honor from the old HarperCollins/Zondervan book still ring so true.

To Martha and everyone else who dove in and came up with helpful changes, I deeply appreciate your thoughtful input.

Mario Murillo, you've taught me so many things which have made this process infinitely easier. One was, "God gives you a great and mighty challenge, and then He makes it seem impossible." This concept of divinely-driven destiny lifted me through many of the impossible times. May you always be engulfed in the fresh fire you so passionately seek . . . as you unleash the Lazarus Generation!

And to you, gentle reader, thank you for staying with me. See ya again soon . . . in *Paradise.*